T0277045

THE
PAIRING

ALSO BY
CASEY McQUISTON

Red, White & Royal Blue

One Last Stop

I Kissed Shara Wheeler

THE
PAIRING

A NOVEL

CASEY
McQUISTON

ST. MARTIN'S GRIFFIN
NEW YORK

This is a work of fiction. All of the characters, organizations, and events portrayed in this novel are either products of the author's imagination or are used fictitiously.

First published in the United States by St. Martin's Griffin, an imprint of St. Martin's Publishing Group

THE PAIRING. Copyright © 2024 by Casey McQuiston. All rights reserved. Printed in the United States of America. For information, address St. Martin's Publishing Group, 120 Broadway, New York, NY 10271.

www.stmartins.com

Designed by Devan Norman

Map design by Rhys Davies

Cityscape art © Shutterstock.com

The Library of Congress Cataloging-in-Publication Data is available upon request.

ISBN 978-1-250-36584-2 (trade paperback)
ISBN 978-1-250-86405-5 (ebook)

Our books may be purchased in bulk for promotional, educational, or business use. Please contact your local bookseller or the Macmillan Corporate and Premium Sales Department at 1-800-221-7945, extension 5442, or by email at MacmillanSpecialMarkets@macmillan.com.

First Edition: 2024

10 9 8 7 6 5 4 3 2 1

For pleasure

It isn't possible to love and to part.
You will wish that it was.

You can transmute love, ignore it, muddle it,
but you can never pull it out of you.

—E. M. FORSTER, A ROOM WITH A VIEW

Initiating slut mode.

—ROBYN, "FEMBOT"

THE
PAIRING

UK

LONDON

DOVER

THE TOUR

PARIS

FRANCE

BORDEAUX

SAINT-JEAN-DE-LUZ

SAN SEBASTIÁN

CINQUE TERRE

FLORENCE

NICE

MONACO

PISA

CHIANTI

SPAIN

BARCELONA

ITALY

ROME

NAPLES

MEDITERRANEAN SEA

PALERMO

THE BEGINNING

(Theo's Version)

The first time I kiss Kit, he tastes like jalapeños and apricots.

We're drunk enough to be brave. Some guys from the restaurant have thrown a Halloween party at their rental house in Cathedral City, and there is a trash can full of mystery punch, and we're twenty-two, the age at which trash-can punch sounds genius instead of evil. I did add a few glugs of apricot brandy from the liquor shelf to take the edge off, at least.

For the last four months since Kit moved to Palm Springs and in with me, we've been talking Halloween costumes. Slutty M&M's. Ralph Macchio and the bully from *The Karate Kid*. Kit came up with Sonny and Cher—he's Cher, I'm Sonny. He found the perfect slinky silk shift on consignment in LA, even made me lace him into a waist corset before he slipped the dress on, because he's never met a bit he couldn't commit to. Not even trash punch could erase the texture of his skin from my fingertips.

After, when we're eating delivery pizza off our coffee table, Kit decides it's time to finally talk about it.

We've never addressed it, not since he returned to California for college and we slipped into each other's pockets like we'd never been apart, right to the synced, steady heartbeat of us. *Theo-and-Kit, Theo-and-Kit, Theo-and-Kit.* It was so easy to find the pulse, we didn't talk about where it had gone, or why.

Kit looks at me over a stuffed crust with extra jalapeños and asks, "Why didn't you ever want to go to Oklahoma City?"

Because it's Oklahoma City, I almost say. But the place was never what mattered; it was the promise. When we were fourteen, a year after Kit's mom died, his dad decided to move the whole family to New York. Kit and I got out a map and found the midpoint between Rancho Mirage and Brooklyn. Oklahoma City. We promised to meet there every summer, but I always found excuses not to go, and they were never that good.

His brown eyes are so sparkly in the lamplight, framed by his stupid Cher wig, that I tell him the truth, partly: When he left, I realized I'd fallen in love with my best friend when I wasn't looking. And then he was five hundred miles too far for it to matter, telling me about first dates over the phone, and it hurt too much. Oklahoma City would have broken my heart.

"I'm sorry," I tell him. "It was shitty of me. I was shitty to you."

"Oh" is all he says.

"I'm totally over it now," I say, which is a lie. I've never been more under it. I thought living with Kit would be great exposure therapy, that nobody could stay in love with their best friend after watching them scratch their ass through sweatpants. If anything, I love Kit *more* now. "So you don't have to worry. I'm not gonna make it weird."

Kit sets down his slice and studies me, my stick-on mustache, hair braided back to fit under my bowl-cut wig. He bites out a smile, tucks Cher's hair behind his ear, and says, "I was in love with you too."

"You—what?"

"Back then, I mean."

I nod, trying to keep my voice steady. "Right. Back then."

And he laughs, so I laugh, and I put on Sonny & Cher to cover up how weird mine sounds. We dance around the living room with grease-slicked lips to "I Got You Babe" until my hand brushes Kit's cinched waist.

I catch the ends of shiny, synthetic hair between my thumb

and finger, touch him without touching him. He reaches up and peels off my mustache.

"What if we tried it?" he asks softly. "Just once, to see what it would be like?"

And then I'm in my best friend's bed, kissing him dizzy. Just to see what it's like.

At the bottom of my belly, I know this will change me in a permanent way. Maybe it's wrong, maybe it's completely fucked up to let him do this when I know how I feel and how he doesn't, but it's Kit. Kit loves to make people feel good, and when he buries his face between my legs, I feel good. I feel so good it's awful.

He'll laugh about it tomorrow, and every person I take to bed from now on will be fighting his ghost for my attention.

In the morning, the kitchen smells like cinnamon and butter and yeast, and Kit's at the sink, doing dishes. He's wearing the apron I bought him when we road-tripped up to the Santa Maria Valley to find out if the barbecue was worth the hype. It says, *THIS GUY RUBS HIS OWN MEAT.*

The table is set with two plates, steam curling and icing dripping from golden-brown dough. Kit bakes from scratch every weekend, and he's been in pursuit of the perfect cinnamon roll recipe for years.

I made a lot of promises to myself when I was falling asleep next to him. I would be cool. It was nothing but a laugh. Two old friends hooking up for old times' sake, pouring one out for the lovestruck kids we used to be.

He smiles at me from the sink, still wearing the bruise I bit into his neck, and I say, "I lied. I never got over it."

Kit lets out a long breath. He turns off the water. And then he says the most incredible thing he could possibly say.

He says, "Neither did I."

THE END

(Theo's Version)

There's a dildo on the luggage carousel.

It's not *my* dildo. Not that I didn't bring one, but Kit would never pack ours so carelessly that it could just flop out of my suitcase and go tumbling through baggage claim. There are rules for these things.

I'm alone in London Heathrow, watching the dildo go round and round. It's purple, shortish but a perfectly respectable girth. On its fourth rotation, I finally step forward and pull my bag off the belt, but I don't move toward the exit.

I don't know where Kit is.

Seven, eight, nine, ten times the dildo goes around before a straight-faced airport employee snaps on some gloves and takes it away in a plastic baggie.

I check the time: thirty-five minutes since Kit walked away. I'm too angry to cry, but I have about half an hour until I come completely, spectacularly unglued. I'll email the tour company later to explain why we never made it, see if I can get a refund. Right now, I just want to go home.

From the British Airways ticketing line, I watch a nervous young couple approach the lost and found to collect their wayward dildo. They're in the kind of love worth getting humiliated at baggage claim. They leave together, pink-faced and laughing into each other's shoulders. How fucking sweet.

I ask the agent behind the counter, "What time is the next nonstop to Los Angeles?"

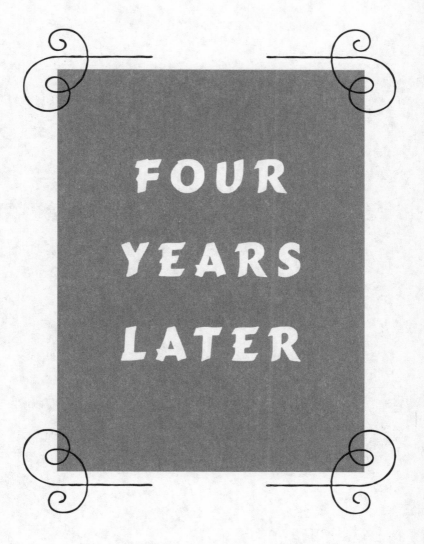

FOUR
YEARS
LATER

LONDON

PAIRS WELL WITH:

Pimm's Cup, tea-dipped scone
eaten in a furious rush

LONDON

"I don't care if you give me two hundred pounds and a hand job, Trevor, you're cut off." I push the crumpled notes back across the bar, smiling sweetly. "Go home. Work on yourself. Your personality is bad, and not in a fun way."

At last Trevor relents, allowing himself to be hauled toward the pub's exit by two other West Ham fans as the crowd cheers another goal on the overhead telecast. One of the Spurs lads he was harassing raises his beer in gratitude. I shake my head and toss a towel over my shoulder, ducking down to finish detaching the blown keg.

"It's always Trevor," sighs a bartender. "Absolute fucking wet wipe."

I snort. "Every bar has one."

The bartender gives me a commiserative wink, then does a double take.

"Hold on. Who're you?"

"I'm—" I finally get the keg unhooked and drag it out with a grunt. "—Theo."

"When'd they hire you, then?"

"Oh, he let me behind the bar because I can change a keg." I jerk my chin toward the sweaty manager doing his damnedest to keep up with orders. It didn't take much to convince him to accept some free help. "I don't work here. I don't even live here. I got off a plane like two hours ago. Hey!" I snap my towel at a

Spurs fan trying to climb on top of his barstool. "Come on, man, be smarter."

The bartender frowns appreciatively.

"Been to London before?"

I grin. "No, but I've seen a lot of movies."

Truthfully, I haven't been much of anywhere outside California. There was that close call a couple summers ago when Sloane was filming in Berlin and invited me to come live for free in her hotel suite, but—no, I wasn't ready. I don't typically trust myself in unfamiliar places or circumstances. I've lived in the Coachella Valley almost my entire twenty-eight years, because it has mountains and desert and huge skies and ravens the size of dogs, and because I already know all the ways I can fail there.

But I'm ready now. I think—I *know* I'm ready. Every muscle in my body has been coiled for weeks as the squares on the calendar went by, ready to spring, to find out what I'm capable of. I *love* knowing what I'm capable of.

Other than one cataclysmic morning at Heathrow, this is my first time overseas, which is probably why I've put myself behind the bar in a crowded pub during a football grudge match. I jumped off the airport train with all of London at my feet, and instead of museums or palaces or Westminster Abbey, I cut a straight path to the nearest pub and elbowed my way into my element. I'm capable of *this*, mediating bar fights and slamming valves and shouting friendly insults at guys named Trevor, learning the local drinking customs, tasting the regional spirits. I study fauna at their watering hole like it's National Geographic. I'm the Steve Irwin of having a pint with the lads.

The whole idea of this trip, when Kit and I first booked it, was exactly that: learning. We used to fantasize about opening a restaurant one day, and one night after our fifth consecutive episode of *No Reservations,* Kit had the idea. He found a guided European food and wine tour where we could experience the best and richest of flavors, the most storied traditions of breaking bread, the perfect full-senses immersion to inspire our work. *The full Bourdain,* he said, which made me instantly fall in love with him all over again.

We saved for a year to book it, and then we broke up on the flight, and Kit fucked off to Paris, and I never saw him again. The reservation was nonrefundable. I came home with a broken heart, a travel-sized bottle of fourteen-year whiskey we'd planned to drink at the final stop in Palermo, and a trip voucher valid for forty-eight months. I told myself that, on month forty-seven, I would take the trip by myself, for me. I'll stand on the beach and drink our whiskey to mark how far I've come. To commemorate being finally, completely over Kit.

And here I am, in a pub five minutes from Trafalgar Square, muscling a new keg into position, being incredibly brave and independent and sexy of my own volition.

I can do this. I'm the Crocodile Hunter. I will *learn,* and I will have *fun,* and I will take it all back to the Somm at work and my kitchen at home where I come up with my own recipes. I will be my best, most confident, most competent self. I will not cram my stuff into my pack in a big tangled wad every morning or drop my phone in the Arno or leave my ID on an airport toilet paper dispenser (again). And I will not, at any point, wish I was doing it with Kit.

I barely even think of him anymore.

I kick the keg the final inch into place with the toe of my boot, then twist the coupler in and push the lever down.

"Guinness is back!"

When I stand, the manager is watching, his face ruddy and bemused. He pulls a half-pint from the new keg and passes it to me.

"You work in a pub back home?" he asks.

I take a sip. "Something like that."

"Well," he says, "you're welcome to finish the shift. Match's almost over, but Liverpool's on at three."

"At—at three?" My stomach drops. "Is it already—?"

Over a tattered leather booth by the door, a clock shaped like a Scottish terrier declares sixteen minutes to three.

Sixteen minutes until my tour bus leaves for Paris. Sixteen minutes until I lose my last shot at this trip, and a mile of unknown, untested London streets between this pub and the meeting point.

I whip the towel off my shoulder and do the unthinkable: chug my Guinness.

"I'm—*eugh*." I suppress a burp that tastes like pure Irish vengeance. "I'm supposed to be at Russell Square in fifteen minutes."

The manager and bartender exchange a grim look.

"You'd better get your skates on, then," the manager says.

I hand him my empty glass and scoop up my pack.

"Gentlemen." I salute. "It's been an honor."

And I take off running.

— — —

Someone yanks me back onto the curb just before a black cab clips me.

"Fuck!" I gasp, my life flashing before my eyes. Mostly swimming pools and cocktail shakers and casual sex. Not bad. Not impressive, but not bad. I look up at my savior, a tower of flannel and blond hair. "Forgot which way to look. I promise I'm about to leave the country and none of you will ever see me again."

The man tilts his head, like a curious boulder.

"Do I look English to you?" he says in an accent that is certainly not English. It's not Scottish or Irish either, though, so at least I probably haven't insulted him. Finnish? Norwegian?

"No, you don't."

The light changes, and we keep walking in the same direction. This isn't a meet-cute. Is this a meet-cute? I'm not into beards. I hope it's not a meet-cute.

"You're on the food and wine tour too?" the maybe-Norwegian guesses. I take in the pack on his broad back. It's a big cross-country pack like mine, though mine looks twice as big on me. I may be tall, but I'm not genetically coded to push warships off beaches into the Nordic surf.

"Yeah, I am! Oh my God, I'm so glad I'm not the last one."

"Yes," the guy says. "I slept on a hillside last night. Did not think it would take so long to hike back."

"To London?"

"Yes."

"You—okay." I have several questions, but no time. "I'm Theo."

He grins. "Stig."

It's 3:04 when we reach Russell Square, where an older woman with a peppery, no-nonsense haircut is loading the final suitcase into the luggage compartment of what must be our bus.

"Are you needing help with the bags, Orla?" a rich voice calls in a thick Italian accent. A handsome bronze face appears in the doorway of the bus.

"Don't you worry your pretty head," the driver, Orla, returns. Her own accent is Irish.

"Do not seduce me unless you mean it," the man says cheekily before catching sight of us. "Ah! The last two! Meraviglioso!"

As he bounds down the steps, the London gray erupts into steaming Napoli amber. This must be Fabrizio, the man listed as our guide in the email the tour company sent out with all the final information. He's outrageously good-looking, dark hair waving over the nape of his neck, coarse stubble across his defined jaw artfully blending into the hair at his open collar. He looks made-up, like the guy who gives Kate Winslet her first orgasm in a movie about a divorcée in Sicily.

He flips a page on his clipboard, looking at me.

"You must be Stig Henriksson."

"Uh—"

He tosses his beautiful head back and laughs. "Joking! Only joking! Ciao, Stig!" He steps up to Stig and kisses the cliff face of his cheek. "And that makes you Theodora!"

And then he's pulling me in too, drawing his mouth across my cheek.

"Theo." I rest my hand on his bicep and kiss his cheek, assuming that's the right thing to do. When he pulls away, he's smiling.

"Ciao bella, Theodora." Almost no one calls me Theodora, but I like how it sounds in his mouth. *Tay-o-dooora,* with the R flipped on its back and the second O drawn out slow and tender, like he's taking it out for a drink. I wouldn't mind if *this* was a meet-cute. "Andiamo!"

Orla slams the luggage compartment.

"Very full, this tour," Fabrizio tells us onboard. "Maybe a seat in the back? And I have one next to me!"

From beside the driver's seat, I can see every row of passengers, my companions for the next three weeks. I glance over at Stig—we're the only ones who came on this trip alone.

Of course. A trip like this is meant to be shared. Float together down the Seine, toast champagne glasses, take windswept photos of each other on a beachside cliff, eat from the same plate and talk for the rest of your lives about that one incomparable bite. Those are the kind of memories built for two to live inside, not one.

I tip my chin up and march down the aisle, leaving the seat for Stig.

I pass two Australian guys shouting with laughter, a pair of older women with matching visors speaking Japanese, a few retired couples, two girls in crop tops, several sets of honeymooners, a Midwestern mom and her bored-looking adult son, until finally, I see it. The very last aisle seat is empty.

I can't get a good look at the person huddled against the window, but I don't catch any red flags. They wear a soft-looking T-shirt and faded jeans, and their hair hides their face. They might be sleeping. Or at least pretending to sleep so nobody sits beside them. They probably want a seatmate as much as I do, which is not at all.

I take a breath.

"Hi!" I say in my friendliest voice. "Is this seat taken?"

The person stirs, brushing loose waves of brown hair back from their face. The only warning I get before they turn to face me is a smudge of paint on their left hand, from the first to third knuckle.

I know those hands. They're always stained the same way, with ink or food dye or watercolor pigment.

Kit looks up, furrows his elegant brow, and says, "Theo?"

— — —

Maybe that cab did hit me.

Maybe I was flattened in a zigzag crosswalk, and afternoon commuters are gathered around saying what a shame such a hot young piece of ass should have to go out as roadkill outside a Boots. Someone at *The Sun* is drafting a headline—GOOD NIGHT FLOWERDAY! "Theo Flowerday, oldest and most disappointing daughter of Hollywood director power couple Ted and Gloria Flowerday, dead after wandering into traffic, to no one's surprise." Maybe everything since has been a dying fever dream, and I've arrived in hell, where I'll be forced to share three weeks of the most sensuous, romantic sights and flavors of Europe with a stranger whose perineum I could describe from memory.

All that seems more likely than the reality that the person seated in the last row is actually Kit.

"You—" I keep staring at him. He keeps being there. My ears are ringing, suddenly. My legs have gone numb. "You're not here."

He holds up a hand as if to prove he's corporeal. "I think I am, though?"

"*Why* are you here?"

"I have a ticket."

"So do I. They—they gave me a voucher, but I—"

"Me too, I—"

"—never got around to—"

"—didn't want it to go to waste, so—"

In some cobwebby corner of my brain, I must have known we had the same vouchers with the same expiration dates, but I never imagined that somehow we would—we would—

"Please tell me," I say, shutting my eyes, "we didn't book the same fucking tour."

The bus jerks into drive, and my knees buckle—half of me lands in the empty seat, the other half in Kit's lap. My backpack swings around and smashes squarely into Kit's face.

Into the hair behind my ear, voice thick and muffled and gently amused, Kit says, "So you're still mad at me, then."

I swear, clawing toward my own seat. Kit's eyes are scrunched shut, his hand clamped over his nose.

"Orla's got a lead foot. Are you—?"

"I'm fine," Kit says, "but don't panic when I show you."

"Show me wh—" He removes his hand to reveal an absolutely spectacular nosebleed. *"Jesus!"*

"It's okay!" Blood dribbles out of his left nostril, already pooling in the hollow of his Cupid's bow. "It's not as bad as it looks."

"It looks pretty fucking bad, Kit!"

"My nose just does this now." He sneezes out few tiny red bubbles. "It'll stop in a second."

Now. Now, as in there was once a *then,* in which we were in love and I knew what his nose did and didn't do.

When someone is your best friend for sixteen years, your boyfriend for two, and your first and only love, it's not easy to edit them from your life, but I've done it. Everything that could be erased or deactivated or deleted has been: every number blocked, every Polaroid and souvenir T-shirt packed away in cardboard boxes in one of Sloane's spare closets. I've curated my own life to know nothing about his, not his job or his haircut or whether he ever finished pastry school in Paris. I'm pretty sure he *does* still live in Paris, but until this moment, he could have joined the Navy and had an arm bitten off by a shark for all I knew.

If I *do* think about Kit, in the fantasy I don't have, because I don't think about him enough to have a specific fantasy scenario, we're colliding at the door of a restaurant in Manhattan. He's on a date, and I'm on invitation to sample the wine list, and whatever tragic artist he's with gets bonked in the head by the door when he sees me in my bespoke suit and knows I've finally made it, that I have a fulfilling career and an endless parade of lovers, that I've gotten my shit so comprehensively together I'll never need him or anyone else ever again. And I don't even notice him.

In real life, people are staring.

"I'm okay, Birgitte!" Kit says with a little wave at the retirees across the aisle. He's already befriended some elderly Swedes.

It's never like this in my head, like I'm the same old catastrophe he couldn't put up with anymore. He's supposed to see that I'm *somebody* now. A brave new Theo, in control of every situation. The damn Crocodile Hunter.

I untie the bandana from my neck.

"Come here," I say, wetting the cloth with water from my pack.

"It's really fine," Kit insists. "It's already stopping."

"Then let me clean you up."

Kit's expression flickers, somewhere between cautious hope and the queasy, trapped look of a man being charged by a grizzly.

"Okay."

I reach for him from the right, but he turns his face to the left. I go to reach from the left, but he corrects too fast and turns his face to the right. We miss each other two more times before I clamp a hand around his chin and tilt his jaw directly toward me.

Our eyes lock, both of us caught by surprise.

Bad move. Steve Irwin never went around grabbing crocodiles by their handsome little jaws. At least, none that he'd had sex with.

"Hold still," I say, refusing to look away first. Kit blinks slowly, then nods.

I dab away the blood, aware with every second that I've made a grave miscalculation. From this position, I have no choice but to study his face and all the ways it has and hasn't changed from twenty-four to twenty-eight. Mostly he looks the same, just a bit more mature and defined. He has the same architectural cheekbones and curious eyebrows, the same soft mouth, the same lash-fringed brown eyes with that familiar flung-open brightness they've held since we were kids. The most noticeable difference is the slightest curve to the statue-straight nose from my memory, which I'm pretty sure is not my fault.

He's looking at me, and I wonder if he's doing the same. I've changed more than he has. No more makeup, unrulier brows, more freckles. A few years back, I stopped trying to make all the disparate features of my face work together the way I thought they were supposed to and started appreciating each individual piece. My wide mouth and its upturned corners, the angles of my jaw and cheeks, my slightly oversized nose. I love the way I look now, but I don't know if Kit will. Not that I care.

I release him and tuck my hand under my leg before it can do anything else stupid.

"Huh, you were right," I say. "It did stop. That was fast."

"I broke my nose a couple years ago," Kit tells me. "It bleeds easy now, just not for long."

A weird spark of loss swirls up, like when Kit and I would watch a show together and I would find out he'd skipped ahead without me. Like I should have known this, somehow.

I don't ask. We sit a foot apart, a bandana full of his blood in my hand as the bus trundles past the white plaster rows of Notting Hill Gate. I'm trying to remember the tour destinations I was so excited about this morning, Bordeaux and Barcelona and Rome, but Kit's hair keeps falling into his eyes.

"Your hair is shorter," Kit says in a strange, neutral voice.

"Yours is longer," I point out.

"We almost have—"

"The same haircut."

Kit exhales a sound between sigh and a laugh, and I have to grit my teeth to keep from screaming.

This is supposed to be *my* Saturn return voyage of self-realization. And now I'll have Kit in every frame, doing nauseating Kit things. Charming old Swedes, waxing poetic about sfogliatella, fondling the foliage, summiting Tuscan hills in the glow of dusk, smelling like—is that lavender? *Still?*

"This is unbelievable," Kit says, shaking his head like I'm an acquaintance he ran into at Trader Joe's and not the lifelong love he abandoned at an airport in a foreign country. "How are you?"

"Good," I tell him. "Really, really good, until about, oh"—I check the time—"fifteen minutes ago."

Kit takes this in stride. "Sure. That's good."

"And you? You look . . . healthy."

"Yeah, more or less intact," Kit says with an enigmatic smirk that makes me wish my pack had hit him harder. "I'm—"

Fabrizio's romance-novel voice croons over the bus's PA system.

"Ciao a tutti ragazzi! How are you today? Good? Yes, good! If you do not know, my name is Fabrizio, and I am your guide for the next three weeks, and I am very happy to be sharing with you the flavors of France, Spain, and Italy—and yes, the sights, also!"

And in that moment, Kit does something unfathomable: he pulls a paperback out of his backpack, opens to a marked page, and starts *reading*. As if we weren't in the middle of our first conversation in four years. As if the only remarkable thing about our two-hour ride from London to Dover is that it must be passed with a book. I just got kicked through the doors of my own personal haunted nightmare mansion, and Kit is reading *A Room with a View.*

The pages are yellowed at the edges, like he got preoccupied with his chic Parisian life and left it in a windowsill for a few months. I'm less interesting to him than a book he forgot he had.

Fabrizio tells us about his childhood in his parents' restaurant in Naples, explaining that we meet in London because it's an English-speaking tour, but the tour won't officially begin until tomorrow morning in Paris. We're pulling off at Dover to see the cliffs before sunset and then pushing on to Paris for two days in the City of Lights.

He moves on to the story of his most memorable night in London, when a bottle-wielding bartender chased him from a pub for making out with his girlfriend ("My favorite girl in England, so nice for kissing, but we could not be together. Allergic to garlic!"). The bus is eating from the palm of his hand.

I'm barely listening. I'm gripping my knees with both hands, staring straight ahead at the seat in front of me. Not wondering what kitchen Kit has been baking in, not feeling his weight in the air he displaces, not waiting for him to turn his page so I know he's not just pretending to read. He never looked back before. I shouldn't be surprised.

Kit turns a page.

If he's fine, I'm fine.

— — —

In the movie, you never see the cliffs in color.

The 1944 Irene Dunne film is all I know of Dover. The one about an American girl who marries an English baronet in World War I. I can't remember when I saw it—probably when Este was small, because our parents thought anything filmed before 1960 was age-appropriate entertainment for babies. Near the beginning, Irene stands on the deck of a ship and gazes tearfully over the sea at the white chalk cliffs of Dover.

In real life, there are a lot more sheep, and the cliffs' grassy tops are too green even for Technicolor. The land curves and sways and breathes with the wind and then suddenly, it stops. The rolling English hillside hits some sharp, immediate edge, and where there should be more hills, there's only a straight, tooth-white, three-hundred-foot drop to the blue sea below.

It would be such a gorgeous view if Kit wasn't in it. A taste of what's to come, I guess.

I'm walking with the two Australians by default. Everyone has split into pairs, even Stig and Fabrizio, although Stig looks like he's regretting it. Part of Fabrizio's job is making sure none of us get lost, so to be easier to find, he carries a telescopic pole stuck up the ass of a little stuffed Pinocchio puppet. (The puppet, he explains, is because *Pinocchio* is an Italian story, and he's Italian, and also, "some Italians do not mind so much from behind—joke! A joke!") And so Fabrizio and Stig lead the group down the trail, Stig with the gait of an Alpine hiker on a short leash and a puppet getting cheerfully penetrated three and a half feet above his head.

Shortly behind them is Kit, wearing the same leather and canvas sling bag he's owned since we were fourteen, and then the rest of the group, and finally, the Australians and me.

"It's Florence for me," I tell them when they ask what destination I'm most looking forward to. "They'll have the best wine. And the best collection of butts carved out of marble."

"Ah, you've never been to Spain, have you?" says the blond, whose name is Calum. "There's nothing like Spanish vermouth, it'll change your life."

"*You've* never been to Spain!" says the ginger, whose name is also Calum.

"I went to Bilbao with *you*, two years ago," Blond Calum argues.

"No, you didn't!"

"Yes, I did, you just don't remember because you were off

your tits for three days straight. *I* was the one who found you when you went off to sleep with the cows."

While they're cheerfully arguing, I take the opportunity to text Sloane without Kit six inches from my screen.

tell me, I type, why the fuck kit fairfield is here.

There's a weird taste in my mouth. I don't know the last time I typed those letters in that order. I can't stand to look at them, so I put my eyes on the horizon, where I can just make out France in the distance.

Kit always dreamed about returning to France, ever since his family moved to the States when he was eight. He was born out-side of Lyon to a French mom and an American dad, bilingual from birth, and whenever he got bored, his dual citizenship was waiting behind break-in-case-of-emergency glass. I should have seen it coming.

I remember the day the kitchen phone rang at Timo. It had been three days since Kit left me at Heathrow, and I'd taken back-to-back doubles to avoid being alone in our apartment. I heard the shift manager say Kit's name—I'd set him up with a part-time gig helping with desserts and doughs on weekends—and then I heard him tell the pastry chef that Kit had called in to quit because he was moving to Paris.

That was how I found out. All our lives together, and he didn't even tell me himself.

I marched into the walk-in and screamed at a bin of pota-toes, then clocked out early to put Kit's shit in boxes. I pulled his baking pans out of the kitchen drawers and his clothes out of our closet and his plants out of the windowsills. I blocked his number and texted his sister that his stuff was ready to be picked up, because I wasn't paying to ship it to France, not when I had Kit's half of the rent to cover.

With time, the anger subsided into the sort of lazy, funny grudge you joke about. If a friend asks me what Kit's up to these days, I'll say *fuck if I know,* and we'll laugh. But he wasn't wrong earlier. I *am* still angry.

"Hey, Theo," Ginger Calum says.

I blink back to Dover.

"Yeah?"

"Anyone ever tell you, you look just like that bird from the Beatles movie that came out last year? The one who played George's girl in the sixties? Joan something?"

Fuck. Not this, not now.

"Sloane." I hoped on this side of the Atlantic people would be slower to put it together. "Sloane Flowerday."

"That's the one!" Blond Calum says. "You could be her! Or the other one, doesn't she have a sister who's an actress? What's her name?"

"Este."

"Yeah! Wow, if they had a sister who was normal, you could be her. Like the third Hemsworth brother."

My jaw clenches for more than one reason. "I get that a lot."

I turn away, squinting at the sun while the Calums debate which of my little sisters is hotter.

"Hey, Theo?"

Kit has appeared in front of us, salty breeze swirling his hair around his face, hands tucked politely into his pockets. He looks like a hero from one of his romantic paperbacks on the way to ravish someone in a field of violets. I'm already exhausted.

"Can I talk to you for a second?"

Oh, he wants to *talk* now.

He leads us out of earshot, to a small outcropping through a gap in the trail's wooden fence. From here, I can see the sheep grazing near the castle, and I wish more than anything I could be one of them. Not a care in the world, no struggling freelance gigs or famous relatives, no fraught reunions with exes who fucked your life up so much you had to make a new one. Just grass.

Kit arranges himself atop a small boulder, crossing an ankle over his knee. I wait for him to say something, to start apologizing for what happened between us, to act like it happened at all. He doesn't.

"What did you want to talk about?" I finally ask.

"Oh," Kit says. "I didn't. I just—I overheard."

He overheard.

This isn't about us. It's about Kit saving me from strangers asking questions about my family, knowing better than anyone how that makes me feel. And now I have to stand here and receive his annoying fucking empathy.

"Am I supposed to thank you?"

"What?" Kit says. "No, I just didn't want those guys to say anything weird to you about Este or Sloane."

I shrug. "People say plenty of things to me all the time."

"I'm sure they do," Kit says. "I just felt—"

"Bad for me, yeah, I got that," I say, "but here's the thing. You stopped being part of my life. So you don't get to jump in when you feel like it now."

Kit touches a finger to his lips. "Okay."

"I mean," I go on, anger spiking in my chest, "if you wanted to look out for me, I can think of a few times you could have deigned to speak to me the past few years."

"Theo."

"In fact, if you're gonna say anything to me now, how about"—I put on an imitation of Kit's musical voice, complete with the faintest hint of a French accent, once lost but now brought back from the dead by Paris—"'Theo, I'm so sorry about everything, I really fucked you over, that was pretty shitty.'"

"Theo."

"'I never should have left y—' Are you laughing? Seriously?"

"It's—"

Something wooly nudges my thigh.

"That," Kit says.

That is a stout white sheep, who has apparently escaped the castle flock. The bell around her neck suggests this isn't her first jailbreak.

"Oh," I say. She stares up at me with her watery black eyes and prods me again with her nose. The bell rattles. "Hi."

"I was trying to tell you," Kit says.

I pat her fluffy head like she's a dog. She bleats approvingly.

"As I was saying—"

The sheep butts my leg, harder now.

"Hey! Okay, okay." I try to pet her, but she ducks and butts me again. "Really?"

"Baa," she replies.

"The point is—ow—you can't just act like I'm the same and you're the same and everything's fine, because—"

"Baa!"

"—because it's not."

Kit's face is serious, even as the sheep clamps her teeth around the hem of my overalls.

"I'm not the same," he concedes. "And I'm sure you're not. And I would have liked to talk to you, but, Theo, what part of blocking my number was supposed to make me think that was welcome?"

I look down at the sheep in time to see her cough up a clump of grass on my boots. Nearly missed my bus, almost hit by a car, committed assault and battery, heard a man call my little sister "a top sort," regurgitated on by a sheep, and now trapped with my ex, who is making an inconveniently good point.

"I am sorry," Kit says. "For all of it."

Kit was born with a sincere face. He means everything he says, and he looks like it.

When I look at him, I believe he really is sorry. Not that it's enough, but it is at least true.

"And I'm sorry if I overstepped," he says. "Old habits."

I think of Kit, age eleven, plucking a bee stinger out of my foot. Kit, age twenty-three, waking me up when I overslept for work.

He opens his little bag, and the sheep finally turns her attention from me, eyeing Kit curiously as he shakes a few orange bits from a foil pouch into his palm.

"Hi, beautiful," he says in his softest voice. "Would you like to leave poor Theo alone and have a snack?"

She plods over and starts eating out of his hand, as happy and gentle as a lamb.

"Dried apricots," he tells me.

Against my own wishes, my jaw unclenches. Maybe, if I'm being honest, I needed Kit away from me because it's so hard to stay mad in his presence. Anger doesn't like to hang around him.

"Look," I say. "You being here—this isn't the trip I had in mind."

"Me neither," he says, still feeding the sheep.

"But this is important to me, okay?" I say. "So I'm going to do it."

"Yeah, of course it is. You should." He's nodding, still horribly sincere. "I was thinking, if you're uncomfortable, I could . . . hop off in Paris? Stay home?"

So he *is* still in Paris.

Even worse, he means this too. It shows not only on his face but in the set of his shoulders, the plaintive tilt of his chin.

He really isn't the same. Something has firmed up, like the center of a crème brûlée that was sloshy custard the last time I saw it. He seems . . . completed, somehow. The Kit I knew was restless and hungry. This person is steady, self-sustained.

This new Kit thinks he's doing me a favor. He thinks he can handle this, and I can't.

Fucking Sheep Boy over here wants to be the bigger person.

"No, that's stupid," I say. "Don't do that."

He blinks. "Why not?"

"Because we both paid for our own ticket," I point out. "And besides, I don't know anyone else on this tour. Do you?"

Kit shakes his head.

"So, if anything happens, at least we'll have . . ." What's a non-committal way to describe what we are to each other? "Someone who knows our blood type, or whatever."

Kit considers that. The sheep licks his palm.

"Are you saying you want to be friends?"

"I'm *saying* I didn't fly across the world to feel weird and bad for three weeks. I came to drink champagne and eat cannelloni until I throw up. So, we could try . . . peacefully coexisting."

Kit tucks the inside of his cheek between his back teeth, hollowing it out prettily.

"I'd like that."

"And maybe we don't have to talk about everything that happened," I say. "Maybe we just get through it. And then it's done."

After a long moment, Kit holds out the hand not covered in sheep saliva.

"Okay," he says. "As long as that's what you want."

I take his hand in mine, and we shake on it.

"AB positive," Kit says. My blood type.

"O negative," I say back. His.

"Baa," says the sheep.

PARIS

PAIRS WELL WITH:

Ulysse Collin "Les Maillons" Blanc de Noirs
Extra Brut poured by a flustered waiter,
brioche mousseline

PARIS

I've learned a lot from taking the Court of Master Sommeliers certification exam three times. Most important: I have a naturally gifted nose.

When I'm sweating in front of stone-faced judges for a blind tasting, the faint distinction between fennel and anise calms me down. When Timo closes for the night, and the dishwashers are scraping forty-two-dollar hand-stuffed tortellini into the trash, and the chef sommelier sets down a glass of white and tells me to identify it, I can clock the spiciness of a grape grown in red slate soils or the airiness of a sandy coast.

Some of that is practice—sniffing produce, licking rocks on mountain hikes, a Rocky Balboa training montage through every botanical garden in Southern California—but you can't teach instinct. I didn't have to be taught to match the note of white pepper in the chef's new special to a bottle of Aglianico, or to concoct a gimlet that tastes like a bride's memory of her mother's perfume. My nose just tells me. When I'm uncertain, or intimidated, or worried I'm about to fuck something up, I can count on that.

So, I prop open the window of my single room in Paris, close my eyes, and take a deep breath. Notes: dark roast coffee, fresh bread from the café down the street, garden aromas of foxglove and elderberry, sulfur from the igneous rock in the cobblestones, car exhaust and ivy and cigarette smoke.

My heart rate slows. My fists unclench. I open my eyes to

see Montmartre's rosy bricks and slate mansard roofs, the city splayed at the foot of the hill.

I can do this. It'll be *fun*. It's a morning pastry tour through Paris, not The fucking Hague. It doesn't matter that Kit literally left me to study Parisian pastry. It doesn't matter that I once whispered to the universe, *I don't ever want to know how Kit is doing, I'd rather imagine him sitting alone in an empty room forever,* and instead the universe has answered with a live-action role-play of Kit's daily life, starring Kit.

"I'm in Paris," I say, pulling on light wash jeans and a boxy linen button-up. "I'm in *Paris*," I say, checking the mirror, thankful for short, effortless shag haircuts. "*I'm* in Paris," I say on my way out, like if I say it enough, it'll stop feeling so weird and big.

I'm here. I'm unbothered. I'm peacefully coexisting. I look great, I smell nice, and I'm going to eat my weight in chou à la crème.

Kit appears as I'm waiting for the jangly old elevator.

I'm surprised to see a creature of comfort like Kit in our tiny Montmartre hostel when he has his own pied-à-terre a few miles away, but he *has* always loved committing to a bit. He's probably all juiced up to play tourist. Tasting everything like it's the first time, falling in love all over again, aesthetically jerking himself off.

"Morning," he says with a small smile.

"Morning," I say.

I note his drapey linen shirt and pale blue trousers. Then I look down at myself and try not to swear out loud.

"We're wearing—" he begins.

"—the same outfit," I conclude. "You know what? I'm gonna take the stairs."

— — —

"Mark your name off, love, so I know I've not left anyone behind," Orla says as she thrusts a clipboard at me.

I draw a check next to *Flowerday, Theodora,* take my seat in the last row, and pull out my phone. Sloane's texted, We just got new pages and Lincoln has twice as many lines now. He's definitely fucking the director. How's Kit?

Last night, she called between shoots and demanded to hear everything. The Kit subject is tricky with my sisters: They've known him as long as they can remember, and he's, well, Kit. Even after everything, I know they only stopped speaking to him and his siblings out of loyalty to me, and we were the only exception to Sloane's opinion that love is a waste of time. She might actually be enjoying this.

oh, you know, I reply, he's kit. Then, have you considered also fucking the director?

Not every problem can be solved by sleeping with it, Sloane replies.

not with that attitude.

I see Kit coming and move to the window seat before he has the chance to magnanimously offer it to me.

"I was going to tell you to take the window," Kit says as he sits down, "since it's your first time in Paris."

I force myself to smile.

"How do you know I haven't been to Paris since the last time we saw each other?"

"I don't," Kit concedes. "Have you?"

I fold my arms. "No. But I could have."

Orla takes us to our local guide by way of a scenic tour. We careen around the wide, lawless circle of the Arc de Triomphe and down the Champs-Élysées to the gardens that fringe the Louvre, then over the silver-green Seine and around the island that holds Notre-Dame. It's a nearly cloudless August morning, and the sun glitters on the golden dome of Les Invalides. Fabrizio tells us how Napoleon divided Paris into arrondissements, this pretty grid of uniform limestone and slate. Everything is peach and lilac and cream, except for the gardens, which are riotously green.

When we arrive at the park across from Le Bon Marché, a woman is waiting at the carousel in the chic, all-black ensemble of someone who'd prefer to be anywhere but next to a children's amusement ride. Her lavender hair is cut in a severe chin-length bob, and she's petite, but her boots add a few inches. She eyes Fabrizio's puppet on a stick with long-suffering distaste and gamely accepts an air-kiss from him, even when one of Pinocchio's dangling feet kicks her smooth, stern forehead.

"Group, this is Maxine!" Fabrizio says. "She is a pastry chef here in Paris! She leads our Parisian pastry tour since last year. Knows the best pâtisseries, orders the best for us. Maxine, will you introduce yourself?"

"I'm Maxine," Maxine says with finality, and Kit stifles a laugh.

"Okay!" Fabrizio claps his hands. "Andiamo!"

Maxine leads us out of the park and to a small corner shop with a simple black sign declaring HUGO & VICTOR.

"This," Maxine says, in brusque English, "is where we begin. My favorite pâtisserie in Paris."

The pâtisserie is so small that we can only squeeze inside in shifts, but it smells heavenly. One section is all house-made chocolates in boxes made to look like Victor Hugo hardcovers. Another is dedicated to artisanal marshmallows. Glass cases hold pavlova clouds topped with split figs, bubbles of sunshine-yellow yuzu cheesecake, and precise triangles of tarts—grapefruit, lime, apple and caramel, tonka bean, passionfruit. Maxine orders a mountain of pastries, and at the sidewalk tables outside, she floats around telling us about everything.

"These are called financiers," she says of a small loaf-shaped almond cake, explaining that some say their name comes from their ability to hold shape for hours in the pockets of Parisian stockbrokers. "And this—could you—" She gestures.

And Kit, who's closest, takes the financier and swaps her a tube-shaped pastry with a golden crust and a kiss of icing sugar at its peak. It kind of looks like a dick.

"Merci," she says. "*This* is my favorite brioche in Paris. Will you?"

At her polite cue, Kit carefully cuts the brioche open to reveal bouncy, round air bubbles and a pocket of raspberry compote.

"Parfait, mon cher," she says to him. He smiles, pleased to have pleased her. Teacher's pet. "The typical brioche you buy from the store is a loaf, yes? This is brioche mousseline. It is traditionally baked in a cylinder mold or even a tin can, and it has twice as much butter as most brioche. A rich man's brioche. You will taste—"

Someone at another table interrupts, calling out a question for Maxine. Kit murmurs something to her in French, and when she nods, Kit trots off.

"I can answer that for you!"

Maxine's pretty lips quirk into a smile as she describes the process of brioche dough, and I squint from her to Kit, suspicious.

Kit has this thing—we used to call it his "condition"—where he accidentally makes people fall in love with him. He never *knew* he was doing it. He just happened to be born with the face of a fancy little god-prince and a way of approaching every interaction with total, sincere interest. Attempting a casual flirt with him is like trying to discuss the weather with the sun.

If my first experience in Paris is Maxine falling for Kit right in front of my dick brioche, I might jump in the Seine.

We carry on through the 6th and 7th Arrondissements, visiting pâtisseries and boulangeries and chocolateries. My thumbs almost can't keep up with the notes on my phone. At a narrow chocolate shop lined with antique cigarette machines, Maxine hands out paper cones of creamy one-hundred-percent dark chocolate. At a sleek pâtisserie owned by a famed French chef, we try glass-smooth cakes shaped like mangoes and hazelnuts and, my favorite, a complex olive oil cake in the shape of a green olive.

I try to focus on flavors, but it's hard to ignore how Kit travels the streets of Paris like he was born in them. It's one thing to share someone's life and then find yourself spectating on it, and another to watch him live the dream he left you for. He buys groceries here. He picks up loaves of bread and makes plans for lunch. While the rest of us are gawking at the Eiffel Tower, he's ducking back into a pâtisserie to chat with the head chef like an old friend. If he ever stands on these cobbles and thinks of his life with me, he probably considers it quaint. Small, cute, a bit embarrassing.

Our penultimate stop is a macaron shop, and we sit in the square around Fontaine Saint-Sulpice passing them around, tasting flavors so much bigger than their delicate packages: banana and acai, lychee with raspberry and rose, yuzu with wasabi and candied grapefruit.

I'm looking at the fountain, inventing names for the saints inside the niches—St. Edna the Indignant, patron saint of stabbing your ex with a chocolate spoon because you've been cast as quaint backstory—when someone says, "You look *really* familiar."

It's one of the two twentysomething girls I noticed when I first boarded the bus, the shorter one with shiny black hair. I'm gathering that she and her friend are some kind of travel influencers.

"I don't think we've met before," I tell her, praying I'm not already two for two on getting clocked as a Flowerday.

"No, I think we have," she says. "You were making drinks at the Coachella after-party at the Saguaro, right? The bar that was, like, in a big van?"

I blink a few times, amazed. I *was* hired for that party. One thing about a freelance mobile bar in a Volkswagen Microbus is, influencers love it. I'd hoped one of them would book me for another job, but no one seemed to remember me.

"You were there?"

"Oh my God, yes!" She turns to her friend, a beachy blonde in a micro-cropped sweater-vest and cargo pants. "Ko! I was right!"

The blonde pauses her scroll through her phone to regard me for one blank second over her skinny sunglasses.

"You made the best Bloody Mary I've ever had in my life," she says in complete monotone. "I would literally kill for you."

"That's Dakota," the first girl says. "I'm Montana."

I instantly love this. Did they come as a combo pack?

"I'm Theo."

"Theo! You're so cool!" Montana says. "Who's your brand partner? Do they rent that van out?"

"Oh, just me," I say. "The bus is mine. I got it secondhand and converted it."

"Wow, slay," she says. "Listen, I go to a lot of parties with a lot of open bars, and you are literally so talented. That blood orange margarita, with the peppers? You should be doing, like, Bella Hadid's birthday or something. Why aren't you in LA?"

"Thank you, wow," I say, meaning it. "But it's honestly just a side hustle. Weddings, parties, catering on weekends. I have a regular job at a restaurant in Palm Springs."

"I was telling Dakota—"

Over Montana's shoulder, I notice Kit talking to Fabrizio. His voice separates from the chatter and drifts to my ears.

"—that's what I think, at least," he says.

"You know so much about the French pastry," Fabrizio says. "How is this?"

"I'm a pâtissier at a hotel in the First Arrondissement," Kit says. "I actually graduated from École Desjardins with Maxine."

"Oh! You know our Maxine!"

"I know her *very* well. I told her she should apply to be a local guide when the spot opened up. She might not show it, but she loves doing this."

"Finally, I can thank someone for sending Maxine to us!" Fabrizio says. "She is a goddess."

"Isn't she?" I can hear the smile in his voice. The way he used to sound when he talked about me.

The morning shifts into focus. I never needed to worry about Maxine falling in love with Kit. Maxine and Kit are *already* in love. Their eyes probably met over a tart, and Maxine knew her life was about to turn to gold dust and candied petals, and now purple hairs cling to Kit's shower curtain, and—

"—so anyway, now he's on house arrest," Montana is saying.

I snap back to our conversation.

"Sorry, who?"

"The guy who did Bella Hadid's last birthday," Montana says. "So there's an opening, if you want me to ask my friend who knows her friend?"

"That's—really generous!" I hedge, unsure how to tell Montana that I prefer to avoid the celebrity circuit without telling her why. "But—what do you do? Travel content, right?"

As we walk to our last stop, Montana tells me about getting paid in sponsorships to eat crab legs in Bali and make out with scuba instructors on international waters. She's deeply cool, and she thinks I'm cool. I hold my chin a little higher, like I did yesterday when I heard there was a keg I could change.

Afternoon light spreads like caramel down Boulevard Saint-Germain, burnishing the flowers that drip from silk café canopies. At the head of the group, Kit and Maxine glide in step under a brown sugar sun. He plucks down a blossom and tucks it into the side pocket of her bag, a secret to find later. This is part of peacefully coexisting with your ex, I guess: watching them move on with someone else. Watching them find love in the city that was too much for you.

I may not be in love in Paris, but I'm not backstory either. I can tell the difference between an Austrian Riesling and an Australian Riesling by smell alone. I bought a bus that didn't run and turned it into a bar. I make the best Bloody Mary in California, excluding one guy with an ankle monitor.

Paris can't make me feel small, and neither can Kit. Not again.

— — —

Dinner is a traditional seven-course affair in a basement brasserie near the Eiffel Tower, secreted away from tourists. The whole thing is leather and velvet and aged wood, dusty chandelier light glinting off oil paintings and yellowed photographs in baroque frames, heavy air simmering with butter and marjoram. The kind of place where Tony Bourdain would camp out with a bottle of Burgundy and a pack of Reds. I wasn't sure I'd ever eat again after all that pastry, but suddenly I'm starving.

In the back, tables have been pushed into two long fifteen-tops for us. Maxine has joined us at Fabrizio's insistence, and by some cruel whim of the pastry gods, she's squeezed in next to me. Kit takes a chair several seats down and across and is immediately enveloped into conversation with Ginger Calum.

When your parents are director-producers and your godfather is Russell Crowe, it's rare to meet someone who intimidates you. Maxine, though—Maxine, with her orchid-and-moss perfume and permanently unimpressed expression—is intimidating. We're sitting hip to hip, but she doesn't seem aware of me at all. She's scrutinizing her hair in the back of her soup spoon.

Thankfully, I grew up with Sloane Flowerday. My little sister was twelve the first time she sent script notes so harsh the screenwriter left LA altogether. I can handle an ice queen with an expensive manicure.

"Hi," I say to Maxine. "I'm Theo."

"Yes, I know," she says, turning to me at last. Her tone gives nothing away.

"Right. I heard you and Kit went to pastry school together."

"We did."

"That's so cool," I say. "How did you meet?"

"Introduction to Dacquoise."

She's giving me nothing. I prop my elbow on the table and lean my chin against my fist.

"Dacquoise . . . the one with the layers of hazelnut and almond meringue, right?"

Maxine lifts her chin. Packed in like this, her face is inches from mine. She really is pretty in a Shirley Jackson sort of way, like she lives in a haunted mirror. If she didn't belong to Kit, I'd be making a move to smear her perfect mauve lipstick, but it'll be enough to get her to like me.

"You were paying attention."

"You're a great teacher."

She takes a long look at me, like I've earned a proper assessment. Then she nods once, as if satisfied, and says, "Now I understand."

Before I can ask *what,* the waiters arrive with our first course, and the tables explode with oohs of delighted surprise. A silver tray appears between us: burgundy snails the size of plums, overflowing with garlicky green parsley butter. Two more waiters bring the wine pairing, and I clock the label— champagne, Ulysse Collin, Les Maillons. A low whistle escapes my lips.

"Hm?" Maxine inquires as she picks up a snail with a tiny set of tongs.

"That's a three-hundred-fifty-dollar starter wine."

Course after course spills from the kitchen, followed always by new wines. After we've loosened the snails from their shells and sopped up the buttery persillade, out come platters of roasted sea bream with beurre blanc sauce and charred lemons. A straw-colored Muscadet splashes into my glass, followed by a Châteauneuf-du-Pape to go with the coq au vin.

At the end of the table, Kit is the prince of dinner. He laughs as Ginger Calum does his best impression of the bream's googly eyes and makes sure the Swedes try the brandy-glazed carrots.

He switches effortlessly to French for the waitress and leans in smiling when she whispers her answer in his ear. He loosens the buttons of his shirt. Fabrizio starts affectionately addressing him as "Professore" and begs him to explain the physics of a domed mousse we tasted earlier. He pulls out a pocket sketch pad to draw a diagram.

I drain my glass and turn to Maxine.

"Your accent—is it Canadian?"

"Montreal, originally," she says. "I grew up speaking English and French."

"Oh, like Kit. The bilingual part, not the Canadian part."

"Yes." She moves her glass in a little circle to swirl her wine. "Although I don't miss the continent as much as Kit does."

That I doubt. It doesn't seem like Kit cares if the continent lives or dies.

"What do you think of the wine?"

"I have been known to enjoy a Châteauneuf-du-Pape moment," she says primly.

"Oh, me too, especially with a gigot d'agneau."

"Mmm. There's something in it that brings out the herbs in a stew, but I can't remember what the French call it."

"The garrigue," I say. "The flavor you get when you grow grapes in the southern part of the Rhône Valley, because of all the sage and lavender and rosemary down there."

"That's the one." She considers me, politely ignoring the champignon that bounces off my plate and under the table. "Where did you learn these things?"

I could flex, if I wanted. Tell her I spent the last ten years working all the way up from busser to assistant sommelier at Timo, the only Michelin-starred restaurant in Palm Springs. But there's a new ember of curiosity in her eyes, and she's the kind of woman who'll only take your hand after you've laid it open before her.

So I say, "Kit probably mentioned my family to you, right?"

Her lashes twitch. "I know of them."

Of course she does. I'm the unfamous Hemsworth.

"And did you know when I was seventeen, I almost killed my dad's Best Picture campaign because the cops raided one of my house parties and TMZ reported it?"

"I was in Canada at the time," Maxine says neutrally. "But I'm sure it's a good story."

I smile.

I tell her how Este and Sloane both started getting steady work around the time I started high school, which meant my parents were usually either on their own sets or my sisters'. Kit was in New York, and I was alone in a house with a pool and eight bedrooms and a wine cellar. So, I threw myself a fifteenth birthday party.

Nobody cared much about Theo Flowerday, but everyone likes the kid from the famous family with the unchaperoned party mansion. I'd wanted to feel *special.* Like I had something to offer of my own. So, I made myself the house-party king of Palm Valley Prep, a magician with my parents' credit card and a fake ID. My big trick? I could make *any* drink on demand.

It didn't matter that I spent hours studying cocktail books instead of SAT prep, or that when I missed my family, I'd go to the cellar and look up every varietal and appellation from wherever they were shooting. What mattered was, you had to be at my parties, and my parties had to have me.

"So, yeah," I finish. "Plus, I work at a restaurant and handle the wine there."

Maxine delicately places her empty glass on the tablecloth, concealing my gravy stain.

"I was alone a lot too, at that age."

Over the next course of salad and a dewy Sancerre, Maxine casually explains that her parents died when she was fifteen and left her and her older sister to raise three younger brothers in a secluded mansion on the edge of Montreal.

She tells it like a morbidly funny children's story. Two teenage girls managing an estate, chasing geese out of the garden so they wouldn't hunt her youngest brother, fending off overly helpful aunts and uncles. She talks about learning to bake the family recipes—both the Japanese and the French Canadian ones—for the boys, who in turn forced her to go to pastry school. I don't tell her I'm sorry. I do ask follow-up questions about the geese, which seems to make her like me more.

I wave over more wine, and we keep talking. About Maxine's favorite things to bake (fussy breads), about my thoughts as a first-time visitor to Paris (great wine, big fan of the eating-croissants-outdoors industrial complex), about Fabrizio (yes, he's always like that). The cheese course arrives with a nice-ass Pomerol, and it's this wine that finally pushes me over the edge into drunk. I stumble through an explanation of Bordeaux's vintage report until Maxine says, "It's important to me that you know you sound like an ass," and I laugh so hard that wine almost comes out my nose.

As I'm wiping my chin, I find Kit watching us like he's not sure what we're up to and even less sure he wants to find out.

Maxine raises her glass to him. "Theo and I are friends now!"

Kit replies, "That's what I'm worried about!"

But the look on his face isn't displeasure. It's something a lot more pinkish and complicated.

I give him a real smile, the first he's gotten from me since before we boarded that plane four years ago. He touches his palm to his heart, then slips away again.

This is my opening to ask Maxine about Kit. What his new friends are like, what he likes to do around the city, if he's still in search of the perfect cinnamon roll. Instead, I concentrate on my cheese plate.

I'm finishing the Pont l'Évêque when Maxine says, "Oh God, he's flirting with the waiter."

Across the table, Kit is talking to the waiter refilling his

water. The smile on his lips is soft, intrigued, like he's just noticed the waiter is hot and is curious how he missed it. He murmurs something, and the waiter misses Kit's glass entirely and
has to run off for a towel.

"I don't know," I say. "That's just how Kit is."

"Please." Maxine rolls her eyes. She doesn't seem jealous,
more like fondly exasperated. "Do you know how deliberately
you have to flirt to get your water refilled in Paris?"

Except, Kit never knew what he was doing. He was deliberate
in a lot of things, but never, what? *Seduction?*

"He does that a lot?"

"You mean Kit?" Maxine arches a brow. "The Sex God of
École Desjardins?"

I nearly spit out my wine again. "The—what?"

"Oh, only the most annoying thing about him," she says. "He
had *everyone* he wanted. It was like a rite of passage in our year to
have one glorious night with Kit and then be in love with him
for a week. I know three different men who thought they were
straight until him."

"That's," I reply, "something."

Now the dessert course is coming out, and I'm confronting
the idea of Kit distributing life-changing orgasms to his entire
pastry school class.

Of the thoughts I don't have about Kit, the memory of what
he's like in bed is one I keep inside a steel-reinforced vault. I was
born a dumb, hot, horny creature who will abandon all reason
if I think too long about the kind of sex we used to have, so I
don't. Not an inch of skin, not a flash of pink tongue, not one
hot, slutty breath on the side of my neck.

I'm not about to start now. If Kit has become some kind of
minor sex celebrity, that's none of my business.

The waiter returns to mop up the spill, but Kit takes the towel
and insists on doing it himself, which only flusters the waiter

more. He backs into a waitress and gets a citron tart smashed into his shirt before beating another retreat.

"Get off your knees, man," Maxine says in a low voice. "Have some dignity."

I make sure to laugh at the right time.

— — —

After Fabrizio has pressed kisses to the cheeks of every waiter, we gather on the street. Maxine steps away to pull a silver cigarette case from her purse and light up.

"Theo."

Kit is waiting for me, half lit by the orange streetlight glow.

Longer hair suits him. It curls at his collar and kisses the highest points of his cheeks with a languid grace all his own. I wonder hopefully if it irritates him when he's baking, if he has to tie it back to get it out of his face.

He holds out a small paper shopping bag he's been carrying since the afternoon.

"It seemed like this one was your favorite," he says. "I thought you should have one to yourself, in case you're not in Paris again for a while."

Inside is a shiny olive oil cake, packed tidily in a ribbon-tied box.

"Did I get the right one?" he asks, and I realize I've been staring into the bag in stunned silence for five full seconds.

"Yeah, you did," I say. "How did you know?"

He glances away, up at a flower box in a window across the street.

"Lucky guess."

As if waiting for her cue, Maxine appears and links her arm through his, and now I understand. She probably takes note of what guests like on her tours, and she slipped him a hint. This is a couple gift. A conciliatory treat. An olive-cake olive branch.

"Thank you," I say to them, resolving not to feel pitied. "I heard the Calums and some of the others are going out for another drink, are you guys coming?"

Maxine takes a drag and exhales a cloud of smoke that smells like tobacco and lotus and high-end weed. She smokes hand-rolled herbal spliffs. Jesus, she's so fucking chic. I can't even remember to charge my vape.

"Darling, I just worked a full day," she says. "I'm putting myself to bed."

"Are you walking back to the flat?" Kit asks her. *The* flat, not *your* flat.

"It's a nice night for it, don't you think?"

"I'll walk you," he announces, like I'm stupid. Obviously he's going home with her to their apartment, so they can put *each other* to bed. We can be adults about it. "Maybe tomorrow night, Theo?"

"Sure," I agree. I put on my most suggestive grin. "Have a nice walk!"

Kit gives me a weird look, but they turn and leave together.

"Theo!" shouts Blond Calum as I watch them disappear arm in arm around the corner. "You with us?"

"Nah," I decide in the moment. "I'm gonna go see the Tower."

I set off on my own, across the street and through the wide green lawn at the foot of the Eiffel Tower, past amorous couples and teenagers with cheap champagne and guys selling light-up rubber balls that bounce thirty feet in the air. It's five minutes to eleven, which means five minutes until the lights on the Tower sparkle.

It's funny. I've seen this tower on so many screens, I assumed it'd be underwhelming in real life. None of those establishing wide shots capture how complicated it is up close, all the flourishes and arches and curlicues and starbursts of intersecting ironwork. It's not so bad being romanced by something familiar.

Sloane answers my video call on the second ring.

"Oh, hello," she drawls in a Katharine Hepburn voice. "I do hope you received my latest telegram."

"Sorry, I was trying to reach my sister, but I must have dialed the *Titanic*."

"The director thinks I should try more of a Transatlantic accent. I've been practicing."

"By God, I think you've got it."

"Yes, I believe I do," she agrees. "How's Paris?"

"Well, Kit and his hot girlfriend gave me a cake. Also I drank a lot of wine and now I might have to pee in a bush under the Eiffel Tower."

Sloane drops the accent and sighs, "Oh, Theo."

"I know," I say. I flip the camera to show her my view. "But look, it's sparkling."

— — —

I briefly consider staying in my room the next morning.

I have a few concerns, based on my track record. I'm concerned I might get pickpocketed because I'm not paying attention on the metro and wind up hopelessly lost with no way to find my way back. Maybe all the beautiful, feminine Parisian women might glare at me on the street, and not in a sexy way. I could discover I was right four years ago when I believed I couldn't handle a city like this, that I belong in my familiar valley and the closest I should ever get to the wide, curious world is the label on a bottle.

And then I think of how many things I'll never taste or smell, and I put on my boots.

I hike up to Sacré-Cœur to see its glistening white scallops and sit on the steps where John Wick died, then climb back down to gawk at the Palais Garnier. I ramble the old stone paths along the banks of the Seine, poking around secret corners and watching day drinkers on floating wine bars. Everything is different here, in small details I never thought of as changeable before, but

I find the city easier to navigate than expected, and I don't even embarrass myself when I order coffee and a croissant.

I'm beginning to suspect that a flirtatious smile and a genuine love of food and drink might get me anywhere.

The tour meets back up for lunch on a gourmet sightseeing cruise on the Seine, and I talk to Fabrizio for an hour about spaghetti Westerns while licking caviar off a spoon. We're served an Irouleguy Blanc so carefully sculpted, I write down *built like Swayze in 1989* in my notes. I'm in such a good mood, I don't care when my eyes meet Kit's across the dining room. I don't even think about his pity cake or new relationship. In fact, I decide I'd be more concerned if Kit *wasn't* dating anyone. He's so good at it, it would be a waste for him to stay single forever, like Meryl Streep quitting movies.

I, personally, am single by choice, not lack of opportunity. I get plenty of opportunities. At my last wedding gig, I pulled a bridesmaid *and* a groomsman, and we gave one another so many opportunities that I had to have Gatorade for breakfast.

For the evening, we have tickets for the Moulin Rouge dinner cabaret, so I change into the nicest outfit I packed, a sleeveless black linen jumpsuit that plunges down my chest in a deep V. I turn in the mirror, pleased with the clean, subtle lines of my chest. I look good, strong, androgynous. Like someone who's not afraid of this city and never has been.

My luck runs out under a glittering chandelier. Inside the theater, the space arches in lush, carpeted tiers with crisp white linens and lamps with opulent silk shades on endless tables. We've been divided into tables of six and eight, and as Fabrizio hands us off to our maître d', I realize who I'm seated with.

"Hello again," Kit says.

I bite the inside of my cheek. "Hi."

He does clean up nicely. Or, he's always clean, always neatly groomed and preternaturally fresh-smelling, but he knows how to make himself look like art. A cream linen shirt with a Cuban collar and delicate accents of embroidered flowers, tapered trousers cinched at his narrow waist, some of his hair twisted back into—did he *braid* it? Did he sit in his little room and lovingly braid his hair like he used to braid his sister's?

To add insult to injury, dinner comes with one bottle of champagne for every two people, and we have to share.

Across the table, Blond Calum eyes his champagne. "What, no absinthe? We don't get to meet the green fairy?"

"I reckon Kylie Minogue was booked tonight," Ginger Calum says.

Kit and I let out identical, simultaneous laughs. Both Calums look at us with eyebrows raised.

"Got that one, did ya?" Ginger Calum says. "Most Americans I've met don't even know who Kylie Minogue is."

"Heathens," Blond Calum adds.

"We're—" Kit says. "*I'm* a massive *Moulin Rouge* fan. It was my favorite movie growing up."

I've been trying not to think about it, Kit at thirteen, obsessed with a high-camp, high-saturation tragedy about forbidden love and dying of consumption. He's always been so completely himself.

"Once," I say, "in the eighth grade, he made me watch it four times in one night."

"I didn't *make* you," Kit teases, and then he flinches, like he doesn't know if this is allowed. His voice softens as he adds, "You were the one who wanted to learn every word of 'Elephant Love Medley.'"

"And you were a full-grown adult when you convinced me to do it with you at someone else's karaoke birthday."

"Crikey," Ginger Calum says. "That'll kill the party."

"Oh, *tanked* it," I say.

"Very poorly reviewed," Kit agrees, beginning to smile.

"We pulled it out, though, with—"

"'Can't Stop Loving You,'" we finish at the same time.

Our eyes meet, and I feel my mouth slipping into a smile. God, we got some mileage out of that song. So many nights in smoky bars or house parties, the two of us laughing into squawky microphones over an instrumental track. I haven't been able to think of it in years, but strangely, it doesn't hurt the same right now.

"Phil Collins," Blond Calum says with a sage nod. "Good lad."

"Good lad," I agree.

When the lights go down and the curtain rises on the luminous heart-shaped stage, I remind myself not to get sappy. I don't watch Kit's reactions from the corner of my eye. I choose the loveliest dancer on stage, and I focus only on her. It helps.

But it doesn't prepare me for the way Kit catches my elbow as we stand for the final bow. I find him gazing at me, golden in the chandelier glow.

"Do you still want to make up for last night?" he says under the cheers of the audience.

"What?"

"When I couldn't go out with you," he says. "Do you want to have that drink now? My favorite bar is around the corner, if you want to see it."

It's the fault of nostalgia, of my surprisingly successful morning, of blurry memories of Ewan McGregor's earnest belting and Kit spinning me under a disco ball, that I hear myself say, "Yeah, why not?"

— —— —

We head off from the Moulin Rouge's red windmill, down the wide Boulevard de Clichy, past sex shop after topless bar after sex shop. Girls grasp their heaving bosoms in portraits over shop fronts full of mannequins in lacy red chemises. Flashing displays advertise vibrators in every imaginable shape and size, and some I've never even thought to imagine.

"I hope that's where we're going," I say, pointing at a three-story emporium, ominously emblazoned with the name SEXODROME in neon red letters. I'm nervous and searching for jokes. "I've always wanted to go to"—I drop my voice to the guttural register of monster truck announcer—"THE SEXODROME."

Unable to resist a bit, Kit replies, "You need a Parisian mailing address to get into THE SEXODROME."

"Canceling THE SEXODROME for discriminatory business practices."

He laughs and takes a left at a violet-painted club called Pussy's, down a sloping side street with ivy-covered apartments and fenced private gardens. At a bright red door beside a window promising pints for four euros, he stops.

"This is it."

Kit's favorite bar is the width of my room at the hostel.

"Are we gonna fit in there?"

Kit just smiles and pushes inside.

My love of cramped dives is extensive and well-documented, but I don't see anything unique about this one. Standard-issue scuffed bar top and sagging liquor shelves, the usual worn barstools. Maybe Kit has cultivated a sentimental attachment to absinthe drippers. It's too loud to hear each other, so he has to lean in and speak right into my ear.

"I'll get you a drink." His breath hits my neck, tangling in my hair. "Still the same?"

I do want my usual whiskey ginger, but I don't want him to think he can use the same old map to navigate me.

"I'll have a boulevardier, actually," I say. Kit pulls away, blinking. "Are there tables in the back?"

"Ah, yes, should be," he says. "Go through the doors at the end of the hall."

I squeeze past the bar and down a crowded little hallway, where an antique wardrobe stands against the back wall, its doors carved with scrolls of leaves. These can't be the doors Kit meant, but they're the only ones here. At the risk of looking like I'm raiding coat check, I grab both handles and pull.

Oh.

The back of the wardrobe has been cut out, revealing a hidden room decorated like a hotel suite Oscar Wilde would have done opium in. Violets and palms fan out on the peeling wallpaper behind red-shaded sconces. Two men drink cognac on armchairs draped with dustcloths. Beside them, a group of women gossip atop nightstands piled with cushions, coupe glasses glinting on a battered travel trunk. A couple toasts champagne in a sawed-open claw-foot tub. And at the center of it all is a huge antique bed.

It's exactly the kind of place I love, the kind of place Kit *knows* I love. I'm a speakeasy person. I love a brilliant secret.

The only open seat is a corner of the bed, and when I sit, my ass plummets into the downy mattress. Kit finds me wriggling out of the abyss, elbowing cushions to pull myself upright.

"Oh, you got the bed," he says, setting the drinks down on a nearby stool. "I've never gotten to sit here before."

"I should warn you, it's not very supportive—"

Too late. Kit sits, and the mattress collapses under his weight, dumping him backward and sideways until we're piled on top of each other.

Except for the collision on the bus and our cease-fire handshake, Kit and I haven't touched. Now, he's everywhere. All of his body covers all of mine at once, his body heat and the scent of lavender surrounding me. His knees crash against my knees, his hips pushing mine deeper into the bed, and the only way out is for him to twist around and plant his hand on my other side, bracketing me in his arms. He's so close, I can almost make out the threads of the flowers on his shirt.

"Ah," he grunts, eyes dark and unfocused. "Hi. Sorry."

He exhales a short puff of air that ripples the hair around his face. An evil part of my brain tells me to tuck it behind his ear.

"I like the bar," I say conversationally.

"I thought you might."

"Almost as exciting as the Sexodrome."

"It's actually pronounced THE SEXODROME."

"Oh, really? Is that the local tongue?"

"No, the local tongue is what you get when you go in."

My laugh comes out as a hoarse bark, and Kit finally pushes up and away from me. For good measure, I grab a pillow and shove it between us. We both reach for our drinks.

"Corpse Reviver?" I ask, watching the liquid disappear between his lips.

He swallows. "Necromancer."

"So, the same thing, but with more absinthe," I conclude, pleased that *his* drink order hasn't changed much. My boulevardier swishes across my tongue, perfectly bitter.

Kit watches me over his glass, lashes lowered, almost smiling and almost not. It's a look he'd get when he was building a recipe around one ingredient, like he was rotating it in his mind and imagining it as part of a whole. He's seeing me in a scene from his life in Paris and deciding whether I complement the flavors.

Immediately, intensely, I don't want to let him reach a conclusion. Instead I say the first disruptive thing that comes to mind.

"So, how did you break your nose?"

He blinks. "Sorry?"

"Your nose. You said you broke it a couple years ago. How did it happen?"

"Oh." He lowers his glass. "On a water taxi in Venice."

I have feelings about two parts of his response: the part that means he's already had his first time in Italy without me, and the part where he was on a water taxi, which is objectively funny. It's easy to choose which to focus on.

"Let me guess," I say. "The boat passed under a window and you were struck by a falling wheel of Parmesan."

Kit laughs. "I wish."

"Turf dispute with a gondolier."

"No."

"What, then?"

"I hooked up with a water taxi driver while I was staging at a restaurant in Venice for a few weeks. He was distracted while driving and overestimated the height of a bridge."

"Oh my God. Please tell me the distraction *was* the hooking up."

Kit's eyes sparkle. "It was my birthday."

"Incredible. Wow. So glad I asked."

"What about you? Any broken bones?"

"No, but check this out."

I hold out my right hand, palm up, showing off the thin ridge of a scar from thumb to wrist. "Longboarding accident. Heard an ice cream truck and hit a curb. Stitches and everything."

"Longboarding? I thought you stopped skating when we were sixteen."

"That was until I got rid of the Soobie," I say. My old silver Subaru hatchback, may she rest in peace.

"No!" Kit gasps, genuinely aggrieved. "The Soobie? When?"

"A few years ago. Traded it for a Volkswagen bus."

"Now *that* I can see," Kit says. I flip my hand over, and his eyes land on the tattoo on my forearm. "That's new too."

"Oh, yeah." Neither of us had tattoos when we broke up, but I'm so used to mine now, I forget I haven't always had them. The one on my right arm is a kitchen knife, spanning from elbow to wrist. "I got it year before last. It's—"

"The knife from *Halloween,* right?" Kit guesses, with the deadpan delivery of someone forced to sit through the movie with me every October. He's the first one to ever get it right on the first try.

"Everybody assumes it's a chef's knife because I work at a restaurant. Like, what if I just love *cinema*?" I point to his left wrist, where a tiny whisk is inked in fine black lines. "Is that your first?"

"Third, actually," he says. "A bunch of us from my pastry school year got them together when we finished."

"Cute. I have three too." I pull up my left sleeve to show him the saguaro on my bicep. "This one was my first, for my twenty-fourth birthday."

We both know that my twenty-fourth was a month after we broke up, so he can probably guess how this one happened. Late night, empty apartment, twenty-four-hour tattoo shop with a flash sheet of cactuses in the window.

Kit looks at me with something like sympathy, then pulls up his own sleeve on the opposite arm.

"I got my first in the same spot, kind of."

The tattoo on the outside of his upper arm is a woman's hand holding three violets. He doesn't explain, and I don't need him to. Kit is the middle child of three. His mom was named Violette.

"Oh, Kit," I say. I have to stop myself from reaching out to touch it. "I love it."

"I think she'd like it," he says with quiet satisfaction. He tugs his sleeve down. "Where's your third one?"

"Oh, uh." Abrupt pivot. "I'd have to take off my pants to show you."

"Oh."

"Yeah," I say. A thought solidifies behind his eyes. "It's not an ass tattoo."

"I didn't think it was an ass tattoo."

"Really?"

"Okay, I thought it might be an ass tattoo."

I roll my eyes. "Come on, it's on my *thigh*. Where's *your* other one?"

"Under my shirt."

Under his shirt. Where his body is, of course.

"Hmm." I take another sip. I don't think about his body. "This is like the scene in *Jaws* where they compare scars."

"Does that make me Quint or Hooper?"

"Don't be ridiculous, I'm clearly the deranged shark man. You're the fancy research boy."

"Well," Kit says, raising his glass, "I'll drink to your leg."

"I'll drink to *your* leg," I quote back.

Is this—Kit and me, sitting on a bed, clinking glasses—how peacefully coexisting exes should feel?

It took so long to stop wanting him in my life. That feels like such an important, hard-won thing, and I don't know how to protect it from this moment. But I also don't know anyone else in the world who could have had those last ten minutes of conversation with me.

"Hey," I say.

"Hey," Kit says back.

"Bonsoir, kiddies," says a third voice, and we look up to see Maxine, dressed in black silk and holding a chambord martini.

"Maxine!" Kit says, standing so fast to greet her that I almost tip over again. He kisses her on each cheek, then turns to me, smiling wide. "I told Maxine where we were going and she wanted to come say hi."

"That's awesome," I say, trying to mean it. "Hi, Maxine."

Maxine kisses my cheek and sits down between us. Kit mutters something to her in French, and I catch a few of the words I know from growing up around his family—*thank you* and *the best*. She does an inscrutable hand gesture and hooks her ankle around his.

I like Maxine. I do. But now I'm wondering if the point of this whole outing was to remind me that Kit is with someone else now.

"The bartender is hot," Maxine declares matter-of-factly. "Did you see how hot the bartender is?"

"Kit got our drinks," I say.

"They're hot," Kit confirms. "Very hot."

Something twinges in my gut, a memory gone sour.

When Kit and I were together, our favorite bi-for-bi pastime was pointing out hot people to each other. It was silly and fun, but it meant something to me. It made me feel close to him, like all my incomprehensible, hidden feelings and wants were totally clear from his specific point of view.

Maybe the problem is that he can have the same thing with Maxine, someone who's a woman in all the ways I'm not. Kit likes boys, and he always liked my most boyish qualities, but every now and then, a worry crept in. When he kissed his flat-chested best friend with bitten-down nails, did he think of someone with plush curves and shiny hair, someone who touches with only the tips of her manicured fingers and leaves a lipstick print in the exact same spot on her glass with every sip? Someone who could be his girl? Someone like Maxine?

I look down at my own glass, covered in smudgy, oily finger-prints.

"I need to see this hot bartender for myself," I announce, suddenly in need of a break.

Back in the front room, the bartender is as hot as promised. Sharp jaw, broody eyebrows, androgynous. They're wearing a half-buttoned shirt and pleated gray trousers, and their hair gives the impression of a classic men's cut growing wild. They work with a cool efficiency I have to admire, as someone inti-mately familiar with handling a late-night full house. I hope that's how I look when I do it.

"Whiskey ginger," I half yell when they lean in, thankful they serve enough tourists to know the English.

I let my eyes drift, scanning for a distraction. Then the door opens, and in she floats: the dancer from Moulin Rouge.

Her hair is down, and she's swapped her costume for a simple cotton dress, but it's her. Her face is a dewy, freshly scrubbed pink, red stain lingering on her lips. I turn my body sideways to open space at the bar, and she goes right to it.

"Hi," I say, before remembering what country I'm in. "Parlez-vous anglais?"

She looks me up and down, then smiles and says, "Enough." Which answers more than one question.

"I'm Theo."

She takes my hand, brushes a kiss against my cheek. "Estelle."

I buy Estelle a drink—she wants a white wine, and she touches my arm when I suggest the one I know to be the best in the bar—and we talk. I tell her that I was at her show earlier and how great she was, and she explains that she lives across the city but likes to come here after work. When I tell her that's lucky for me, she sneaks a finger through my belt loop.

Once I've finished my drink and the hot bartender has poured Estelle a second glass, I consider bringing her through the wardrobe and introducing her to Kit and Maxine. It could be a double date. She and Kit could talk art. I could slip my hand around her waist while Kit presses a kiss to Maxine's throat, and then I could watch Kit and Maxine go home together again.

Instead, I push Estelle's hair behind her ear and ask if she wants to leave.

She laughs as we climb up the hill to the hostel. I hold her hand above her head for a pirouette, watching her dress whip around her thighs, then reel her in and kiss her. She tastes like cigarettes and Muscadet, smells like hairspray and setting powder.

I take my phone out to let Kit know I'm not coming back, then remember I still have his number blocked.

My thumb hovers over the blue letters of Unblock this Caller. Not much point to it anymore, is there?

left with someone i met at the bar. good night! I hit send.

In my room, my shirt lands on the floor, Estelle's balconette bra on the nightstand. I tell her she's beautiful, because she is, and then I tell her to lie back for me. I like the way she settles herself on the pillows, how everything she does is graceful. I like how her hair falls in her eyes.

I walk her out to her cab after, kiss her good night.

Usually sex helps me sleep, but tonight I'm awake for another hour. I can hear my own heart, and there's a cadence to its beating, a steadily repeating one-two-three-four.

It sounds unsettlingly like *Theo-and-Kit*.

— — —

"Have a good night?"

I gasp, nearly fumbling my croissant. The last person I was expecting to see in the hostel hallway this morning is Kit, but here he is, ambushing me at my door. Technically he's just emerging from his own room looking underslept, but it feels like an ambush.

"What are you doing here?"

"This is my room?" he says. "We've been over this, Theo, we're on the same tour."

I roll my eyes. Someone's in a mood. "No, I mean why aren't you at home with Maxine?"

"Why would I be with Maxine?"

"Because she's your girlfriend."

"*What?*" he says so loudly that a passing housekeeper shushes him. He lowers his voice. "You think— Theo. Maxine is not my girlfriend."

They—

No. What about last night? What about the flower in her bag? Why is he wearing his sincere face? How can he have his sincere face on at a time like this?

"But . . . you live together."

"No, she's plant-sitting for me while I'm on this trip."

"You went home with her after dinner."

"I walked her home because it was *late*," he insists. "I don't think of her like that, Theo, she's my best friend."

"Yeah, so was I."

The words are out of my mouth before I realize what I'm saying, and we both wince. Kit looks like he'd have preferred a punch in the face.

Before I can recover, a rumpled person in an unbuttoned shirt and gray trousers appears in Kit's doorway. I watch, dumbstruck, as they bid Kit a cheerful farewell in French. Then they slap his ass and stroll off toward the elevator.

I stare at Kit. Kit stares at the ceiling.

"Was that—?"

"The bartender, yes. Like I said. Nothing between Maxine and me." He turns for the stairs. "I need a coffee."

He leaves me there, alone with my croissant and the realization that I've made an absolute rollicking ass of myself.

If Maxine isn't his girlfriend, then—then he gave me a cake out of genuine kindness, and he invited me out because he wanted to show me his favorite bar, and Maxine really did want to see me again, and I acted like a rude little freak for no reason when I ditched them. I was supposed to be showing Kit how much I've grown without him, and instead I got jealous of the first person he smiled at and decided she must be sleeping with him. Maxine probably only sleeps with low-level royalty.

I wasn't like this before we were together. There were so many years of wanting him and thinking I could never have him, of watching him date other people and hearing about every fuck, feeling every complicated feeling you can have for a person, and I still managed to be his friend.

Maybe I can't do peacefully coexisting exes. Maybe it only works when we're friends.

I can try, I think. We're adults. I can set my anger aside and try to be his friend.

BORDEAUX

PAIRS WELL WITH:

Fourteen-month Pomerol,
minimum half dozen canelés

BORDEAUX

I dropped out of college two months into my first semester.

It was supposed to be fun, going to college with Kit—and the Kit part *was* fun. UC Santa Barbara had a good art history program for him, and their swim team had scouted me, and I missed him. I'd tried so hard to get over him, but I missed him like tea misses honey, boring without him.

It had been easier than I expected to have him back. I'd anticipated the gut punch of our first reunion, how New York had made him taller and surer and even more sparkly, but then he had just been Kit. As much a part of me as the rest of me.

Lectures were boring, and I kept forgetting exams, but I could stick it out as long as I got to keep swimming. The pool was the one place I was really, truly great, so great that my coaches threw around words like *college record* and *Olympic trials.* Then I wrecked my shoulder at invitationals and the doctors benched me for good, so I didn't see the point anymore. I didn't tell anyone I was leaving; I just cleared out my dorm and silently moved back into my parents' house in the Valley. That was the closest Kit and I ever came to a real, adult fight, when he found out I'd made the decision without him.

(You'd think he'd have known better about the apartment in Paris after that, and we could've avoided the breakup altogether. But here we are.)

All to say: Higher education didn't work for me. *Wine* education, though. I was fucking mint at that.

It began with aggressively befriending the chef sommelier at Timo, a mystifying sixtysomething man with a collection of leather dusters and a psychosexual obsession with Chablis. I was bar manager then, but I pestered him into putting me in charge of the cellar map and inviting me to spit in buckets at his after-hours blind tastings. Then there were flash cards and wine-encyclopedia audiobooks and almost setting myself on fire practicing decanting, and it turns out I'm great at learning things I actually want to know.

Now, I know what it means to stand here on the Pomerol plateau, on the right bank of the Gironde estuary. I know about its pockets of rare blue clay, and that when my boots crunch through the crumbly marl, a million little merlot babies drink from the dense earth beneath, ripening navy and opulently sweet so fast they'll never lose their newborn zing. We follow Fabrizio down a tree-canopied road through the most fuck-off magnificent morsel of southwestern France, grounds sprawling in green and green-gold and copper, orderly rows of vines in one direction and fringes of ancient trees in another. The whole sky wants to climb in when I open my mouth. Tasting notes: clay, plums, the sea.

I catch Kit craning his neck, admiring the sun through the leaves overhead. He's wearing washed-out linen. His mouth is soft and happy, parted with wonder.

A frisson of *yes-no-yes* courses through me.

Kit has always encountered the world with a pure, wholehearted eagerness to be amazed. A cool rock, a dog in a park, a song in a shopping mall, the rolling grounds of an eighteenth-century chateau. My first instinct, the thing I learned before I could find France on a map, is to love how Kit loves.

Then there's the miserable ordeal of everything else.

But after that comes the second yes: I'm going to try to be his friend.

I fall into step beside him and ask, "What's that tree?"

His jaw drops when he sees me, which is honestly funny. Like a dumb baby in a Renaissance painting.

"I—I think it's a Norway maple."

"Really?"

"Best guess. I thought it was a field maple at first, but the leaves have points."

It's a skill he picked up from a childhood running around the French countryside and his mom's greenhouse. Anytime I saw an interesting flower or a funny-shaped cactus, I could text Kit a photo and have it identified in ten minutes or less. I've had to get used to not knowing the names of trees.

It's nice to know this one.

Neither of us says anything else, but we don't drift apart either.

The path ends at a massive château with a limestone facade and dark mansard roofs, elegant but unpretentious. Somewhere in LA, a location scout is crying because they shot a wistful French period romance without knowing about it. Ten-foot stone walls separate it from the gardens, and in their opening stands a white-haired man in a chambray shirt and olive trousers. His straw sun hat manages to look jaunty despite also looking like he's sat on it a bunch of times.

"Amici," Fabrizio says, "this is Gérard! His family owns this estate for generations. Today, we learn how wine is made in Bordeaux!"

Gérard, who has an accent like a cognac-drunk fiddle suite, leads us through the arching entrance of the château. We glimpse the interior—antique chaises and damask wallpaper and *is that a nude oil painting of Gérard*—and then we're in a courtyard framed by the house's long, narrow wings. Here, a dozen or so wooden worktables are arranged on the packed dirt, bowls of flour and dough set out on each one.

Another man awaits us there. From the way Gérard saunters up to him (and from what I saw of that painting, though it's hard to tell with his pants on), this must be his partner.

"Before our tour, we have une petite surprise for you," says Gérard. "Baguettes! My husband will teach you how to make baguettes, and then we will tour the grapes and taste the wines. Et à la fin, we will have lunch in the garden, and you will eat your baguettes." He leans in and stage-whispers, "And if you cannot make the baguette, you must leave France. It is the law."

He winks outrageously and leaves us with his husband, who's draped in a menagerie of floaty earth tones.

"Bonjour!" Baguette Husband says.

"Bonjour!" everyone calls back.

Baguette Husband demonstrates how to form the provided dough into three small baguettes, explaining that they'll be rested and baked for us during our tour. Everyone divides up, two people to each numbered table. Maybe if I had sat with Fabrizio that first day I'd be sharing his table instead of Stig, but as it is, Kit and I are the only two left.

"Ah, together?" Baguette Husband coos at us.

"No," Kit says with a readiness that's almost insulting.

Baguette Husband gets a twinkle in his eye and says, "Not yet, maybe?" and nudges us to the last open table like we're two fourth graders with a crush. The worst part is, we *were,* once. He's eighteen years behind.

We flour our table in silence, and I riffle uselessly through my brain for something to say. Everyone else is laughing and chatting with their table partner, flicking flour at each other or trying to recall the instructions, while Kit and I are pointedly not having a cute time.

The problem is, we've only ever been everything or nothing to each other. I don't know how to start being *something* to him.

I also don't know how the hell this lump of gluten is supposed to move through three-dimensional space to become a baguette. The dough and I are in a fight. I fold one edge toward the center, then seal it down with the heel of my hand, then turn the dough around and do it again, and then—fold it? How? Save me, Baguette Husband.

I peek over to cheat off Kit's work and discover, with no small amount of horror, that he's already finessing his last baguette. His hands move like a magic trick, precise and swift and certain.

He was always a gifted baker, but he's gotten staggeringly good at this. It's like the dough *wants* to be touched by him. It gives under the heel of his hand, swells affectionately back into his palm, relaxes again at the gentlest pressure. The muscles in his forearms flex with the plain, steady purpose of doing the exact thing they were developed to do, which is when I realize how *much* they've developed, how they taper down to the same elegant wrists, the dusting of flour there, the little whisk inked just under the knob of bone—

"Theo," Kit says, "you're overworking it."

I look at my dough. Half of it is flattened under my fist.

"Oops."

"It's okay," he says, "you can still fix it, you just have to—"

His hands move toward mine and stop, hovering an inch above. A speck of flour floats down from his palm and settles on my skin with the weight of one of Gérard's antique sofas.

"Like, um, like this."

His left hand does a funny sort of circular motion, and I catch the hint and mirror it with my right. My misshapen lump of dough starts to resolve into a loose ball.

"That's good, just like that," he says. When I glance up, he meets my eyes and gives me a small, encouraging smile. "Don't stop."

"I bet you say that to all the boys," I say, which is an overcompensation, but Kit gives a bright, permissive laugh.

"Keep going."

I stare down at the dough, at our hands. He expertly guides me through each step without ever touching me, his fingers so close I can feel their warmth. It helps. He moves, I move. He gives simple and patient directions, I follow them. His thumb almost brushes mine, I classify the twinge in my chest as acid reflux.

Together, we roll out three lopsided baguettes.

"Not perfect," I observe, "but not bad."

"Better than the Calums," Kit says in a low voice. At the next table, Ginger Calum's nose is smeared with flour, and Blond Calum has made the courageous choice to eat a hunk of raw dough.

"How do *all* of theirs look like penises?"

Kit puts his hands on his hips. "Sometimes baking is about what's in your heart."

— — —

Gérard returns, accompanied by a scruffy gray terrier, and at last we amble into the vines. When I realized we'd be touring the vineyard in the first week of August, this was the part I couldn't wait for: Bordeaux in veraison, when the vines are as colorful and alive as they'll ever be.

We visit the merlot first, the main grape of Pomerol's eponymous wine, which we're allowed to taste off the vine even though it'll be weeks until they develop their biggest flavors of cherry jam and strawberry and, because it's been a hot year, lush black fruits. Next, Cabernet Franc in a riot of lavender and fuchsia and the juicy green of a cut-open lime. We hear about warm, dry summers and mild harvest seasons, the life-giving clay and the salty kiss of the Atlantic, how it all comes together to yield grapes with a lot of personality. That's how Gérard talks about his grapes—like kids he's trying to raise into strong-willed grown-ups with something to say at a party. Every morning, he plays Édith Piaf for them.

Beside me, Kit is smiling. If there's one other person in the world who'd get lost in this vineyard teaching plants to love French torch songs, it's Kit. The *yes-no-yes* happens again, like that unripe grape bursting sour across my tongue.

"Ah, here is one of our farmhands!" Gérard says. "Florian!"

A pair of work boots tromps down a row of vines, and a young man bursts onto the path.

My God, what a young man he is. Square-jawed and faintly stubbled, with sweet brown eyes and dark curls falling across his sweaty golden forehead. He's carrying a crate of grapes on one muscular shoulder, straining the fabric of his dusty white shirt. Suspenders hang around his hips, apparently shrugged off to allow full range of motion for cinematic deadlifting.

"Salut!" Florian says, wiping his face with a gloved hand. Soil streaks his cheek. "Welcome!"

On pure reflex, my head snaps toward Kit. His does the same, and our eyes meet in the raised-eyebrow look of unspoken agreement we used to share in moments like this: *He's hot!* We turn away just as fast.

Gérard invites Florian to join us, and Florian tells us how his parents met working on this vineyard and let him race around the vines when he was small. He lives in an apartment in Bordeaux proper now, but he happily makes the drive five days a week to tenderly coax vines up their trellises.

Kit leans into my ear and says, "I don't think we're the only ones who noticed the Florian situation."

Dakota and Montana are exchanging conspiratorial whispers, and at least three different brides are visibly contemplating leaving their new husbands. One of the Calums asks if he knows any good bars in Bordeaux. Even the old Swedish lady starts cleaning his cheek with her scarf.

"Do you think he's always part of the tour?" I ask Kit. "Like, when they know guests are coming, they have him come in to provide an immersive hot farmhand experience?"

"I think they buried a bunch of French romance novels in the garden and he's what sprang up."

In the wings of the château, Gérard takes us through the vat room and the aging cellars to a narrow, stone-walled tasting room. Then, one by one, Gérard pours us each a glass of their signature Pomerol.

I give mine a baby sniff, swirl it around the glass and whiff it again, slower this time. Damn, it's intense. Black cherry, crushed pepper, oak, and something else. Something lower, farther back on the nose. What is that? Is it—

"Worn saddle," I think out loud, and Gérard pauses, his bottle suspended over Kit's glass. Behind him, Florian perks up.

"Yes, I smell it too with this vintage," Gérard chuffs. "Good nose!"

I bite my lip, trying not to look too pleased with myself, but I couldn't be happier if Gérard invited me to move into the château as Florian's full-time suspenders wrangler. When I lift the wine to examine its color, I see Kit through the glass, funhouse-y and frowning into his wine.

"You got all of that?"

He looks vaguely hurt, as if his nose has betrayed him by not providing the richest possible sensory experience. Instead of answering, I take a sip, and he watches me pull the wine over my palate, turn it over in my mouth, settle its weight on my tongue. His eyes follow my throat as I swallow.

"Hm. Yeah, definitely black cherry on the front." I lick the back of my teeth. "Dried, though. And some plum jam."

Kit says gently, under his breath, "C'est quoi, ce bordel?"

The other wine is a younger Pomerol, a round, fruity summer wine that Gérard promises will go perfectly with lunch. This time, Florian pours.

"Hello," Florian says as he fills my glass, his voice close and warm and earthy.

"Thanks so much," I say, smiling at him.

It happens so quickly, it's hard to say if it happens at all. Florian finishes my pour, and then he flutters his eyelashes in what could be interpreted as a flirtatious wink. He moves on to Kit, who says something in French that makes him laugh, and he *winks at Kit too.* Before I even have time to summon indignance, we're whisked out to lunch.

Blankets and quilts spill across the sun-soaked lawn, each with a numbered serving board and our lopsided baguettes. Two more farmhands emerge with platters of meat and cheese and fruit. Kit and I have been assigned to a blanket so small, I have to wonder if Baguette Husband was involved.

We sit one careful inch apart and pile our board with little pots of seedy fig jam, orange crescents of melon, slices of Jambon de Bayonne, and hunks of soft, stinky cheese. Baguette Husband returns to laugh at the dog as she runs happy laps and sniffs everyone's ham.

Kit procures a tiny jar of cloudy honey from his bag, and I can't resist the urge to roll my eyes.

"Did you really bring your own special honey from home?"

"The restaurant where I bake sources our honey from a lavender farm," Kit says. "It's ruined me for all other honey."

"Oh, sure, we can't have you eating just any old honey."

As lunch goes on, Florian stays busy refilling everyone's wine. When he kneels beside us, I catch a hint of his scent on the midday breeze. Soil and sweat and a bit of thyme.

"Do you like the wine?" he asks me.

"Oh, it's gorgeous," I answer honestly. Then I think about him winking at Kit. I look into his eyes and sink to the bottom of my voice to add, "Structured. Muscular, even. I can tell you work hard."

Florian stops pouring a second too late. When he leaves, Kit is staring.

I tear a piece of bread off and smear it with cheese. "What?"

"You know what. You were flirting with Florian."

"So?" I shrug. Kit's face is unreadable. "Are you jealous?"

"No," Kit says instantly. "I mean—yes, because he was flirting with *me* at the tasting. I thought he and I had something special."

"Sorry, he's mine now. Look at this pour." I gesture extravagantly at my half-full glass. "Maybe if I show a little leg he'll give me the whole bottle."

Kit looks down at one of my legs sticking out of my shorts, blinks slowly, then drains his glass.

"Pardon, Florian!"

He says something that must be French for *Can you top me off?* Florian's eyebrows say Kit has found a way to make it sound just as suggestive as it does in English.

This time, when Florian holds the bottle over Kit's glass, Kit loosens one of his shoulders and tilts his head to the side. He slips Florian a languid smile, letting the sunlight gild the ridges of his jaw and throat.

Oh. That's someone I haven't met before. The Sex God of École Desjardins.

When Florian leaves, Kit's glass holds more than mine. He turns that smile toward me, eyes bright with laughter and something else I can't name.

"Well." I take a swig that's somewhat bigger than necessary. "We'll see who wins the next round."

"In the meantime," Kit says, passing me a honey-soaked piece of baguette, "taste this."

I take it in the name of friendship, doubtful his boutique honey can possibly be as good as he says. Kit is the kind of person always pursuing the most of everything—the highest thread count, the ripest peach—but sometimes he gets lost in aesthetics. I'm not expecting much when it hits my tongue, especially not with my mouth still coated in sugars from the wine.

But then the flavor blooms.

"*Damn.*"

"Right?" Kit says, positively beaming.

"It's actually fucked up how good that is," I say. "The lavender with the floral notes from the wine, the violet and peony."

Kit sags onto his elbows, gratified, and regards me from under heavy eyelids. "When did you become so good at wine tasting?"

Unlike with Maxine, I have no problem flexing for Kit.

"I'm the assistant sommelier at Timo now."

His eyes widen. "You are? Since when?"

"Unofficially, like, three years? But I didn't fully switch over from bar manager until last year." I pause, then decide to just say it. "After I took the certification exam."

"You—" He sits up. "Theo, you passed the sommelier exam?"

"Yeah," I say. It's technically a lie, but just barely. My exam is scheduled for the day after I get home, and I know I've learned enough to pass now. There's no way I'll fail a fourth time. And I'm not going to walk it back, not with Kit marveling at me like this.

"That exam is insanely hard, isn't it?" Kit says. "The somm at my restaurant said he threw up his first time."

"It's not that bad," I say, as if I didn't serve the table counter-clockwise instead of clockwise the first time I failed, or forget the thirteenth German wine region the second time. (See you in hell, Saale-Unstrut.) I drain my glass. "I have some other stuff going on, but sommelier is my day job now. Or, night job, I guess."

I wave over another refill and ask Florian how many crates of grapes he can carry at once. Kit wonders out loud how far Florian could carry *him*. When we compare glasses, they're exactly the same level of two-thirds full.

It goes on like that for the rest of lunch, Kit and Florian and me. We mop up the fig jam and honey and melon drippings with our bread, ask for refills until we've lost count, make Florian laugh and blush, turn our mouths purple. I smile at Kit. Kit smiles at me.

And every time we hold our glasses together, every time the lip of his glass almost touches the lip of mine, I try not to think, *This is the closest we'll ever come to kissing again.*

— — —

We spend the afternoon at the Musée des Beaux-Arts in the city of Bordeaux, where I float from room to room, not bothering with most of the plaques.

It's not that I don't care about art. I *love* art. But prestige art is my parents' shop talk, and eventually, you get bored of it. While my dad was directing contemplative period pieces and my mom was adapting *Lady Chatterley's Lover,* I was watching every *Friday the 13th* sequel. My favorite is the one where Jason is cryogenically frozen for 445 years and goes to space. The day I said that to my dad was probably one of his top ten parental heartbreaks.

The art I like best is unpretentious, highly saturated, and fully committed to what it's doing even when it's bad. *Especially* when it's bad. I like B movies and slashers and eighties action flicks, anything with a synth music cue and a cocaine-fueled screenplay. I don't want to analyze the creator's intentions. Subtlety is for wine; I want to feel what the art wants me to feel and feel it big. Kit got so upset that I refused to read *The Lord of the Rings* when we were kids, but the movies had all the feelings in them.

For me, it's enough to look at a painting and think, *I like it.* Or, *This makes me feel sad.* Or, *This reminds me of myself.* Or, *That's a fucked-up looking dog.*

When I enter the next room, the first thing I notice is the huge painting of a woman kneeling on crumbling stones. She's wearing a dark blue coat with a gold sash over a billowing white dress, and her arms are uplifted, her palms out-turned. The look on her face is sad but vengeful. Her tits are mostly out.

The second thing I notice is Kit, transfixed before her, a fountain pen and a little sketchbook in his hands.

I used to always catch Kit like this when I'd visit him at work, back when we lived together after he finished his degree. His front desk job at the Palm Springs Art Museum wasn't stimulating enough for him, so he'd take extra-long breaks to sketch the exhibits.

Why did I find that so charming? He was just posing, wasn't he? Too cultured and deep to sit at his desk on his phone like a simple receptionist.

I imagine asking him about this painting. The tragic look

he'd give me for not knowing the painter, for not having my eyes turned to the greatest heights of artistic expression. I imagine him explaining it like I'm a toddler, making references that only someone with an art history degree would get. That's what the version of Kit in my head would do, the Kit who's an ex I don't talk to anymore. Pretentious, erudite Kit, always too highbrow for me.

A piece of hair falls in his eyes, and he pushes it back with the eraser of his pencil.

That motion, the way the rubber skids across his brow. I'd forgotten, but I remember it now. Kit-the-ex never does that in my head. But Kit-in-real-life did when I knew him, and this Kit does too.

As far as I know, there are two ways to get over someone: Surrender to the anger that's already there, or invent something to get angry about. Sometimes it was always wrong, and the only thing to do is stop believing it was good to love them in spite of it. But sometimes they were good to you. Sometimes you go looking for kindling and find that green leaves won't burn, that the garden was watered too well. Sometimes you have to rearrange the truth into something you won't miss.

And sometimes, when enough time goes by, it gets hard to remember which one you did.

— — —

After, on the museum steps, Fabrizio unspools a list of local recommendations: La Cité Du Vin, the ancient crypt under Basilique Saint-Seurin, the bronze horses of the Monument aux Girondins. A few of us decide that the medieval Saint-Pierre district sounds most interesting.

"Mind if I come too?" Kit asks me.

I'm post-tipsy, relaxed enough that it feels silly for him to ask permission. I roll my eyes and wave him to my side. This feels good, like the picnic shook something loose. Florian gave us a gift: mutual assurance that we're only interested in fucking other people.

We head past Cathédrale Saint-André and onto a wide, tram-lined street, where Kit asks, "How's Sloane?"

It's strange to hear her name from his mouth, but of course he would ask. Sloane's the most important person in my life, and he's known her since she was five, which is two whole years longer than the rest of the world has known her.

"She's good. Busy, but that's how she likes it. I'm sure you've, you know. Seen her around."

"Yeah, I have," Kit says, and I wonder, not for the first time, how many times he's seen my sisters' faces on a screen and thought of me. "She was incredible in that thing with Colin Farrell last year. How long did it take her to get her Irish accent that good?"

"Like a *week*. I swear she's not human. She just started working on this new one, like a turn-of-the-century, high-society New York accent."

"What's that one for?"

"Oh, you'd be into it. It's an adaptation of *The Age of Innocence*, but like, weird. Very A24. The script is nuts. Her agent says it'll be her first Oscar nomination."

"That's incredible!" Kit says sincerely. "Is she playing May or the countess?"

"Winona Ryder." I haven't read the book, but I've seen the Scorsese film from 1993. "She really wanted to be Michelle Pfeiffer, but the director said she comes off too friendly."

"Sloane? Sloane who wanted her audition monologue to be Glenn Close in *Fatal Attraction*? When she was ten? That Sloane?"

"Curse of the former child star," I sigh. "What about Cora? How's she?"

Kit laughs under his breath, and I smile. Cora's still Cora, then.

"Last year she stole Dad's credit card and charged seventeen hundred dollars at Dave & Buster's," he says. "This year she unionized the staff of her Dutch Bros."

"Hey, that's really cool!"

"She doesn't *work* there."

We talk about my youngest sister, Este, who just wrapped a five-episode run on a big-budget HBO show, and his older brother, Ollie, who's now in marketing at a publishing house in New York.

Near an intersection, the road branches diagonally, like whatever lies this way is too old to abide a grid system. It starts as a secret alley, then opens wide, dark cobblestones giving way to the big, smooth, pinkish tiles of the Place du Palais.

Tourists filter through arched antique doors with paper shopping bags and ribbon-tied candy boxes. Cafés overflow onto smoke-tinged terraces. A delivery man zips between Kit and me on a butter-yellow bicycle, fresh loaves of bread bouncing in its basket. It's like its own tucked-away village, forgotten by time and walled off by rows of lavender and peach buildings that sparkle in the evening sun. At the edge of the square stands a massive, medieval gate topped with a truly fantastical number of pointy turrets. We go under it and down another storybook street, toward one of the historic churches Fabrizio mentioned, Église Saint-Pierre.

We're almost there when I glance down a side street and notice the letters over a bright blue restaurant entrance: A CANTINA COMPTOIR CORSE. Corse like Corsica, like the island.

"Kit," I say, stopping. He stops too, even though the rest of the group is leaving us behind. "I have to go try something. For work."

Kit simply nods and follows. It's not until after we've pushed deep into the noisy pub, grabbed the last two leather stools at the bar, translated the menu, and put in an order that he finally raises a question.

"You said this was about work," Kit says, "but you didn't order any wine."

I cross my ankles under the bar. My boot grazes the cuff of his pants.

"You know how I told you I traded the Soobie for a Volkswagen bus?"

I tell him about my bus, gutted and built out by hand into a bar I can drive around the Valley, how I design custom cocktails for weddings and bachelorette parties and influencers that come in for Coachella. Then I tell him about next month's monster wedding gig: 350 guests, eight bespoke recipes, and a bride who emails me five times a day expecting prompt responses to questions like *Did I mention one of the drinks must be served in these custom tiki mugs that look like my pet schnauzer?* and *Can you make a drink that tastes like the vacation to Corsica where we fell in love?*

I leave out one major detail: I'm barely bringing in enough money to make back what I spend, and before I got hired by Schnauzer Bride, I was close to packing it in.

"*Anyway,*" I finish, "I need to find out what Corsican flavors are like so I can design a cocktail that reflects 'the complexity of our love,' which, you know. He's a hedge fund manager named Glenn, but sure."

"Theo, this is . . . wow." Kit stares at my phone, which I've opened to the Instagram page for my bus, a grid of cocktail money shots and my hands holding drinks out of the service window I installed. His eyes are wide and sparkling when he looks up, and a wave of warmth sweeps through me. The only thing bigger than Kit's capacity for wonder is how it feels to be at the center of it. "You built that yourself?"

Obviously, it was harder than I'm making it sound. Almost a year of sweating and swearing, watching hours of tutorials online. I got on a first-name basis with my local Home Depot sales associates. I ripped out and replaced the floors, put in a new engine, scraped the rust off and repainted, rigged tanks and pipes and sinks, pasted wallpaper and sanded the countertops and salvaged coolers from work.

Some people dye their hair when they go through a breakup. I got a bus.

Kit doesn't need to know it was a breakup bus, that I was nail gunning my heartbreak out while he was licking crème anglaise off some pastry classmate's abs. Or that I might never have been fired up enough to take the risk if he hadn't said what he did on that plane.

"I mean, it did help that I was briefly hooking up with a carpenter." I see the food coming and pull my elbows off the bar. "But what about you? What's the pastry game like?"

Over cuttlefish in a garlicky red-wine tomato sauce and cheesecake with orange zest (*fiadone,* I add to my notes), Kit describes working at a gourmet restaurant inside a five-star Parisian hotel. Early mornings, precise milligrams of ingredients, arranging ribbons of white chocolate with long tweezers like a brain surgeon.

"Honestly, the worst part is the tweezers," Kit says. "I'm so much better with my hands. When I can get my fingers in, there's pressure, you know? You can tell from touch if something will give, or if it's too soft, or— Oh, here." He passes me a napkin, for the bit of drink that has dribbled from the corner of my mouth.

When I'm finished taking notes—*acid, tomato, citrus, island mist, maybe a spritz?*—we skip the church and head straight to Place du Parlement in the heart of the district. We stand at the fountain under wrought iron balconets, where Kit points out the sculpted stone faces keeping vigil on the corners of each building.

"They're called mascarons," he says, "not to be confused with macarons," which fills me with another swell of affection.

I can't believe how much better I feel than I did last night. Can it really be only twenty-four hours since I was at the Moulin Rouge, trying to crush the bloom of nostalgia? Does time move differently in France?

France. I'm in *France*. Four years later and we're in Bourdeaux together after all.

"Man," I say. "We're really here. Look at us."

"Look at *you*," Kit says. "A sommelier and a bar owner."

"And you're a gourmet pastry chef," I counter, feeling my grin spread. "Crazy the difference four years can make."

"Yeah. A lot changed." He returns my smile. A couple of children dart past, racing around the fountain. "Not some things, but . . . still, a lot."

"I guess it's kind of good that we broke up, so we could become these cool fucking people."

Kit's smile stays fixed, but something changes in his eyes.

"Yeah."

Shit. We were doing such a good impression of old friends who've never seen each other naked, and now I've dumped our nudes on the cobblestones.

I search our surroundings for something to break the silence, an emergency fire axe.

At a table outside a bar on the edge of the square sits a man with a head of dark curls. He's wearing a T-shirt and tan trousers instead of farmhand regalia, but he really looks like—

"Is that Florian?"

Kit follows my line of sight, and his mouth pops open in surprise. "I—I think it is."

"Is he with—?"

One of the two other men at the table lets out a cackle that unmistakably belongs to Blond Calum.

"Of all the people to get Florian out for a drink," Kit says, "my money was not on the Calums."

"Oh, mine was. Those two are trouble. The ginger told me he can never return to Belgium for legal reasons."

Just then, Dakota and Montana appear on the terrace with matching flutes of pink champagne. Florian waves, and the Calums start pushing tables together so everyone can sit.

"Oh," Kit says, "this is interesting."

"It's like *The Bachelor*," I say, fully invested. "Which of those girls do you think wants the fantasy suite most?"

"How do you know it won't be one of the Calums?"

"Those men are terminally straight."

"Nobody's straight on a European vacation."

"Sounds like you're speaking from experience," I observe, picturing Kit picking up tourists at bars in Montmartre.

"Historic precedent. They switch everyone to bisexual at passport control."

"Damn, that's what the stamp's for? Could've skipped the line."

Kit laughs, rubbing a hand across his forehead in a kind of *oh Theo* gesture that makes the nerves in my fingertips buzz. "The real question is, which one is most likely to succeed?"

"The one with the dark hair—Montana—she's perkier, which gives her an edge, but Dakota's a wild card."

"The blonde?" Kit asks. "She looks bored."

"Some guys are into that. Should we start a pool?"

"I think—" Before Kit can reveal what he thinks, Fabrizio manifests on the terrace with a bottle of wine and a basket of frites. "Hold on. Game changer."

We watch as Fabrizio sits next to Florian and throws an arm over the back of his chair. He joins the conversation with a salacious grin, tosses a frite into his mouth, and then dips another in sauce and feeds it to Florian.

Kit outright gasps. "Oh my God."

"That's the game, folks."

"Fabrizio by a mile."

We both fall apart in laughter, mine shot through with relief. The tension is gone, and that easy current from lunch gushes in like water in the fountain. As long as we can keep finding our way back here, we'll be fine. We just need an endless supply of Florians.

Which gives me an idea.

"You know who else might have a chance?" I ask Kit.

"Who?"

"One of us." Kit's still half laughing, like he doesn't think I mean it. "I'm serious! He was flirting with both of us. We have a head start."

Kit shakes his head. "I don't know."

"Come on, I'll prove it."

"Theo, don't—"

He grabs a handful of my sleeve to stop me. I raise my eyebrows, and he lets it go, pauses, then smooths it back into place.

"Why not?"

"I—I just mean—" His olive face has taken on a faint tinge of mauve. "If it's going to be one of us, why not me?"

Oh. I recognize this approach. Back when we were friends, we used to occasionally compete for the same people. Occupational (bisexual) hazard.

"Is that a *challenge,* Fairfield?"

"Maybe," Kit says. "But then, if Fabrizio could pull Florian, maybe the true challenge would be Fabrizio. By the transitive property."

"Fabrizio's more available, though. We're always with him," I say. "With Florian, there's a finite window of opportunity. A Florian Fuck Window."

"Sure, but let's say one of us succeeds within the Florian Fuck Window," Kit counters. "The other could just do the same with someone else in the next city. It wouldn't be a meaningful victory."

"What are you suggesting? A tournament bracket?"

"I'm not suggesting anything," he says, though he doesn't look disinterested, "but if I *was,* I think it would be a matter of seducing a local in the greatest number of individual cities."

Huh. Now *that's* an idea.

I touch my chin with two fingers, thinking. It started as a bit, but now I'm seeing the potential benefits of a friendly-but-horny rivalry. I like us like this. If having sex with other people will keep things with Kit stable enough to enjoy my trip, *and* we both get an outlet for any leftover sexual friction, then why not?

"A body-count competition," I muse.

"You don't have to phrase it like we're murdering them, but yes, essentially."

"We *do* both already have one, from Paris . . ." The more I think about it, the better it sounds. In fact, the longer I look at Kit, the more I want to have sex with someone.

"Wait," Kit says. "You're being serious? You actually want to compete?"

"It sounds fun. I'm down. Are you?"

When I look into Kit's eyes, I can practically see the pleasure receptors in his brain crackling. He can't say no, not a hedonist like him.

"Define *hookup*. Does that include making out, or over the clothes, or—?"

"At least one person has to come," I say.

"Oh." Kit blinks. "That's easy, then."

"Is it?"

"What, is it not easy for you?"

"No, it's easy for me."

"I personally do it all the time."

"So do I," I say. "That's what makes it a competition. I'm like, the number one seed. Of fucking."

Kit touches his chin. "Proud of you for resisting a seed joke."

"Thank you, I'm very strong," I say. "So, what do you think? A little sex wager between friends?"

For a long moment, Kit doesn't say anything at all. He just looks at me, searching my face so intently that I feel his gaze like a touch.

Then, like he did on that cliff in Dover, he puts out his hand.

"Okay," he says. "Let's do it."

I grin. "Let's do it."

When I take his hand, it's smudged with ink from his sketch-book. His skin burns hot against my palm.

"One more thing, though," Kit says. His thumb presses into the back of my hand. "Is that star of *Fatal Attraction* Glenn Close?"

I turn to look, and Kit takes off toward the bar.

SAINT-JEAN-DE-LUZ

PAIRS WELL WITH:

Green Izarra (neat, after dinner),
gâteau Basque made with fresh cherries

"Ah, finally!" Fabrizio sings when I board the bus late the next morning. "Our little conquistadore!"

Orla shoves the clipboard at me.

"Go on, we haven't got all day."

"Be kind to my Theodora," Fabrizio says. "It is not her fault. She is in love!"

"I'm not—"

"I am always so happy when my guests sample the local cuisine on their own," Fabrizio says, winking lavishly. "And when it becomes love! Orla, do you remember the German girl two summers ago, who tried to tell us to leave her in Barcelona with the sailor? Ah, they are married now!"

I push on down the aisle, accepting a round of applause from the Calums and envious but not unfriendly looks from Dakota and Montana. At my seat, Kit is against the window wearing a patterned terry button-down and very small matching shorts.

I heave my pack into the overhead, grab the nearest small item from the outermost pocket, and chuck it at him.

"Ow," Kit says as a jar of pomade hits him in the arm. He pulls out his headphones. "Good morning."

"Morning!"

I'm wearing my most shit-eating grin as I flop down next to him and Orla whisks us away from Bordeaux.

"So." Kit's tone is light and indecipherable. "How was Florian?"

"He was . . ." I hold a pause to build suspense. "Surprising."

"In what way?"

How to explain it? Kit and I may have set the terms of a sex competition yesterday, but we haven't yet laid out rules for talking about sex with each other. We're friends, though, and the last time we were friends, we told each other everything.

What happened with Florian was, we went back to his apartment to share another bottle from the château. Then he took me to his bedroom, showed me the contents of the top drawer of his dresser, and asked me if I would use it on him.

"Surprisingly well prepared," I say, thinking of the supple leather harness he buckled around my hips, the vial of oil he poured over my fingers. "I mean, I knew he had the knees for it, but I didn't think he had the range."

Kit's eyes widen incrementally. "You mean he let you—"

If anyone would know, it's Kit.

"That was *all* he wanted." A strange, small part of me almost wishes Kit could have seen how nicely my hand fit between the two dimples at the small of Florian's back. Kit is the only one who could truly appreciate how my technique has improved. "I guess you could say I hadn't pegged him for it."

Kit's expression of covetous wonder twists into a grimace.

"Not a pegging pun."

"He took it really well," I go on, all eyebrows. "Such a *strapping* young man."

"You should be banned from sex for that. You should have to become a monk."

"Score's two to one," I say, cheerfully ignoring his disdain. "Advantage me."

"I hope you're enjoying yourself," Kit says, taking out his book. "It won't last."

It's two hours to our next stop, Saint-Jean-de-Luz, a fishing commune on the southwestern coast of France near the Spanish border, so I decide to catch up on my most pressing notifications.

One, the family email chain. Two, a text from the bar manager at Timo. Three, an email from the Somm. Four, an email from Schnauzer Bride. Five, a text from Sloane. I close my eyes, take a deep breath, and put the part of me that wants to ignore them all in a chokehold.

I address the bar manager's crisis first, even though I specifically told everyone at work not to bother me while I was—and I used these exact words—up to my nips in Brie. It shouldn't be that hard for the guy with my old job to read my notes, but I guess an assortment of random sticky notes in the back office isn't as intuitive for him as it was for me. I remind him that our small-batch-bitters supplier has to get free tiramisu once a month or he'll stop giving us a discount, and that those two barbacks can't be scheduled together because one fucked the other's girlfriend.

In the family email chain, Dad has sent a long-winded update from set in Tokyo, Mom is location scouting in the Texas Panhandle, Sloane is thinking about leaving a horse's head in her costar's bed, and Este is meeting an ambassador's son for dinner in the Maldives via chartered helicopter. I send back a short report about Paris and Bordeaux, leaving out Kit completely.

After is the Somm, asking if I've registered for a distributor portfolio tasting next month. Trade events are important for serious sommeliers, but I hate networking and being expected to look feminine, and I really hate listening to men in blazers and dark jeans jerk each other off about Burgundy. And I can't give up a weekend of bus bar sales to kiss ass in Scottsdale. I tell him I can't make it, already hearing his lecture, do I really want to make it in this business, et cetera and so on.

Schnauzer Bride is next, wanting to incorporate at least three but no more than five botanicals from her florist's samples into her menu. My endurance is fading, so I grind out a few cocktail pitches and lock my phone. Sloane can wait until my brain isn't so hot.

I press the cool glass of the screen to my cheek and breathe

out slowly, soothed by the expanse of French countryside rolling past the window, the funny, skinny trees with puffs of leaves
bursting from their tops like dandelions.

Sometimes it's embarrassing that this is peak performance
for me, that I spent the past few years kicking my own ass to
achieve twenty minutes of executive function and a fear my life
will collapse if I breathe wrong. But most days, I'm proud of
how far I've come. Everything up to age twenty-five was a series of small-to-medium fuckups, until I decided to get my shit
together.

I got my shit together because I had to, because I didn't like
myself or my life. But I also did it because every time I lost my
keys or forgot a promise, I missed Kit.

Living with Kit was like living in a pixie nest. Every night,
I'd find my phone charger relocated to my nightstand and my
water bottle beside it, refilled at the precise temperature I liked.
Dates circled themselves on the calendar. Fresh flowers appeared
whenever the old ones wilted. And no matter how carelessly I
unloaded the dishwasher, when I checked the back of the utensil
drawer, the measuring spoons were always there.

I loved and resented how good he was at the parts of life I was
worst at, and once he was gone, I let resentment win. I made my
love into a power drill and built a life I could keep in order myself, because you can't miss something you don't need anymore.

But every so often, after an eight-hour shift and an all-night
gig, I'll stumble home to a pile of dishes and think, *Kit would take
better care of me than this.* And for a second, he'll be there. Putting
the cereal bowls away, waiting up with a book, kissing the tension from my shoulders, picking up my slack.

"Theo?"

The real, present Kit is watching me, one headphone out, his
book face down on his lap.

"You okay?"

I shake my head.

"Yeah! Yeah, just thinking," I say. "What, um, what are you listening to?"

"Oh"—Kit glances at his phone—"you'll laugh."

"Probably not."

He gets this tender look on his face, the way he used to when he'd look up at the very top of Mount San Jacinto from the valley floor.

"So, before the trip, I had this idea to make a list of composers who wrote music in each of the tour stops. Because I—" He pauses, searching for the words. This is new. He used to talk in long, breathless sentences until he chiseled down to his point, but now he sifts through his thoughts. "Everywhere we go, I want to experience it entirely. All the way out to its edges. I want to touch it, taste it, drink it, eat it, climb it, swim in it. You can hear a place by walking down the street or sitting next to the ocean or opening a window, but I think if you want to *listen* to it, it's in here. Like how bread can taste like the kitchen it's baked in. Or—"

"Or how wine can taste like the barrel."

He smiles.

"Yes. Yes, exactly. So, I'm listening to Ravel."

Without another word, he hands me a headphone. I put it to my ear, and he starts the track over.

— — —

I've never seen a movie set in Saint-Jean-de-Luz, but I've seen sandcastles and dollhouses and ripe white peaches, so, close enough. The buildings cuddle together around narrow streets, some made of pink stone and others crisscrossed with bright red timber and matching shutters. Lazy morning sunlight drips from the pink-orange roofs to the promenade curving around a huge crescent-shaped beach, which Fabrizio says is simply called La Grande Plage. In the hazy blue distance, the Pyrenees rise toward endless sky.

We start our day at the village's central market. In winespeak, Les Halles has a robust, varied nose, with high intensity aromas of the sea—salt water, abalone shell, wet stones, seaweed, fatty fish. Notes of brined pork and smoked sausage, yeasty bread and burnt crust, fresh clover and geranium and bird of paradise, wild sage. Another elusive note slips in between, something juicy and sharp, like lemongrass or verbena.

That's the one I follow.

I weave around cheese cases and pans of steaming brioche, past an old woman ordering lamb from a mustached butcher, to a vibrant fruit stand. It reminds me of my go-to frutería back home, except there's a type of pear I've never even *heard* of, which is rare when you spend your spare time tasting wine with guys competing to name the obscurest berry. These fruits can *teach* me something. I pick up an apricot and press my nose to its skin.

"Bonjour!"

I startle up from the note I'm tapping into my phone (*orangé de Provence: intense, sweet, tart*) to see a shopgirl in an apron.

She's pretty the way Saint-Jean-de-Luz is pretty, breezy and sensuous, her brown face soft and relaxed. Her dark hair is in an informal knot at her nape, and the loose bits have the crispiness of sun-dried seawater. She's holding a speckled green-red pear and a paring knife, a slice balanced on the blade. She has an air of wife about her. Maybe not my wife, but certainly someone's.

"You want?" Fruit Wife says.

"Oui." I nod eagerly. "Wow, yes, please."

The petal-pink flesh of the pear melts on my tongue like butter with a kiss of cinnamon, and the woman watches me suck juice off my thumb. If my French were better, this is the part where I would go, *Are we about to make out?*

She points to a sign over the bin of pears.

DOYENNÉ DU COMICE.

Hiring a hot girl to feed fruit to customers is an excellent business model, because next thing I know, I'm being rung up for two pounds of cherries as Fruit Wife waves goodbye.

"Lining up number three already?" asks Kit, who has apparently witnessed the whole thing.

I shake my head. "I think I just got hustled."

"Understandable," Kit assesses with a nod. "She's lovely."

"What'd you buy?"

"Fromage de brebis," he says, holding up a chunk of wrapped sheep's milk cheese. "The guy at the stall was hot too, but I can't sleep with any more cheesemongers. Trying not to pigeonhole myself." I open my mouth, but Kit has a hand raised. "Theo."

"Don't use words that end in 'hole,' then."

He huffs out his *oh Theo* laugh. I'd forgotten how nice it sounds.

"There's a sexy fishmonger," he says.

"Ooh, show me."

We loop the market, admiring glossy pastries and dishes of stuffed peppers, ribbing each other. Kit's laughing, I'm laughing, the air between us is fresh and light. We feel like friends. My sex competition idea is fixing us. I am, I decide, a genius.

At the back of the hall, the fish counter is as pungent and glistening as an oyster shell and as busy as the Grande Plage. Bins of ice brim with gleaming prawns, scallops in brick-red shells, deep ruby cuts of tuna, slender little silvery-pink fish and flat fish and fish with stripes. Customers line up three bodies deep and point at squids.

Behind the counter, a strong-nosed brunette in coveralls heaves fish onto the bar, wrapping and weighing and taking orders in a crisp, friendly voice. A man lobs a question at her; she punctuates her answer with the crunchy thump of her cleaver on the chopping block.

"That's her," Kit says unnecessarily.

When the crowd clears, the fishmonger cleans her hands and

turns to us, addressing Kit in French. I understand just enough of Kit's response to know he's telling her I don't speak the language.

"Ah." The fishmonger switches effortlessly to English, confident but with a light, unplaceable accent. "Sorry, I didn't think you were American!"

"Thank you," I say, meaning it. "You're very good at your job."

"I've had this job since I was twelve. I very much hope I'm good at it by now." She grins, flashing a gap between her front teeth. "He says you're on a food and wine tour? What will you eat in Saint-Jean-de-Luz?"

"Lunch is at a restaurant in a hotel on the Grande Plage," I say. "Do you know it? It has a Michelin star."

"Ah, Le Brouillarta." She does a begrudging frown of approval, and I get the sense that nothing short of a fresh-caught fish roasted by a local grandmother would have satisfied her. "And where will you go after you leave here?"

We take her through the destinations ahead. Along the coast and over the Spanish border to San Sebastián, across Spain to Barcelona, back up to the southern coast of France and east until we hit Nice and Monaco. After that, it's Italy the rest of the way: Cinque Terre and Pisa on the northwest coast, inland to Florence, south through Tuscany to a villa in Chianti and on to Rome, further south to Naples, and a ferry to Palermo for the final stop. By the time we're done, she releases a French swear so colorful it surprises a laugh out of Kit.

"Lucky bastards!" she says, patting her stomach through her coveralls. "My mother was born in Barcelona. I'll tell you where to go." She goes on to describe in detail, with total confidence, the precise and mandatory experience we are to have in Barcelona. The only bar for vermouth, the only tapería for patatas bravas. "And then, if you like pastry—do you like pastry?"

"I do," Kit says.

"He's a pastry chef in Paris," I add.

Kit casts me a look, his eyes bright and curious. "And Theo is a sommelier."

Finally, we've impressed her. She leans over a bin of pearly anchovies, examining us with renewed interest, before concluding, "I like you."

I'm not easily thrown off my game, but something about her keen gray stare makes my face warm. Kit's elbow nudges mine.

"So few travelers respect food and drink the way they should!" she goes on. "Oh, you must see the port, where we buy our fish. I can show you after the market closes, if you want? My name is Paloma, by the way."

Which is how we leave Les Halles with two pounds of cherries, a hunk of fromage, and directions to meet a sexy fishmonger named Paloma at sunset.

— — —

"I'm gonna be honest," I say. "I love a menu that's just a list of nouns."

Kit and I are sitting together in Le Brouillarta, soaking in the ocean breeze through the open window as I study the menu. Lobster cake. Bergamot, mint, cucumber, and citrus. Foie gras. Smoked eel, chanterelles.

"You could be ordering *anything*. Look at the tuna—leek, fir, marigold! Is it a dish? Is it a community garden? Is it a candle? Do words mean things? Can't wait to find out."

The smile tugging at Kit's mouth makes something flare in me.

"You said the wine yesterday smelled like worn saddle, right?" he says.

"Honestly, it was more like assless chaps. I was being polite. Why?"

"Illuminating, is all." He doesn't begrudge me for it. We're the same way about food.

Kit and I have always shared a need to know what we're getting into. Kit takes leaps, once he's confident he can control how he'll land. I generally prefer the ground. But what's on the plate—what's in the glass, what melts into the palate, what plays nicely together in the pan—that's where we both like to be surprised.

It started with Del Taco.

We were ten, and I was sure an American fast food cultural education would help Kit fit in. That was the fall my sisters got their first gig together, so I was having all my dinners with Kit. One afternoon when his mom asked what we wanted, I said, "Miss Violette, can we get burritos?"

Frankly, Del Taco isn't even *good*. But I watched Kit across the back seat as he took that first bite and slipped into another dimension. One mediocre mouthful of refried beans and he was hooked on discovery. He had to know what other wild and astonishing shit was out there. We worked our way through every shape of french fry at every major fast-food chain, until Kit's mom told us we were frying our taste buds with American sodium and plonked a pot of coq au vin in front of us. Then it was my turn to be astonished.

While my sisters were making a divorce drama with Willem Dafoe, I was at Kit's house, discovering French cuisine. Kit's mom was a garden fairy, a kitchen witch, and everything she cooked was some great-great-grandmother's jealously guarded recipe. She introduced me to the five mother sauces, let me caramelize onions at her stove, and made what I still think of as the platonic ideal of bœuf bourguignon.

And so, Kit and I became curiosity gluttons together. Fifty percent of our friendship was sitting at tables going "ooh!" and shoving bites at each other. When we exhausted every cuisine in the Coachella Valley, we drove all over the state for roadside stands and chili festivals and beachside fish shacks. We'd take any risk, as long as it was something you ate or drank.

We were twenty-one when we first started daydreaming of a restaurant of our own, a small bistro with a simple, seasonal menu and new cocktails every week. We'd call it Fairflower. And from then on, everything we tasted had a bright, new tang of possibility.

I miss that flavor sometimes. I haven't been able to find it since.

"Do you remember the fancy-ass restaurant in LA?" I ask Kit. "The one we went to for your birthday?"

I know not to bring up our relationship now, but this was before, when I was still in what I thought was unrequited love. It was Kit's twenty-second birthday, and he wanted to try this restaurant he'd read about. God, we both wanted to like it so much more than we did.

I watch his face, waiting for the shadow I saw when I mentioned the breakup yesterday, but he brightens.

"Oh my God. The molecular gastronomy place."

"Now *that* was a nouns-only menu."

"It was less of a menu and more of a poem."

"All the portions were, like, microscopic."

"The *octopus foam.*"

"Who thought of octopus foam?" I say, the same thing I said when it arrived at our table that night.

"Octopus should never be foam!" he says, the same reply he had then.

"The bill was three hundred dollars, and we were still so hungry after, we went to—"

"Original Tommy's, for chili cheese fries."

"*Yes.*" I picture us in our nicest outfits, eating chili cheese fries out of the back hatch of my car. Hollywood, neon glow, Olivia Newton John on the parking-lot speakers, and a big, scary, brilliant secret in my heart.

I finish my tiny glass of room-temperature water, still smiling. Kit slides his over to me, and I finish that one too.

— — —

After lunch, we're set loose on the beach. Kit turns to me and asks, "What do you want to do?"

I'm mad at myself for leaving my swimsuit at the hostel, but I refuse to let that come between me and a place like this. I shade my eyes and scan the blue horizon, all the way to the rock formations rounding out the bay.

"I want to go see those rocks."

Kit nods. "Then let's go see those rocks."

He flags down a delivery guy for directions, and we leave the beach to climb uphill along a narrow, snaking road hidden among the trees. We go up and up and up, until we reach a little white chapel at the crest. From here, I can see everything from the green knees of the mountains to the horizon, and over a shambly wooden fence, the grass gives way to striations of gray rock cascading toward the water.

"Well," I say. "Just as I thought. Rocks."

Kit laughs and shakes his head. "Come on."

He ignores the locked gate and the sign barring visitors from the area and flits through a gap in the fence posts, heading downhill.

"What are you doing?" I yell.

He turns, grinning over his shoulder, light on his feet. "You wanted to see the rocks. I'm getting you to the rocks."

This has always been the difference between us. I look at a mountain and think, *What a nice view.* Kit looks at a mountain and thinks, *I wonder if I could climb that.*

I sigh, duck through the fence, and follow.

I catch up to him at the shoreline, where the rocks flatten into a shelf pummeled by waves, mist shimmering over our faces. Kit pushes his sunglasses up into his hair and plants his hands on his hips, pleased with his work.

He's found us our own private cove.

A long, narrow, concrete breakwater juts out from the shore, its surface slick and dark from catching the tide. We walk it until we can see the Grande Plage around the edge of the rocks, and then we sit down on its edge. I lay my bag of cherries from the market between us, and Kit unwraps his cheese. With help from my pocketknife and Kit's traveling jar of honey, we share both. The cherries are fantastically tart with a plummy sweetness, better than any cherry I've tasted before. Shout-out to Fruit Wife.

We don't discuss any of this. It just happens, like any of the thousands of meals we've eaten together. We've lapsed into our shared first language.

"That book you've been reading," I ask Kit. "What's it about?"

Kit swallows a bit of cheese.

"It's about this English girl named Lucy who falls in love with a man she meets while traveling to Florence," he says, "but of course everyone is being very Edwardian about it, so now she's engaged to another man who's a better match but a total drip."

"Man, I hate when the girls get all Edwardian." I pretend to sigh, and Kit laughs. "Is it good?"

He leans back on his hands and contemplates the question.

"I like reading E. M. Forster because it's always gay, even though this one is about a man and a woman," he says. "Do you know how sometimes when you read or watch or listen to something, there's a . . . resonant homosexual flavor? Not even in anything the characters are explicitly doing or saying, but in the voice, or how the flowers are described or a character looks at a painting, or the way they see and react to the world. Like when Legolas and Gimli walk into Minas Tirith and immediately start criticizing the landscaping."

I turn the idea over in my head. "Sort of like how I love older action movies because they're inherently homoerotic."

He exhales a short laugh through his nose. "I can't wait to find out what you mean by that."

"Kit. Come on. How many times have you watched *Point Break* with me? And how many times did we watch *Speed*? Those are two of the best action movies of the early nineties, and at their heart, both are about Keanu Reeves having this intense, soul-deep connection with the other lead, this crazy chemistry engine that works so well it's basically sex. The only difference is that one is Sandra Bullock and one is Patrick Swayze."

Kit touches his fingers to his lips, like he's thinking hard now. "I never thought of it that way."

"Or *Road House*! Or *Top Gun*!" I go on, propelled. "All the greatest action movies of the eighties, the most grab-ass, baby-oiled, hyper-masculine movies ever made, don't work without this underlying sense of everyone's dick being hard the whole time. That, *that* is fucking gay! They made the loop all the way around to gay! And that's the secret sauce. Nowadays everyone's so afraid of accidentally making a gay movie that *nobody's* dick is hard, which is why there hasn't been a truly iconic action hero in the last twenty years." I spit out a cherry pit and add, "Except John Wick."

The corners of his mouth tuck under into an appreciative upside-down smile.

"I like how you brought it full circle with Keanu."

"Right?"

"You really landed that plane."

"He doesn't get enough credit for what he's done for the community," I say. "*The Matrix*? Gender."

"Mm," he hums in amused agreement. "You're making great points."

Of all the things I missed about having Kit as my best friend, this might be the biggest. The forever *yes, and* of our conversations, every thought a continuation of the last, every random inconsequential detail of our lives dominoing into one another. Especially here, in our big, swirling, mutual soup of sex and gender.

We came out to each other four years apart—Kit first, to my absolute lack of surprise. Based on how he moved through the world, I'd always suspected he was either fruity or engaged in some kind of spiritual romance with the cosmic essence of the earth for which there were no human words. I should have known then that I was bisexual too; we understood each other too well to not be the same. But I was only fourteen, and I wasn't ready to know that about myself until eighteen.

He was so happy when I told him, pulled me so close that my Slurpee exploded all over us both. We had to jump the fence of the apartments behind the 7-Eleven to rinse off in the pool. It was like our world became twice as wide, like we could finally talk about colors no one else could see.

There's a second coming-out that I haven't done yet with Kit. Something I wasn't ready to know about myself until a few years ago. I watch him scrape the meat off a cherry pit with his teeth. Is this the right moment? Our first time alone together as friends again?

"Hey."

Kit turns, his eyes the color of top-shelf whiskey in the sun.

"The cherries," I say. "On the fly."

An old game of ours, invented when we first started fantasizing about Fairflower. I watch him recognize it, whiskey eyes glittering like I've dropped in a sugar cube.

"Oh," he breathes. "Okay, let me think."

I make a game-show-buzzer sound. "No thinking!"

"Okay, okay! I'm making an éclair. Cherry and mascarpone filling, quince and cherry jelly on top. And a mirror glaze, just to be sexy."

"Very nice." I pull my knees to my chest. "I'm taking the quince, and I'm making a ginger-quince syrup and putting it in an old-fashioned, with Angostura bitters and Four Roses and orange peel."

"Then I'll take the bitters and put them in a dark chocolate cake. Chocolate ganache with cayenne and cinnamon."

"I'm mixing the cayenne with salt and gochugaru and putting it on the rim of a persimmon margarita."

"Persimmon compote and blitzed hazelnuts for a cinnamon-roll filling, with persimmon–cream cheese frosting when it's fresh out of the oven."

"Fuuuck." I press my forehead to my knees. "I wanna eat that."

"So do I," he agrees. "Do I win?"

"I think so. I don't know how to top that."

"That's—" He interrupts himself with a cough.

"A first for me, yes," I say. "And you tried to shame me for *my* dirty jokes."

"It's not my fault," Kit sighs. He tips his head up, letting the sea breeze sweep his hair from his flushed face. "It's too nice out here. I can't work under these conditions."

"It really is." I gaze out over the water, imagining I could see a seaweed-wrapped starfish washing up from the ocean floor, the wiggling dots of the Calums on borrowed surfboards, a pod of dolphins, someone swimming home for dinner. "What must it be like to live here?"

Kit considers it. "I think I'd like life by the water. Especially out here on the Côte d'Argent, where you get the mountains and the ocean, and the flora too. It almost reminds me of Santa Barbara."

I haven't wanted to ask. I didn't want to hear him lie to save my feelings, but he's brought it up now.

"Do you ever miss California?"

"Oh, yeah," he says, eyes closed to the sun. "All the time."

I don't know what to say, so I don't say anything. We sit in companionable quiet for a while, just us and the cherries and the ocean.

"I wish I brought something to swim in," Kit says, as much to himself as to me.

I think of our talk about experiencing places—swimming in it, he said. I can hear the Ravel piece he played for me, the flute trills and strings rushing in and out like sea-foam. If he can give me that, I can give him something back. That's what friends do, isn't it?

I spring to my feet and face the rocks, my back to him.

"Stand up."

A surprised laugh bubbles out of him. "What?"

"Stand up and turn around. Face the horizon."

Over the whoosh of the waves, I hear the crinkle of paper, the rustle of leather, a zipper. Kit, tucking our things safely away before he does whatever ridiculous thing I have in mind. I'm glad only the rocks can see me smiling.

"Okay," he says. "Now what?"

"On three, we take off our clothes."

I can't see his face, but I know the exact velocity at which his brows just shot up.

"Sorry?"

"I won't look at you, you don't look at me. We take our clothes off and jump in as fast as we can."

A pause. The waves roll in again.

"Specifically how naked am I getting?"

"As naked as you want to get, I guess."

"How naked are *you* getting?"

"Underwear only."

Another pause.

"Underwear only," he repeats, his tone neutral. "Okay."

"Ready?"

"I hope so."

"One, two, three!"

I rip my shirt off over my head, drop my shorts, and leap. The water is cool, but not the shocking cold I expect from a lifetime swimming in the Pacific. It swirls around me in smooth, strong whorls, and I stay down for as long as I can, letting it hold my body and push up on the bottoms of my feet. I kick to the surface just as Kit splashes in.

"You hesitated!" I yell when he comes up.

"No, I didn't!" He pushes wet hair away from his face. "I just didn't know if you meant it."

"Why, because I can't be spontaneous?" I say. "I'll have you know I've become *very* spontaneous. You know how they say to do one thing every day that scares you?"

"You do that?"

"Well, I'm working my way up. Right now I'm at one a week."

"I see," he says. "What scares you this week?"

This, something in me answers automatically. *You.*

"Bull testicles," I say. "I'm gonna eat some in Spain."

I dive under and swim a quick lap, five meters out and back, just to pop up behind Kit and startle him.

"Ah, okay!" He spins around, paddling backward. "You win, you're spontaneous. I'm sorry I doubted you."

I laugh, swallowing the words down with a blazing gulp of air.

"It's good to see you swimming," he says.

Kit was at the swim meet where I messed up my shoulder, and he was there for the years after, when I hated the thought of learning to swim again. He was there before too, so many chlorine-scented summers. He's missed the past few years of chin-ups every morning to shore up my muscles and exploratory dips at Corona del Mar, but he knows what it means for me to be back in the water.

"Yeah. It feels good."

We tread water for what feels like ages, our bare shoulders rising and falling with each swell, just talking. I feel sun-roasted and salt-brined, like a tomato in a jar. Life is silly and random and magnificent, and I'm experiencing it all the way. I'm in it up to my nips. I'm in Saint-Jean-de-Luz, a delirious pink tide pool of happy accidents, and despite it all, I'm glad that it's Kit here with me. I can't think of anything happier or more accidental than that.

When an especially big wave rolls in, Kit twists around to catch it head-on, and I see the thin, straight line of black text on the top of his left shoulder, running horizontally between the base of his neck and the shoulder joint.

"Oh, hey," I say, "there's your third tattoo."

Kit tucks his chin back to look at it. "Oh, yeah, I forgot about it back there."

"What does it say?"

"Just a line from a book."

"What book?"

"The Silmarillion."

"Ah, of course," I say. Kit's family introduced me to genre fiction and Renaissance festivals after a childhood of Serious Art. His parents used to say they stole Kit from Rivendell, on account of how he had the air of like an ethereal elf child. Tolkien was always his favorite. "Nerd. Can I read it?"

He turns, and I push myself closer, glad I'm a strong enough swimmer to keep our naked skin from accidentally touching.

The words read, *surpasse tous les joyaux.*

"It's in French," I say, a little disappointed.

He's quiet while the ocean laps against his chest.

"I read the book in French first," he says finally. "It means, 'surpasses all jewels.'"

"Huh. Cool." It's been ages since I read *The Silmarillion* for Kit, but the phrase sounds familiar. I'm more fascinated by the linework, the delicate, featherlight script. Whoever did this must have barely dug into his skin at all, but the black is stark and clean. "I love the lettering."

Without thinking, I run my fingertip over the ink. Wet skin meets wet skin. Kit shivers.

The sense memory crashes in like a rogue wave. I see our skinny legs, grown too fast and not filled out yet, kicking together against the tide. I see a teenaged Kit levering himself out of my parents' pool. I remember a flat tire in the pouring rain on the side of the Pacific Coast Highway, peeling his wet shirt off in the back seat. I feel my back pressed to his chest in a too-small bathtub, and I see his face, slick with me from nose to chin.

Oh, fuck.

Kit kicks away as if he can sense the deluge of uninvited horny thoughts. God. Why can't my fear of spontaneity manifest as impulse control? Why do I have to *touch* things?

"Sorry, that was—" I start, but then he turns. "Oh my God, Kit, your nose."

It's bleeding, this time from both sides. He wipes it with the back of his hand and examines the red swirling through the seawater. "Ah. Yeah. I thought so."

"It looks . . . pretty fucking gnarly. It'll stop, right?"

"It should," he says, attempting an apologetic smile, "but it might stop faster if I get out of the water?"

"Okay," I agree. He looks at me like he's waiting for something. "Oh, right. I'll close my eyes, just let me know when you're decent."

I listen for his strokes through the water, and the sounds of him climbing onto the breakwater. Something soggy splats against the concrete—the underwear he swam in.

"I'm decent!" Kit calls out.

When I open my eyes, his back is to me as he settles his shorts on his hips. I very deliberately do not have any emotions or observations about his silhouette against the distant watercolor foothills or the fact that he's no longer wearing anything under his terry shorts. Kit's build has always been graceful and lithe, but his ass is, as the poets say, bodacious. The poets, not me—I'm not choosing any adjectives. I swim in and get myself dressed, very decidedly not looking.

"Sorry to kill the mood," Kit says, his head tilted.

"No, it's okay, there was no mood." I pull on my shirt, feeling mildly delirious. "Except, you know, a friendly mood. The mood of friendship."

"Yes, my favorite Wong Kar-wai. *In the Mood for Friendship.*"

"Tony Leung is so hot in that one."

"He always is." He turns just as I do, scrunching up his nose and sniffing. He hasn't put his shirt on yet. I look everywhere but him. "I think it stopped."

"Cool. What do we do now?"

Kit considers. "Do you want to go pick up some things for when we meet up with Paloma?"

"What kind of things?"

"I was thinking pastry," he says, "in case she wants to keep hanging out."

He puts his arms through the sleeves of his shirt, and I narrow my eyes, finally thinking clearly.

"You're trying to sleep with her."

"I simply *think*," he counters, "it seemed possible she might want to sleep with one of us, and the right pastry might tip things in my favor."

"Or the right bottle of wine."

"Sure," he says noncommittally, half smiling, "maybe."

"Let's go, then." I slide my feet back into my Birks, grinning back. "May the best slut win."

— —— —

I stand outside the bakery, cradling a bottle of screw-top red and watching through the window as Kit charms every single person behind the counter. He emerges flushed, waving to the shopgirls as they blow kisses. He really is some kind of world wonder.

"What'd you get?"

He opens a white paper box to reveal two dozen thin, pale, informal cookies with crinkly cracks around their edges. When I take one, it's surprisingly light and tastes like almonds.

"Mouchous," he says. "Basque macarons. Chewier than the Parisian ones, right?"

"Mmm. And better, I think."

"The secret is potato flour." He closes the box. "And you?"

I hold up my bottle. "A cheeky Croatian Plavina. Should be cute and beachy, a little juicy."

Kit sighs.

"This isn't fair. You're just going to do your thing, and it'll be over."

"What thing?"

"Your sommelier thing, where you lower your voice and tell

them the grapes taste like elderflower because the wind blew in a southeasterly direction in Provence last July, and then everyone wants to have sex with you."

I raise my eyebrows. "Everyone?"

"Theo!" a crisp voice calls out from above. "Kit!"

We look up to find Paloma leaning out of the open window of the apartment over the bakery.

"I was about to leave to meet you at the port," she says, "but then I look out my window, and there you are! And I see you went swimming, well done!"

The shutters of the window above Paloma's rattle open, and a bearded old man's head pops out. He looks at us, then calls down to Paloma in a language that sounds like both Spanish and French and also nothing like either.

"What's he saying?" I whisper to Kit.

"I think he's speaking Basque."

"Isn't your mom's family Basque?"

"Yeah, on her mom's side, but she didn't speak the language."

"This is my great-uncle Mikel," Paloma says to us. "He wants to know if either of you are fit for marriage."

"Uh—"

A much smaller but equally curious face appears in another window, a girl around twelve with a flute in one hand and a cookie in the other.

"What's Papa Mikel yelling about?" the girl yells to Paloma. "Who's here?"

"Just some friends!"

Paloma's cousin squints at us. "They don't look like any of your friends!"

"They're visiting! I met them at the market! Stop being nosy or I'll tell your mama!"

"Tell me what?" says a middle-aged woman in the window beside Great-Uncle Mikel.

"Léa isn't doing her flute practice!"

"*Palomaaa!*"

"Léa!"

"I'll come down," Paloma says to us, closing her shutters. The only one left in a window is Great-Uncle Mikel, lighting a cigarette.

"I love this fucking town," I say to Kit, who shakes his head, breathless with laughter.

Paloma bursts out of the street-level door beside the bakery wearing short-sleeved coveralls identical to the ones from this morning, sans fish guts.

"Sorry for my family," she says. "We have lived in this building for seventy-five years, so it's very interesting when someone new comes around."

"I guess you won't be impressed by these, then," Kit says as he shows her the bakery box.

"No, these are my favorites!" Paloma says, touching his arm. "And we must enjoy them while we still can."

"Is something happening to the shop?" I ask.

"Not yet, but the owner is a thousand years old, and she has no children to pass it on to. I think I'll die when she finally stops baking."

Paloma takes us away from the ill-fated pâtisserie and soon enough we're at the port, air brimming with salt and seagrass and the eye-watering smell of fish. We bob like buoys behind her as she shows us around red-and-green fishing boats, stopping to banter with a fisherman and help a deckhand heave a sack of ice off the pier. It's deeply dreamy.

I should be bringing her my A game, but Kit's presence—the scent of salt water on his skin, the faint stain of cherry juice on his lips—is disrupting my process.

Paloma has family throughout southern France and northern Spain, all married to the sea. Her parents met at this very port when her mother was working on her family fishing boat and her father was pulling fish for his family market stall. She says she was born smelling like anchovies.

"I speak five languages in all," she tells us. "French and Spanish were always my best. My Basque is okay. My Catalan is awful. English I learned in school, and then I lived in Sydney for a while."

"Sydney, Australia?" Kit asks.

"Yes, I went to culinary school," she says. "I thought I would be a chef at a famous restaurant, but I hated it. Every day I wanted to come home, until I did. I like it better here. Nobody ever tells me what to do."

Finally, as the sun begins to set, Paloma asks, "Do you have plans now? I'm meeting friends on Plage de Ciboure, if you want to come."

Kit and I exchange eye contact.

Tour dinner is optional tonight, I say with my eyes. *Skip it?*

Skip it.

"We'd love to," I say.

Paloma lights up. "Quelle chance!"

On a small, secluded beach away from the Grande Plage, one with big rock outcroppings and a view of an old fort on the water beyond, Paloma's friends make a loose circle in the sand. We're not the only ones to have brought an offering of food or drink—at the center of the circle, a blanket is spread with plates of oil and soft cheeses, brown paper parcels of jambon and saucisson, loaves of bread, round golden-brown cakes with burnt edges, jugs of lemonade, and a jumble of half-drunk bottles.

Paloma introduces her friends in rapid succession, each lifting a glass from atop fraying pillows or beach towels or slingback chairs. There's a bartender, a surf instructor, a butcher, the cheesemonger from the market, a few beachside hotel staffers, a line cook, a bookseller, and a gardener.

"Ah," Paloma says, "and here is Juliette!"

A woman appears from the direction of the water, her dark hair falling damp and loose around her shoulders. Her sundress is darkened in patches, like she threw it on over her wet swimsuit. She's carrying a mesh bag of oranges over her shoulder.

Fruit Wife. Her name is Juliette.

I turn to tell Kit, but he and Paloma are already chatting in French with the cheesemonger. Maybe I should institute some kind of weighted system in our competition, like a half-hour head start if only one of us speaks a mark's native language. Kit should have to sit quietly and let me make the first run at anyone who speaks French, or at least take a disadvantage. Maybe an ugly hat.

But I'm standing before a buffet of the most sexually compelling characters of the Saint-Jean-de-Luz hospitality industry, and Paloma is not the only dish. I plant myself in front of the bartender and hold out my Plavina.

"Salut!" I say. "Your glass is empty. Wine?"

By a stroke of delightful luck, he's Croatian, so he speaks a few languages and is thrilled to see a wine from home. He calls over one of the hotel guys and the gardener, and I pour everyone a round of ruby red. In turn, the bartender offers me a glug of local white wine aged in underwater tanks beyond the seawall. Naturally, I have five hundred questions about this. Soon, I've been absorbed into a cluster of English-speaking oenophiles.

Camping lanterns illuminate the circle as I taste a bit of everything and ask question after question, tipsy and eager and rolling around flavors. The butcher tells me about the nineteen months of aging to create Jambon du Kintoa, which tastes faintly of chestnuts because the pigs roam free on the green Pyrenees slopes eating whatever they find. The line cook passes me a hunk of cheese that tastes almost like caramel. Even Kit drifts by on a slow lap around the sand to tell me the history of the gâteau Basque, with its buttery crust and tart black cherry filling.

Kit comes by more than once, actually. We've gravitated to opposite sides of the language barrier, but he seems exclusively interested in the cheese and wines closest to me. At first I suspect competitive sabotage, until I realize he's checking on me. He's making sure I'm okay in an unfamiliar place. It holds the comfort of before, when we'd lock eyes across a party and know that whatever happened, we'd get each other home.

On his fifth visit, after someone's pulled out a speaker to play Kylie Minogue and we've all gotten up to dance in the sand, Kit and Fruit Wife find their way to me at the same time.

"Hi, Kit," I say. And then, with significantly more interest, "Hi, Juliette. It was nice to meet you at the market."

Juliette smiles, looking ever the wife with her hair down and her dress slipping off her shoulder. I'm not looking at Kit, but I can sense him finally putting together who she is. My hand finds his thigh, and I dig one blunt fingernail into his skin as a warning not to blow this for me. Juliette keeps smiling. My head goes a little wobbly, and I pull my hand away.

She produces an orange from the folds of her skirt and holds it out to me, saying something in French.

"Oh, merci," I say, taking the orange. "I—sorry, je ne parle pas français."

"Ah." A pucker appears between her pretty brows. "No English."

She says something else in French, and Kit shifts closer.

"She was saving this one for you," Kit translates, looking at me. "She's happy she got to see you again."

"Oh! Moi aussi!" I turn from her to Kit. "Can you tell her that I loved the cherries?"

Kit translates dutifully. "She says—ah—she says she thought you would like them because they're beautiful, and so are you."

"Oh yeah? Tell her I'd buy anything from her."

He does, and when she answers, he translates, "You should come back to the market tomorrow, then."

"I'm leaving tomorrow, but I have all night."

Kit translates, and Juliette answers, but he doesn't take his eyes off me for the entire exchange. It's almost like he's asking for himself when he translates, "What do you want to do that will take all night?"

I look directly into his eyes and say, "Something I'm very good at."

For a second, Kit's face goes completely immobile. Then he lets out a laugh that's all breath.

"You know what, I don't think I'm needed here anymore," he says, holding his hands up.

Juliette and I laugh, which doesn't need any translation. As everyone begins to collapse into the sand, I find myself sideways on a flower-patterned towel with my head in Juliette's lap. Kit falls on the other side of the circle with Paloma, talking quietly in the lantern light and sharing the last mouchous.

It feels so natural here, like we're among our people. Right now, I can imagine us here forever. Theo-and-Kit side-by-side in Saint-Jean-de-Luz. A perfect hyphenate daisy chain. We could have neighboring apartments down the street from Paloma's and lunches of cheese and fruit from the market. I would swim in the bay every morning, and Kit would go out to the mountains every weekend to sketch plants. We could become best friends again, spend the rest of our lives together.

I realize I've never felt this comfortable before, outside of the Valley. I didn't know it was possible.

My phone buzzes from my hip pack: another email from Schnauzer Bride. I ignore it and open my texts instead, replying to Sloane's message from this morning.

you know all those times you said i need to get out of the valley? I type. maybe you were onto something . . .

When I'm done, I look up in time to see Kit take Paloma's face in his hand.

It's a gentle, exploratory touch, his fingers lacing into the hair at her nape. His thumb brushes her jaw. She's still for a moment, and then her hand covers his.

His gaze shifts away from her face, to mine.

It's fleeting, but I catch it. The question in his eyes. The genuine need. It's a fair trade for earlier, with Juliette. He wants me to watch.

He leans forward and kisses her.

I go under.

In the moment of suspension after the plunge, we're everywhere. A hundred thousand memories of a hundred thousand touches circle like shoals of little iridescent fish. Kit's lips against the bridge of my nose. Kit holding the side of my face in the laundry detergent aisle. A slice of cake on a bad day and Kit's apron smeared with buttercream, a grateful kiss to each of his fingertips. Passed dishes, stolen covers, a thumbprint of strawberry juice on my chin. My hand pinning his shoulder to the wall, his mouth livid and wet and starving. The way he kissed me at the kitchen table the first morning we were honest.

Air runs out. I kick to the surface.

Up here, he's still kissing Paloma, and my head is still in Juliette's lap, and we're friends again. Just friends, just barely.

I sit up and pull Juliette's mouth to mine.

It's easy to kiss her. So smooth and sweet and uncomplicated. She puts her hand on the side of my neck and kisses back, and I slip my tongue into her mouth and taste nectar and buttery bread. There's nothing hidden here, just pure curiosity and desire, no sense memories to flood my body or ghosts to stick in my throat, and it's nice, isn't it? Is this what Kit felt? Is he watching the way I watched him?

I open my eyes to see for myself, but his spot in the sand is

empty. When I scan the beach, I can't find him or Paloma anywhere.

I break the kiss and try to remember the French words for
Where the fuck did they go?

"Où—" Shit, I only know present tense. "Où est—" Wait,
that's singular. "Où sont Kit et Paloma?"

Juliette gives the group a perfunctory once-over and shrugs,
her dress falling farther down her shoulder.

"Je ne sais pas," she says, kissing me again.

I kiss her for four seconds, five.

"Sorry, I just—do you think she took him home?"

Juliette chases after my mouth.

"Je ne sais pas."

I close my eyes, trying to focus on the feeling of her breath
on my skin, but—

"Do you know if she likes him? Like, really likes him?"

She pulls away this time, sitting back with a sigh. She regards
me from under her long lashes with an expression that's soft and
almost sad, almost kind, with a bitter finish. The crease between
her brows reappears.

She calls out to the bartender, who crawls over to kiss her
cheek and listen as she tells him something in French. He looks
at me with that same strange expression and says, "She wants you
to know you don't have to do this if you love someone else."

The words land like a sprained ankle.

"What? I—" I glance between them, a laugh bubbling up
from my chest. "Oh, that's—no, it's not what you think. Kit's my
friend."

Juliette and the bartender exchange a look.

"She says you're lovely, but she doesn't settle for second place."

I try to argue, but it's useless. Whatever Juliette saw between
Kit and me, whatever broke inside my brain when I saw him
kissing Paloma, whatever was cut loose when my skin touched

his in the water—Juliette has decided it's love. It doesn't matter how much I insist it's not.

She presses a kiss to the back of my hand and gives me a pity-ing smile, and the bartender passes me a bottle.

SAN SEBASTIÁN

PAIRS WELL WITH:

Txakoli poured high above the glass,
tortilla de patatas

SAN SEBASTIÁN

The short version is, I'm pissed at Kit.

The long version is, we're on a pintxos crawl through glorious, sun-soaked San Sebastián, and everything is sumptuous and salty and soaked in oil and piled atop the most delectable morsels of crusty bread, and Kit looks happy, and I'm pissed.

I've read the San Sebastián portion of *World Travel* five times, so I know exactly what Bourdain said about this place. He wrote that it might be the greatest culinary destination in Europe, and that he imagined himself living a perfect life here. I get it—I feel it in every corner of this city, every sand-dusted tile and fuzzy green stone, every brick in every Gothic arch, whiffs of saffron and clove and guindilla at every overstuffed pintxos bar.

We've arrived on the last day of Semana Grande, the city's end-of-summer festival, and the streets are fucking *alive.* Street performers balance on milk jugs with puppets on their hands, cooks under tents pound balls of dough into pans, giant-headed mascots chase screaming children through the squares. The chaos is incandescent and overwhelming and viscerally of its own place, like a cava waterboarding.

And still, I'm pissed at Kit.

I don't want to be pissed. I want to feel the way I did yesterday. I want to be here, on the small peninsula of San Sebastián's Old Town, in a dim bar with ham hocks hanging from the ceiling, slurping buttered clams and enjoying the company of my friend Kit.

"Oh my God, Theo," Kit's saying, passing me a skewer of pickled olives, peppers, and anchovies on a slice of baguette. "You have to try this one."

Fabrizio pops up beside us in an even more spectacularly good mood than usual. I'm surprised his shirt's still on.

"La Gilda! Excellent choice! This is the first Basque pintxo in history. Do you know the film *Gilda*?"

"With Rita Hayworth?" I ask.

"Yes! This is named for her, because it tastes like how she was in the film. Green, salty, and spicy."

We find ourselves sharing a little table with the old Swedish couple Kit befriended on the first day. Plate after plate of pintxos pour from the kitchen—slices of tortillas de patatas, mushroom croquetas, velvety goose liver and herb-flecked anchovies on bread topped with duck eggs—so many that Fabrizio sweeps in to help the waiters. Kit sits sideways in his chair and laughs at everything, his body loose with the unmistakable contentment of the recently fucked.

It's all so *easy* for him. Leaving me for a shiny new life, kissing sexy fishmongers and abandoning me to be cockblocked by my own unresolved feelings. Even when we were together, I could see the vines of potential spiraling out of him, reaching for taller trellises in bigger fields. He gets everything he ever dreamed of, and I'm where I've always been, one step behind.

It would be such a relief to create a problem for him, even a small one.

Fabrizio drops off a plate of croquetas and compliments Birgitte's blouse, and when he saunters off, Birgitte says, "Den där Fabrizio, he is like a painting we have in the Nationalmuseum in Stockholm."

"Which one?" Kit asks.

"I think I know," says her bespectacled husband, Lars. With the jolly mischief of a man wearing a straw fedora indoors, Lars pulls up something on his phone and shows it to his wife.

"Ja! This is him!"

She shows us an extremely horny painting entitled *The Youth of Bacchus,* featuring a bunch of naked, nubile, wine-drunk revelers in a forest, either dancing or warming up for an orgy.

"Oh, yeah, I definitely see it," Kit says. He zooms in on the central figure, a muscular, bronze-skinned man with a tambourine-waving child on his shoulders and a leopard hide barely concealing his dick. "Especially his, uh—his—"

He points at the grooves of abdominal muscle near the figure's hips and takes a sip of wine, trusting me to choose the appropriate phrase. Iliac furrows? V-line? Adonis belt?

I say, "Cum gutters."

Kit chokes.

"Kümgütter?" Birgitte asks. "What is this word, kümgütter?"

I thump Kit between the shoulders, smiling beatifically. "Kit, care to explain?"

"I—" Kit shoots me a look that's half glare, half terrible delight. My smile widens. "It's, ah, American slang for the lower muscles on the stomach."

"Oh!" Lars exclaims. "We call this bäckenspåret! In America, I should say kümgütter?"

"No no no," Kit says, distressed, "it's *vulgar* slang."

"Is it?" Birgitte asks. She leans in with a twinkle in her eye. "What does it mean?"

Kit looks to me for help. I open the translation app on my phone and press the mic button until the digital bleat sounds.

"*Cum gutter,*" I enunciate loudly enough for the next tables to hear. "Huh, no results."

"Please, you will not embarrass us," Lars says. "Go on!"

Kit takes a breath. "So, during sex, when a person with a penis finishes on their partner's stomach, and—"

"Ahhh, I see," Lars interrupts, alight with glee. He says something to his wife in Swedish, and she nods knowingly.

"Cum *and* gutter! Two words!"

Despite my best efforts, this seems to have permanently endeared us to Lars and Birgitte. They ask us so many questions that I'm half expecting a Christmas card from Sweden this holiday season.

"And you two," Lars says, gesturing between Kit and me, "you are—?"

"Friends," I say.

"Old friends," Kit elaborates.

"Very good! And how did you meet?"

Kit and I exchange a look, waiting each other out.

"We went to grade school together," I say.

Kit weighs this answer, pushing an olive across his plate. He's not letting me off this easy, not after the cum gutters.

"That was *where* we met," he says, "not *how* we met."

I remember the day Kit showed up. Second grade, a skinny little changeling trying to explain to a bunch of California kids named Josh and Taylor how to pronounce his name—his real, French name, not the one he goes by. He was *different*. He had big, daydreamy eyes and a gentle accent that none of us had heard, and he spent every recess reading books in trees.

I was different too, a tomboy in the extreme, always wearing cargo shorts and insisting on being let into the boys' games. One day I found Kit in a stairwell, cornered by two of the boys who wouldn't play with me and trying not to cry. Maybe if he had been crying already I would have just gotten a teacher, but he was biting his lip, holding the tears back. Those little assholes didn't deserve the satisfaction.

When I was called to the principal's office that afternoon for fighting, he was there, waiting for his mom. She called him a different name than the one on the classroom roster, a family nickname. Kit. I asked him if I could call him that too, and when he said yes, I told him to call me Theo.

The Swedes adore this story.

They reward us with their tale of meeting each other at a ski lodge in the Alps, where they were celebrating their respective divorces. After three nights of discussing art by the lodge's fireplace, they realized they'd met before on a hiking trail in Croatia in their early twenties. They married within months, and they've been inseparable for fifteen years now.

"I was a fool the first time we met," Lars says. "Proud, crude, always one woman after another."

"And I was married!" Birgitte adds. "It was the wrong time. But he was the right man."

Lars wraps his hand around hers. "Still, I wonder what life would be if I had asked her to run away with me that day at Jezero Kozjak." He looks at us intently. "Learn from an old man. Take care of good love when you find it."

Kit glances at me with something soft in his eyes, like we could still be those kids in California.

The Somm once told me how he came to love wine. *Everyone has that one bottle,* he said. His was a red that sat in his mother's kitchen window for twenty-seven years, until one day he looked up the vintage on the sun-bleached label and discovered it could have been worth forty thousand dollars if stored properly. Instead, it's a window decoration, a precious thing that spoiled because nobody thought to take care of it.

I do, despite everything, want to take care of this. There's never been another person who could fill Kit's place, and I know there never will be. I've been living around that gap, never looking at it, always feeling the draft it lets in. Yesterday was so warm, though.

I want to be his friend—not because it'll make the trip easier, but because I *want* to. But I can't do it like this. If I'm going to do it right, there are things I have to say.

— — —

The green peak of Monte Igueldo towers over San Sebastián, and a little amusement park sits on top. In the packed crowd of

Semana Grande tourists, I feel my first moment of gratitude for
our navigational beacon of butt-fucky Pinocchio puppet. At least
when it's time to regroup in an hour, I'll only have to look up.

Before Kit can be swept away, I grab the strap of his sling bag.
I point to a sign advertising a children's boat ride with once-in-
a-lifetime views.

"Wanna be my co-captain?"

"Yeah," he says, smiling. "Yeah, let's go."

At the front of the line, a teenaged ride operator waves us
into a miniature boat and pushes us off down the long, winding
flume. Greenish water carries us forward, alone together, Kit in
the front seat, me in the back.

At the first big curve, the trees fringing the flume give way to
open air, and the view spreads into panoramic widescreen. It's as
spectacular as promised: water glistening for miles into the horizon
of the Atlantic, the distinctive seashell-shaped bay of La Concha,
small white sailboat triangles, jutting green islets, lush mountains
cupping the city and fading off into distant blue-gray shadows.

The boat rounds another corner and floats into a rocky cave,
and then, as if to wake us up from a dream, our boat bangs into
the one in front of us.

The river is stuffed bumper-to-bumper as far as I can see,
each boat full of confused tourists and cranky children. Another
boat collides with ours, and when I turn to check, it's Stig waving
at me apologetically.

"Hey buddy," I say.

"Hallå," Stig replies. His boat is sitting dangerously low in
the water.

"I think we're stuck," Kit says.

We wait, sitting in silence except for the rush of water and
the conversation of the Portuguese tourists in the next boat. Stig
hums to himself. I study the inside of the cave.

It appears to have been decorated to appeal to children some-
time in the late '90s, but not in any way that makes sense. In the

recesses of the cavern, someone has propped up plywood cutouts of a random assortment of Disney characters—Peter Pan, Quasimodo, Hercules flexing his biceps, all looking conspicuously un-trademarked. Between them are a few topless mermaids, a stuffed stork, and a plaster crocodile with glowing red eyes.

"Interesting decor," I comment, eyeing a mannequin dressed as a pirate and a hauntingly out-of-place skeleton.

"Sort of Disneyland meets Willy Wonka's nightmare tunnel," Kit replies.

"'It's a Small World' on ayahuasca."

Kit laughs, and I think, *fuck it*. There's no good place for this conversation. Might as well have it in a cursed mermaid-nipple dimension.

I take a breath and say, "Kit."

He twists in his seat to face me like he's expecting another joke. I can see the moment he registers the serious look on my face, and the quarter second after, when he calculates how rarely I look serious about anything.

"Oh." He pushes a piece of hair behind his ear. "Are we . . . ?"

We are.

"I know I said I didn't want to talk about what happened," I say. "And I honestly don't see the point of getting into what we said on the plane, or the Paris thing, because I haven't changed my mind, and you obviously haven't either." I pause. He doesn't contradict me. "But I do have to talk about what came after, if we're going to be friends."

Kit absorbs that.

"Okay," he says, nodding thoughtfully. "After. What do you mean? Heathrow?"

My face flashes hot. I'm already irritated on reflex.

"Yeah, Kit," I say, making an effort to keep my voice polite, "weirdly enough, I would like to know why you left me at an international airport with my dick in my hand."

A pause.

"Theo, you flew back to America without me."

"It wouldn't have been without you if you had shown up."

"What are you talking—?" Kit pinches the bridge of his nose, like he's thinking very hard. "Hold on. What do you think happened that day?"

"What do I *think*? I know what happened."

"I thought I did too," he says slowly, "but now I'm not so sure."

I suck in another deep breath and recite the sequence of events, even though I'd prefer to do almost anything else.

"We fought," I say. "We said a lot of stuff there's no coming back from. By the time we got through passport control, I didn't even want to go on the tour anymore, and you said you didn't either. I said I wanted to go home, and you said you did too. And then you said you needed some space to think, and you walked away."

Kit says, "And then I came back."

My mouth opens automatically, but whatever I was going to say disappears into the damp cave air.

For four years, my life has been directed by the simple fact that he walked away. He turned around and never came back. That was the one-line answer when anyone asked, the simple truth.

"You came back?"

"I came back," he says again, "and you were gone."

"That was—" I shake my head. "That was because I had already gotten our tickets home, and I had to check our bag."

Now Kit's staring at me, the way I was just staring at him.

"*Our* tickets?" he says. "You got one for me?"

"Of course I did, Kit. I checked us both in, and I texted you your ticket, and then I waited at the gate until the very last call, but you never came."

Kit closes his eyes and says, "Theo, you sent me *your* ticket."

"What? No, I didn't." I distinctly remember how my fingers

shook as I checked into our combined reservation, pulled up both of our boarding passes, and sent him a screenshot of his.

"Yes, you did."

"No, I didn't, I remember, distinctly."

Kit pulls out his phone and swipes through his messages to our conversation. Unlike me, he hasn't deleted it, so he can scroll directly up from the text I sent him in Paris to our last exchange. I catch a glimpse of one undelivered message from him to me, gone from the screen too fast to read, before he taps on the image above it. The boarding pass I sent him, taken straight from the British Airways app.

At the top, where it should say Kit's name, it says mine.

I stare at it. Read it three times before I believe it. Of all the idiotic, badly timed, baby-brained fucking accidents, this is the last one I ever thought I could make and maybe the most important one in the entire course of my adult life. I feel faintly nauseous.

"Okay, well, obviously that was a mistake," I insist, pushing his phone away. "You had to have known that."

"What I knew," Kit says, his voice tight, "was that it sounded like you didn't want to be with me anymore, so I went to have a cry in a very damp airport bathroom, and by the time I got back you were on the other side of security, and you'd sent me a message that clearly—to me—meant you were going home without me." He touches a hand to his temple, like the memory is stressing him out. "I thought that was your way of breaking up with me."

"I—I can't believe you would—" I shake my head. "Kit, does that sound like something I would do?"

"Honestly, yes."

I—

I think of all the lies I told to get out of meeting him in Oklahoma City. The look on his face when I told him I'd left Santa

Barbara. The crash of his coffee mugs when I threw them in a box. How fast I left that bar in Paris.

"Well, I didn't," I say to the taxidermied stork over Kit's shoulder instead of having to look him in the eye. "Why didn't you just ask? We had agreed we were going home."

"I didn't think we had."

"I did. And I thought—" All this time, I'd been sure. "—I thought you had your ticket and just decided not to get on the plane. I thought you left me."

Kit says, "I thought *you* left *me*."

I count to three in my head, collect myself.

"Okay, well," I say, "what about the rest? Why did I have to find out you were moving to Paris from a shift manager at Timo?"

Kit blinks, surprised into a whole new line of confusion.

"That's how you heard?"

"I was at work when you called in to quit."

"No, it was a Tuesday lunch shift," he says. "I specifically called then, because you never worked Tuesday lunches."

"I picked up a double."

"Fuck." He sighs. "I didn't know. I mean, I figured you'd heard somehow—"

"Yeah, that was obvious."

"Theo, I wanted to tell you," he says, sounding like the softer side of miserable. "I did. When you left, I didn't know what to do. Every time I thought about having to see you and say good-bye, having to—to go into our apartment and disentangle our lives—I couldn't do it. I took the train to Paris, and I went to the flat. I must have written and thrown away a hundred letters until I got one right."

He looks into my eyes with a sincerity that's nearly frantic, like it'll kill him if I don't believe him.

"And then," he says, "the day I was going to send it, Cora called to say you'd packed my things. And when I tried to text you I realized you'd blocked my number, and I thought, that's it. Theo's done with me. I'd taken too long and lost my chance to change your mind. And after what you said on the plane, I thought I should respect what you wanted. I should let you go. I should live with it. So, that's what I did."

He leaves it there, letting me pick it up and do what I want with it, like I have the first idea where to put this piece I never knew was missing. This unexpected fucking complication. The idea that I survived losing him with an anger I hadn't even earned.

The whole thing, my story where Kit plays the traitor—it doesn't make sense with two broken hearts.

When I find my voice, I ask, "What about the rent?"

"What?"

"We were splitting rent. I had to cover your half when you left."

He scrubs a hand over his face. "Sloane said she was going to help."

A memory comes back to me: Sloane, taking me out for dinner after the breakup, gently suggesting over dessert that she could help with bills until my lease ran out. I should have known.

"*You* asked Sloane to bail me out?"

He holds up his hands before I can get going. Apparently, this is the one thing he won't allow me to get mad about.

"I sent one text to your sister," he says flatly, "who was also my friend, who loves you and is a literal multimillionaire, asking if she would be willing to help you."

"I can't believe—"

"Theo," he interrupts. "If I had sent money, would you have taken it?"

For the first time, I imagine how it would have felt to have Kit cut me a check after he broke my heart.

"No."

"Right," Kit says. "I thought Sloane had a better chance, but I'm guessing not."

I don't say anything. Slowly, boats begin drifting forward, one by one. Someone must have unclogged the river.

"Okay," I say at last. Kit's eyes are fixed on the plywood mermaid, his brows set in a rueful arch. He tips his chin up to listen. I squeeze my knees with both hands. "Okay, so, I left you, but only because I thought you left me. And you left me, but only because you thought I left you."

Ripples of light flash off the water and across Kit's face, catching on the soft curve of his smile.

"C'est à peu près ça." I know this one; he always said it growing up. He's picked it back up since Paris. *That's it, more or less.*

All I can do is laugh. "What a dumb fucking series of events."

Kit laughs too, and finally, we begin to float on.

"So, are we friends?" Kit asks. He's not even mad. He's not mad at me for any of it.

Our boat drifts out of the cave and into the sun. I take a breath and try to make my answer come out resolute, but the truth is, things feel less resolved than ever now.

"Yeah," I say. "Yeah, I think so."

— — —

Later, we crash into Fabrizio on the beach.

He's a few drinks in, a crust of sea salt and sand up to his knees, his bare chest glazed with sweat like the outside of a spritz glass. When he kisses my face, his skin smells like chinotto oranges. We're both so happy to see him. Our human aperitivo.

"Do you know a good place to watch the fireworks tonight?" Kit asks him.

Fabrizio grins and pulls me into his right side, Kit into his left.

"Stay with me, amori miei. I will show you."

A thick, slow crowd carries us from the beach like flies in honey, across a plaza jangling with carnival games to a hole-in-the-wall corner bar. Kit and Fabrizio ravish the pintxo counter, and I order a wine I've never had, a straw-colored Basque Txakoli that the bartender pours from high above his head into the precise center of my glass without looking. At our table outside, I tell Kit and Fabrizio about the bartender's pour, how pouring from a height accentuates the tiny, delicate bubbles in the wine. Kit leans in so closely to listen that he nearly tips my glass into Fabrizio's lap.

We feast, and we laugh, and the sun goes down. Kit reclines in his chair to listen to Fabrizio, a hand buried in his hair to keep it off his face. My mouth waters from the acid of the wine and three helpings of sour La Gilda.

When we're done, Fabrizio takes us to one of the nicest hotels along the beach, one with spires and arches and Gothic embellishments up its front, where he knows a concierge who lets us onto the rooftop. I wait until the first firework explodes over the bay, until Kit's eyes are fixed on the sky, to let myself look at him the way I've wanted to since Monte Igueldo.

When I do, I see Kit. Not a memory that can be bent or shrunk or cut up into paper snowflakes, but a whole, living person. I see lights flickering over a face I woke up to every morning and shoulders I slept on when I was exhausted from growth spurts. Here, now, under a shower of sparks, he looks just like the person who would have missed me, the one who wouldn't have left.

The truth is, I never stopped loving that person. I only stopped believing he existed.

— — —

I raise my glass, cross myself, and call out, "Here's to swimmin' with bowlegged women!"

Fabrizio smiles bemusedly while Kit and I chug our ciders.

"American toasts, very strange."

"It's from *Jaws*," Kit says as he sets his empty glass down. Affronted bubbles stream into my cider—I have never understood how an elf prince like Kit can drink me under the table. "Theo's favorite movie."

"Ah! One of my favorite American movies too!" Fabrizio says. "Have you seen the Italian one?"

I drop my own glass and swallow a burp. "*L'Ultimo Squalo,* 1981. Fucking classic."

We detour into an impassioned review of the movie's greatest moments, from all the extended windsurfing sequences to the scene where the mayor tries to catch the shark by dangling a steak out of a helicopter. Kit is laughing so hard he's nearly weeping.

We're at a disco so close to the beach that I can almost hear the surf over the pounding bass, crowded around one of the tiny tables fringing the dance floor. Fabrizio brought us here to dance, but instead we're sitting under the flashing lights, learning how he picked up English while studying Italian history in Rome.

"I am nineteen years old then, staying with my zio Giorgio, yes?" he says. "And it is winter, and I get—what is it called—when clouds make me sad?"

"Seasonal depression," Kit prompts.

"Seasonal depression! So I am inside all the time, and the only thing Zio Giorgio has to watch is videotapes of an old American show. *Hawaii Five-O.* So, this is how I learn English, from Detective McGarrett. 'Book 'em!'"

He procures another round of cloudy Basque apple cider and tells us about his pursuit of eternal summer, how he learned Portuguese and some Māori so he can lead tours in Brazil and New Zealand while it's winter in the northern hemisphere. He tells us how he was almost a professional footballer but was too bored by the training schedule, how he always dreamt of traveling for a living even while his brothers worked in the family restaurant.

"I can relate to that part," I tell him. "My family sort of has a business too, but I never wanted to be in it."

"Yes, I know," Fabrizio says.

"You know?"

"Your father is the director, no?" Fabrizio says. "I have seen many of his movies. He is very good."

"You've known this whole time?"

"Of course," Fabrizio says, one of his always-moving hands flapping dismissively. "It is not a common name, Flowerday."

An incredulous laugh slips out of me, and Kit smiles, teeth gleaming.

"But I must ask you," Fabrizio says, leaning in so he doesn't have to shout, cheekbones flashing. God, he is irresponsibly hot. "You two know each other, but you do not arrive together in London. Why is this?"

My drinks are catching up to me. Kit looks at me, and I say the first thing that floats to the surface.

"We used to date." It feels comically, unforgivably small to call it that, but I'm at least two ciders beyond a better explanation. I'm still looking at Kit, not Fabrizio. His gaze is fuzzed out around the edges. Maybe the drinks are getting to him too. "We actually haven't seen each other in years."

"And you did not plan this?"

Kit says, "Complete surprise."

"Che bello!" Fabrizio sings, relaxing back onto his barstool. "My tour has brought you back together! How is this for you? How do you feel?"

"It's had its ups and downs," I say, "but it's been nice to have my friend back."

Kit presses a knuckle to his lips and says nothing.

"In all my years of this tour," Fabrizio says, hand over heart, "I have seen many kinds of love. Family, friends, just married. New love, much too soon for so many days together—these hearts are always broken before Toscana. Couples together for fifty years. Even some who find the love of their life on my tour. But I have never seen two people who once were in love, making peace. It is a marvelous thing. I am so happy you are here."

I look at Kit, whose expression is still too complicated to read.

"I think we're happy to be here too."

"Yeah," Kit agrees. He smiles. "We are."

"Tell me, what surprises you most about each other now?" Fabrizio asks us. "What is most impressive?"

I quickly take a long gulp of cider so that Kit will have to answer first. I feel his gaze travel the line of my jaw, my wet bottom lip.

"I'd say . . ." Kit begins, speaking not to Fabrizio but to me. "Your confidence. The way you carry yourself. You seem . . . in command of yourself."

My heart does something horrible behind my ribs, but the words make my shoulders feel broader, my grip stronger. Kit holds my gaze. I hold his.

"Huh," I say, "I was going to say the same about you."

Someone's knee nudges mine. I'm not sure whose.

"Meraviglioso," Fabrizio says, slapping the table so loudly that we both jump. "More drinks, yes?"

He's gone before we can answer, disappearing into the wall of dancing bodies between our table and the bar.

"Jesus," I say, managing to catch my breath. "Hate to see him go but love to watch him walk away."

Kit laughs. "He really is something, isn't he?"

"Yeah," I agree. "Who do you think he likes more, you or me?"

"What, are you putting him back on the menu?"

"Oh, baby, he was never off it," I say. "I could show him a nice time."

Kit raises his eyebrows.

"What?" I ask. "Why do you look so skeptical?"

He shrugs. "I just don't know if you're compatible."

"I'm not talking about marrying him."

"Neither am I."

I set the dredges of my cider down with a slightly sticky thunk.

"You mean we're not sexually compatible? What are you, the Fuck Whisperer?"

"I know people like him, and I don't know if you're up to it," Kit says, the tip of his middle finger skating around the rim of his glass. "That's all."

"Up to what? Does he want to put my toes in his mouth or something?"

"He wants to *make love.* Light a hundred candles, sprawl out on a Moroccan rug, massage oil onto each other's bodies for hours before you even get into it. I don't think you have the patience."

"You'd be surprised how patient I've become," I say. Kit's fingertip slips from the edge of his glass and smudges down the side. "And what if you're wrong, huh? What if he wants to be, like, manhandled?"

"Then I would manhandle him."

"You're not a manhandler."

"That's not true."

"Who have you ever manhandled?"

Kit's eyes lock on mine. "You."

A server brushes past with a tray of shots. A woman at the next table laughs, sudden and loud. Something sour and hot rolls down the inside of me and begins to pool.

"Like, three times. Barely. At specific request."

"Maybe I've been practicing."

Where is Fabrizio with that drink?

"So, that's what you'll do if he wants you to rough him up?" I ask. "Spank him twice and bake him croissants in the morning so he knows you didn't mean it?"

"You liked those croissants," Kit says, the corner of his mouth tugging upward. "And if he wants you to be sensual? Will you give him the Flowerday Special? A mixtape and a hand down the pants by track three?"

"I'd wait until track twelve."

"Wow, you *have* gotten patient. Did you start meditating?"

"I have simply learned how rewarding it can be to take my time," I say. "It's called having range."

"Range," Kit repeats, leaning closer. "Sure."

"In fact, if you want any tips, let me know." I shift toward him. "I'm happy to help."

"If I ever need advice on using spit as lube, I know who to ask."

"And I'll hit you up next time I'm trying to, like, fuck a poet."

"Oh, poets are easy," Kit says, breath warm against my cheek, all apples and spice. "They just want to be thrown around."

"Sounds like you've been throwing some poets around, Kit."

"I told you, I've been practicing."

"Still finding that hard to believe."

"I have references."

"And I have doubts."

"Give me an hour and I can prove it."

"An hour's not nearly long enough."

The eye contact is overwhelming, so I look at his lips instead. They part to reveal pink tongue against white teeth, and for one smothering moment, the only thing in Spain is that mouth, the plush promise of it, the way it would feel to push inside.

It crushes me then, slams into me and pulls me down: I want him. I still want him.

I kick my stool backward and jump to my feet at the same moment Kit does.

"There has got to be someone in this club who wants to fuck me," I say.

Kit looks away, eyes wild. "I'm sure you're right."

We split up, not bothering to fight the crowd blocking Fabrizio. Instead, I find someone leaning against the back wall with a beer. I chat them up in clumsy Spanish, and at the first sign of interest, I ask if they want to get out of here. When they say yes, I turn to declare victory, half expecting Kit to be there.

He isn't far, but he's not waiting for me. He's on his way out of the club with a group of hot locals of various genders, his arm over a woman's shoulder, being swept away into the night. I left him alone for ten minutes, and he got himself invited to some kind of polyamorous Spanish sex party.

He meets my eye and smiles, fingers tangled in a stranger's hair.

"That still only counts as one!" I call, but he's already gone.

BARCELONA

PAIRS WELL WITH:

Spanish vermouth over ice with
an orange garnish, turrón de yema tostada

BARCELONA

I turn the bombone over on my tongue.

The chocolate is dark and rich, almost peppery. The wet warmth of my mouth melts it down to the caramel and citrus-kissed cream at the center. I focus on how it coats the flat of my tongue, the body of it, the nuttiness.

A bead of sweat rolls down my spine and into the crack of my ass, breaking the last bit of my concentration.

We're standing in the arched doorway of a chocolatería on La Rambla, the wide, busy, tree-fringed walk that runs from central Barcelona to the Mediterranean Sea. The buildings here are a strange mix of new and old, incongruent pieces of a long-lived city keeping up with its people. A sixteenth-century church across from a shop serving dick-shaped waffles, a McDonald's wedged between saints. A dog lies panting in the alley nearby, stealing shade from the big market, La Boqueria. Old women in booths sell fresh flowers and cups of sliced fruit, young men zip by on electric scooters, and the sun scorches every cobble and brick.

Magical, vibrant Barcelona has welcomed us with a heat wave. It's thirty-six degrees Celsius, which means nothing to me but made Kit go "Holy God" when he saw it on his phone. I've been covered in a sticky layer of sweat since I stepped out of the hostel.

"Barcelona," says our local chocolate guide, a thin Catalan woman with dyed red-orange hair, "is the city that brought chocolate to Europe."

This is the first stop on our afternoon chocolate crawl: a confectioner built in the shell of a historic pasta shop, jade and gold mosaic glass glittering on its facade. Inside, wooden filing drawers and glass shelves of chocolates cover the back wall, and the long case holds elaborate cheesecakes the size of my palm. Our guide sent around boxes of bombones—bonbons—for us to try, and I've picked a gem-shaped chocolate filled with crema catalana.

As our guide explains how crema catalana differs from crème brûlée, I reach into my pocket for my phone and find . . . nothing.

"Shit," I whisper. We had an hour of siesta between arrival and this tour, and I thought I was being so responsible by plugging my phone in to charge. "*Shit.*"

Kit nudges me, brow raised in question.

"Left my phone at the hostel." I wipe my hand across my sweaty forehead, which doesn't help since my hand is also sweaty. "I was gonna take notes—Fabrizio said the tour is ten stops, I'll never remember it all."

I shouldn't be surprised, not after the last twenty hours. My hookup from the bar couldn't get me off, and then I had to pass six hours on a bus next to Kit, fresh off whatever beachside orgy he must have had. I may have created an untenable situation. My blood is not spending a lot of time near my brain.

Kit takes out his pocket sketchbook and his fountain pen.

"I'll take notes for you."

I stare. "You want me to—dictate?"

"Yeah, I'd like to experience your sommelier process. Tell me what to write. Tastes like the spirit of a wild stallion, or something."

I know he'd let me take the pen and do it myself. But this is the kind of thing Kit likes to do for his friends. He gets this satisfied little smile when he's solved someone's problem, and I want to watch it tug at his mouth.

His mouth. Last night, at the club. Apple and spice. *I want him.*

"Make sure you write down the filling," I say, resolving to

smother the memory in chocolate. "And there are notes of black pepper, can you put that?"

The tour takes us across La Rambla and into the Gothic Quarter, the oldest part of the city, where mosaic sunflowers and stone flourishes burst out of shops between displays of souvenir magnets. The roads are so narrow that the apartment balconies on either side can't be more than a few feet apart, flags and laundry and tendrils of green plants strung from their iron railings like a hanging village, a thin strip of blue sky visible only when you look straight up.

We wander into a glossy shop that specializes in turrón—Spanish almond nougat—where we taste soft turrón topped with burnt egg yolk and creamy marzipan striped with candied squash. We crunch into chocolate-dipped churros and chew chocolate-coated slices of blood orange, rind and all. At the oldest chocolatería in the city, a handsome young chocolatero gives us cava bombones made with the shop's two-hundred-year-old grinding wheel. These are so incredible, I can only watch in mute bliss as Kit uses his charm to get two more just for us.

By the time we reach the ruins of the city's Roman wall, half of the group is going slightly wild from the heat and the sugar. Stig looks on slackly while Montana slips a morsel of chocolate between Dakota's lips with her fingers. One of the Calums is singing Spanish love songs. Birgitte and Lars might want to get a room, though I can't tell if they need a nap or a quickie.

Kit stays close so I can describe flavors and textures into his ear, his pen gliding over the page, his presence as suffocating as the humidity. Everything is overwhelming. The thick air, the richness melting on my tongue, the radiating warmth of bodies around us, licks of damp hair at Kit's temples when he sweeps it up off his neck. My words go sluggish and slurred, and Kit puts his lips to my ear to ask me to repeat myself, which only makes me dizzier. My body wants to sink into his voice like a fever dream.

The chocolate crawl rolls directly into a tapas crawl near the water, this one led by Fabrizio, whose eyes are already dark and glazed before the first round of drinks. Somewhere on a sidewalk embossed with a pattern of almond blossoms, I find myself briefly in Montana's orbit, watching her watch Dakota and the Calums ahead.

"You know what's funny?" she muses. "How sometimes you look at a man and it's like, *Oh, yeah, that.* And then you look at a woman and it's like, *Ooh, yes, this.*"

I nod, mostly knowing what she means. For me, it's more that I like different genders from within different parts of me. Like I turn to face the light from a different direction every time.

Kit illuminates me entirely. Today, I'm catching all that light. I'm catching so much, I'm nearly cooking.

We drift from back rooms to basements in a haze. Crispy patatas bravas in red-brown salsa, hunks of fried dogfish, blood sausage, Manchego with fig jelly, heaps of paella, one million varieties of ham. Blond Calum passes me my first glass of Spanish vermouth, dark brown over ice like Coca-Cola. Its flavor is almost too deep and fragrant to describe to Kit, a heady mix of marjoram and coriander and sage and a hundred other things. I immediately order another.

I think distantly of Paloma's guide to Barcelona, but I can't recall any of it now. I only remember Kit's thumb on the hinge of her jaw. I see her pulling Kit into her bedroom that night after the beach, tasting the salt left by our swim, covering his mouth so he won't wake her family. I can almost hear his muffled moan like I'm listening from the next room, and—

Fuck.

I'm not listening. The door is closed. *The way is shut,* I think, so delirious that one of Kit's Tolkienisms bobs to the surface.

And it *is* delirium. The soft-focus overfullness of decadence. I'm not the only one losing my mind—the atmosphere inside our last stop, a century-old restaurant called El Sortidor, is palpably erotic. Dusk filters through the stained glass windows, bringing out everyone's finest features. Have the Calums always been so ruggedly handsome? Did I never notice how well Montana wears a sundress? Fabrizio could be Apollo as he demonstrates the technique for pan con tomate, rubbing garlic and a freshly split tomato over oily bread. I watch Kit's fingers move, always so good at following instructions, applying pressure until the tomato is nothing but juice and pulp.

As I'm staring at a chunk of potato to get ahold of myself, Kit tucks his face into the side of my neck.

"Do you think," he says in a low voice, "the Calums have ever explored each other's bodies?"

This too is unbearably horny, even as a joke. Down the table, the Calums are absorbed in a conversation so intense they're speaking almost directly into each other's mouths.

I laugh and gulp down humid air, turning to Kit. He's wearing the shirt with the embroidered flowers from our second night in Paris, and it makes me think of him braced over me on the bed in the back of that bar. I can still feel his breath cooling the sweat on my nape.

I keep my voice steady as I say, "All the best friendships get there sooner or later."

— — —

I don't have it in me to find a hookup for tonight. I'm too full, and the day was too long. I'm overdosing on Barcelona. It's like being too tired to sleep. Too horny to fuck.

Instead, I return to my room and unlock my phone to fourteen emails and six missed calls from Schnauzer Bride. Her custom schnauzer tiki mugs have fallen off a shipping barge.

I scroll as I wash my hair, one arm out of the shower to keep my phone dry. My single room is so tight that I'm dripping on the nightstand from the en suite bathroom. I feel around my soup pot of a brain for something coherent to say.

A text from Kit pops up.

is the air conditioning in your room working?

I frown.

yeah why

hm. second question: how good is your spanish?

"What's going on?" I ask when Kit picks up.

"My aircon doesn't work," Kit says. I hear him climbing onto his bed, whuffs of breath and rustling linens.

"Oh, shit."

"Can't say I'm shocked," he says. "I was honestly more surprised they have air conditioning at all."

"How bad is it?"

"Well, the room is about sixty square feet and was facing the sun for the last eight hours; I'd say it's . . . not ideal." More sounds, like he's poking at the air conditioner. "I opened a window but it isn't doing much."

"What are you gonna do?"

"I might see if they have any other rooms? That's why I asked about your Spanish."

My Spanish is significantly better than my French thanks to four years in high school and a lifetime in Southern California, but even I can't help. Earlier, I overheard the front desk guy telling a couple of backpackers they're full for the night.

The only other option is such a bad idea that I shouldn't even consider it. Before Kit texted, I was planning to slide my freshly clean body under the crisp top sheet and get myself off until the fog of horniness dissipated. I don't know how I'll survive without some sort of release. But I feel bad for him.

"Do you wanna crash in my room?" I offer before I can talk myself out of it.

"Your— Oh." The rustling on his end stops. "Really? Are you sure?"

No. "Yeah, fuck it."

"That's— Thank you, Theo," he says. "I'll be down in five."

He hangs up, and I stand there in my matchbox of a room, staring at the black glass of my phone screen.

"Okay," I say out loud. "Okay. That's fine."

I throw my phone at the bed and do a lap, pulling on sweatpants and the first shirt I can reach, toweling my hair, sweeping lip balm tubes and pomade into my dopp kit, shoving clothing into my pack so Kit will think I've stopped leaving my laundry wherever it falls. By the time he knocks, my room looks like it belongs to a real adult.

I open the door to Kit in a rumpled T-shirt and soft cotton joggers. His hair is half wet. He smells like lavender and the same soap he used to keep in our shower.

"Hi," he says, smiling apologetically.

"Hi."

"Thanks, again. I hope this isn't too weird."

"No, of course not," I say, even though it feels a little like my head is floating away from my shoulders. I step aside to let him in. "We're friends, right?"

"Yeah, we are."

"So, no biggie." I shrug. "It's a sleepover. We've had a million of those."

"Yeah." He doesn't look at me, busy stepping out of his shoes. "Of course."

The room suddenly feels too small, too hot from the lingering shower steam. I pace over to the window and open it.

"I don't know if it's much better than your room."

"Trust me, it is." He hovers near the en suite, holding his shaving kit. "Do you mind if I . . . ?"

"Yeah, knock yourself out."

"Amazing, thank you." He steps toward the sink, pauses, then turns back. "Oh, I forgot to give this to you earlier." He reaches into the pocket of his joggers and hands me his flimsy little sketchbook. "Keep it."

"You don't have to—I can just copy the pages down or take some pictures."

"Theo, I packed twelve of those. I don't mind."

I run my fingers over the blue stripes on the sketchbook's brown paper cover, the neat letters spelling CALEPINO. I imagine him picking it out at a stationery store in Paris, stuffing a whole bundle of them into his pack, his face shining with anticipation. The first few pages are loose sketches of streetlamps and stray dogs, then notes from that first chocolatería. And—

"Kit. What is this?"

I flip forward—the rest of the pages are the same. For every stop, he's transcribed my notes in his slanting script, and on the opposite page, sketched a simple illustration.

"Yeah, I, ah, I thought it might help to have visual references?" He leans out of the en suite with his toothbrush in his mouth, toothpaste foaming along his bottom lip. "I mean, you always hated books without pictures, didn't you?"

"Fuck off." I go back through the pages—the crescent of a dipped orange slice, the churro's rough ridges. He even did a cross section of my first bombone to show the layers of caramel and cream filling. "Kit, this is . . . really cool."

"I'm glad you like it."

I wish I could see the look on his face, but he's spitting toothpaste into the sink.

It's strange and strangely calming to stand next to the bed and look at Kit's drawings while he does his skincare routine. I listen to the soft clicks of bottle caps and splashes of water, sounds I used to hear every night. I could close my eyes and be in our old apartment. I could smell his plants. I could feel the weight of his head on my chest.

I reach the last page and stop. There, an unfamiliar hand

has written a series of digits, smudged like the writer was in a rush.

"Whose phone number is this?"

The water shuts off, and Kit releases the short *oh* of someone caught in the act.

"That would be the, ah," Kit says, appearing in the doorway, "the number of that chocolatero who gave us extra chocolates. I meant to tear that page out."

Ah. Of course. Almost forgot I was dealing with the Sex God of École Desjardins.

"Kit Fairfield, you dog." I rip out the page and hold it out, showing him all my teeth when I grin. "You gonna use it? Ask him on a hot date tomorrow?"

Kit folds the page up and zips it into his shaving kit without looking at it.

"I don't know. Do you think I should?"

"Well, what's the score?"

He sits at the foot of the bed, right on the edge. He's never been so cautious with a bed of mine before. Even when we were friends, he'd pour himself across the whole thing. I want to push him onto his back for the sake of consistency. Instead, I sit down next to him.

"One for each of us from Paris," he says. "Florian, that makes two for you. And Juliette for you in Saint-Jean-de-Luz."

I let him think it's true. "And Paloma for you."

"Mm. And with last night . . . God, was that only last night?"

"I know."

"That makes four for you, three for me. So I guess, if I want to catch up, I could message him."

I stand up and pull a pillow off the bed.

"Sure, I mean, why not?"

"Yeah, why not." He sounds distracted, watching me open the tiny closet to dig out an extra blanket. "What are you doing?"

"I'm sleeping on the floor."

Kit's eyes go wide in horror. "No, you're not."

"Come on, Kit. The bed is barely a twin."

"It's your room, Theo, let me take the floor."

"One of us spent the entire camping trip in Joshua Tree bitching about how hard the ground was, and it wasn't me. You just let me know if you find a pea under there, okay?" I drop the blanket at my feet.

"Theo Flowerday," Kit says, serious as the grave, "if you lie down on that disgusting carpet, I'm going back to my room."

His sincere face is on. I sigh.

"Okay, fine. But I don't want you sleeping down there either. So, what?"

We look at the bed. Again, there is an unthinkable solution, and there's me, and there's Kit, and I still don't have it in me to do what I ought.

"Should we . . . ?" I say. Not a question. If I don't ask out loud, I'm not responsible for whatever happens next.

Kit says, "We're friends." Not an answer either.

"Yeah, okay," I say. "But . . ."

"But what?"

"Remember how, if I get too sweaty in my sleep, I'm really cranky the next day?"

"Yes, vividly."

"So," I say, "I was gonna sleep in my underwear tonight."

Kit nods several times in rapid succession. "Yeah, that's—of course that's fine. We're friends. It's your room, you should be comfortable."

"Cool," I say, also nodding. Just two friends with a normal dynamic, nodding and nodding. "And you too, of course, if you want to."

"Yeah, it's—it'll be warm, with both of us."

"Okay. So, I'm gonna . . ."

"Sure, me too."

I turn around and tug my sweats off, trying not to listen

to the creak of the mattress when he shifts, the whisper of his clothes coming off. I leave my tank on, but from the waist down, I'm only wearing a pair of soft boy shorts.

I feel an unspoken agreement settle between us. This time won't be like the breakwater in Saint-Jean-de-Luz. This time, we're going to look.

Ninety-nine days out of a hundred, I love my body. I like my long legs and strong thighs, the bands of muscle in my back and shoulders, the hint of what could be abs, if I tried. I know what I look like in my underwear, and I enjoy watching people experience it for the first time. Kit has seen me so much more naked than this.

Still, when I turn to face him, my heart is thrumming.

His shirt and joggers are folded neatly on the nightstand. He sits on the same spot at the edge of the mattress, wearing only a very small pair of black boxer briefs. The lamplight touches the highest points of his shoulders and chest, the tops of his spread thighs, the dimples of his knees. Shadow pools in the dips of his hip bones. Every bit of him. That elegant, graceful body I knew.

He's looking at my body in the way only Kit can look at something, like he could eat the world up with his eyes. It's not just that I want him. It's that he taught me what wanting was. Anyone would have a weakness for that.

It occurs to me that if I want to have sex with Kit—if I *have* sex with Kit—it doesn't mean I love him. Sex doesn't have to contain love. Those things don't even need to be in the same room.

"Hey," Kit says, "there's your third tattoo."

I blink a few times.

"Oh!" My hand moves automatically to the spot on my left side. Part of it is still hidden by my underwear, but my third and biggest tattoo runs from my hip down the outside of my upper thigh. "Yeah. It's sick, isn't it?"

He peers through the low light. "Is it a snake?"

"It's a rattlesnake." I move closer so he can see the details of a western diamondback coiled around a coupe glass. "And look, his cocktail has a little orange slice for garnish." When I look up, Kit is biting back a smile. "What?"

"Nothing. Just, you said it wasn't an ass tattoo."

"What—it's not!"

"It kind of is."

"It is an upper thigh tattoo! It's on my—my—my haunch!"

The laugh he lets out is so delicious I want to swallow it whole. "Your haunch? Are you a pony?"

Maybe it's the heat, or all the skin, or his laugh, or his attentive pen strokes and the ink stains on his knuckles, but in this moment, I want to find out what he'll do. If he's as close to the edge as I am. If he'll back away from it.

I take his hand and place it right over the ink.

"Does this feel like my ass to you?"

His laugh subsides.

"No," he says. "No, I guess not."

He doesn't take his hand away, but he doesn't move it either. It just stays, his palm flush and warm against my skin, the tip of his thumb nearly brushing the elastic of my underwear. His eyes hold on to mine. I imagine him pulling me into his lap and parting his lips, think of his fingers and oil and the wet, red flesh of a cleaved tomato. Spit pools in my mouth.

He does nothing.

I shove his shoulder hard enough to play the whole thing off as a joke.

"Move over," I say. "And stay on your side."

He makes a sound in his throat and rolls off toward the wall as I climb into bed.

"That's the plan," he murmurs.

I switch off the light and crawl under the sheet, hooking my leg over the side of the mattress to anchor myself as far from him as possible. Behind me, Kit settles in. I wish my body didn't still recognize the exact pitch of the mattress sagging under his weight.

"Good night, Kit," I say, instead of screaming into my pillow. A long moment goes by before Kit says, "Good night, Theo."

— — —

I'm in the desert.

We're on a blanket in the back of my car with the seats folded down, the hatch open, our boots lined up in the dust by the back tire. These deep summer days in the valley are so long, but Kit wanted to wait up for the Milky Way. He once said it was like a huge butter knife had spread the galaxy across the sky, swirls of stars like blackberry jam.

He tips his head back to moan. I see stars in the shine of sweat on his throat.

His legs are around me. I'm gripping his waist with one hand while the other works him, my hips against the backs of his thighs, his mouth already open when I bend to kiss it. He's so pretty like this, coming apart. His body follows mine like a disciple.

Sometimes when I'm on top of Kit, when I'm making him sigh and shiver and beg—when I'm fucking him like this—I feel more present in my skin than I ever have. All the pieces in their right places. I wonder if anyone else in the whole blackberry-jam galaxy has ever loved someone so much that it made their soul feel fixed in their body.

Then, in a heartbeat, I'm not in the desert anymore.

I'm with Kit, but we're inside a restaurant with stained glass windows. I'm atop a wooden table at the center of a feast, surrounded by overflowing dishes of melting chocolate and ripe tomatoes and fruit in spiced syrup. Kit sits on a chair between my parted legs, devouring an apricot, nectar glistening on his lips and chin.

He throws away the pit and brings me to his mouth, and I—

I wake up to a yell on the street.

Fuck.

I'm—where, again? Spain. Barcelona. A hostel near La Rambla. In a single bed, next to Kit.

Only, I'm not next to Kit. I'm wrapped around him, my face on his chest, my arm thrown over his waist, his arm around my shoulders. And I suspect, from the way one of his thighs is pinned between mine, I've been grinding against him in my sleep.

Fuck. *Fuck.*

Sunlight presses on my eyelids, but I'm too afraid to lift them. This is what I get for going to sleep horny—and for bringing up our camping trips, which were mostly an excuse to have sex in creative new locations. One of our memories got out of the vault, and now I'm having wet dreams.

Kit's breathing is deep and slow, so at least he's still asleep. If I can manage not to wake him up, he never needs to know.

Carefully, gradually, incrementally, I disentangle myself and roll away toward the other side of the bed.

Just when I think I've made it, Kit lets out an unhappy grumble and turns onto his side, pulling me back into his chest.

When Kit and I were together, his body became so familiar that I stopped sensing it as separate from my own. Every inch came as naturally as the slice of my hand through water. Now, I can feel all the subtle changes: his longer hair brushing my skin in new places, the impression of a new scar on his knee. All those hours kneading dough and throwing around sacks of flour—and poets, I guess—have added a layer of lithe muscle to his chest and shoulders.

His hips shift against me. My heartbeat skips as I realize: He's hard.

He is not, I tell myself, hard for *me*. It's a bodily response, like goose bumps, or a sneeze. But if he *was* hard for me, if he woke up right now and pressed himself against me and scraped his teeth over my pulse, I know I wouldn't stop him. I'd welcome it. I would send this creaky, too-small bed to the big Ikea store in the sky.

I have to get the fuck out.

I try wriggling away, but with every inch I gain, his body instinctively closes the gap. He's making unconscious sounds of frustration, whimpers that do absolutely nothing to strengthen my resolve. Every time I feel him hard and heavy through our thin layers of fabric, I have to concentrate on how mortified he would be if he knew what he was doing. I'm saving both our dignities here.

Or at least that's what I'm trying to do when we tip over the side of the mattress and crash to the floor.

Kit startles awake with a shout that could be a mixture of English and French or just a bunch of affrighted vowels. His arms momentarily tighten around me, and then he goes absolutely still.

"Theo?"

"Yeah."

"Oh. Oh, *no.* Oh God, did I—?"

"No, nothing happened, you're fine," I say as Kit releases me and scrambles backward.

He looks like he wishes he had been born a slug, which is obviously how you want a person to look after they've spooned you. I think I might start laughing. "It's not a big deal. It's, like, muscle memory, and I think I started it anyway."

"I'm sorry," he says miserably. "I didn't mean to."

"It's okay!" I am laughing now, hysterical, insuppressible hiccups.

"Why are you laughing! I'm embarrassed! This is embarrassing!"

"Sorry!" I gasp. "I'm sorry, I'm just—I'm so glad it's not me."

"*Theo.*"

"Who were you dreaming about? Was it the chocolatero?"

"I—" Kit begins, but he's cut off by the blaring jingle of his phone alarm. I take it from the nightstand and toss it to him, wiping a tear from my eye as he shuts it off.

"I guess we're awake," he says.

"I guess so."

"Can we please," he says, "pretend this never happened?"

I look at him, wide-eyed and crumpled against the wall in

his underwear, his hair mussed from sleep and falling into his beautiful face. I want to smooth it away with my hands. I want to keep laughing forever. I want to pretend nothing happened, but only because he does.

"Yeah," I say. "Of course, Kit. Of course."

He fixes me with a plaintive look. "You mean it?"

"Kit. Come on. It's us."

At last, he smiles weakly.

"It's us."

He gets dressed to head upstairs, already talking about Sagrada Familia, how he's read an entire book about it but pictures can't do it justice. Once he's gone, I walk over and slide the window shut. My reflection is full of color, my eyes dilated like I've had too much to drink. On the street below, two people are kissing.

— — —

There aren't words for Sagrada Familia.

Maybe, if you could fold everything a person can see and know and experience in on itself, every face, every feeling, if you could max out all the bars on how much a thing can exist, it would be this five-hundred-foot-tall church. Millions of stone details on its facade. Figures and foliage and symbols and painstaking wrinkles of cloth. And somehow, inside, there's more.

Every last inch has a complex, deliberate geometry, no straight line or unadorned surface. Groves of columns spiral up, transforming from squares to octagons to sixteen-sided shapes to circles, splitting into a canopy of bursting stars. Immense stained glass panes pour rainbows of light through the naves, fiery reds and oranges to one side and drowning blues and greens to the other, tunnels of color deep enough to swim through. Every feature is one detail on top of another and another, strange curves and jagged edges and joining corners that seem impossible.

We're led around with little transmitter boxes on lanyards,

Fabrizio filtering out through tinny earbuds, voice sweet as ever. But I listen instead to the echoing murmurs of hundreds of voices in a hundred languages, the slaps of sandals against marble.

Kit lags behind, and I let myself fall to his side. His earbuds are loose around his neck. The look on his face is pure, slack, sparkling wonder.

I think of the museum in Bordeaux, the painting of the woman on the rubble. How I told myself he'd answer if I asked about the painting.

"Hey," I say, quiet as the group moves on without us. "Tell me what you read about this place."

Kit smiles.

In a low, gentle voice, he tells me everything. How the columns and their branching vaults are meant to evoke the feeling of walking through a forest, their double-twisted design inspired by oleander branches. He talks about Gaudí, the artist and architect who devoted forty-three years of his life to building this church, the only love of his life and his great unfinished project, how he lived on the grounds and is buried in the crypt below to be with her forever.

There's no pretense in his voice, no arrogance, only naked joy and generosity. Happiness to open up a world and share it with me. I turn away so he won't see me blink the sudden wetness from my eyes. I left that room in Bordeaux specifically to avoid this: the terrible, undeniable, shattering fact of his goodness.

When the rest crumbles—the worst angles, the meanest versions of events, the lies I told myself—what's left is only Kit. Only the great unfinished love of my life, and a floor I'm still lying under.

— — —

"You can't use a whole dish as an ingredient!" Kit says, gesturing so expansively that his vermouth almost spills. "That's cheating!"

"Not even if I buy it prepared and incorporate it?"

"That's against the spirit of the exercise. On the Fly is for *raw materials.*"

"Then you shouldn't be allowed to use chocolate," I counter. "You should have to march your happy ass down to the shops and crank up the bean grinder, baby."

Kit's smile blooms even brighter, color splashing into his cheeks. He's always loved when I get belligerent for his entertainment.

"You know that's not the same—"

"Do you churn your own butter too? Do you have a chic little Parisian butter churn? Does it have a holder for chic little Parisian unfiltered cigarettes?"

"Okay!" Kit says, showing me his hands. "Okay, you can use crema catalana to make a milk punch! And I'll take the only the orange zest from it—"

"Boooo."

"—and I'll mix it with ricotta to fill cannoli, and—" He sees the look on my face. "What?"

"Did you make the ricotta, Kit?"

He looks like he might scream, half frustration and half delight, all Theo-and-Kit.

"Yes, Theo, I rode my bike down to the village sheep farm, and I made sweet, tender love to the farmer's wife all night long so she would let me milk the sheep, and then I carried the pail home and made the ricotta."

"Then I'll take the salty tears of the sheep farmer whose wife leaves him for the village hole—"

Kit gasps theatrically. "*Hole?*"

"—and use them to make a salted Negroni, with a tangerine twist."

"Campari tangelo marmalade," Kit says instantly. "Glazing a tangelo-and-five-spice pound cake."

"I'll take the Chinese five-spice and steep it in rum and then use the rum to make a Cable Car."

Kit sets his glass down, still smiling.

"Cable Car. That was ... that was what we drank that time we drove to San Francisco for your birthday, wasn't it?"

"Yeah, at that dive in North Beach," I say. "It was cash only, and we were out of cash."

"And I pretended to propose so they'd comp our drinks."

We were only twenty-three then, and we always joked about getting married, like it was so obvious that it wasn't worth taking seriously. I laughed when he did it. But after, he told me he'd marry me that night if I wanted. That he'd have married me the night we first kissed.

"I'm definitely not beating that one, then," Kit says. He tips his chin up at me, and I want to press my thumb to the center of it. "You win. I'll drink the absinthe."

"Discúlpeme, señor!" I call to the bartender. "Una absenta, por favor!"

We're in Bar Marsella, the oldest bar in Barcelona, allegedly a haunt of Picasso and Hemingway. Humid night clings to wood-paneled walls and peels away brown paint, steaming cabinets of antique bottles and mirrors mounted behind wobbly tables. A chandelier blinks dustily above as the soles of my sandals stick to the mosaic floor. The bartender drops off a crystal glass of pale green absinthe, a bottle of chilled water, and a paper-wrapped sugar cube, and Kit sets about expertly melting the sugar into the glass.

Down the bar, an older man sits alone with a glass of pale beer and the kind of book you'd pick up at an airport. His khaki shorts and polo scream American tourist. When I check the cover, I do a double take.

"Check it out," I say. "Three seats down. That's one of Craig's, isn't it?"

Kit spots the glossy paperback. *The House on the Lake,* a John Garrison novel.

"Ah, yes. The one where the wife dies."

"Isn't that all of them?"

"Sure, but in this one she comes back as a ghost, which he's only done two other times."

I laugh. "How *is* your dad?"

"He's alright. Moved into a nice town house in the Village. Still ghostwriting, clearly. His last one was on the list for forty-seven weeks. *The Anchorite of Venus.*"

"Oh my God, that was him?"

"The most prolific author no one's ever heard of," Kit says. He's looking down into his absinthe, the cloud of sugar slowly clearing. "Truthfully, I haven't spoken to him in about ... six months?"

I don't say anything. I don't have to. We both know how out of character that is for him. I swill my sangria and wait.

"Remember that book he was working on when my mom died?"

I think back to that awful summer before eighth grade, climbing into Kit's bed five nights a week and reading *The Silmarillion* out loud so he could fall asleep. Ollie had a fresh license, so he did the grocery shopping, and Kit baked a cake once a week in whatever flavor Cora asked. And every day, his dad stayed in his office with a manuscript that couldn't be delayed.

"It was supposed to be his first book under his own name, right? But his editor hated it, or something?"

"Yeah, that was the story," Kit says with a grim smile. "So, you know how Ollie works for Dad's publishing house now? A year ago, he had lunch with Dad's editor and asked him what he really thought of that book, and the editor had no idea what he was talking about. And so Ollie asked Dad, and it turns out the manuscript never actually existed."

I frown. "What do you mean?"

"He never wrote it. He never wrote anything that summer. He only pretended to."

I think of Kit, age thirteen, braiding Cora's hair for her.

"Holy shit," I say.

He's still wearing his small, grim smile when he continues.

"After that, I started thinking about everything," he says. "I always trusted there was some design to the choices he made for us. Moving across the world because he got bored, moving across the country when he didn't want to be in the old house. He was always so *impressive* to me, this romantic genius who might take us anywhere. Every second of his attention was so shiny and important."

He takes a sip of absinthe, grimacing at the burn.

"But it was always just whatever he wanted," Kit finishes. "And he wasn't there that summer because he didn't want to be."

I swear earnestly. "So you haven't spoken since Ollie told you about the manuscript?"

"Actually, I tried to talk to him when he was in Paris a few months ago," Kit says. "About all of it. He kind of blew it off, said a lot of words about how much he loves me, which is not at all what the problem has ever been. Afterwards, I had to put him away on a shelf until I can, I don't know. Process. Figure out what kind of relationship I want with him as an adult."

"Well, fuck," I say after a long pause. I feel like bare-knuckle fighting Kit's dad right now. "Kit, that's . . . that must be a lot. I'm really fucking sorry."

"Thank you," Kit says, giving me a small, tender smile.

His gaze shifts to the door behind me, and he suddenly swears in French.

"What?"

"I kind of—I forgot that I invited Santiago to meet up tonight."

"Who?"

"The—"

"¡Hola!" says a smooth voice, and I recognize the chocolatero just as he swoops in to kiss the air beside Kit's cheek. Kit looks at me with wide, apologetic eyes.

There's no reason I should be disappointed. I'm the one who told him to call the guy. I put on my most easygoing smile.

"Sorry," Kit murmurs, "I—"

"Nothing to apologize for," I say. The chocolatero turns to me, a handsome, dark-skinned man in simple beige and gold linens, and I let him air-kiss me too. "¡Hola, Santiago, qué bueno verte!"

"You remember my friend Theo," Kit says, and really, after all the work I've put in, it shouldn't sting to be called that.

"¡Sí!" Santiago says warmly. "And this is my neighbor, Caterina."

A woman appears beside him, tall and graceful and smiling. She pushes her wild hair behind her ear with a paint-smudged hand.

"Caterina," I say. I glance toward Kit and find him watching me. "Can I buy you a drink?"

— — —

Caterina is a painter. She smells like almond blossoms and turpentine and just broke up with a Dutch girl who captains sunset sails out of the main port. She lives in a skinny apartment building in the Gothic Quarter, one so old its door still has a bronze knocker shaped like a hand holding a persimmon. At the top of the stairs, as she unlocks her flat, I kiss her behind her silver earrings.

Her apartment is a magpie's nest. Dried flowers hang from the chandelier, strings of translucent citrus slices in every window. Half-finished paintings lean against velvet armchairs and side tables heaving with books. It's as hot here as it is outside, so she brings out a pitcher of cold water and pours two glasses.

When she presses one into my hand and guides me onto a kitchen chair, I think: *I'm not even thinking about Kit right now.*

I'm not seeing him and Santiago ahead of us on the walk from Bar Marsella, or the way he glanced at me when Santiago pulled him into the apartment building across from Caterina's. I'm not even thinking of the way he looked last night on the edge of my bed, or the heat of his hand against my tattoo.

There's so much to like about Caterina. I like how she floats around the apartment, emptying the rest of the pitcher into her houseplants. I like the paint stains on her hands.

She asks, "What do you want?"

I spread my legs wide, feet planted on either side of my chair. All my unsatisfied need rises to the surface, thick in the sweat on my skin. God, it'll be good to finally get it out.

"Take off whatever's under that dress, and come here."

Caterina does as she's told, straddles my lap, and kisses me. I kiss her back, hard, her tongue swiping into my mouth, her hands cradling my jaw. I guide her hips with both hands until I can feel her slick and needy against my thigh before I've even touched her, which is extremely fucking hot.

Everything is extremely fucking hot, actually. Suddenly, urgently, the heat between our bodies is nearly suffocating. My shirt sticks to my back. Sweat beads in the hollow of my throat. I break off to catch my breath.

"Okay?" Caterina asks, wiping my brow with the back of her wrist. "Do you need air?"

"Sorry, yeah." The unsteadiness in my voice surprises me. "Could we open a window?"

"I have even better."

She crosses to a tall, street-facing window and parts the gauzy curtains to reveal a set of narrow French doors.

"Come, look."

When I join her, we're on one of the Gothic balconies I admired yesterday. It barely fits us with all the flowers and plants crowded along the railings. Every building on the street has rows of tiny balconies like hers, pressed right up against one another like you could pass a cigarette to the person next door. The balcony across is so close, I can almost touch the curtains drifting from the open door.

As I pull Caterina's body to mine, I hear it. A voice, close but slightly muted, shockingly familiar. A soft, open moan.

"Uh, does—does Santiago live in that apartment across from you?"

"Hm?" Caterina slips her hand up my shirt. "Oh, yes. Why?"

Another sound, a second voice saying something too low to decipher. Kits voice is rough when he answers, but this time I can make out "yes" and "please."

Fuck.

Caterina laughs, her nose bumping my shoulder.

"Santiago does this all the time," she says. "Estoy acostumbrado a eso. Is it bad for you?"

There are about one million reasons why it's bad for me, but right now, all I can feel is thrumming need, and all I can see is the pitying look Juliette gave me on that beach.

"No," I say, and I crush my mouth into Caterina's.

I don't waste any more time. I press her to the leafy railing and kiss her, my hand slipping under her dress to palm the wet heat between her thighs. She grinds against the heel of my hand.

Someone swears into the night, and I'm pleased with myself until I realize it's not Caterina but Kit. His is the only voice behind the wafting curtains now, and I can imagine what's happening. Kit, laid out on his back, lost in Santiago's mouth.

"Fuck," I murmur out loud this time, feeling insane. I drop to my knees.

This will work. Going down on an attractive woman always does it for me. Watching the pleasure dawn on her face, feeling her knees start to shake, burying myself in her taste. I shove Caterina's dress up with one hand and push the other past my waistband.

I narrow my focus to my mouth on her, my own fingers, the hot blood rushing in my ears, her gasps and sighs, the roll of her hips. I give her everything I've got until she finishes, hands fisted in my hair, and I start her over again.

I want to—*need* to get off so fucking badly. Needed it for days, *especially* since last night, but I—*can't*. Can't get close enough.

Can't chase down the mind-numbing, maddening horizon, the touch of someone who's not here.

I hear Kit again, whining through clenched teeth, and I know, I *know* what it fucking means when he sounds like that.

There's not a sound inside of Kit that I haven't worked loose. I know the low, imperious tone that means he wants control, the filthy mid-register drawl he uses when he's feeling indulgent, the huffy swears when he's pushed to the brink of his patience. When he sounds raw and wrecked like he does right now, it means he wants to *take it*.

It's heartbreaking how gorgeous he is like this. Pliant and glassy-eyed, head thrown back. Spreading himself out, offering himself to be pushed down and swallowed up, teased and twisted until he's begging, gasping, nearly weeping for it.

A shudder courses through me, and I close my eyes and see Kit's face, the look when he kissed Paloma on that beach, like he wanted me to watch.

I let myself listen. I open the vault.

There he is. There we are. Light spills across our skin. My hand grasps for his, and everything unfolds at once.

On the next swipe of my tongue, I hear three simultaneous gasps: Caterina with her knee hooked over my shoulder, Kit across the alley being sucked off by another man, and Kit bent over our old kitchen counter with my spit sliding down his thighs.

My hand quickens to match my mouth, to match the rhythm of Kit's breathing. To match the beat of my heart one summer night on a beach blanket in Santa Barbara when I sank down onto him. The click-click of the hazards while he ate me out in my back seat. The kick drum through the speakers as he snuck his hand down my jeans in the middle of a crowd. Caterina's pulse on my tongue, Kit's pulse against mine. I push two fingers into her, and his push into me, and mine push into him.

When Kit comes, I hear him, and I see him in our bed, wrists pinned, bright tears in his eyes. I lean my forehead against Caterina's hip—against Kit's shoulder—and finish with a rough, punched-out cry.

In the quiet after, I'm left with the part of the memory that tipped me over. It wasn't how Kit begged me that night, or how he couldn't walk straight in the morning.

It was in between, when he told me how much he loved me.

That's exactly what I was afraid it would be.

— — —

I don't sleep in Caterina's bed.

It's not a long walk back to the hostel, but by the time I pass the spires of Cathedral La Seu, I'm running. I sprint all the way up La Rambla, through the huge wheel of Plaça de Catalunya and all its bosomy statues, up four flights of stairs to the room where I woke up tangled in Kit.

When the door is locked behind me, I take out my phone.

I might be falling back in love with kit

Sloane texts back within a minute.

Would that be such a bad thing?

NICE

PAIRS WELL WITH:

Pastis and chilled water in a highball glass,
pain au chocolat

Would that be such a bad thing?

On the highest plateaus of Provence, in the mountainous countryside above Nice, lavender grows like a motherfucker. It's purple for miles, purple for years. Purple up to my nips. Every breath smells like lavender, and so every breath smells like Kit.

Sault is a scenic detour on the way to Nice, where we'll spend two nights before beginning the Italy leg. Everyone's hangover seems cured by the cool mountain air, except for Ginger Calum, who is throwing up behind a goat pen. Even Orla has climbed down from the bus to explore the lavender fields.

I bend to touch my toes, stretching my back and hamstrings. My knees ache from being tucked to my chest for the last four hours so I wouldn't accidentally touch Kit. If he knows I heard him last night, or if he heard me, he's unmoved. He napped all the way through Spain and back into France, lazily picturesque in his soft jeans and a sand-colored T-shirt, lashes fanned serenely against his cheeks.

Meanwhile, I can barely *look* at him. The fog of horny war has lifted, but I'm still in the trenches. I'm down here, dying. I've got trench foot of the heart.

Kit is walking with Orla now, somehow wearing her safari hat on his head. He spreads his arms wide, palms up to the sun, and Orla laughs.

Would that be such a bad thing?

The thing about loving Kit is, it's objectively the best thing that could happen to anyone. There's a reason it's happened to so many people by accident. Loving Kit is like being the strawberry in a flute of champagne. Just floating forever on sparkling bubbles, making dizzy circles, soaking up complexity and being sexy by association.

Being with Kit was different. I can admit it now: The only thing better than loving Kit was being loved by him.

Life with Kit was a good dream. It was just—it was inevitable. It made sense. I'd met him so young and loved him so long that everything I'd ever learned about love had grown into him, until I couldn't tell where he ended and love began. We used to look at each other with constant astonishment, like no matter how many times we kissed, we couldn't believe it was happening. And he made me happy, or at least as happy as I could be back then. It was good. We were good.

I've had a million temporary lovers since, but the truth isn't that I haven't needed something real. It's that I haven't wanted it. The thought of starting from scratch, the ordeal of rebuilding something I already spent my whole life building with someone else—it's exhausting. It's a fucking Olympic triathlon of mortifying vulnerability, and at the end, I might not even like them as much as I liked Kit. It'd be a relief if I never had to do it.

It'd also be a relief to get back the parts of me that live inside of him. To have somewhere to put all of him contained in me. There are so many things we couldn't fit into boxes, pieces of ourselves that we can't access anymore because we could never return them. I'd like to be whole with him.

And that whole me—the Theo of Theo-and-Kit—I like them. They have the best jokes, the most nerve, the biggest ideas. I'd have spent weeks coming up with the recipes I've pitched Kit on the fly. It's possible I wouldn't even *be* here if not for Kit. I never would've booked this trip on my own, and if I'd been able to get my money back, I don't know that I would have tried again. I might never have felt the world open wide to me.

Would that be such a bad thing?

Logistically, it would be stupid to fall back in love with Kit. For one, we live 5,600 miles apart. He loves his job and would never leave it, and I've never seriously imagined myself doing anything more than what I've been doing back home. And even if we lived on the same street, it wouldn't matter, unless Kit still has feelings for me. And I have every reason to believe he doesn't.

He said it in San Sebastián: *I thought I should let you go, so that's what I did.*

Maybe something more than friendship still shimmers between us—a friction, the tension of two people who know they're the best at fucking each other—but I know the difference between sex and love. I don't know which he feels when his body is close to mine, or what he sees when he looks at me. It's been so long, and I'm not the girl he wanted to marry anymore.

"Theo!"

I spin. Kit's only a few feet away now. He's ridiculous out here in a sea of lavender, a sprig between his thumb and forefinger. I shift my weight to steady myself on both feet.

"Did you have anything in mind for the afternoon?" he asks me.

"I—um, the Calums invited me to climb Castle Hill with them." I glance toward the goat pen. Ginger Calum is now lying flat on his back, halfway under a shrub. Blond Calum prods him with a stick. "But I have a feeling they're not gonna make it."

"A friend of mine from pastry school opened a boulangerie in Nice a few months ago," Kit says. "I thought I might pop in. Do you want to come?"

"Sure," I say, because there's no reason to say no. "Yeah, that sounds fun."

He looks me up and down, like he's taking his first opportunity to get the whole view of me this morning. My tan work pants cinched at the waist, the dust on my boots, the open collar of my shirt. He reaches up and tucks the lavender sprig behind my ear, his thumb brushing the topmost hoop in my earlobe.

"You're very handsome today."

My heart kicks in my chest.

I could ask him. If there's a lesson to take from the aftermath of us, it's that. Not here, not now, but maybe during one of our nights alone in a dimly lit bar, I could put my hand on his and ask if he could ever love me again. And if he said no, at least it would be an answer.

But if he said yes—

If he said he could fall again, I'd tell him I already have.

—   —   —

At the corner of two streets in Nice, a young woman slumps on a doorstep under a sign that says BOULANGERIE in gold letters. She's staring at a cup of tea like she might start crying into it. A huge splatter of pink-red covers her apron and shirt and mats the ends of her blond hair. She looks like hell.

"Apolline?" Kit says.

She looks up and sees Kit, her exhausted eyes going wide in surprise.

"Kit? Qu'est-ce que tu fais là?"

He answers, and gestures to me and says in English, "This is Theo, we were coming to see the shop, but—are you okay? What happened?"

She looks down at the grisly stain on her chest and sighs.

"Raspberry."

Apolline—whose accent suggests she's spent a few years in England—has had a clusterfuck of a day. Her entire staff is out with food poisoning from a party the night before, so she's been running the register and the kitchen by herself since early morning. She barely got half of the day's bread baked before opening, and she's sold out of almost everything. She also knocked a five-liter tub of raspberry filling off the top shelf of the walk-in and caught it with her face.

"We open for the afternoon in thirty minutes, and we need the business." She glances at her watch. "Je ne sais pas quoi faire."

Kit looks at me. I nod.

"Let us help you," Kit says to Apolline.

Inside, I clean up the debris of the morning shift while Kit and Apolline strategize in rapid French. When they're done repeating the words *feuilleté* and *pâte à choux* over and over, Kit sends her home to change clothes, and I meet him in the kitchen.

"Okay." Kit pushes aside a pile of mixing bowls that appear to have been dumped in a panic. "We're going to be making eight things at once. Apolline's on the register, so I need you."

His eyes shine with the eager determination of Kit on a mission. I forgot how thrilling it is to be on the receiving end of that look. I grin at him, and he grins back, wolfish and ready.

"What's first?"

He hauls over a tub of dough, its domed surface jiggling.

"I've got to roll this out," he says, turning the dough out onto the workstation, "and cut and assemble—croissants, pains au chocolat, pains aux raisins, all those boys. While those are rising, I'll make the pâte à choux. Can you handle glazes?"

I shrug. "I can handle most liquids if you give me a recipe."

"Perfect. I'll pipe chouquettes and éclairs, and you make the glazes. We'll do breads in between, and fillings are already prepped." He's working the dough now, pressing it out into a large rectangle. "There should be some sheets of butter in the walk-in, can you—?"

I'm already pulling the door open before he can finish. "What shelf?"

"Left side, second from top."

"Heard." I bring the butter over, and he unwraps a big, flat piece from its parchment paper. He folds the dough around it, picks up a rolling pin and whacks it so hard that dishes across the room rattle.

"Sorry!" he says to my surprised yelp, pounding away with his rolling pin with a fervor that I find upsettingly hot. "Makes it easier to roll! There's a recipe binder in the cabinet over that prep station, can you go to the éclair section and make the chocolate and white chocolate glazes? Pistachios are already prepped in—"

"Dry storage, I see them," I say, thankful for the distraction. "On it."

I take the binder down and fly through the instructions, bubbling with adrenaline. Once I've translated the phrases I don't know, I lay out the ingredients the way I do when I make drinks, so I can see everything at once.

"Nice mise en place," Kit says, glancing over. He tips his head back to shake hair from his eyes.

"Thanks, you good?"

"Yeah, I just—I don't have anything to tie my hair back."

I unwind a rubber band from some sleeves for to-go cups and bring it to him. He looks down at his butter-slicked hands and back to me.

"Could you?"

Could I—could I slide my hands into Kit's thick, soft hair while he's busy maneuvering dough with the calm agility of a professional?

"Sure," I say evenly.

I sweep my fingers up from his temples and gather the front pieces of his hair into an untidy knot, tying it off. I could swear he shivers at the touch, almost leans into it. When I give the knot a tug to make sure it's secure, his hands falter on the rolling pin. *Oh.*

"You still like that, huh?" I comment, my tone light, uninvested.

"Don't *tease*." He's aiming for firm, but his voice cracks on the second syllable. My hand is still in his hair, and I have the overwhelming urge to plant a kiss on his crown.

Instead, I lean close to his ear and whisper, "This is just like *Ratatouille.*"

"Good fucking God, Theo."

He elbows me away, half laughing and half groaning as I yell, "What! We're in France!" on the way back to my station. But I tuck the moment into my apron, the breath he held before he knew I was joking.

Kit cranks the butter-filled dough through the rolling press four times, folding and turning, letting me peek at the paper-thin layers of lamination before he cuts it to shape. He rolls triangles of dough into croissants and tucks bits of chocolate and raisins into pockets with nimble hands. Eight sheet pans of pastries settle into the proofing rack, and he switches seamlessly to the stove beside me to make choux dough. I babysit saucepans like my life depends on it.

Apolline returns as I'm pulling the éclair fillings out of cold storage and Kit is piping the last dollops of choux. She thanks us with a kiss on each cheek, then heads out front to reopen with the few pastries left in her cases. I notice the whisk tattooed on her ankle, a match to the one on Kit's wrist and presumably somewhere on Maxine. I remind myself what happened the last time I got jealous of one of Kit's classmates before I lose focus.

"That's good," Kit says, watching me roll out baguette dough. "Much better than last time."

I feel useful and lit up inside. I dart from station to station, from cold storage to dry storage, to the front of the shop with chouquettes and cream puffs, to the back to tell Kit what's needed. I've been spending so much time by myself in the wine cellar and the bus bar, I forgot how much I thrive in good, competent, back-of-house madness.

The shop fills with locals picking up afternoon snacks and tourists filling boxes to carry away to their beachfront hotels, and we make it work.

It helps that Kit is extremely good at this. He's so deeply in his element, it's like Swayze in *Road House* when he finally gets to bust out his tai chi. The pastry school training keeps his lines neat and his measurements accurate, but the rest is all him. The flick of his wrist, the clear, decisive tone of his voice as he thinks out loud, the way I know from a shift in his hips or shoulders exactly how to follow in harmony. I put out my hand, and Kit pushes a piping bag into it; Kit tilts his chin, and I pass the oven mitts. If I could see us from above, I'd see two bodies, two aprons with the same stardust patterns of flour and cinnamon, one set of choreographed steps.

Our friends used to say they could tell we'd grown up together because we have the same gestures and tics, like two branches of the same nervous system. Outside of sex, I don't think I've ever felt that more than I do in this kitchen.

It makes me think of our old dream. Fairflower. The restaurant Kit believed we could open and that I thought of as an unattainable daydream. If I had let Kit convince me, would it feel like this? Would it be possible still, if I asked and he said yes? Maybe we could still open our own little shop somewhere, anywhere. Make up new menus every weekend, bike home from the market with baskets of fruit, stay up all night experimenting. Stay up all night doing all kinds of things.

Kit looks up at me over a steaming pan of croissants, a stray bit of hair falling across his brow. When he smiles, it's the pleased smile of a job well done, and I'm struck by a memory of him smiling like that between my thighs.

"One more hour!" Apolline calls.

The final rush goes in a flurry of pastry flakes and sugar nibs, éclairs boxed as soon as they're finished with pistachio dust. By seven o'clock, when Apolline turns over the sign in the front window, we're all sweating through our shirts, but we've done it.

"Mes sauveurs!" Apolline cries, sweeping Kit up to kiss him ferociously on each cheek. She does the same to me, and I find that I like her, her fiery eyes and the vivid color in her round cheeks and the way she still smells like raspberries. I also find that I don't really have any desire to try to sleep with her.

We gather around the central workstation and feast on left-over pastries, which is the first time I've actually gotten to taste Apolline's recipes. They're incredible, perfectly buttery and sur-prising and complex. I can't believe Kit and I made these.

"Do you have anything to drink?" I ask Apolline.

"In the case by counter, anything you want."

I leave the kitchen to fetch a Perrier for myself, then grab another for Apolline and a sparkling lemonade for Kit. Hands full, I have to shoulder the kitchen door, so I don't see them at first. It's not until I step inside that I realize what's happening.

The small of Kit's back is against the edge of his workstation. Apolline is pressed close to him from chest to hip. Her hand is in his hair, and they're kissing.

I drop one of my bottles, catching it with my boot before it smashes on the floor. It bangs into a proofing rack.

Kit and Apolline spring apart.

"Sorry!" I say, my voice unnaturally high. I cough and overcom-pensate, unnaturally low. "Sorry, I—I didn't mean to interrupt.'

"Theo—" Kit starts.

"You guys clearly have some catching up to do," I say. Fuck, is that why we came here? Does Kit have history with her? *It was like a rite of passage in our year. . . .* "I'm gonna— I'll see myself out."

"Theo, you don't—"

"No, no, it's totally cool! Really great to meet you, Apolline."

I leave the bottles and shove out of the kitchen, out of the boulangerie, and away from Apolline's street.

— — —

Castle Hill is only open for another half hour by the time I reach it, so I climb the steps two at a time. For some reason, it feels right to get as much topographical distance as I can from this afternoon.

I didn't even consider that Apolline might be one of Kit's pastry school lovers, or that this is why he wanted so badly to help her. I was in her kitchen fantasizing about a life with him while he was baking croissants for her. He was thinking of their pastry school hookups while I was contemplating pulling him into the back of a bar and asking if he could find it in himself to love me. That is . . . deeply fucking embarrassing.

I stare out over the sparkling rush of the Riviera and feel like the biggest jackass in the south of France. So, I do what I usually do when I feel like a jackass: I call Sloane.

She answers from set, tucked into a director's chair with pages of sides folded in her lap, her hair in rollers. I squint at the screen—that doesn't look like a wig.

"Hello, world traveler," she says, biting into a carrot stick. "Reunite with any old flames lately?"

"Did they make you dye your hair?"

"Oh, this?" She gestures to the dark brown hair, which was the same orange-blond as mine last time I saw her. "I did this out of self-defense. Less time in hair and makeup with Lincoln."

"It looks good."

"No, it doesn't, I'm shaving my head when this is over. Why do you look like someone pissed in your pinot gris?"

I sigh. "So, that text I sent you yesterday about Kit—"

A banner at the top of my screen interrupts me. It's an email from Schnauzer Bride.

Panic stabs between my ribs. I never responded to her that night in Barcelona, did I? And the next day I was too fucked up over Kit to think about it, and today I got caught up at the boulangerie, and—

The subject line reads "TERMINATION OF CON-TRACT <3," with a bunch of sparkle emojis.

"Fuck!" I swear, opening the email. "Fuck, goddammit, I just got a really bad fucking email."

"What? From who?"

I skim Schnauzer Bride's record of every time I ever missed a call or took too long to answer an email, ending with my two days of silence following her shipping-barge crisis. My heart rate accelerates at every bullet point, all the way down to the last line, where she wishes me luck in the future and demands her deposit back.

"I just lost my biggest client of the season, and I—I already maxed out my credit card ordering all the shit for that gig, and there's no fucking way I'm breaking even now. God, I'm such a fucking—" Idiot, jackass, piece of shit, dumb fucking disaster, pathetic failure. I scrunch up my fist and grind it against my forehead. "*Fuck!*"

"Oh," Sloane says. "Bummer."

I drop my fist and stare at her face on the screen.

"It's kind of significantly more than a bummer."

"No, it is," Sloane says, looking more sincere now. More like she feels sorry for me. "Should we discuss the nuclear option?"

"I'm not borrowing money from you."

"Why not? You can't spell Sloane without 'loan.'"

"That's not funny."

"It is," Sloane disagrees, biting into another carrot, "but as I have told you a million times, it wouldn't be a loan. I could be your investor. I'd be buying in. I could have our guy draw something up and wire you fifty grand tomorrow."

Jesus. "Fifty grand?"

"Okay, a hundred? Two hundred? What do you need?"

"I don't want any money, Sloane," I insist. "The whole point of the bus was—is—I mean, it's because I love doing it. It's a creative outlet, and people think it's hot, but it's also—"

"To prove you can do something by yourself," Sloane finishes. "I know. You're not ripping the curtain back on any secrets here, Theo."

"Then you know why I can't take the money."

"I get why you won't take money from Mom and Dad, but I don't get why you won't take it from me."

"It's the same thing."

This is absolutely the wrong thing to say to Sloane in any context, but I'm not currently my best self.

"It's actually fucking not, Theo," Sloane says acidly. "It's *my* money. Did you seriously just—do you think I have what I have because of Mom and Dad?"

I shrug. "I mean, it doesn't hurt."

"Let me remind you that I am a *good* fucking actor." Her expression is dead serious, the way it gets when we really fight, when I've actually managed to wound her. A pang of guilt and self-loathing shoots through me. "I studied. I did Shakespeare. I fucking did workshops, and I am very expensive, and directors want to work with me—"

"I know, I know, that's not what I meant—"

"—and you know what I don't have to do? I don't have to show my tits unless I want to. I never had to play Crying Girl Number Two just to get my name on a desk. I don't have to put up with any bullshit. And that's because I am very fucking talented, *and* I know how to use what we have, so you could be a little more grateful for it."

"I *am* grateful," I say, sounding awful even in my own ears. "I know I'm lucky. But I don't want to be that person. I don't want to be fucking Chet Hanks. I don't want to be another jerk-off with a trust fund and a famous family who gets them embarrassing gigs at fucking influencer festivals in Ibiza."

"Well, it's better than being broke on purpose so you can feel morally superior."

I feel her words like a punch.

"Jesus, Sloane, that's a bit fucking harsh."

Sloane sighs. The rollers in her hair wobble. "Look, Theo, I love you. But you get in your own way. You have this—this nepotism chip on your shoulder, and you make your life harder on purpose just to prove to yourself that you're not what you are. But you're a Flowerday. You have options other people would fucking kill for. You're just too proud to use them."

I hate this. I hate that I don't have anything to say in response.

"The offer stands," Sloane says. "Let me know if you change your mind."

She hangs up, leaving me alone on Castle Hill, feeling worse than I did before I called. And I was feeling pretty fucking shitty.

You get in your own way.

Kit said the exact same words to me in the fight that ended our relationship. I can hear the jet engines rumbling, the crinkle of a biscuit wrapper. I can see the look on his face when he said it, the gentle fucking pity.

I worry that sometimes you get in your own way.

This is why I had to keep myself away: As soon as I look into Kit's big sparkly brown eyes, I forget that I had every right to be angry.

The aftermath of our breakup may not have been Kit's fault, but it doesn't change the fact that the breakup *was.* He did what he did, and he said what he said on that plane, because he thought he could decide how my life ought to be.

That's what everyone thinks, isn't it? Everyone thought I should be in the family business until I was in front of a camera. Everyone thinks I need to be saved from myself, like I don't know I'm a fuckup. I know. I *know.* Every day I wake up in the town I grew up in, and I put on my boots and roll up my sleeves and work so hard to be pretty good at a few things, because I know I'd fuck up anything bigger. I would be so much braver if I was someone I could trust.

But what's the point of trying not to be a fuckup, if everyone thinks I'm one anyway? If I'm ruining my life, there are more pleasurable ways to do it.

I climb down Castle Hill and wander into bars, one after

another until I find a guy who looks enough like Kit. After a few rounds, I pull him into the bathroom and put my hands in his hair. I laugh until I mean it.

I won't ask anyone for help. And I sure as shit won't ask Kit for love.

MONACO

PAIRS WELL WITH:

Stolen champagne, a very ripe peach

MONACO

I'm the wrong Flowerday for Monaco, but today, I'll be good at it.

Everything about this place, from the marble palace to the luxury cars, screams Este. The Princess Grace of it all, the pink glow of family money. My baby sister would swan into Monte Carlo and giggle over Dom Pérignon until someone invited her back to the VIP suite. She'd pick out the archduke of whatever made-up principality by clocking his Loro Piana cashmere baseball cap and be on a yacht by lunch, sun shining on that Flowerday strawberry blond hair.

Fuck it. I could do that for a day.

I slept like shit and woke up feeling like I do riding my longboard home after a long day of inventory: delirious, clammy, careening too fast, head swimming in languages I can't speak. On the bus, I pulled my bucket hat down low so Kit wouldn't try to talk to me for the thirty minutes between Nice and Monaco for today's day trip, and now I'm sitting at our four-course champagne brunch, pretending not to listen as Kit explains our dessert to Dakota and Montana.

I watch the cream sploosh out of the strawberry mille-feuille under my fork and think it looks like me, like how there's barely room left for me in my body. I'm a splat on the plate of life. If I'm nothing, I could be anything. I could be the car crash I'm always trying not to be. I could be one more renegade nepo baby in Monaco.

When Kit glances across the table at me, I smile, all teeth. I finish my champagne in one go and let the buzz take over.

After lunch, Kit magics up a paper bag of fried pastries and follows me down to the harbor. He's wearing a miniscule pair of tight mustard swim trunks and an insane spindrift-blue silk shirt with a trim of yellow and blue waves and a nude woman riding a dolphin over the pockets. His hair is loose, caught up in the breeze off the water, and I'd like to either put my legs around him or push him off a pier.

"Nice shirt," I say. "You look like you suck dick at Caesars Palace."

"Thank you," he says, adjusting his sunglasses. "I've been saving it for Monaco."

My own shirt is an afterthought, all-purpose oversized linen open over a black two-piece swimsuit. Part laziness, part need for Kit to look at my body.

Falling back in love doesn't mean I forgive him, and not forgiving him doesn't mean I stopped wanting him to want me. It might even be more delicious if he wanted me now. I feel equally likely to reject him or fuck him to destroy myself, and today, unpredictability tastes good. A bright tang of possibility.

I hop up on a pier railing and bite into one of the half-moon pastries. Inside its flaky crust, it's stuffed with swiss chard and ricotta.

"They're the local thing," Kit says. "Barbagiuan."

"I guess every culture really does have their own dumpling."

Kit chews and swallows, watching me teeter on the railing.

"Hey, are you okay?"

"I'm great." I stretch my arms wide like Kit did in the lavender fields, as if my fingertips could graze the Alps if I reach far enough. "Monaco is fucking beautiful, isn't it?"

"Yeah, it is," he says, not looking at the mountains. "Listen, about what you saw yesterday—"

"Oh, right, we need to update our numbers. With Santiago and Apolline, you're at five now, right?"

"Well—"

"And then I've got Caterina and my guy from last night."

The paper bag crunches in Kit's hands. "Last night?"

"Didn't catch his name. That's six to five."

"Six to four."

"Six to . . ." I drop my arms, counting again. "No, it's five."

Kit sighs and tosses the last bite of his barbagiuan into the water. Fish bubble up to finish it.

"Nothing happened with Apolline. She got—I don't know, caught up in the moment, and she kissed me, but that was all. After you left, I helped her close up and got dinner on my own. What you saw didn't mean anything."

The look on his face isn't unlike the one he gave me in that cave in San Sebastián, but I don't know why he'd care so much about being believed now. He certainly hasn't minded any of the other times I've seen him with someone else.

Unless I was right about what kind of friends they were.

"So, that was the first time you kissed?"

His beat of hesitation confirms it before he does. I have to laugh.

"There was— Yes, we did hook up years ago, but it was only once, and I wasn't—"

I hop down. "Kit, I don't care."

"You don't?"

"Of course not. Except for, you know, prior history would have disqualified her from the competition anyway, for the record. But, no, why would I care? Does it seem like I care?"

". . . No?"

"Exactly. Anyway, what do you want to do today? Can't really go to Monte Carlo in that slutty little swimsuit."

He looks down at himself, at the trunks that end just below the crease of his thigh. "It's not slutty. It's European."

"For you, that's the same thing."

I can't see the look in his eyes when his chin tips up, but faint color gathers in his cheeks. *Do you like that?* I wonder.

"Okay, then, what do *you* want to do with me in my slutty little swimsuit?"

Oh, he likes it.

"I want . . ." I say, savoring those two syllables. I could be anything. I could be a tease. I could be a Flowerday who does Molly on boats with Formula 1 drivers. "I want to be on a yacht."

"A yacht?" Kit repeats, bemused. "Okay. Should only be about a quarter million to charter one."

"I don't need to pay," I say, gesturing at all the rich men milling about their fancy boats. "Look at these guys. It's like a Tom Wambsgans casting call. I could convince any of them to let us on."

I scan the harbor for what Este would notice. She wouldn't waste time with any yacht small enough to fit in a slip. I narrow in on the 150-foot behemoth at the very end of the pier.

"That one," I declare, hopping down from the rail.

"Theo, what are you doing?" Kit asks, eyebrows high over his sunglasses, but I'm already walking backward away from him.

"I just told you."

"No, I mean . . . what are you *doing*?"

"I'm taking risks! Aren't you happy?"

Beside the slipway up to the megayacht, a man speaks animated French to a passing caterer, a bottle of wine in each hand. I can tell it's his yacht by the weight of his flax linen shirt and his Cartier watch, but what really convinces me is the label on the wine: Pétrus, the only winery on the Pomerol plateau situated entirely on a blue clay deposit. Every somm I know would shiv their mom for one taste of that wine, and he's waving it around like it's Franzia.

"What's the vintage?"

The man turns at the sound of my voice. Sunlight flashes on a thin gold chain against sandy chest hair.

I'm pleasantly surprised to see he's strikingly good-looking, in a Cary Grant or Marlon Brando kind of way, old Hollywood with a palpable air of bisexuality. Angular jaw, full lips, dirty blond hair, eyes the same clear blue as the harbor. The crinkled corners of his eyes and salt-and-paper stubble place him around forty.

"2005," he says, a curious tilt to his smile. "Have we met?"

"I'm Theo. Theo Flowerday, of the Ted and Gloria Flowerdays. Do you know of my parents? Eleven combined Academy Awards? If you've ever been to Cannes, I'm sure you've seen them around."

In case none of this is enough, I point toward Kit, who is helpfully bending over to tighten his sandals.

"He's with me."

— — —

Émile has an utterly unplaceable accent. It's part Greek, part Swiss German, part Ivy League American, and a secret fourth thing, a sumptuous quality that brings to mind silk ties and dessert wine. He reminds us to take off our shoes before we step on the teak, then tours us around his enormous yacht, stopping in the chef's kitchen to taste a sprig of lemongrass for the canapés and give us each a flute of champagne. Then he takes us out onto the main deck, where the party is well and truly raging.

Models lounge on chaises, drinking vodka on the rocks and rubbing coconut oil onto their skin. Grand Prix drivers throw down euros over a poker game. Some people swim in the pool on the deck, while others jump from the back of the boat into the sea. Waiters bring around trays of high-concept hors d'oeuvres and glasses of pink champagne. Music throbs over the speakers, clouds of vapor and cigar smoke waft from laughing mouths, and everyone is so goddamn hot.

"Enjoy yourselves," Émile tells us, his hand skimming Kit's waist. Something between possessiveness and arousal buzzes in my veins.

When he leaves, Kit turns to me in disbelief.

"You got us onto a yacht," he says. "What now?"

I suck down my champagne and grab another from a passing waiter.

"Unbutton your shirt," I say, already taking mine off and throwing it over the nearest chair.

"Why?"

"I want to see if I can get someone to do a shot out of your belly button."

"Oh, sure," Kit says reasonably, complying.

We drink, and we dance, and we swim, and I find, to my slight annoyance and much greater pleasure, that being a renegade Flowerday is actually pretty fun. The daughter of the Belgian ambassador shows me how to take bumps of caviar off the back of my hand. Kit takes to yacht partying like a fish to water, swanning around in his little yellow swim trunks, flirting outrageously with anything that moves. He's from another world. I want to bite him.

At some point, Émile rejoins the party, and he seems to gravitate back toward Kit or me every time someone pulls his attention away. Kit notices too, giving me a significant look when Émile puts his hand on my thigh during a card game. By now, I've had at least a bottle of champagne and a few hits off someone's designer blunt, so I let myself enjoy Kit watching someone want me. I enjoy watching someone want Kit too.

When Kit and I were together, we were known to take someone home with us every so often. We weren't *open,* but we did sometimes enjoy watching each other receive pleasure from a third-person perspective, or competing to see who could get someone off first, or—well, there were a lot of things we liked doing.

I'm kind of starting to think we might like doing Émile, a suspicion confirmed by the tone of Kit's voice when he leans into my ear and says, "We've just been invited up to the private deck."

I gaze at Kit, trying to read his vibe, except for how I'm mostly staring at his nipples.

"Should we go?" I ask.

"That depends," Kit says. "He's definitely trying to have a three-way with us."

"I mean," I say. "It's not like it would be our first."

"Those were different," Kit says with a significant look. *We were also having sex with each other separately at the time.*

"I'm not worried about it," I say airily. "Are you?"

Kit tosses a lock of hair out of his eyes. "Oh, you know me. Daddy issues. Try anything once. We're firmly in my wheelhouse."

"How far are you willing to go?"

He looks at me for a long moment. Just looks at me.

"As far as you want," he says. And then, "If it's just me, will you watch?"

I imagine sitting in a hot tub while Kit and Émile tangle up on a chaise nearby, Kit's competent fingers undoing Émile's belt. Heat licks lazily at the base of my spine.

"As long as you do the same," I say. I feel something here, something dangerous. I wonder if Kit feels it too.

"And if he wants us both?" Kit asks.

Well . . . then I guess I'm having sex with Kit today.

"We'll do thumbs," I say, meaning the system we used when we were fooling around somewhere too quiet or too loud for verbal check-ins. Thumb on the chin for green light, thumb on the earlobe for red. Kit nods.

"Okay. How do we keep score?"

"Well, if we all have sex together, I think it cancels out," I say. "PEMDAS."

"Sure, no points, then," Kit says, charitably allowing this reasoning. "But if it's just one of us, there should be a bonus. Double points."

"I'll take that action," I say.

— — —

Up on the private deck, Émile uncorks a bottle of two-thousand-euro champagne, and we discover that he's surprisingly good company. He's interesting in the way only a very wealthy man can be, full of stories of impossible views and spiritual yurt retreats and five-digit tasting menus on private islands accessible only by boat. For a long time, we just talk—about art and wine and travel, about Malibu, about the horse ranch in the Dolomites he built with his own hands.

To me, he gets sexier by the second. I've been around plenty of rich fucks, and few of them take the pride Émile does in doing things for himself. He can filet a fish and sear a steak, saddle a horse and mix a mean old-fashioned. I catch Kit's eye and think he's fallen under the spell too. In a way, Émile almost reminds me of an older Kit, a collector of the finest things and richest experiences.

Actually, now that I'm considering it, I see an older me in him, too.

"What is the point of having everything," Émile asks us, luxuriantly sweeping his gaze over us, "if you're not open to *everything*?"

There it is. The reason we're really here.

We glide easily through the preamble, the feeling each other out, the flirting. It's nobody's first time, and all three of us are loose-limbed and quick to confidence. Then Émile calls us a beautiful couple, and Kit says, "Oh, we're not together."

I shoot him a glare, and he quickly recovers.

"I mean, we're not *exclusively* together."

"I am glad to hear that," Émile says. "I wonder if you would let me watch."

Of all the scenarios discussed, I didn't consider the possibility of Émile simply wanting to watch us together. I glance at Kit, wondering if he'll back down, but he looks calm, so I decide to be calm. I reach down to the platter of fruit laid on the table between the canvas-cushioned daybed where Kit and I sit and Émile's deep leather chair.

"What would you like to see?" Kit asks.

The grape I'm grasping nearly slips out of my fingers.

Émile shifts the ice in his cocktail glass. He turns his gaze to me.

"Does he know how to show you pleasure?"

What a fucking question.

I look at Kit as I answer, daring him to keep his composure. "Yes."

"Will you show me?" Émile asks Kit.

Kit's eyes search my face. He's deferring to me, letting me decide what happens next. If this is a game of chicken, I won't lose. But I also won't beg.

"I'd rather him teach you," I say to Émile.

I watch as Émile climbs to his feet and takes off his shirt, revealing sculpted, tanned muscles, including what could undeniably be described as cum gutters. He tosses the fine linen over his chair and turns to me with his hand offered, his manicure pristine but his palms meaty with a working man's muscle.

I'm tracking Kit's reaction as I let Émile pull me to my feet. I see the way he leans forward, how he sucks on the rim of his champagne flute.

When Émile presses his lips to mine, I taste custom leather interiors and syrup-soaked fruit. He kisses with the directness of a man who has fucked more people than I've ever met and the thoroughness of a lover who still cares about making it good. I find myself looking forward to when he's kissed Kit and we can compare notes.

Kit watches it all.

He parts his thighs at an instruction from Émile, and I have to stop my reflex to praise him for how well he takes directions. Like this, his little gold swim trunks leave nothing to the imagination, and I can see just how much he's into this. My eyes skim over his taut stomach, up the graceful planes of his chest and the gentle curves of his biceps and shoulders, to his mouth, slack with anticipation, and his dark eyes, which are fixed on my face.

I touch my chin with my thumb. Kit does it back. Green light.

"Good," Émile says, unaware of this little conversation. He guides me down between Kit's splayed legs on the daybed, my back to Kit's bare chest, my legs falling open against the sun-warmed insides of Kit's thighs. While my senses are overwhelmed with all of *that,* he leans in and kisses Kit.

It's happening inches from my face, so close that I can feel the vibration of Kit's moan in my own chest and see the pink flash of Kit's tongue as it slips into Émile's mouth. I'm so thankful for champagne, for reckless spite and the rush of salt water, because watching them doesn't sting like it might have yesterday. It makes me wet.

They break apart and Émile returns to the platter of fruit, all of it ripened to softness by the evening sun. I stare down at my open legs between Kit's, wondering what comes next, wanting whatever it is. Kit's heart is pounding fast against me, but his hands rest at his sides, not touching me at all. What happened to the Kit who was unable to keep his hands off me, who couldn't go three days without going down on me? What kind of Sex God has this much restraint? What do I have to do to get him to fucking *touch* me?

Experimentally, I tip my head back and let it rest on his shoulder, my face tilted toward his. I watch his pupils dilate, his lashes flutter as his gaze drops to my mouth, my exposed throat. Still, his hands stay where they are.

Émile kneels between our outstretched legs, the gold around his neck and the saltiest bits of his stubble catching the sun as he edges forward on his knees. He holds half a peach, its flesh wet and golden, a raw opening at the center where the pit must have been, and tells Kit to use it. To show him what I like.

Jesus *fucking* Christ.

Kit takes the fruit, examining its contours, palming its velvety skin. I begin to wonder if he's stalling, if he's forgotten how

I like to be touched. But then he slowly traces the pad of his thumb around the rim of the peach's red center, making a loose, messy circle, pressing harder when he reaches the darkest flesh at the crest. I swear to every god, I feel the touch between my legs.

A wounded sound catches in my throat.

I lay my hand on Kit's thigh to tell him I'm hot for this—so incredibly fucking hot for this—and when he nods, I know it's more for me than Émile. It almost feels like I'm dreaming when he brings the peach to his mouth and puts out his tongue.

Émile and I both watch with rapt attention as Kit laps at the peach's livid center. His hesitance is gone, absolutely no shame in the way he laves and sucks, only a familiar, voracious enthusiasm. Juice runs down his chin. I can barely believe what I'm seeing, that I get to watch him put on such a pretty show.

With a hand on the side of my neck, Émile leans in and follows Kit's example until their mouths meet. Then they're kissing, nectar and spit dripping onto my shoulder and down my chest. Kit keeps *moaning,* letting out these desperate little whines, and he's hard against me as Émile's tongue fucks into his mouth, and I'm imagining putting something else in his mouth, imagining Kit trailing nectar-sticky kisses from Émile's mouth to mine.

Then Émile is kissing me with the same mouth that was kissing Kit, peach juice in his rough stubble, Kit all over his lips. I know Kit is watching, that I'm pushing myself into his familiar hardness, and it's too late for me to stop. I'm too fucked up and buzzed and catastrophically turned on to entertain shame. Everything is happening through an iridescent haze of unreality, and my hand is moving on instinct, slipping down between my legs. Finally, *finally,* Kit makes deliberate contact with me, his fingers ghosting over my jaw, and I respond automatically, close my eyes and lean my face toward his touch and—

A foghorn, of all stupid fucking things, interrupts before I

get my hand down my swimsuit bottoms. The yacht has returned
to the harbor. More guests are coming aboard. I sit up, and Kit's
hand vanishes from my face.

"Ah," Émile says, reluctantly drawing away. He gets to his
feet, stretching athletically as if he were out for a light jog rather
than trying to initiate a three-way. "The host must attend to his
duties. I will return."

He takes my hand and kisses the back of it.

"When I do, I hope you will have begun without me."

And then he's gone like a god of luxury linens, and we're suddenly, inescapably alone. And I'm suddenly much more sober
than I was two minutes ago.

That was—

We were—

Kit pulls away first, but I pull away harder.

"Theo," Kit starts, breathless and dark-eyed.

Something you need to know about Kit is, his name isn't
actually Kit. His parents started calling him Kit because he
was quick and wily like a little fox, and it was easier for his
older brother to say, so it stuck. But his real name is Aurélien.
The golden one. It fucking suits.

The golden one doesn't make careless mistakes. The golden
one doesn't twist himself into knots over long-lost love. The
golden one wasn't about to jerk off in front of the ex he still
wants because he had one too many caviar bumps and needed an
outlet for his frustrations. The golden one is kind, and reliable,
and thorough, and so unruinable that even this could barely per-
suade him to touch me. It's not fucking fair.

"You know what would be so funny?" I say.

Kit barely reacts. I notice with some satisfaction that he's still
hard.

"What?"

"If I did this."

I snatch a bottle of Dom Pérignon from the ice bucket on the table and take off running.

I run all the way down the stairs to the main deck, through the party to scoop up my shoes and our shirts and, for the hell of it, some expensive-looking coasters, and soon I'm sprinting down the spillway and onto the pier, sandals slapping wildly against the planks. Kit is only a few seconds behind, chasing me down the pier, and I feel like screaming with hysterical laughter. I feel like flying. I want to be golden too.

We race through the streets of Monaco, our shirts billowing and a bottle of Dom in my fist, and we start to laugh. We ricochet between alley walls, drunk on the rush of adrenaline, and I pop the cork out of the champagne. Bubbles stream down my forearms and over my feet until I fasten my lips on the opening and catch them in my mouth. I pass it to Kit, and he drinks, and I sing at the top of my voice, "Farewell and adieu all you fair Spanish ladies!"

We nearly drop the bottle, fumbling it between ourselves so that we crash together to catch it. My sandal comes halfway off, and Kit catches me before I trip, propping me up smoothly against the nearest wall.

In the pink bloom of a Monaco sunset, Kit is as breathtaking as he's ever been. We've slowed now, laughter still on our lips but beginning to fade into soft, lilting breaths. My back is against the bricks, and Kit's hands are on my shoulders.

I bite my lip and look into his face, his dark eyes and expressive mouth, his every unforgettable angle. I love him. I don't want to, but I do.

He touches my face like he did before, his fingertips soft on my cheek.

And he kisses me.

THE BEGINNING

(Kit's Version)

Just northeast of Lyon, overlooking the Ain, there sat a medieval village called Pérouges surrounded by walls of honey-gold stone. And within those walls, there was a house.

The house was smallish and modest, with flower boxes that spilled green vines down its cobbly front like tipped watercolor pigment. The garden too was painted a lush, impossible green, and the hills outside the village's walls were green and amber and the bruised bluish black of wet soil. Somehow the flowers never wilted or browned when I pressed my fingers to their petals, even though we'd been told not to touch them when they were in bloom. When I opened the shutters each morning, the air tasted of irises and sage.

(One day, the love of my life would say this explained everything about me. *You can take the boy out of the fairy-tale hamlet, but you can never take the fairy-tale hamlet out of him.*)

When we came to California, nothing was green. It was all dust and sand, all rocks. Brown and pale slate, pebbly and craggy, like the alien planets my dad wrote stories about. The only familiar things were the ones we'd brought from home, the mixing bowls and big wooden spoons, the eggbeaters that had to be turned by hand, the dimpled ceramic trays cradling eggs on the pantry's highest shelf. When I missed home, my maman would open her book of French pastry recipes, and we would stand together at our new kitchen counter and bake something. Still, I missed the colors.

Then came Theodora.

The first time I ever saw her, she was the brightest thing in the classroom. The only spot of full saturation I'd seen since we got to the desert. Brassy orange-blond, rose flush and cinnamon-dust freckles, her lip bitten angry red by the bumpy edges of new teeth. She had eyes like the hills of Rhône, blue-green on the outside and honey-gold at the center. I wouldn't find the right English word for her until spring, when Maman took us out to Antelope Valley to see explosions of wildflowers on the hills. It was the biggest thing I'd ever seen, bigger than the ocean out of an airplane window or the bottom of my own heart. So deep and wide, so much of everything at once. We were eight years old, and Theodora was smiling.

I learned the names of all the growing things I never would have seen back home. Lupine, fiddle-neck, Western blue-eyed grass, California poppy, Theo. Superbloom.

Love took root in me before I even knew its name. Theo was a superbloom. The petals stayed.

THE END

(Kit's Version)

"Kit," says Thierry, "did you know that parrots taste with the tops of their beaks?"

My uncle is reclined on his favorite chair, reading a guide to bird behavior loudly enough for me to hear from the kitchen. I don't mind. It's been nice, after so long, to hear his Lyonnais accent between the soft thumps of cold butter against sifted flour.

I switch on the oven light and ask, "Is that right?"

"It says here that most of a parrot's approximately three hundred taste buds are located on the roof of its mouth." He closes the book and holds it to his chest, turning his face to the sun in the vine-fringed windows. "Such a strange, wonderful creature, don't you think?"

On my mother's side, from her father's father's father, come two inheritances: a love of all beautiful living things and a pied-à-terre in Saint-Germain-des-Prés. The latter is how Thierry can afford to live in a Haussmann apartment in the 6th on a part-time ceramicist's salary, and the former is why he's filled every windowsill of it with leafy plants.

Some of my favorite childhood memories happened in this apartment: sprawling on the herringbone floors while Thierry told Maman about whichever woman he'd fallen in love with that month, waking up to the bells of Saint-Sulpice, writing postcards to Theo. I haven't been back since high school, but when I got the letter from École Desjardins, I booked a ticket.

"Only three hundred taste buds? Seems a bit tragic, compared to our ten thousand."

"They can still taste many foods, though. They even have favorites! Constança says her gray one likes mangoes. Benny, I think. Or—no, the gray one is Anni-Frid." He jots down a note on the side table, determined to remember which of Constança's birds are named after which member of ABBA.

Constança, Thierry's latest girlfriend, lives in Portugal and hates long distance, so Thierry is moving out of the pied-à-terre and into a two-bedroom home in Lisbon with a menagerie of birds. I really do admire how devoted he is to believing every woman he meets is his soul mate. This is the third country he's moved to for love, after Belgium for Lydia and Japan for Suzu. But this is the first time he's been so sure that he started looking at selling the place.

"Lisbon is glorious this time of year," Thierry says. "I'll hardly miss Paris."

"That's the first lie you've told all day."

"No," Thierry says. "I also lied when I told you I didn't buy any ice cream at the store this morning. I just didn't want to share."

"That's alright," I say. I lift the cake out of the oven and set it down on a tea towel, then carry it into the living room. It's a galette de Pérouges, made with my grand-tante's recipe. "I made dessert for both of us."

Thierry eyes the cake, then my face. "What is this for?"

"Can't I just do something nice for my favorite uncle?"

"You have your mother's eyes," Thierry says. "And I could always tell when she wanted something."

"Well," I say, reaching into my pocket, "I know you're thinking of selling the place, because there's no one in Paris to pass it down to. But, what if there was?"

I give him the paper and watch as he unfolds it. Within the first few lines of text, he's beaming.

"Is this true?" he says. "You are coming to Paris?"

I nod.

"Oh, lovely Kit." He jumps up to hug me, spinning me around like he did when I was much smaller. "Oh, of course, of course it is yours. And Theo? Tell me Theo will come too."

I smile. "I haven't told her yet. But I have a plan."

CINQUE TERRE

PAIRS WELL WITH:

Sciacchetrà, Ligurian focaccia with fresh basil

The first six months after Theo left me, I lived on sex, croissants, and a volume of Rilke's collected poems from Thierry's
bookshelf.

I sat up at night and drew circles around the lines that most
made me think of Theo, copied down the best ones until they
stitched together a new verse. *Dream in the eyes, the brow as if in touch
with something far away.* And, *Was it not summer, was it not sun—all that
heat from you, that measureless radiant warmth?* And, *Alone: What shall I
do with my mouth?*

Well. Sex and croissants, that's what.

It was Maxine who, at the end of a long evening that could
have been a first date if she hadn't seen right through me, went
scouring my notebook for a recipe and found the page with the
Rilke. She asked, "How long have you loved them?" And I said,
"Almost my whole life." And she said, "Putain de merde," and
opened her cigarette case.

That was the night we became friends, and it was the night
I told her about the tour. On the first day of every subsequent
summer, she asked if this was the year I'd redeem my voucher,
and every year I told her I couldn't, because I was waiting. I
was holding out hope that someday, somehow, Theo would come
back.

It isn't as if I've loved the same cold memory all this time.
Rilke wrote, *Even your not being there is warm with you.* I'm in love

with Theo's residual warmth, the indentation she left for me to grow around. All those living petals, never falling.

That's my life, in the kitchen and the café and the épicerie every morning thumbing orange rinds, nights looking into empty corners of the apartment where a liquor cabinet or a pair of boots might fit, mornings waking up on the left side of the bed. I leave space for Theo to be something that's still happening to me.

But four years *is* a long time, and this year when Maxine asks about the ticket, I say I'll do it as a farewell tour. I'll take my unsent letter to a beach in Palermo and bury it at sea, and I'll return to Paris and spend the rest of my life loving someone I'll never see again.

And then Theo walks out of a dream and onto a bus in London, fiercer and stronger and screamingly hotter than ever before. She can't stand to be next to me, but she wants to try, so I say yes, because I'll take whatever she'll give me. She calls me her friend in the same breath that she proposes having sex with other people, and I say yes to that too, because it's a good distraction. Because as long as we're counting, we have something to talk about, and I've missed the sound of her voice.

And she's looking at me while I'm touching someone else, and we're sleeping in the same bed, and I'm thinking of her every time I sink into another person's body, and she's sighing into my palm on the deck of a yacht. I have no room left in myself to hold it all. It has to overflow. And so, I kiss her.

I kiss Theo because I'm in love with her. I always have been. I always will be.

— —— —

I'm still getting used to how different Theo looks.

The last time I saw her, her hair fell past her shoulders and down her back. She wore nail polish until it chipped away and she painted over it, shadowed her eyelids before work for better tips, wore skirts on weekends. Sometimes I would notice her checking her posture, as if she could soften the natural breadth of her shoulders, make herself delicate.

Now, she stands with her shoulders back, moves as if she knows a thousand ways to use her body and fears none of them. Her face has hardened and sharpened slightly, but it still holds a raw, hardy friendliness that makes strangers tell her their secrets, and there's never anything on it but freckles. She wears practical boots and overalls with cargo pockets and ugly bucket hats, and her hair is so short that her neck and jaw are always on display.

A month ago I'd have sworn I could never want anyone more than the Theo I knew. Then I saw this new Theo, and suddenly want wasn't big enough. This is more like *need*.

We're in Monterosso al Mare, the northernmost of the five villages clustered along the curve of Italy's northwestern coast, Cinque Terre. Here, pastel palazzos cascade down steep cliffs to the bright blue Mediterranean Sea. Terraced farms line green hills, growing olives and lemons and basil, and rows of striped umbrellas cram the pebbly beaches below. It's wilder and warmer here than on the Côte d'Azur, but the salt on the air is the same, and the resort beaches are almost the same, and so I am thinking—miserably, inescapably—about Monaco. About yesterday, about need.

I'm thinking about Theo between my open thighs, nothing but dried sweat and salt water between our skin. About how casually she settled there, ready for anything, while it took everything in me to keep my voice steady and my hands still. The weight of her gaze on my mouth, the pressure of her hand on my thigh, her damp hair on my shoulder, all the hysterical need I poured into Émile so Theo wouldn't feel it. I was so completely willing to do anything she wanted, and so afraid that the moment I touched her, she would know it meant so much more to me.

I wonder, as I watch her ruthlessly shred basil leaves, if that was the last time we'll ever be that close.

Theo's wearing boots today—her sensible Blundstones—
with hiking shorts and yesterday's linen shirt, still smelling of
sea salt and expensive champagne. Perhaps she chose them for
this morning excursion on a basil farm because a good viticul-
turist is always prepared. Or maybe it's because I kissed her, and
she's going to kick me off a palazzo.

I hold a leaf between my thumb and forefinger and squeeze
until the fibers collapse, but its new, wet bruise only reminds me
of the shine on Theo's lower lip in a dark alley. Theo's mouth
against mine for five long seconds before I broke off and I started
apologizing. The cool laugh she forced when I swore I was drunk
and caught in the moment, that I hadn't meant it.

We walked back to the hotel in silence, and she hasn't spoken
to me since. Not on the bus here, not during our tour of the farm,
not when we were set loose to gather our own basil, not even during
our adorable old farmer's lesson on making pesto. Presently, she's
focused on crushing leaves with a righteous, wholehearted fury.
The table creaks under her mortar and pestle, bottles of olive oil
rattling nervously.

"Are you alright, Theo?" Stig asks.

"I'm great," Theo says brightly, which means she's angry, and
when she's angry, she breaks things.

My hands are graceless on my own pestle, the taste of regret
too thick in my mouth to get the flavors right. It took time to
understand how I'd made Theo so angry she could leave me back
then, but this time it's simple. I'm supposed to be her friend,
and I kissed her. All the flirting and innuendos, the platonic nudity and almost threesomes—I made them mean something she
never agreed to. I'd kick myself off a palazzo if I could.

When we taste everyone's finished pesto, Theo's is vibrant
and complex and perfectly balanced, exactly as creamy as it
should be because she whisked in the olive oil at the end instead
of dumping everything together like half of us did. Theo has

never encountered a straightforward, useful skill she couldn't instantly master by will and instinct. *Jack of all trades, master of cunt,* she once said. I've never liked anyone more than her.

I dip a corner of bread into my bowl and discover it doesn't taste like much of anything. It's the most pitiable, anemic thing I've made since pâtisserie school.

"You didn't crush the basil hard enough," Theo says, working her lip with her teeth. She slides a finger around the rim of my bowl, then sucks oil and herbs off her fingertip. "It tastes apologetic. Fucking commit to something, man."

I don't have an answer for that. She's right, but even if she weren't, I deserve to be bullied today.

When I took her hand on the cliff in Dover, I wondered how I could give her a reason to keep me this time. This new person with carpenter calluses where each finger meets her palm, who packs light and crosses oceans alone, the sturdier, broader Theo who cut off her hair—what would she see in me?

She saw friendship, and I was lucky for that. I shouldn't have asked for more.

— — —

On the train that will whisk us down the coast to Cinque Terre's four other villages, Theo sits across a little gray table from me and says nothing. She puts her headphones in, her knife tattoo flashing ominously as she folds her arms over her chest. I look at her and miss her twice, once as a lover and once as the friend I had yesterday.

Rilke wrote, *Whispering sweetness, which once coursed through us, sits silently beside us with disheveled hair.*

All day, I see double. The next village, Vernazza, is full of weathered stone stairs and beachgoing tourists. I see it, but I also see San Sebastián. I see Theo beside me in the sand, both of us fresh with the revelation that we hadn't been abandoned after all, the sun laying itself over her shoulders, and wishing so badly I'd taken the next flight out instead of wallowing around an empty apartment for a week composing dramatic letters.

Farther inland, in the hills of Corniglia, we drink Vernaccia made from local white grapes. Fabrizio tells us how Michelangelo once wrote that Vernaccia "kisses, licks, bites, slaps, and stings," and Theo says, "Damn, is she single?" I think of Bordeaux and a belly full of wine, standing before a fountain and daring to hope, the sting of hearing Theo say that losing each other was a good thing. And I think of Theo's hands on a farmhand's hips and wonder if heartbreak will fuck you if you learn to love it enough.

The bigger, busier coastal village of Riomaggiore reminds me of Barcelona, with its Gothic churches and street carts selling paper cones of calamari. I remember that second hot night, begging Santiago to fuck Theo out of my mind for long enough to catch my breath. How I heard her across the alley and raised my voice, knowing she probably wasn't listening, pretending she was. How the thought made me come so hard I passed out and had to buy Santiago an apologetic breakfast.

By the time the train drops us in Manarola, I am half agony, half hard. We wander dusty trails through the terraced hillside vineyards and climb to a pink trattoria with sweeping views for dinner. I expect Theo to leave me for another table, but she isn't *avoiding* me—she's aggressively ignoring me, which is at least familiar. She drops into the seat beside me on the rooftop terrazzo, across from the Calums.

The Calums have been uncharacteristically quiet today, and they simply nod their chins at her in approval. I don't spend much time with traditionally masculine men unless they're, quite frankly, fucking me, but I like the Calums. They exude a certain harmlessness, the earnest and beefy benevolence of Channing Tatum, or a cow. Theo loves them, of course, because Theo was a frat daddy in a past life.

Waiters bring around bottles of cold white wine and a parade of seafood antipasti—fileted anchovies brined in lemon and olive oil, squid braised in their own ink, herbed octopus. Then come plates of fresh-cut pasta drenched with cuttlefish ink and clattering with mussels and clams, and then fat-bellied amberjack that gleam like they're still dewy from the fisherman's hold.

It's an incredible meal, and we're all sitting around it, barely talking.

Finally, Theo jabs her fork at the Calums and says, "What's going on with you two? Did you get drunk and have sex or something?"

Ginger Calum's face pinkens and Blond Calum suddenly becomes fascinated with a prawn. My interest is piqued.

"Oh my God," Theo whispers, leaning in, "you *did*."

"We didn't," Blond Calum says to his prawn.

"Right," Ginger Calum agrees, "because you were too busy stabbing me in the back with your cock, mate."

I lower my eyebrows. "Sorry, did you have sex or not?"

"I did not stab you in the back!" Blond Calum snaps, rounding on his fellow Calum. "I seized an opportunity!"

"Pause." Theo holds up both hands. "What happened?"

Neither Calum says anything, both scowling. Finally, Ginger Calum speaks.

"Last night in Monaco, we were out with two birds, and we were both trying to . . . well, you know."

"Do the ol' rudie nudie," Blond Calum provides.

"But then Calum took *both* of them home while I was in the toilet. And he didn't even *ask* me first."

"It was their idea!"

"I liked her!"

"You couldn't even decide which one you liked better."

"They're both lovely women!"

"You would have done the same thing if you hadn't been fucking munted," Blond Calum says. "I told you, you can't hold your champagne."

"Can I say something?" I interject before Ginger Calum can go off. "In my experience, group sex with a close friend can get a bit . . ." I deliberately don't glance at Theo, but I can feel her eyes on me. "Emotionally complicated."

Ginger Calum frowns. "What do you mean?"

"Calum," I say, "is it possible you're not upset about the girls, but that Calum had a threesome and didn't invite you?"

Both Calums are silent again. Theo is quiet too, arms crossed, swirling her wine around in its glass.

"Is that it?" Blond Calum asks Ginger Calum.

Ginger folds his arms. "We promised that if we ever did it, we would do it together."

"When we were fifteen, Calum! It didn't mean anything!"

"It meant something to me!"

Theo presses her knuckles to her lips. The Calums share a long moment of intimate eye contact. I share a long moment of intimate eye contact with the branzino on the table, reflecting on the week I've had.

"I didn't know it was that important to you," Blond says softly. "Honestly, I didn't think you'd mind."

Ginger says, "Well, it hurt my feelings."

"I'm sorry, mate. I was just—I was caught up in the moment, I guess. I wasn't thinking."

"In Calum's defense," Theo chimes in, leaning forward. It seems like the phrase *caught up in the moment* may have activated something in her. "I think we all probably made some question-able decisions in Monaco."

She looks directly at me. I clench my jaw.

"It was something in the air, wasn't it?" Blond Calum says.

"Definitely," Theo agrees. "I mean, Kit *kissed* me. Can you be-lieve that?"

My heart drops.

"No!" Ginger Calum shouts, instantly lit up with laughter. "Naughty lad!"

Blond Calum jumps in too, and I order myself to laugh along and take my ribbing, but my sinuses are beginning to sizzle, which can only mean one thing. Theo is watching my face closely over her glass.

"Yes, very funny, what was I thinking," I say, pushing my chair back. "Excuse me."

I leave the terrace as quickly and discreetly as I can, praying nothing happens until I'm out of sight. Through the dining room, down the stairs, out to the street—I don't stop until I'm on the gravel, where no one but an old man sitting by the road in a kitchen chair will see if my nose starts to bleed.

Most of the time I find it romantic and even somewhat sexy that, ever since that water taxi in Venice, my nose sometimes bleeds when I feel an especially powerful emotion. It's like being the victim of a curse in a Greek tragedy or Satine in *Moulin Rouge*. But Theo isn't stupid, and if this keeps happening, I'm going to give myself away even more than I already have.

I tip my head forward and lean against a garden wall, waiting for the feeling to subside. It works: When I swipe my thumb over my upper lip a few minutes later, it's dry.

I release a sigh and contemplate calling Maxine, or even Paloma, just to tell someone what I can't tell Theo.

There was a moment, a month after Theo and I settled into our apartment in Palm Springs, when things began to shift. I glanced up from my morning reading and I caught her staring at me with a private sort of tenderness in her eyes, and for the first time in a long time, I wondered if she loved me the way I loved her. If this was how she always looked at me when she didn't think I could see.

For all my regret, I felt that bud of hope last night too. It was only a breath, a quiet swish in through her nose and then a softening of her mouth, as if she might have pulled me deeper if I hadn't already been staggering away. But I'd be a fool to hold on to that after how she talked at the table just now, as if it was all a *joke* to her, as if—

The door behind me flies open.

"Kit!"

Theo charges out into the street, hair wild and amber in the windy dusk.

Her boots pound against the stones, and my first thought is, *good*. Theo should always walk with heavy footsteps. She should leave deep tracks wherever she goes so everyone can know she was there, like a historical event. Archaeologists should put tape around her footprints and study them with brushes.

She draws close and demands, "What are you doing out here?"

"Nothing," I tell her. "I just—I needed some air."

"We have an outdoor table," Theo points out.

"Different air."

"*Why?*"

Every day of this trip, I've wanted to tell her. And every day, I've told myself no. But I've been so close to her, and everything has been so beautiful, and I've swallowed so many words already. I've made meals of my heart. If she keeps pushing, I'm afraid I won't last.

"Theo, I know I fucked up last night, and you have every right to be angry," I say, closing my eyes, "but was that necessary? In front of the Calums?"

"I didn't think you'd mind," Theo says, "since you said it didn't mean anything to you."

And I hear myself say, "I meant it."

Rilke wrote, *Who hasn't sat trembling before his heart's curtain?*

"I meant it," I say again. "I'm sorry I did it, and I wish I could take it back, because I have loved being your friend again, but I have been going out of my mind trying to hide this from you, and then on the yacht, when I thought we might—when we almost—it was too *much*, Theo. And for one moment, I couldn't keep pretending that I haven't wanted to kiss you since you walked onto that bus in London." I take a breath. "But I will never do it again if you don't want me to."

Theo stares at me, lips parted, chest falling and rising. The trees above us shiver in the wind.

"I *knew* it," she says at last. I was braced for that, but not for the furious triumph in her voice. "You feel it too."

My heart thumps hard in my chest. She can't mean—

"Theo," I say, "what do you feel?"

"This—this—thing between us," Theo says. "This *problem*."

Ah.

Theo continues, beginning to pace.

"We've had sex in the past," she says, "and now we're not having sex anymore, but we're talking about sex all the time, and thinking about sex, and thinking about each other having sex with other people, and I thought that would help, but it's doing the opposite. Not fucking each other is making us both stupid. And I think we have to do something about it. Like, get it out of the way."

I put my hands on Theo's shoulders, stopping her pacing. A cloud of dust settles around her boots. Her face is inches from mine, eyes bright.

"What are you saying?" I ask her. "That we should have sex?"

"No, that would be too much like getting back together, and we're not getting back together," Theo says plainly. "That's out of the question. Right?"

"I—" I remove my hands. "I do see how having sex would feel like getting back together."

"Yeah," Theo says, nodding hard. "But we have to do something because—" She sucks in a breath and pins me under her steady gaze. "Because I do very much still want to fuck you. So, do you want to fuck me?"

"Theo," I say. "Worse than you can possibly imagine."

"Great," Theo says. Color bursts high in her cheeks, her breath short like she's about to take off running. I love her. "Then, I think—I think we should have sex, just . . . without actually having sex."

"Yes," I say immediately. "Or—I don't know what you mean, but yes. Tell me how."

"*Pretty Woman* rules. No kissing on the mouth." She thinks about it. "But no skin-to-skin contact from the waist down either."

I nod, feeling my pulse in my fingertips. In other places. I can do this. I *want* to. If this is the most I can have of her, I'll gladly take it. And if this is all she wants from me, it's easy to give.

"Anything else?"

"I don't think we should do it in our rooms," she adds. "That's—that seems like a slippery slope."

"Sure," I say, as if I wouldn't love to slip. "Are we allowed to make each other come?"

"It would be fucking encouraged."

"Then yes. Absolutely yes. When?"

Theo considers the question for all of one second.

"Now?"

— — —

We don't have a plan; we pick a direction and hike back into the vineyard trails. I have half an idea of finding a secluded clearing or rocky alcove or even a decent-sized gap in the grapevines, but then it appears. A groundskeeper's shed, carpeted with ivy like it's been abandoned for some time.

We exchange a look. The door handle is rusted through. It'd only take one good push.

"Good enough?" I ask Theo.

"Good enough," Theo declares, shoving me through the door.

Inside the shed, it's nearly dark. A strip of sunset through one high, narrow window reveals rickety shelves of plant pots and sacks of gravel and a cluttered worktable. It smells of mulch and wet granite, and I immediately bang my elbow into two different shelves.

"Ow, fuck," Theo swears, punting something noisy and metal

out of her way. I push aside a bundle of trellis wire, and Theo knocks over a rake, and then it's quiet. All the obstacles are gone. We're alone, in a pocket of privacy, nothing between us but air.

As my eyes adjust, I make out the lines of Theo's face. Her expression is focused, her jaw working like she's tonguing the sharp parts of her teeth.

God, I've missed her.

"I don't even know where to start," I confess.

She says, "Anywhere."

And we crash together.

At first, it's more a fight than anything. Two people who know each other's bodies better than anyone else ever could, with years to think about all the weak spots. She pushes the full strength of her body against mine, and I push back, kicking dirt and pebbles across the slab floor as we scramble for purchase. She pins my thigh between hers, and I bury my face in the side of her neck and take her weight. I thought it would be harder to do this without kissing, but hands go where mouths would—her fingertips at the corner of my mouth, my thumb at the center of her lower lip. We swear, and we groan, and we fit the way we always did.

When I would dream of holding her again, I imagined taking my time, undressing her inch by inch, a kiss for every night apart. That, I realize, was the wrong fucking idea. I should have pictured us starving and delirious from consuming everything but each other, no self-control left to take it by spoonfuls. I want to rip the cloth off the table and feast. I want her to open wide like an animal and take a bite out of me. Everything I've held back since London was only an apéritif.

I touch her lips and think of how she took the wine into her mouth in Bordeaux and sucked the taste of cherries from it. I bite a bruise into her neck the way I wanted to under the dance floor lights in San Sebastián, swipe my tongue over her collarbone like I wanted when I saw the cut of her neckline in Paris. The fingers that grazed my skin in the water near Saint-Jean-de-Luz, the rough voice from the next balcony in Barcelona, the capable hands from that kitchen in Nice—I let myself have it all, for now.

In one violent shove, Theo clears the worktable and throws me against it. Shears and trowels clatter to the floor. A pail clangs into the wall. My knees buckle, and then she's straddling me. She presses the heel of her hand to the ridge of my throat, her thumb digging into the vulnerable flesh under my chin, her breath crashing through her teeth. My hands claw across her back, grabbing fistfuls of her shirt and tugging it down her shoulders.

Her teeth nearly graze my bottom lip, and I remember this, the pause before a kiss, the way she liked to wait me out until I begged or closed the gap myself. I want it more than anything—a good kiss, an intentional one, the kind of kiss Theo deserves. Instead, I tilt my hips up to show her what she's done.

Her mouth skids sideways, close to my ear as she feels how devastatingly hard I am and swears.

"Is that for me?"

"*Yes,*" I tell her, and she grinds against me, giving me both the relief of friction and the agony of not enough. My voice is dark and crumbling, like butter burned into the bottom of the oven, but I can't keep the smoke trapped when she's easing the door open like this. I'll give her anything she asks. I'll turn the kitchen walls black. "You're—you make me like this. You always do."

"In Barcelona, that morning—" Her breath hitches, short nails nipping my neck. I slide a hand under her shirt to grip her hip for leverage. "Were you hard for me then too?"

"Yes," I say again. I'm moving with her now, or she's moving where my hand guides her, or maybe it's both. Maybe we've only ever been this one continuous, gasping thing. "I was dreaming of you."

"Tell me. Tell me what I did to you."

"We—we were in the bar, in Paris. On the bed. But I was

under you, and—" And she was kissing me, telling me she loved me. "—you were touching me. You had me in your hand."

Theo snaps her hips forward. "Can I tell you a secret?"

"Yes."

"I dreamed about you that night too."

I bite down a moan. "How? Where?"

"I dreamed we were at that last restaurant, and you ate me out on the table."

"Fuck."

We're moving faster, pressing harder. Theo kisses my pulse again and again, and a whine falls from my mouth each time. She's so *warm* at her center, warm and yielding but strong, the ridge of her zipper hard through the soft terry of my shorts.

"I can't—I've been thinking about it so much," Theo says. "About you. About you inside me. About me inside you. Do you think about it too?"

"All the time," I say, barely even knowing what's I'm saying, "all the fucking time, Theo, it's like I'm—I'm made of it, I've wanted you so much."

"Ah, fuck—" A desperate, cliff's edge sound, half groan and half whimper. I feel her hand between us, her fingertips dipping beneath the waistband of her shorts. "Can I—?"

It's nearly over for me then, just from the way she asks. I bite my lip so hard I taste sweet metal.

"Yes, please, touch yourself."

Her hand plunges, and I feel the movement of her knuckles against me when her fingers find their place, listen to her sigh of relief and the sigh after, the one that's pure, renewed need. She'll be close soon. I remember how she unfolds, where the creases are.

"Fuck, thank you," she says, hips and fingers moving, so wet I can *hear it.* "You can too."

"Don't need to," I admit, getting closer, closer, so close just from her sounds and the incredible realization of how badly she's wanted this. Wanted me. God, all this time and she *wants me,* and I get to have her like this. "Just—just keep doing what you're doing."

"Tell me again," she gasps. "Say it."

"I want you, Theo, I want you, I want you, please, please, please, I—"

—*love you.*

By some divine mercy, Theo comes before the words do. I'm right behind her, and she locks her arms around my neck until it's done washing through me, making soft hums of approval into my hair. I can't believe it. She's finished me without touching me before, but not like this—in *minutes,* without even a kiss on the mouth.

She kisses my chin, just below my lower lip, and starts to laugh.

"What's *my* God in French again?" she asks.

My voice breaks when I answer, "Mon Dieu."

"Mon Dieu, Kit, when's the last time you creamed dans your pantalons?"

I groan and try to push her off, but she resists, squeezing my neck tighter, and I find myself unwilling to convince her otherwise.

"There is absolutely no reason for your French to still be so horrible," I say.

When Theo pulls back, a beam of early moonlight falls across her face and into her eyes. She's so gorgeous like this, laughing and satisfied. I stroke her jaw with the side of my thumb and tell myself to be satisfied with this too. If this is all there ever is with us, I can make it enough. I can learn how to touch her without telling her all the rest.

(Rilke wrote, *How will I keep my soul from touching yours?*)

PISA

PAIRS WELL WITH:

Souvenir leaning bottle of Tower of Pisa
hazelnut liqueur, torta di ceci

PISA

"You said you checked the radiator?"

"That I did."

"And the engine block?"

"Not my first time, love," Orla says. She squints under her safari hat, its drawstring flapping in the Tuscan wind. "The head gasket looks alright too, so we've not blown it."

Theo puts her hands on her hips and frowns very seriously.

We were half an hour out of Manarola when the bus started making a distressing kicked-can noise. Fabrizio came over the speakers to say it was nothing to worry about, never mind all the smoke, but in the spirit of curiosity did anyone happen to know anything about Volkswagen engines? And now Theo's standing with Orla on the side of an Italian motorway, staring into the bus's engine compartment as trucks whip past.

Fabrizio and I are watching from the steps of the bus, sweating through our shirts.

"Do you know, it is not far from here where Genoa defeated Pisa in the Battle of Meloria to begin the decline of the Republic of Pisa," Fabrizio tells me, sounding like he's succumbing to heatstroke. "Maybe Pisa does not want visitors from the northern coast. Maybe they send to us un piccolo fantasma."

"Un piccolo fantasma," I repeat. "A little ghost?"

"Sì, bene," Fabrizio says, stroking my cheek tenderly.

I'm fighting my own Battle of Meloria, which is my desire to help Theo versus the memory of her erotically throttling me in a garden shed last night. The least helpful thing I could be doing is thinking about it happening again. But she's holding a wrench and wearing worn-in jeans, and my maritime empire is crumbling.

"You smelled that, though, didn't you?" Theo asks Orla. "The smoke was sweet. That's definitely coolant." She rubs at her jaw thoughtfully, leaving a streak of engine grease behind. "Do you have a cylinder compression tester?"

Whatever that means, Orla does have one. Theo rigs it up, Orla climbs aboard to turn over the engine, and after a minute of clunking and scowling at some kind of meter, Theo shouts, "I was right! The head bolts are loose!"

Apparently this is an easy fix, because Orla is jolly as she pulls out her toolbox. I watch, feeling wobbly and iridescent as Theo digs through it with the offhanded confidence of a self-taught mechanic. How long has she known how to do this?

"Kit!" she calls out. "Can you give me a hand?"

"You're up, love," Orla says, slapping my hand to tag herself out. She sits beside Fabrizio and gives me an indiscrete wink, and I regret telling her how I feel about Theo when we were strolling those lavender fields in Sault.

Theo smiles as I approach, glistening with sweat and flushing vigorously under her freckles. I try not to remember her weight in my lap.

"Do you have a sketchbook on you?"

We need to tighten all twelve head bolts on the cylinder, she tells me, which I'm sure means something. This has to be done in a very specific sequence, one Theo has memorized from having the same problem with her own Volkswagen bus but can't explain without drawing a labeled diagram. We're going to take turns tightening the bolts and reading the sequence out loud, to make sure she doesn't skip any steps.

"Oh, and it's gonna get greasy," Theo says, eyeing my linen. "You might want to, you know."

To finish her sentence, she peels her shirt off and tucks it into the back pocket of her jeans, safe from stains. All the powerful inches of her swimmer's build are now concealed by only a skin-tight undershirt.

"Oh, sure," I say, going out of my mind.

I strip my shirt off and throw it to Orla, who waves it over her head like a scarf at a football match. Fabrizio applauds. I happen to know that Theo and I are *both* nice to look at topless, and I'm pleased to feel Theo's gaze settle on my shoulders.

"I do love these Tuscan views, don't you, Fabs?" Orla says to Fabrizio.

"Sì," Fabrizio says, eyeing us with drowsy delight.

With Fabrizio and Orla's encouragement—half sincere cheering and half suggestive wolf calls—we fix the engine. Theo explains the torque wrench to me and guides my hands on it, showing me the precise amount of muscle to apply. It's hard, and it's sweltering, and Theo's skin is so close to mine, and this new, resolute, commanding side of her is making me lightheaded, but it also feels natural, somehow. After last night, I was afraid she might pull away, but there's an ease here. She trusts me to help her. I trust her to let me.

When we're done and Orla cranks the engine, a cheer goes up inside the bus. Theo stomps her feet and slaps a victorious hand against my chest. If everything else was different, this is when I would kiss her.

Instead, I put my hand over hers and lift it away gently, squeezing once before I let go.

We roll on to Pisa.

— — —

French buttercream is a very particular color. Italian and Swiss buttercreams have that pure gloss of egg-white meringue, but French buttercream doesn't begin with egg whites. It begins with yolks, beaten until ribbon smooth, then whisked with hot sugar syrup to make pâte à bombe before the butter goes in. When it's finished, it should look richer than its sisters, a shade of white-gold that means it was one degree more difficult.

I'd describe the Tower of Pisa's color in afternoon light as French buttercream. In pictures it seems to stand alone, but in real life, it's in a green square with a matching cathedral, baptistery, and camposanto. They make a neat set. Fabrizio says this is called the Piazza dei Miracoli—the Square of Miracles.

Before the group splits, Fabrizio lines us up so he can take the classic Leaning Tower photo for each of us. I hang back with Theo to watch. Lars poses as if he's holding the campanile in a gelato cone; both Calums pretend to fuck it.

"Don't you want one?" I ask Theo.

"Nah."

For someone so certain of her hotness, Theo has historically been camera shy. I see the way she's watching, though, and I realize that at all these sights we've visited, I've never once seen her take a photo of herself.

"You're not too cool to do tourist things, you know."

Theo lowers her sunglasses. "I could say the same to you."

"Oh, you think I can't be uncool? Because I can."

"Won't they revoke your French passport?"

"Let's find out."

I jump up onto one of the stone stanchions keeping visitors off the lawn and do all the most cliché, embarrassing tower-tourist poses—holding it up, kicking it over, back-to-back lean—until Theo stops taking pictures and starts begging me to stop, screaming with mortified laughter. It works, though. When I tell her she has to do one now, she laughs and sighs and says, "Fine."

I line up the shot: Theo with grease-smudged hands in front of an 850-year-old tower, both of them tall and gorgeous and beaming.

"Oh, wow," she says when I show her the photo. "I actually really like this one."

"Yeah?"

She touches the back of my hand as she passes the phone back. "Yeah."

Theo's been like this about photos since we were eleven, when she still went to premieres for her sisters' projects. It was the big one, the Willem Dafoe movie that both Sloane and Este were in, and Theo wore a blue suit with a flower-print tie. Flowers for Flowerday, she said.

It never occurred to me that it would matter to anyone. It didn't occur to Theo either, and certainly not to her parents, who never cared when Theo asked for haircuts and clothes meant for boys. That was just how Theo had always been. But for some reason it mattered to red-carpet reporters, who wrote breathless articles about how heartwarming and progressive it was for two famous people to let their daughter wear a suit to an event, and what an inspiring gender hero Theo was. They made it into a whole thing. *Diversity win! Child wears clothes.*

Tabloids didn't exist in Theo's household, but if one comes from a famous family, one might look oneself up on one's best friend's family computer eventually. We were thirteen. She stopped posing for pictures after that, and she didn't get a haircut for years.

I've always thought Theo could pull off anything she wanted. I liked her just as much in slip dresses and lip gloss as I did in T-shirts and cotton boxers, and I didn't care if she chose to leave one for the other. But sometimes, when she leaned in to the mirror to put on lipstick or tugged the front of her shirt away from her chest, I would see her eyes go somewhere else, like she wasn't quite inside the body she was dressing up.

In her photo with the tower, I see someone filling up their body all the way to the skin. It's in the loose set of her shoulders under her shirt, her broad stance, the jut of her chin, her short hair flying across her forehead in wild, boyish waves.

"I love your hair this length," I tell her as we walk toward the cathedral. "It's so good on you."

"I like it too," she says, readying her ticket for the guard. Her expression is soft, inquiring. "I feel like I finally look like myself, you know?"

We walk into the cathedral, between huge Corinthian columns topped with acanthus leaves and through Romanesque arches with alternating black and white stripes of marble. Above the central nave is a gilded ceiling, each ornate coffer decorated with flowers and faces of angels. We split at the cross point of the nave and the transept, where the dome is painted with the Virgin Mary gliding toward heaven in a whirlpool of golden clouds.

When I moved to Paris, Dad told me to guard my wonder. He said that the danger of living in a place of dreams is that it can become ordinary. His exact words were, *Novelty is half of sublimity,* the kind of thing that once made me believe he was a genius and now makes me picture Theo doing a jerk-off hand gesture. Still, somewhere during the long hours at work making the same gelée for three months straight, I lost my appetite for taking in the view on my way home. I stopped noticing all the beauty that once astonished me when I read about it in books.

I was full of wonder when I was studying art. The quality that made me choose Renaissance artists as my concentration so I could write obsessive pages about their attention to human emotion and bodies, the part of me so infatuated with the Baroque that Theo made me put a dollar in a jar every time I brought up Bernini—it left me not long after Theo, but much more quietly. I barely noticed until Bordeaux, when I stepped off the bus at the château and felt wonder return like an old friend. Every stop since, I've slowly unfolded, opening to it again.

Here at the apse of the cathedral, I remember how it felt to be eighteen and falling in love with a history of art course catalog. I look at the massive oil paintings and recite pigments of the Renaissance palette, azurite and vermilion, verdigris and gamboge.

I remember when I learned their names, how I imagined being some sixteenth-century cheese maker seeing paint give off light for the first time. I don't know if it's Italy or Theo bringing it all back, but I'm so thankful to both.

I find Theo by a golden casket, reading something on her phone.

"I'm looking this guy up," Theo says, jerking her chin toward the coffin. "It's Saint Ranieri, patron saint of Pisa. I feel like we could be friends. It says, 'He was a traveling musician who played all night and slept all day.'"

I smile, enjoying the way her mind works, and lean in to read the screen. "'His life revolved around food, drink, and partying.' I've slept with this Italian boy before."

She scrolls down. "Oh, but then he joins a monastery and gives away all his possessions. But look, one of his miracles is multiplying bread. You'd love that."

"Depends on the bread. Let's do the camposanto next."

We walk on to the long cemetery spanning the piazza's entire north side. I follow Theo through the arches and thousands of meters of frescos, still thinking of my imaginary cheese maker and those impossible, luminous oil-mixed paints he would have never seen before. They probably looked to him the way Theo looks to me now.

Beside the camposanto is the round baptistery, its domed roof half terracotta tiles and half brown and gray sheets of lead. I read once that the exterior was finished nearly two centuries after it was begun, and it shows in the way the structure literally evolves upward in complexity, starting with simple Byzantine columns and ending in ornate, pointed Gothic arches up top. Inside, it's almost all empty white-gray marble except for the font at the center of the floor and the sculpted pulpit over it. The rest is open, encircled by two tiers of massive arches holding up a high, curved ceiling.

"Kit, look at this," Theo says, pointing to a sign about the mathematics of the baptistery's roof. "What do you think it means by 'acoustically perfect'?"

Before I can guess, a badged guard steps away from her station and declares, "*Silenzio.*"

Theo's eyes widen as the murmur of visitors drops off into silence. From beneath one of the tall arches, we watch the guard walk to the font, directly under the highest point of the ceiling. And then she begins to sing.

At first, she holds one long, clear tone, an open *ah* that unfurls to the yawning ceiling and expands to fill it. Then she sings a second, lower note, but the first note still hangs in the air, resonating among the marble walls as if she's still holding it. She sings a third, higher note. The echoes layer over one another, so loud and rich it's as if a choir of ghosts is in the loggia harmonizing with her. But it's only her own voice lasting on and on, over and over, harmonizing with itself.

An expression of delighted awe dawns on Theo's face, and in it I see layer after layer, old self after intermediate self after current self, the Theo I met as a child and the Theo I got to call mine and the Theo who fills her own body. They're all here, hanging in the air, harmonizing with one another. Maybe they're always here. Maybe she feels so familiar and so new to me now because I'd heard the beginning note but not the completed chord. I knew her before her arches had points, before the paint to finish her had been invented.

What a wonder, what a miracle: somehow, more of her.

— — —

We have tickets to the top of the tower, but we're too heat-drowsy to climb the stairs. Instead, we buy gelato from one of the shops fringing the piazza and admire the tower from the cathedral steps below.

Theo tips her head to see all the way to the top of the campanile, all the repeating Romanesque arches making a pattern of half-moons like rows of pastries from this angle. She spoons amarena gelato into her mouth and hums.

"I feel better than I expected to, about last night," she says casually.

My spoon stops in my cup of fior di latte. I wasn't expecting us to talk about it. My mouth slips sideways into what I hope is gentle interest and not obvious, profound relief.

"What were you expecting?"

"I don't know. I guess I thought I'd be angrier?" She exhales a laugh. "At myself, that I did it, or at you, for making me want to. But I feel . . . good. Relieved, even. I think I'm glad we did it."

"That's good. That's really good, because I . . ." I should hold back. I shouldn't ask for more. But I think I might die if that was the last time she touched me. "I would love to keep doing it."

A pause. Theo stabs her spoon into the lump of gelato.

"Yeah."

"Yeah?"

"Yeah, fuck it, why not?" She looks off into the distance where gold hills meet a big blue sky, a dangerous, punch-drunk edge to her voice that makes my heart pound. "It's like . . . nothing in this life matters except what you want, and what feels good. Right? Taste everything, fuck how you like, nothing else matters. You know what I mean?"

"Of course," I say. "I'm French. We invented that."

"Exactly," Theo says. She angles her face toward me. "But there's one thing I should tell you if we're going to be hooking up."

I brace for a catch, a caveat. "I'm listening."

"So," Theo begins, "I don't know about you, but after we broke up, I sort of wasn't sure who I was anymore."

I think of my own first year after Theo, drowning myself in

poetry and pastry, pouring all my love into person after person and still waking up full afterward, wondering if the problem had always been me.

I say, "Sure."

Theo nods. "So, I went back to the beginning of me. Like, square one. And I started going through everything and figuring out what went where. And one of the main things I found is that—" A pause, a pinch of contemplation between the brows. "I think gender has always been more complicated for me than I wanted to admit."

Oh. *Oh.*

"I don't necessarily see myself as any particular, static thing," Theo goes on, "but if I have to pick, nonbinary is the closest. I just know I'm a lot of stuff, but one thing I'm not is a woman. Does that make sense?"

Truthfully, it wouldn't matter if it made sense. I would accept anything about Theo even if it didn't agree with any laws of this world or the next. But more importantly, it *does.* It's not so much a revelation as an explanation of something I've never been able to put into words about Theo, like the day I learned what a superbloom was.

"That might make more sense than anything you've ever said to me," I say. Theo laughs like I might be joking, but I don't break eye contact. "Really. Of course that's you. That's been you forever."

Theo blinks. "You think so?"

"Theo, you're—do you know how big you are?"

"Yes, I'm five-ten."

"Don't ruin it, I'm being sincere," I tease, bumping my knuckles against Theo's shoulder. "You're . . . expansive. You take up space. You make the world bigger to fit you. So, no, I'm not surprised you can't fit inside one idea of gender."

"That's—that's really fucking kind of you to say," Theo says, voice soft but fierce, knees pulled up to chin level. "But—yeah, I don't always tell everyone I hook up with, but if it's going to be a regular thing, it feels important that you know. And also, I just wanted to tell you."

A regular thing.

"I'm happy to know," I say, meaning it. Then I voice the worry that's been at the back of my mind for a minute now. "Can I ask—have I been using the wrong pronouns?"

"Ugh." Theo sighs, forehead to knees. "Not exactly? I guess I'm still sort of soft launching. I've been *they* to all my friends for three years, but I haven't fully retired *she* yet, because sometimes I can't avoid it. It doesn't feel like something I want to explain to my parents, and I'd rather die than see some stupid head-line about *Sloane Flowerday's Sister, Nonbinary Queen!* I don't want to have to correct every stranger who calls me a lady or ma-demoiselle or señorita. And at work, it would just be—I mean, hopeless. So it's like, if I keep *she* on the table for now, those things don't feel so shitty. I can frame it in my head in a way that doesn't hurt. Like pitching a really wonderful, complex, grippy Nebbiolo to a table and watching them order the house red be-cause it's familiar and they don't have to think about it. It's not *technically* wrong, but . . ."

"You wish they would have tried."

"I just think it'd give them a richer experience," Theo says, smirking a little. "But, anyway, the people who know me best say, 'That's Theo, they're my friend.' And I'd like that to include you."

My hand drifts reflexively to my chest, over my heart.

"That's Theo. They're my friend," I try. "Yeah, it feels so much better that way. Meaty."

They begin to grimace, but they can't hide their laugh.

"Are you giving notes? On the mouthfeel of my pronouns?"

"Sure, yeah," I say, laughing too. "Very nice vintage. Strong finish. Notes of dressing up as Indiana Jones for Halloween in fifth grade."

"At least people knew what I was supposed to be. Everyone thought you were Abraham Lincoln in a dress."

"How could I know that nobody would recognize Gustav Klimt? I was eleven!"

"Where did your mom even find a child-sized druid gown?"

"She sewed it herself," I say, still laughing. "God, sometimes I worry she was *too* supportive."

"She would have loved our Sonny and Cher."

"Yeah," I agree, softening. "That was a good night."

A tour group streams out of the tower and passes us in a swish of sundress skirts and Bermuda shorts. We watch them in comfortable silence, listening to their guide recite the history of the campanile in Mandarin until they're absorbed into the rest of the tourists filing through the square.

"I kind of love that we were both in drag the first time we slept together," Theo says, returning to me. "Sex is better when the person you're with really understands you, and understands how to look at you."

I consider that.

"For what it's worth . . ." I search for the right way to phrase it. "You know how attraction to men feels different from attraction to women? It has a different flavor, or comes from a different place."

Theo nods; we've talked about this many times before. "Yeah."

"Being . . . attracted to you," I say, putting it mildly, "that has always come from another place completely. Or, maybe everywhere at the same time. But it's never been like one or the other."

"I like that," they say.

Sun flashes off the gold in Theo's eyes. The moment settles.

"So . . ." I say. "A regular thing?"

Theo grins. They reach out and briefly tangle our grease-smudged fingers, then jump to their feet. It's almost time to meet Fabrizio.

"Yeah," Theo says. "But I did the work last time."

"Oh, the *work*?"

"Your turn to make a move." They take two steps backward, still grinning, bouncing on their heels. "I'll be waiting."

FLORENCE

PAIRS WELL WITH:

Campari spritz,
cornetti alla marmellata di albicocche

FLORENCE

There is perhaps nothing as true, as enduring, as fitting a tribute to the Renaissance as being so horny you could die on the streets of Florence.

Filippo Lippi was a Carmelite monk when he fell for the nun who sat for his paintings of the Madonna. Botticelli yearned so passionately for his muse, Simonetta, that he painted her as Venus ten years after her death. Donatello was almost certainly unlacing his doppietto for Brunelleschi. Da Vinci wanted to hate-fuck Michelangelo, while Michelangelo was so obsessed with the young Tommaso Cavalieri that he sculpted himself in submission between the nude lord's legs and called it *Victory*. Raphael essentially died of exhaustion from too much painting and fucking.

And I, I am standing on the black stones outside a caffetteria, watching Theo eat pastry.

They're wearing those tan work pants, the ones that make them look like they spend all day working a steam-powered letterpress. Their shirt tugs at the broadest points of their shoulders and nips in at the waist. As they bite off the corner of a cornetto, their brows go down and then up, from investigative to pleased.

We're traveling with a third now: the mutual understanding that sex will happen again. That I get to choose when, and how. Every moment is syrup-sticky with intent and anticipation, sitting heavy on my palate, tasting like *the* moment.

I have a plan, though. I was up late in my little Florentine hostel bed designing the right moment, picking the right place, and we won't reach it for another two hours, so I have to wait. Theo deserves it.

I force myself to stare at the paper cups of coffee Theo put in my hands. Both are dark, one black, the other a shade lighter. Theo finishes shoving euros into their hip pack and takes the darker coffee from me, cornetto flakes swirling through the hot morning air.

As we set off through a narrow alley toward the Duomo, I ask, "You take your coffee black now?"

"Ever since I started having coffee with my somm every day," Theo says. "This is how he takes it. I have a theory it's the source of all his power."

"The Somm . . . is it still the same guy? The one with the pony-tail and the tattoo of a rat smoking a cigar, and the—"

"The leather dusters, yeah."

"Same pastry chef as well?" I ask. I liked the old one.

"Nah, there's a new guy, but he's not as good," Theo says. "Your order's still the same, right? Little cream big sugar?"

I smile. It's an old joke, something I mumbled once when I was too tired for English, the kind of thing that sticks.

"Little cream big sugar," I confirm. Theo's mouth angles into a satisfied smirk. They take another bite of cornetto, revealing an orange jam at its buttery center. "What's the filling?"

"Albicocca," they say in a muffled Super Mario Italian accent. They swallow and translate, "Apricot."

"Black coffee *and* they know Italian? Wow, the Bourdainifi-cation of Theo Flowerday," I say, failing to pretend this doesn't turn me on. I would fuck Anthony Bourdain at any stage of his life and we both know it.

"Yes, like Tony I've picked up all the food words and swears from working in fine dining. Vaffanculo!" A passing Italian teenager whips around. "Not you! Scusa!"

We turn onto another tight street, buildings with the same golden-brown walls and green shutters as the last one and the ones before that. Tourists and taxis and men on scooters crowd the road and the high, cobbly sidewalks, but what dominates the view is the massive structure looming ahead at the street's opening, the side of a cathedral so broad and tall it eclipses the world beyond. A sliver of brick dome peeks out like a red crescent moon.

Theo holds up their pastry, matching its crescent shape to the dome.

"What's the difference between this and a croissant?"

"A cornetto has eggs in the dough," I say. "Croissant dough is all about the butter. That's why croissants are flakier, and a cornetto's texture is more like—"

"A brioche," Theo notes.

"Right," I say, smiling. Maxine did say they'd been un bon étudiant. "Can I try? I've heard apricots are sweeter in Italy."

Theo passes the cornetto to me, and I taste, letting the compote touch every part of my tongue.

"They *are* sweeter," I say. Theo's looking at me with amusement. "What?"

They untuck their sunglasses from their shirt pocket and slide them on.

"You remember what you were doing in that dream I told you about?"

The dream about me eating them out on a restaurant table in Barcelona? I'd sooner forget how to make a baguette.

"Yes."

"Well, in my dream, you ate an apricot too."

Theo grins and takes off running toward the piazza.

When I've pulled myself together enough to catch up, they're standing before the cathedral with their head craned back. Their grin has spread into the silent, incredulous laugh usually reserved for a particularly good stunt in a Fast & Furious movie.

"This might be the coolest thing I've ever seen," they say.

When you spend four years studying Renaissance art and architecture with a special focus on southern Europe, you inevitably find yourself in romantic love with the Duomo di Firenze—the Cattedrale di Santa Maria del Fiore, the Florence Cathedral, the Duomo. I've dreamed of standing here. I knew, intellectually, that it would be nearly three times the height of Notre-Dame and one and a half times the size. I've read about every elaborate detail, from the architecture Brunelleschi invented to make the dome physically possible to the hundreds of thousands of intricate green, pink, and white marble panels placed by hand to adorn the exterior. And still, it shocks me.

It reminds me of a cake. Gum-paste details for the window tracery, sugar lace for the foliage over the portals, precise layers of vanilla and raspberry and pistachio joconde for the polychrome marble. Like the Tower of Pisa, I can only understand the Duomo in terms of dessert.

"I can't believe people made this," I exhale. "I can't believe I get to see it."

Theo turns to me.

"Haven't you—I thought you'd already been to Italy?"

"Only Venice."

"Oh. So, the rest of the places on the tour will be new to us both?"

I forgot they don't know.

"They've all been new to me, except Paris, and I went to Nice once when I was five," I say. "We were supposed to go to these places together. It felt wrong to go without you."

Theo bites their lip, eyes hidden behind dark glasses. I think of the sudden hardness of their voice in Paris, when they said they could've gone without me. I believed them then, but now—je ne sais pas.

Finally, they say, "Do you wanna see something interesting?"

"Hard to imagine anything more interesting than what I'm looking at right now."

"What about four people sharing one cone of gelato?"

I blink. "What?"

I follow their gaze to a gelato stand where the Calums, Dakota, and Montana are passing around a single runny cone of stracciatella.

"Ooh." I frown approvingly as Ginger Calum tongues down the cone, then holds it out to Montana to give her a taste. "They're in the Italian spirit."

"I wouldn't do that with someone unless I was fucking them," Theo says. "The two girls they were talking about, the ones who had a threesome with Blond Calum . . . do you think they meant Dakota and Montana?"

Dakota licks a streak of chocolate off Blond Calum's hand, and I have to hold my applause. Sluts forever. "Good for them, then. Looks like they're figuring it out."

"Maybe they settled the score," Theo suggests. "Maybe we're not the only ones who got some action in Cinque Terre."

We find Fabrizio at our meeting point in the piazza, arguing with another guide in vehement Italian over the best spot in front of the cathedral. He finishes with fire in his eyes and a *fuck off* gesture of his hand under his chin, but he gets the spot he wanted, which instantly puts him back in a good mood.

"Buongiorno, amici!" he shouts, clapping his hands. "We will begin our walking tour of Firenze? Sì? I think today, because we have many lovers in our group"—I swear his eyes land mischievously on mine—"I want to take you on a special tour of the *passion* of Florentine history. The secret affairs, the betrayals, the great loves, the scandals. What do you think? Yes? Andiamo!"

We begin at the cathedral, Fabrizio's voice smooth as he explains every intentional panel and detail, the contrasting stripes of red marble from Siena, green from Prato, white from Carrara.

He points up to where a scorned stonemason secretly mounted a bull's head with its horns pointing at a tailoring shop owned by his lover's husband. Then he ushers us away to Palazzo Pazzi, a rugged palace once home to the powerful Pazzi family, who conspired to stab the even more powerful Medici princes to death at the altar of the Duomo in the middle of Easter Sunday mass. On its exterior is a small door around chest level, a wine window left over from the plague days, which Theo finds so delightful they stay behind to get a good photo for the Somm.

The next stop is—whoa.

The old alleys are so close and gnarled, Piazza della Signoria seems to open wide out of nowhere. It sprawls in a lake of black stone, clusters of tourists swirling like schools of fish. Directly ahead, water erupts from a majestic white marble fountain embellished with bronze figures of fauns and satyrs, a huge, powerful sculpture of a nude man borne on a shell-shaped chariot at its center.

"The Fountain of Neptune!" Fabrizio announces with a flourish.

I've beheld the cheeks of a thousand nude sculptures, and yet I swear this is an extraordinarily hot rendition of Neptune. Maybe it's the ambient horniness, but the full, muscular ass on this Neptune is—

"Bodacious," Theo pants, breathless from running to catch up. "That ass is bodacious."

I turn to see Theo flushed with exertion, shadows of perspiration beginning to show through their shirt. Ambient horniness, buongiorno.

"Sì, very sexy!" Fabrizio says. "So sexy, the sculptor eventually denounces this Neptune and his other nude sculptures for leading people to sin."

"Is that true?" I ask.

"More or less," Fabrizio says with a wink.

At a bronze statue of a man on horseback, Fabrizio tells us

Grand Duke Cosimo I de' Medici was so enraged when his chamberlain leaked his plans to marry his mistress that he stabbed him through the heart with a trophy boar spear in the middle of the Palazzo Pitti. We study the sculptures in the Loggia dei Lanzi: Giambologna's iconic *Sabine Woman* with her supple, achingly lifelike flesh; a bronze Perseus with the severed head of Medusa so difficult to cast that the goldsmith desperately threw his own kitchen chairs and pans into the furnace for fuel. We learn about Cosimo's slutty son Francesco in the courtyard of Palazzo Vecchio, frescoed with Austrian landscapes when he married Joanna, archduchess of Austria—something to keep her company while her husband fucked the mistress he'd installed in a palace nearby.

Past the Uffizi Gallery, we cross the Arno via Ponte Vecchio, where men of the Renaissance furtively fucked in back rooms of butcher shops. We visit the palace of Bianca Cappello, the mistress Francesco loved so much he would've had his Austrian bride murdered, only for his brother to (allegedly) poison them both. Inside Palazzo Pitti, where most of the Medici family's art collection still hangs, we see paintings by Lippi and Raphael, and Fabrizio tells us how insatiable desire ruined them both.

It's all so rich, so warm, so flavorful, that when tour ends at the Boboli Gardens, I feel glutted on Florence. I'm sweating, barely keeping ahold of myself. Theo is pink and shining in the heat. We're nearly to the place I planned for us. *This,* finally, is the moment.

"Well," Theo says. Fabrizio has dismissed us for the afternoon, leaving us beside a leafy pond with a nude statue of the sea god at its center. "Right back where we started. Sexy Neptune."

I can't wait any longer.

"Can I show you something?"

— —— —

I take us away through winding tunnels of holm oak to a place tucked in the shadow of the palace at the garden's north corner.

It's quiet and empty, so far out of the way that no other tourists have bothered to find it.

"Holy shit," Theo says as we draw close, taking off their sunglasses. "What is that?"

"The Buontalenti Grotto."

It's a strange, fantastical piece of architecture, its facade half pillared marble and half dripping, flowering concrete stalactites. If a villa could be swallowed whole by enchanted seaweed, or the earth could come alive and take back its sediment, it might look like this.

"I read about it once," I say. "Francesco Medici commissioned this one."

"No way, Bianca Cappello's slutty boyfriend?" Theo says. "The original nepo baby?"

"The very slut," I say, laughing. "Come on."

I pull them through the unlatched gate and into the first chamber, where the walls are sculpted like a natural cave, spongy coral and stalagmites and flowering branches bubbling toward the vaulted ceiling. Frescos of nature flow from the open skylight into a second, deeper room with a statue of Paris and Helen in the throes.

"Did Francesco ever sneak Bianca in here to fool around?" Theo asks.

"Oh, almost definitely."

The third and deepest room of the grotto is round, with painted birds flitting through vines and roses and irises. Its centerpiece is a marble fountain of Venus bathing, sculpted by Giambologna. Like all his women, this Venus was chiseled with pure rapture, the curves of her body fluid and sensuous. If Francesco and Bianca fucked in any of these rooms, it was here.

Theo drifts away to begin a loop around the room's perimeter, examining the leaves on the walls.

"You know," they say, "I've gotten the impression that the Florentines fuck severely."

I move in the opposite direction, slipping past Theo near one of the mosaic niches.

"That's my favorite thing about Renaissance art," I say. "It's really about sex."

"Even when it's about Jesus?"

"*Especially* when it's about Jesus. What better excuse to hang pictures of naked men around your palazzo?" I say. "I think the Renaissance came out of Florence *because* of sex. Everyone was having it, or wanting it, or trying not to want it so they could be a friar, and it was soaking into everything. It's the perfect environment for an artistic awakening. Sex is in every beautiful thing that's ever happened, and every beautiful thing can become sex."

Theo laughs. "You ever wonder if maybe you take sex too seriously?"

"Honestly, no, I have never wondered if I'm wrong to accept the miracle of tender humanity into my heart," I say, only half joking.

"The fucking Kierkegaard of cock over here," Theo replies.

We circle each other around the room, edging closer to the fountain with each pass.

"What is sex to you, then?" I ask.

"It's . . . physical," Theo says, eyes tracing Venus's breasts. "It's about being in your body, and strength, and stamina, and instinct, and, well, it's kind of about winning."

"You just described sports," I point out, amused.

"Okay, fine, it's more than that. It's like . . . eating a great meal. Short-term pleasure. It's fun and exciting, one of the best ways to spend an hour, maybe you try something new and find out if you like it, and one day you look back and remember how good it tasted. But it doesn't have to be anything deeper."

We pass each other again, face-to-face for a moment.

"Is that really what you think?"

Sweat gleams in the hollow of their throat, and I want them

so much, I'd gather it on my fingers and let them watch me suck
it off. I would lap it up like a dog.

"Well—" Theo says, moving, swallowing. "Maybe it's more
like cooking a good meal. Curiosity, creativity."

"Patience."

"Sometimes."

"All the time."

We're almost to Venus, the space between us nearly closed.

"Sometimes it's just butter and a hot pan," Theo says, voice
hushed. "Or a—a peach and a really sharp knife."

They face me at the fountain's pedestal, turning their back
on the goddess of love.

"I don't know," I say. "What good is a knife if the peach isn't
ripe?"

"What is that, a poem?"

"Sure. It's about impatience."

"I told you—"

"You told me you would show me," I say. Without looking
away from Theo's face, I take hold of their wrists at their sides.
"So, show me."

My grip is light enough that they could break away if they
chose. I wait for them to demonstrate they want this—to lean
forward, to part their lips. Then, I pull gently away.

They watch, brow pinched in confusion, as I lift one of their
wrists to my mouth and deliberately, slowly press a soft kiss to
the inside. For a moment, they go still, their eyes widening. And
then they're laughing and pushing forward, grasping for my
cheek with their fingertips, reaching out with their other hand.
Still, I don't let them touch me.

I don't want to rush. I want to take care, to touch them how
they deserve to be touched.

I direct their hands behind their back, onto the rim of the
fountain. Like this, holding their palms down against the marble, my body brackets theirs. Another inch and our chests would

be flush, our hips aligned, so I make sure to let neither happen when I kiss their neck. Theo sucks in a sharp breath and releases it as another laugh.

They keep laughing as I drag kisses up their neck and across their jaw, to their cheek and temple. Their skin is warm and salty under my lips, tinged with that essentially Theo scent of bitter orange leaves and spice. Soon, they're not laughing anymore.

"Come *on*." Their body strains forward, but I hold myself back, even when they try stomping on my foot.

"Patience," I remind them.

Theo groans, but they don't stomp on my foot again.

I switch to the other side of their neck and treat it the same way, and Theo's grunts and huffs of frustration begin to melt into sighs. I kiss and tease and swipe my tongue until their body goes slack, until I realize they've stopped making any sounds at all.

When I pull back to look at them, there's tension in their brow and the corners of their mouth, the kind I know from trying not to let my own face show what I feel. That's how it looks to be overwhelmed by the enormity of a feeling, afraid it's going to burst out before it's meant to.

My eyes speak for me. *What are you hiding?*

Theirs respond, *Please don't ask.*

Part of me wants to keep teasing until they crack. But so much more of me wants to be sweet. I'd want them to show mercy to me.

"Same rules?" I ask, with my voice this time.

Theo nods. "Same rules."

"Tell me if anything is too much."

I tug on their wrist to turn them around and set their hands on the fountain again, their back to me, their face turned toward Venus so I can't see it. At last, I press my body flush with theirs, chest to back, hips to ass, legs tangling. I nose under their collar and bite at their shoulder until they moan and tilt their hips back and spread their knees apart. My hands skim their forearms, the muscles flexing as they grip the marble, then their stomach, the softness and hardness there.

With my hand on their belt buckle, I ask again, "Same rules?"

"Same fucking rules," Theo snaps, struggling heroically to keep their hips still.

Finally arriving at the end of my own patience, I wrench their belt loose and push my hand down the front of their pants until the flat of my hand finds the warm, soft swell between their legs.

The first contact hits us both hard. Theo chokes out a low, desperate sound. I've been inside someone's mouth this week, slid my tongue over the cleft of a stranger's ass, and still, holding Theo in my palm over their underwear—not even going deeper, not even being touched myself—feels more intense, more intimate.

They're wearing the same kind of silky boy shorts they wore in Barcelona, thin enough to let sensation through, loose enough to allow movement. I delve deeper, trace my middle finger over the contours of the split at their center, the suggestion of a parting. Theo responds with a desperate whine, the treads of their boots scuffling on the stone floor as they widen their stance.

My free hand floats to their throat, not squeezing, just holding with loose, splayed fingers, feeling the quick rise and fall of their breath. I tip their chin to the side, scrape my teeth gently against the hinge of their jaw and then, lower, their pulse. Its thrum is faster now, and I could dissolve with gratitude at being close enough for long enough to measure and compare.

"Have I been patient enough yet?" they beg.

I nod into their hair, smiling at the irascible edge to their voice, and finally give them what they ask.

My fingers easily find their destination, swollen and obvious even through the barrier of dampening cloth, confirmed with

Theo's short, shocked cry. It's simple to adjust my wrist and find the correct angle, like navigating my apartment with the lights off, not needing to see to know where things are in my own home.

I touch them how I remember they like, strong and steady and unrelenting, and they meet every movement, making too much noise as they get closer. My hand moves from their throat to their mouth; they bite into the meat.

When they finally come, it's with a sharp jerk of their hips and a furious growl. I hold them through it, until they spit out my hand with a faint, panting laugh.

"Fuck," they exhale. "I didn't know I could come from that."

"See?" I say, kissing them behind the ear. "Patience."

"Fuck *off.*" They release their grip on the fountain and turn to me, their face flushed and sated, rippled by a half smile. "Do you want me to—?"

They glance down. I'm halfway hard, more than a little aching, but I can't have what I want most. Not here, not now.

"It'll be fine," I tell them. "This was just for you."

An emotion complicates their expression, tightening the corners of their eyes. This time, they smooth it away before I can read it.

"Fine, then," they say. "I'll buy lunch. Are you hungry?"

With them, I always am.

— — —

"Focaccia," Theo says the next day.

"Schiacciata."

"Focaccia?"

"That's *schiacciata.*"

"I really don't see the difference."

I point over the heads of the dozen other tourists crammed into All'Antico Vinaio with us, to the stack of flat, golden-brown schiacciata atop the glass case of sandwich toppings.

"You don't see how that bread is thinner than what we ate in Cinque Terre?"

"No," Theo says. "Explain it again."

Their eyes are bright in the midday light through the open front of the sandwich shop, and I know they see the difference. They just want to find out how many times I'll repeat myself. Nothing gets Theo going like an endurance test.

"So, even though they *look* similar, focaccia and schiacciata have completely different textures. Focaccia should be pillowy and light, almost spongy. Schiacciata gets a longer knead and a shorter rise, so it's flatter and chewier."

"Hmm." Theo taps their chin, visibly fighting a laugh. "I don't know if I believe you."

An old baker emerges from the back and piles a dozen more crusty rectangles of schiacciata on the prep bar. He's sweating and laughing, dusted with flour up to his elbows, and I smile. I know this type of baker well. The kind who thrives on the reliable routine of a simple kitchen run by somebody else, content to keep mixing and kneading and baking the same well-worn recipe every day. They're always the happiest bakers. I envy him.

"Next!"

I order mortadella and stracciatella with crema di pistachio, Theo gets salame toscana with artichoke and spiced eggplant. The line stretches all the way down the alley beside Palazzo Vecchio, past a pharmacy vending machine full of condoms and cock rings, almost to the Uffizi Gallery steps, but when I see my sandwich, I finally understand why Theo insisted on the wait. It's nearly the size of my head.

For the afternoon, we split up: me to the Uffizi Gallery, for the Botticellis, Theo to Fabrizio's guided tour of Michelangelo's *David*. I hang back near a statue of Lorenzo the Magnificent to finish my sandwich, letting the others from the tour slip ahead. I genuinely cherish the Swedes, but I've been waiting my entire life to see the paintings in this museum, and I want to do it alone. I want to make a thing of it. Maxine says I'm "overly precious," but I simply love a perfect moment.

When the clouds are right and the aftertaste of pistachio settles on my tongue and a hot breeze whips up from the Arno, I let the crowd scoop me up and into the museum.

Art is the reason I'm alive. Not even in the figurative sense, although that's probably true too, but in the literal, biological sense.

My dad was thirty-one when he decided to study in Paris. He met my uncle Thierry through grad school classmates while poring over French Romantic poetry on a student visa, and it was at one of Thierry's hazy artist parties in the pied-à-terre that he noticed the watercolor paintings in the kitchen. He was transfixed. As it turned out, the artist was my mother, and Thierry was planning a trip home to Pérouges if my dad wanted to join.

My parents swore it was love at first sight. My mother was ten years younger, living and painting in my grandparents' upstairs bedroom three doors down from the house I'd grow up in. They spent all night walking the village, just talking. At sunrise, they kissed, and by the next sunset, he had told his old roommate in Ohio to sell his things because he was never coming back.

When I was small, I'd sit with my mother while she painted flowers in the garden—or, after we moved, the greenhouse. She'd tell me about her favorite French artists, pull down books from the shelves and show me what they'd painted. Manet, Monet, Van Gogh. She loved Cézanne the most. I always think of her whenever I see a quince in a painting.

After she was gone, I'd sit in her place in the garden and paint watercolors so her easel wouldn't be empty. I'd paint cherry and blackberry juices into tart crusts the way she'd shown me when we learned to bake together. As a teenager in New York, I spent hours wandering museums, looking for quinces. And when I had

the choice to go anywhere to study anything, I chose art history
to be close to her and Santa Barbara to be close to Theo.

I finished my degree full of curiosity and inspiration and
found it was only good for working at a museum, doing the same
things every day and looking at the same handful of pieces. I
wanted to keep discovering, to make things. That was what
brought me back to pastry, and now I get to make things every
day. I spend every day at the same station in one of the finest
kitchens in Paris, repeating the steps of recipes someone else
wrote with absolutely no deviations. And I'm great at it, which
I've heard should make it fulfilling.

All to say, I can't wait to see what the Uffizi will give me.

I wander through long, coffered corridors bursting with
hand-painted flowers and cherubs, trying my best to savor it
all. The golden panels, Lippi's *Madonna*, the Duchess and Duke
of Urbino diptych. I skip the rooms with Botticelli's paintings,
deciding to save them for last. Then it's Da Vinci's *Annunciation*,
the frescoed maps on the upstairs terrace, Michelangelo's *Doni
Tondo*, and *Venus of Urbino*. When I'm satisfied, I turn back, past
oil portraits of dukes and duchesses lining the halls, and into the
Botticelli rooms.

Here, I take my time with each individual painting. I bring
out my sketchbook, but there's no way to capture how ethereal
each piece is, the luminance, how Botticelli's brush could capture every flower petal with scientific accuracy and still imbue
everything with the gauzy grace of a dream. Twenty minutes
pass while I stare at *Primavera*, astounded by the gossamer ripples
of the Graces' veils, the blooms spilling from the nymph's mouth
to become the flowers adorning the goddess's gown, the proud,
serene, gently smiling face of Flora herself.

My phone buzzes with a text from Theo: a grainy, zoomed-in
photo of the *David*'s cock and balls.

Nice, I reply. I send back a photo of *Calumny of Apelles*, a
dramatic painting of hot people in billowing robes fighting

one another in an ornate throne room. This is how I picture Númenor. Theo replies, nerd, and, <3, and then sends a photo of the *David*'s ass.

Finally, when the crowd thins out, I reverently approach *The Birth of Venus*.

As I take my first, long-awaited look at her windswept hair, that iconic, brassy shade of blond, I realize I've seen the color before. Three times, actually, on Sloane, Este, and Theo.

Venus is a Flowerday strawberry blond.

It feels strange to see something of Theo in a depiction of the divine feminine. I've never really seen any woman in Theo (here, Theo would say *well, technically,* and mention one of the times we brought a girl home together), but I have occasionally seen something else. Some eternal, ineffable quality present in this painting. I see Theo in the way Venus leans her weight to one side and juts her hip out in the contrapposto stance, Theo's jaw and chin in Venus's face, Theo's subtle smirk in the shape of Venus's mouth, Theo's laughing vitality in the way Venus's hair flies.

The longer I stare at her, though, the more I begin to see bits of myself too. Her gaze, the fluidity of her body, the way her fingers lay on her breast. If Theo were here, would they recognize me the way I recognize them? Would they wonder, the way I'm wondering, how it can be that we've met here in a Botticelli, curling out of the sea-foam?

I picture them a few streets away beneath *David,* that monument to masculine beauty, finding us in him like I've found us in Venus. Comparing their thighs to his thighs, my lips to his lips, their knees, their shoulders, my waist, our collarbones. I hope Theo looks at that lovingly honed marble and sees the places where their own body holds as much of the divine masculine as he does. I hope it makes them feel known.

I stay there with Venus until two minutes before aperitivo, unwilling to look away. She fills me with dreams of Theo and me on a beach strewn with petals, fills my mouth with the taste of sea salt and rose water and citrus blossoms. An idea for a pastry comes to me unprompted: a featherlight, shell-shaped madeleine infused with rose water and lightly salted, kissed with lemon crémeux and flecked with candied primrose. I write it down, though I don't know what I'd ever use it for.

— — —

In France, we take an apéro before dinner. In my family, it was kir in a juice glass with a splash of Lillet Blanc. Crème de cassis, white wine, a hint of orange peel and honey. Maman said an apéritif should be sweet to ease you into your meal gently, though I suspected she just liked the taste of Lillet.

In Italy, an aperitivo should be bitter. Vermouth, Campari, Aperol. The philosophy is that bitter herbs prime the palate by shocking it into a blank slate for whatever flavors come next. This is what Fabrizio tells us outside a café near the Duomo, where we meet to sip bitter, orange-red Campari spritzes at flimsy café tables that wobble on the piazza's stones.

Evening sun lights Theo from behind as they lean back in their chair. I watch them laugh at Dakota, who discovers that a spritz is the only way to get a full glass of ice in Italy and orders three more in rapid succession. They take notes on flavors, push their fingers through their hair, recline into their typical legs-akimbo Theo posture, take out a bandana and tie it around their neck. When I first moved to the US, I thought Theo might have been one of those cowboys from the American books my dad bought me.

Cowboys, flowers. David, Venus, Theo.

I don't know how I didn't guess it sooner. I certainly felt it long before Theo put a word to it. How could Theo not have always had everything I want? Everything I'm most attracted to, every aspect of masculine and feminine I like best. I don't know if I love Theo because I'm queer or if I'm queer because I love Theo, but I know there's nothing I need that Theo doesn't have. If I'm a man in constant pursuit of decadence, Theo is the ultimate. The most of everything.

I wonder, if Theo had never been on their own, would they have ever discovered this? Or did safety and familiarity keep them smaller? Would there have always been a limit to how much they would know of themself, how much of them I would get to know?

What tragedy that would have been, a comfortable, diminishing love.

I've always agreed with the French that a meal should begin with sweetness, but I'm beginning to wonder if the Italians have it right—if, sometimes, discovery wants bitterness first.

— — —

"Theeee-oh, Theeee-oh, Theee-oh!"

It was the Calums that got the chant started, but our entire table has joined in, banging their fists until plates rattle. Theo stands, flushed but clearly pleased with the attention.

"Fine, I'll do it!"

Fabrizio passes down three empty glasses, and Theo turns away while I pour a different red wine into each. When I'm finished, they sit back down, and everyone leans in to watch.

Theo picks up the first glass and swirls the wine.

"Oh, baby. Deep ruby in color, fading to a garnet rim. Brilliant in the light. Already thinking Sangiovese is the main grape here, and like, duh, Tuscany." They bring the glass to their nose and take a whiff. "Whew. Okay, off the rip, lots of dark fruit. Black cherry for sure. Blackberry, maybe pomegranate. Hold on." They tip the glass to their lips and close their eyes to taste. "Mm. She's got a lot going on. Full-bodied and intense, and those fruits are preserved. Bit of balsamic, bit of oregano, bit of leather. A lot of tannins, but they're gentle, like they've had a long time to think about it. Long finish. Sort of like making out with a sexy nun.

Gotta be Brunello, Riserva. Around ten years. Slightly candied, actually, which makes it a warm vintage, and 2014 was a cooler year, so maybe 2015?"

"2016," I read off the bottle, jaw slack in astonishment. "But yes, you got it."

Montana gasps delightedly, and our table cheers. Ginger Calum puts his fingers in his mouth and whistles. Theo takes a silly little bow.

They taste the other two and correctly identify a Chianti Classico and a Carmignano, each time to riotous applause. A ridiculous balloon of pride swells in me. I spent so long wanting Theo to throw themself into something the way I knew they could, and here they are, being great.

I once read a line in *Mrs. Dalloway* that stuck with me because of how well it described Theo's place in my life. Clarissa sees Sally in her pink dinner frock and, after listing every other visitor and activity in the house, thinks, *All this was only a background for Sally.* To me, Theo is the eternal foreground. I put them at the center of every room. It's gratifying when the room agrees.

Trattoria Sostanza is ours for the night, booked out for an endless Italian dinner. The restaurant barely fits our entire tour group, but that only adds to the experience. Bottles of wine and water flow from hand to hand, plates of oil and herbs from table to table, baskets of bread passed around like the collection at Sunday mass. My back is pressed to Stig's back like we're two travelers from the north crammed into the same carriage on a Grand Tour. Fabrizio is leaning over to the next table, shouting to be heard as he explains the courses of an Italian meal. "That is the beauty, in Italy you do not have to choose pasta or meat! You have pasta for primi, meat for secondi!"

For primi, we have hand-pinched tortellini simmered in butter and rough-cut pasta in a perfectly simple meat sauce, and then comes secondi, when we truly feast. Fabrizio expounds on the subtleties of traditional Tuscan cookery that make a country dish like bistecca alla fiorentina taste so complex: how the charcoal embers must be stoked to the exact right temperature, hot enough to achieve a fragrant crust when the beef is laid close to it for a few short minutes, but not so hot that it cooks out the marbled, ruby-red center. Meanwhile, a skillet of breaded chicken fried in a centimeter of pure, golden butter requires no explanation—it's just fucking delicious.

But as our plates are cleared for dolci, I think the dish that has surprised me most is the tortino di carciofi—eggs swirled in a pan around a cluster of fried artichokes to make a puffy, perfectly round omelet.

"Fabrizio," I say, "do you know the story of Caravaggio and the artichokes?"

He doesn't, so I tell him how Caravaggio, a hotheaded young bisexual street brawler and one of the most masterful Italian painters in history, went to dinner with friends at an osteria in Rome. The waiter brought him a dish of artichokes, some cooked in oil and some in butter, and when Caravaggio asked which was which, the waiter told him to sniff them and find out.

"And so Caravaggio—"

A hand slides into my lap, and my thoughts skid to a halt.

Beside me, Theo innocently sips their wine, as if their other hand isn't on the inseam of my shorts under the tablecloth.

"Go on," Fabrizio says, "what does Caravaggio do?"

"Yeah, Kit," Theo says, smiling. Their hand slips higher. "Go on."

I shoot Theo a pleading look, undermined by the way my legs reflexively spread under the table.

"So Caravaggio's furious, and he grabs the artichokes, and hhh—" The word evaporates as Theo fully palms me through my shorts. I play it off as a cough, reach for my glass. "He throws the whole dish at the waiter's face."

"No!" Fabrizio gasps.

"Hits him right in the mustache."

"Not the mustache," Theo says.

"Non i baffi!" Fabrizio agrees. "And then?"

"And then—" Theo gives me a maddeningly brief squeeze before taking their hand away, leaving me wanting. I forget the end of the story. "And then he jumps up, steals a sword off the guy at the next table, and tries to attack the waiter, and *that's* when he gets arrested."

Fabrizio, delighted, thanks me for a new story to use in Rome. As soon as he's pulled into another conversation, I lean in to Theo's ear.

"What are you doing?"

Theo smiles angelically. "Telling you my plans for the night."

"Oh." I nod. "Good to know."

After that, I expect us to sneak off when dinner ends, but we each get the arm of a Calum flung over our shoulders, and before we can protest, we're whisked into the streets of Florence. Stig is with us too, and Fabrizio, and Montana and Dakota and a few more of the younger people from the tour group. We wind up in a small, dark bar with glittering glass mosaics and red leather booths and a swordfish on the wall. Fabrizio has Theo order for us, and the bartender uncorks two bottles of young Brunello.

After so many days together, conversation flows easily. Theo and Stig compare notes on backpacking through the Rockies versus Jotunheim. Fabrizio and the Calums discuss their favorite New Zealand beaches. I prop my elbows on the bar and beg Dakota and Montana to tell me more about their work trip to Tokyo, where they dropped acid with a Moroccan prince. Theo insists on buying two more bottles for the group, this time a softer, fruitier Morellino di Scansano.

By round three, Stig and Fabrizio are shouting about the last World Cup, and Dakota and Montana are bending their heads together at one end of the bar, whispering behind their hands. At the other end, the Calums unconvincingly pretend to study the cocktail menu instead of eavesdropping. I watch Theo accept a glass from a handsome bartender who eyes them with interest, but they're already turning their body toward mine, bumping our knees together.

"I have a question," I say.

Theo raises their eyebrows as they drink. *Go on.*

"Is our competition still on?"

They swallow. "Yeah, why? You want to call it before you lose?"

"No, I was just wondering how you'll find time to maintain your lead if you're hooking up with me."

A moment goes by. Fabrizio continues talking shit about the Portuguese national team. Dakota makes a move toward the Calums.

"Yeah, about that," Theo says. "I have a confession. My numbers may be . . . slightly inflated."

"What do you mean?"

"I didn't hook up with the fruit-stand girl in Saint-Jean-de-Luz."

"But—" I can still see the intent in their gaze when they told me how well they could get Juliette off, feel the hot twist in my gut. "I saw you kissing her."

"Yeah, we kissed, but then—I kind of got curved. I didn't want to tell you because I was a little jealous of you and Paloma. So, it's not six to four, it's five to four."

I shake my head.

"Five to three."

It's Theo's turn to frown. "What?"

"I didn't sleep with Paloma either."

Theo puts their glass down with force.

"What? You left with her!"

But it's true. As soon as she broke the kiss, she patted me on the cheek like a lost dog and said, "I think I would rather be your friend." And then she invited me over out of charity, and I sat in her kitchen and told her about my job and asked how she knew she didn't want to do what I do.

"Yes," I say. "We made crepes and talked about culinary school. That was all."

I may have also tearfully confided in her how much I still love Theo while Great-Uncle Mikel made me a cup of tea.

"You—but you said—"

"I never technically said I slept with her," I point out. "I just didn't contradict you."

"So, to be clear," Theo says, laying their hands flat on the bar, "neither of us got laid in Saint-Jean-de-Luz."

"No, we didn't."

"Damn." They sit back, laughing in disbelief. "Well, this is embarrassing for us both."

"Is it?" I ask, smiling. "Maybe the only thing better than sex is having friends on the Côte d'Argent."

"A wholesome sentiment from the Sex God of École Desjardins."

The—quoi?

"The what?"

"Oh, don't be coy." They roll their eyes. "Maxine told me all about it."

Oh, no. That could mean anything.

"What exactly did Maxine tell you?"

Theo shrugs. "Essentially, that you sucked and fucked your way through pastry school, and everyone was in love with you."

"In *love* with me?" I repeat, stunned. "Theo, did—did you ever think my best friend might have been exaggerating to make me look good to my ex?"

"Well—" Theo blinks. "I thought she was your girlfriend at the time."

"Oh, God. Oh, Theo, no." I rub a hand across my face. We can't keep doing this. "Do you want the honest truth?"

Theo hesitates for only a second.

"Yes."

"It's true that in pâtisserie school I had . . . a lot of sex," I say. Theo's mouth forms a thin line, as if I'm just showing off. "And I'm sure some of them had feelings for me, because I—I was kind of raw for a while. Kind of pouring out a lot of love in a lot of directions, trying to, I don't know, get it all out of me. Because you were gone so fast and so completely, and I couldn't shut it off."

Theo's gaze drops from my face to a cocktail napkin, their mouth softening.

"But, while that may be an excellent way to get someone into bed, it's a terrible way to get them to stay," I go on. "I was a mess. No one could put up with me for more than a week. I had to learn to be better at picking people up so I wouldn't have to sleep alone in the apartment that was supposed to be ours. That's all. Maxine is a saint, but she's also protective to a fault. She would've told you anything to make it sound better for me."

A pause, only the bar noise around us. Theo seems to be chewing on this information. I thumb the base of my glass, hoping they don't find it too pathetic.

Finally, their voice almost too low to be heard, they ask, "So, it was hard for you? When I . . . ?"

It shouldn't shock me to learn Theo thought their exit from my life was easy for me. As long as we've known each other, Theo's great misconception has been that people don't miss them. It's hard for them to believe that they have so much to offer, that people want them around and think of them fondly when they're gone. They don't expect anyone to care if they leave. It's affected us before, and often—when I moved to New York, when they dropped out of school, when we'd have a tense conversation and they'd avoid me for days. Under pressure, they would vanish, and they loved themself so little they were surprised when it hurt me.

In my memory, I see a small Theo outside my old house in the Valley, dropped off by the family driver with an overstuffed suitcase.

Adult-sized Theo continues: "I kind of figured you didn't think of me once you got to Paris. I thought you found better things to care about, and I was, you know. Backstory."

We've come so far from who we were when we met, but some things hold out.

"Theo, you could never be backstory," I say. "I thought about you every single day. I wanted to spend the rest of my life with you, and you had disappeared. And it seemed so . . . clean. Like you didn't even hesitate. And that killed me."

After a pause, Theo says, "For what it's worth, it killed me too."

As much as it hurts to think of Theo in pain, it is worth something. It helps, in some strange, sad way, to know they were as fucked up as me. That I was alone with it not because they didn't feel it, but because they never told me.

"Can I ask why you did it, then?" I say. "I know why we broke up, and I know you thought I left you, but I still don't understand why you didn't just call me when you got home."

I wait for them to harden, to answer with *You didn't call either,* but they rest their fingertips on the stem of their glass and look thoughtful.

"I think I was always waiting for you to outgrow me," they say. "And it seemed like you finally had. I was humiliated, and angry—I was so *angry*—and part of me just needed a win. Cutting you off felt like *doing* something, like—like taking control of what was happening to me. But, Kit, it wasn't easy for me either. It never could be."

I try to absorb this, wishing for the words to make Theo understand they're not someone I could ever outgrow. I settle for making them smile.

"So, like," I say in the most American strain of my accent, leaning against the bar. "How bad was it?"

Theo smiles.

"Dude, it was so bad," they say, laughing like they're talking about a longboarding accident. "Those first six months, the only time I didn't think about you was when I was working on the bus, so I had, like, blisters in places I never imagined. My stomach was way fucked up, my back hurt all the time, I slept like shit. It was fucking hell, bro."

I nod gravely. "I feel that, bro."

"And even after the worst was over, I couldn't call. I just knew you'd be doing well, and I'd realize I'd been right, that I'd held you back."

I slide my hand across the bar until our smallest fingers meet.

"You never held me back," I tell them. "I hope you know that now."

"I'm working on actually believing it," they say with a brisk shrug. "But this helps. And it helps to see you doing well and know it doesn't have to change how much I like myself."

A twinge in my chest.

"I like you too," I say.

"Thanks! I like *you!*" Theo declares, grinning. "Look at us, sitting here in Italy talking about our lives, and it doesn't even bother me that you're happy and successful in Paris! I'm happy that you're happy. That's growth!"

"Yeah," I say. *Happy and successful*—I am, aren't I? "I'm happy for you too."

We stay there, drinking and talking and liking each other. The rest of our group trickles out, and new faces replace them. We look on with rapt attention as Dakota leaves with a Calum on each arm, and then delighted confusion as Montana pulls Stig after them by one of his enormous hands.

We should leave too, if only we could find the end of our conversation.

"Fuck," Theo says as they search their pockets to pay for another Negroni. "I'm out of euros."

I'm sure I have some coins rattling around the bottom of my bag—except, I don't. I come up empty.

"Should we call it a night?"

"We . . . could," Theo says, toying with a plain gold ring on their index finger. They take it off and hold it in the palm of their hand. "Or there's always the San Francisco Gambit."

The mischievous gleam in their eye lights up the memory: Theo and I, so in love we didn't even have to try to sell a faux proposal. Anyone could see we were in it for life.

"You won't," I say, half because I'm afraid they'll do it, half knowing this is the best way to make sure they do.

"I will."

"I don't believe you."

Theo stands up, banging a spoon against a glass to draw attention. When enough people are looking, they drop to one knee on the floor of the bar and gaze up at me, looking like some handsome young wanderer come to take me away from this provincial life.

"Kit Fairfield," Theo says, presenting me with their ring, "you are the best-looking person in this bar. And you smell so nice all the time. And I like you, and I really missed you. Will you do me the honor of spending the rest of your life with me?"

I'd give absolutely anything for them to mean it.

I put on an easy smile and say, "My love, I thought you'd never ask."

As the crowd begins to cheer, I stand and pull Theo to their feet. They slide the ring onto my left hand, and it fits. The inside is still warm from their skin. We're laughing together, swept up in the moment, clutching each other's hands while the bartender pops a bottle of champagne and someone chants, "Bacio, bacio, bacio!"

"They want us to kiss!" Theo shouts.

I tell them, "Sell it, then."

So Theo takes me in their arms and dips me low. For one dizzy second, all I see is their face, close and complicated with feeling, and I try to tell them with my eyes to just do it. Kiss me, haunt me, handle me recklessly.

They slip their hand between our mouths and kiss the back of their own fingers. Drinkers applaud; the bartender clangs a bell. We know how to make it convincing.

— — —

On the walk to the hostel, we stumble into an alley, my back against a yellow stucco wall and Theo's mouth on my neck. We're loose and hazy from hours of steady drinking, tired and reaching for each other with a desire like returning to an abandoned cup of coffee. It was hot and strong before, but now the sugar has settled at the bottom.

I open my eyes to see dark green shutters across from us, a cat lounging on the sill behind them. It's one of those small details that reminds me these places are real and belong to people we'll rarely meet while passing through, that Florence will forget us even if we remember it for the rest of our lives. I find it terribly romantic, the evanescence.

I rut lazily into the warm press of their thighs. They kiss my neck, my jaw. We're moving slowly—so slowly it's hard to know when we stop trying to fuck and start simply holding each other.

My arms circle tightly around Theo's waist. Theo's hand cradles the back of my head, their fingers clenched in my hair. It's been so long since anyone has held me like this. It's been so long without them. I could cry with relief.

We stay there, not speaking and not letting go, until the cat in the window yells at us and Theo breaks off laughing. They make a joke in a shaky, too-loud voice and stagger away.

But I felt their breath catch against me, and I see the strange brightness in their eyes when they pass through the glow of a convenience store window. When I return their ring, they slip it into their pocket without looking at it. They smile like it's nothing. I don't know if I believe it.

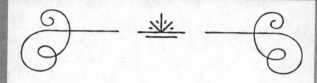

CHIANTI

PAIRS WELL WITH:

Chianti Riserva after a long bike ride,
pesche di Prato

CHIANTI

We go south. Orla drives us through the hills toward Siena, past the tower houses of San Gimignano and the walled palazzos of Montepulciano, along cow pastures and olive groves and patchy wheat fields. In the distance, copper-and-green hills fold over one another like mussed-up linens in a bed as wide as the sky. The motorway exits east toward crunchy gravel roads that bounce us in our seats until the bus pulls off at an overgrown stone gate.

Theo, who fell asleep mid-sentence before we even left, jolts awake against my shoulder and picks up where they left off.

"Sort of a—" Huge yawn, eyes being rubbed. "—a circles and squares thing. Or, I mean, squares and rectangles. All Chianti Classico is made in Chianti, but not all Chianti made in Chianti is Chianti Classico."

"Sure," I say, smoothing a stray piece of their hair, "I'm always saying that."

Theo scowls sleepily. "Are we here?"

"We're here."

Here is Villa Mirabella, a centuries-old Tuscan villa tucked along the edge of Greve in Chianti. Before Theo passed out, they were explaining how important those two details are— something about counterfeiting and subzones and the percentage of Sangiovese grapes, and how only a small cluster of nine communes are legally designated as makers of Chianti Classico. I don't know. Theo's a brilliant person full of interesting thoughts, but I was mostly watching their mouth.

"Ciao a tutti ragazzi, hello everyone!" Fabrizio calls out. He explains that our room arrangements will be as usual—shared rooms for pairs who booked together, singles for solo travelers— and that a dinner prepared with ingredients fresh from the surrounding farmland will be served at nine, or whenever the cook feels like it. "The rest of the day is yours—swim, bicycle, eat, drink, make love, it is your choice."

We pour out of the bus and down the front walk to a hedged gravel terrazzo shaded by crepe myrtle trees, fig trees, lemon, apple, elm, white poplar, clusters of hortensia bushes with pink flowers. Yellow-striped chairs and bistro tables sit prettily under lemon-yellow umbrellas. It all culminates in the villa itself, four floors tall and twice as wide, its white stucco facade engulfed in ivy and hanging wisteria.

An older woman wearing a dress the same shade of yellow as the umbrellas awaits us at the doorstep, bearing a basket of fresh linens and the gravity of someone in charge. Pair by pair, she distributes antique keys as Fabrizio reads names off his clipboard, until Theo and I are the last two.

After much whispering in Italian, the signora retires to the house, and Fabrizio pulls us aside.

"Amici," he says, "Signora Lucia tells me there is a mistake. When we send the names for the tour group, there is—how do you say—a glitch? Because your original reservation is together, you have the same reservation number. It is very rare that guests book together, and then cancel together, and then use the reservation again for the same tour but not together—you see how this becomes confusing for our little office man? And I will tell you, we have a new man and I do not think he is very good. Terrible personality. We are trying to send him to the Germany office." Fabrizio trails off darkly, probably imagining the terrible office man in especially uncomfortable lederhosen. "But, the problem. Lucia has assigned for you the same room."

"Oh."

I glance at Theo.

"That's—"

"And I ask if there are more rooms, but they are repairing the third villetta. I even tell her about your situation, but—"

"It's okay," Theo says firmly. Fabrizio and I both pause. "We don't mind."

"You don't?" Fabrizio furrows his brow.

He looks to me, then to Theo, and to me again.

"Ah, *I see*." A smile takes over his face. "Meraviglioso, then, this is for you! Last room on the top floor. Grazie mille!"

He hands us a heavy brass key with a green silk tassel and leaves with a wink, humming to himself.

"He definitely thinks we're fucking," I say.

Theo's grin is wicked. "Why shouldn't he?"

Almost everyone has left their doors open behind them, so muted laughter and conversations in English and Dutch and Japanese filter up the creaking stairs as we climb them. I catch glimpses past each landing, tufted blue sofas with scrolls of white flowers on distressed rugs, piles of old books tucked into windowsills and scuffed side tables painted with pink rosebuds. It's as if some baronet and his family took the horses out to visit the next village over and will be back any minute with hot gossip about wheat prices.

On the top floor, our room is bright and warm, with a red upholstered bed patterned with the same flowers as the curtains around the open windows. The ceiling is a rugged grid of thick wooden beams and terra-cotta tiles, and fresh flowers rest in a vase by the hand-painted wardrobe. My pack falls beside Theo's on the plush rug.

"This is wild," Theo says. "Like a fucking Guadagnino film."

Below the windows, behind the villa, brick steps and dusty paths connect terrazzos and flowering gardens to make a tiny, crooked village of the estate. The rest of the buildings, all clay-tiled villettas, have their doors propped open to let in guests or let out smells of pressed olives and stewing pork. I take a deep breath in and swear I can hear a romantic piano score in the air.

"You're right," I say, stepping away from the window. "It's unreal."

I turn to find Theo at the foot of the bed, tugging their shirt over their head with the same fluid motion I saw on the motorway outside Pisa. This time, though, they're wearing nothing under it.

Having spent my childhood traipsing naked through the French countryside and my adulthood either studying artistic nudes or living in Paris, nudity doesn't faze me. I have, however, become an Edwardian gentleman for Theo and Theo only. Every re-revealed inch of skin has set my fingers flexing and my heart fluttering in my stomach, a flash of shoulder or navel or peach-fuzzed armpit. When they put my hand on their hip in that room in Barcelona, I had to recite the steps for pâte à choux in my head so I wouldn't lose myself completely. And now, this, their sudden bare chest in the light of a Tuscan morning.

I avert my eyes in case I wasn't meant to see, but they toss their shirt aside and stand there facing me, casually topless. So, I look.

I see the same rib cage with the same thumbprint-sized birthmark on the upper left side, the same splash of freckles down the breastbone. The same pinkish nipples. No new scars as far as I can see, but I can tell they've been training muscle to reshape their chest into something even subtler and more boyish than before. They look strong, lean, gorgeously purposeful and beautifully ambiguous, like Caravaggio's *Bacchus*.

"What—" I swallow. "What are we doing?"

"I'm getting changed. Didn't you see that sign downstairs? Piscina?" Theo bends to pull a swimsuit from their pack. "There's a pool."

I watch Theo drop their shorts next. Only their underwear remains, their thumbs hooked under the waistband. It's so different from how they undressed in Barcelona, so brazenly nonchalant, and I realize they're *showing off.*

"What?" they say. "Did you think I wanted to—?"

"*No.*"

"Because using the room is against the rules."

"I'll remind you tonight that you said that," I say, recovering by taking off my own shirt. Theo hates when the girls get all Edwardian. "I'm coming with you."

"Cool, it'll be nice to just hang out today," Theo says conversationally. They drag their underwear down. "My feet are so tired."

"Mine too." My shorts hit the floor. "And I'm kind of catatonic from seeing so many Botticellis."

"Oh, I never told you about Fabrizio's *David* tour." Theo stands tall, completely naked. I don't hide how my eyes travel their body, ankles to biceps to the place I touched at Venus's fountain. They're still smiling, still chatting. "Did you know it was originally meant for the top of the Duomo?"

I nod. "And Da Vinci wanted to shove it in the back of the Loggia dei Lanzi where nobody would see it."

"He wanted to fuck Michelangelo so bad, it's embarrassing," Theo says.

I slip off my own briefs, intensely aware of the obvious heaviness between my legs. I'm not embarrassed of how badly I want them. I'd show them so much more if they asked.

Theo looks. Theo keeps looking.

"Have you been doing squats?"

"Moving sacks of flour from the bottom of dry storage."

"Hmm."

And then someone knocks on the door, and the spell is broken. Theo laughs and goes "whoops" and ducks behind a wardrobe, and I pull on trunks to accept a delivery from a friendly maid.

"Complimentary wine," I call out, examining the bottle of red I've been handed. Theo emerges in their swimsuit as I turn over the monogrammed card tied to the bottle's neck to find a handwritten note. "Oh, it's from . . . your sister? She must have called ahead. That's sweet of her."

The card says:

Theo,
Might have taken it a bit too far. Sorry. Love you.
                                    —*Sloane*

P.S. Offer still stands.

"Let me see," Theo says, whisking the bottle and card away. Their face hardens slightly as they read, mouth going sharpish. "Oh, nice. Can't imagine where else we'd find wine in a place like this."

They open the wardrobe and shove it inside. When they turn back to me, they're smiling.

"Are you ready?"

Now, that—*that* seems like something I wasn't meant to see.

"Let me get my book."

— — —

Theo is the first in the pool, naturally.

Past the last villetta and a wall of trees, the grounds unfold into a sloping meadow with a wide swimming pool and panoramic views of the surrounding hills. Lemon-striped loungers fan out under umbrellas in the grass, and I sink into one with my shirt open to the sun and my book open to the last place I left it. The air is hot and perfumed with wisteria, and past the birds and the snip of the gardener shears, I hear the clean, quiet ripples of Theo swimming laps.

Soon others wander to the pool, and a man in yellow linen brings trays of antipasti and buckets of chilled wine. Honeymooners cruise off into the hills on borrowed bikes with wicker baskets. A cook leans out of a green-shuttered window, calling to a maid. Signora Lucia floats about, watering plants with a loving diligence that reminds me of my maman, which is more sweet than bitter in a place like this.

"Mind if I join you?" says Ginger Calum, appearing with a fluffy white towel over his shoulder.

"Not at all."

He hands me a glass of cool amber wine and keeps one for himself. "What is it they say here? Salute?"

"Salute," I repeat, endeared.

"Shady day for this ginger lad," he says, arranging himself under the umbrella on the chaise beside mine. I thought he was flushed with drink last night, but now I see he's sporting a spectacular Florentine sunburn. He pulls a tablet and a battered field journal from his tote. "Just as well. Loads of work to catch up on."

I lift my sunglasses to glance at his pages, jammed full of time-stamped notes and hand-drawn data tables.

"What is it that you do, Calum?"

"Me? I'm a wildlife biologist."

"Is that right?" I pictured him as more of a sexy fireman or Olympic shot-putter. "What kind of animals do you work with?"

"Mostly white pointers for the past year or so, but I'm keen on all Indo-Pacific marine predators. I wrote my dissertation on chemotactile social recognition in the blue-ringed octopus."

I can't imagine a more wonderfully surprising answer from a man I heard belch the French alphabet last week.

"You're a doctor, then?"

He grins. "Don't let Calum hear you say that, he'll take the piss. He's an *actual* doctor, or so he says."

In the pool, Blond Calum is doing handstands, only his legs and feet poking out of the water. He has a tattoo on his calf of a prawn wearing a cowboy hat.

"That man?"

"Emergency medicine," Ginger Calum says with a fond laugh,

as if revealing this is one of his favorite activities. "You should ask him about it. He loves telling horror stories."

Water splashes over my feet, and I peer over my book to see Theo poolside, elbows propped near a tray of sweating cheese and fruit.

"Don't get the crostini wet," I say.

Theo snaps off a branch of grapes and lowers one into their mouth like a Roman emperor.

"You're really not getting in?"

I hold up my book. "I'm on the last chapter. Lucy's going to admit she's in love with George."

"Oh, well"—they push up an invisible pair of glasses—"if Lucy's going to admit she's in love with George."

They kick away, grapes held over their head, and I smile.

When we were in Paris, I watched Theo striding down Boulevard Saint-Germain and wondered if I was seeing what it would have been like if we'd gone on the tour like we planned. I held them beside the image that's lived in my head all these years, the Theo in a parallel life who came with me to France.

But here, in Chianti, I see only what is, not what could have been. Us, in two arcs bent toward each other. Theo in the water, me content to sit by the pool with a book and a view.

For the first time, it seems better this way.

I continue reading, watching Lucy and George come back together, confess their love, and return to Florence to marry. By the time I reach the last page, emotion tingles sweet in my sinuses like prosecco bubbles. A droplet of water lands on my page, and I think I've summoned an actual tear until I hear Theo's voice above.

"You done yet?"

They're standing beside my chair, rivulets of water running down their body. I didn't notice them getting out, but I'm very much noticing now.

"Come on," they say, finishing my wine. "I want to see what they have for lunch."

"Almost finished." A slight wobble in my voice. "One more minute?"

They lower my empty glass to regard me properly.

"Are you *crying?*"

"It's a beautiful story!"

"Oh, no, he's crying!" Theo crows, and then they're climbing onto the lounger, shaking their damp head over my pages, dripping with malicious intent. Their wet skin skids against mine, cold where mine is warm. I hold the book over my head and settle them with a hand at the small of their back. They wind up half folded across my lap, their knees hooked around my thighs, laughing.

"I'm not embarrassed," I say.

"I know."

"I'm allowing art to touch my soul."

"Okay," Theo says, doing a jerk-off hand gesture, still smiling.

"I'm being transported. I'm experiencing."

"Go on." Theo tugs my book down. "Experience."

They're teasing, but I decide to be earnest. I smooth the page with my free hand and pick up at the final passage, the one smudged with Theo's pool water.

"'Youth enwrapped them,'" I read aloud, keeping my voice low. "'The song of Phaethon announced passion requited, love attained. But they were conscious of a love more mysterious than this. The song died away; they heard the river, bearing down the snows of winter into the Mediterranean.'"

For a moment, Theo is quiet. Then they sit up, take a bottle from a nearby ice bucket, and replenish my glass before handing it to me.

"Okay, that was actually really nice." Their eyes are a little soft, faraway. "Will you come to lunch with me?"

We crunch the gravel path back to the villa's dining room, where a long antique buffet painted with vines and rosebuds heaves with food: marbled prosciutto, mozzarella on wheels of eggplant, huge garlic-simmered beans, figs and persimmons picked from the garden and sliced open so their flesh shines in the sunlight from the open windows. We fill our plates and carry them out to the biggest terrazzo.

As we eat, I catch Fabrizio watching us from two tables over, clearly noting the practiced ease with which Theo shoves pan-zanella onto my plate. I point this out to Theo, who instantly has that devious gleam in their eye. They make sure Fabrizio is still looking, and then they slide their hand into my lap.

This time, there's no tablecloth to hide anything. Just us in our striped chairs before the green backdrop of the garden, Theo's palm on the inside of my thigh where anyone can see. The tip of their middle finger grazes the stretchy hem of my swim trunks.

Part of wants to move their touch higher, but I think of ear-lier, how they hid the bottle of wine in the wardrobe, how they turned pink when I read the card from Sloane. I wonder what they're trying to conceal behind this.

Gently, I lift their hand up and press a kiss to the center of their palm. I lace my fingers through theirs, resting our hands on the table between us.

They don't pull away, and they don't laugh. They peer into my eyes for a long moment, daring me to act like this too is a bit. When I don't, they put their sunglasses on and return one-handed to their plate as if nothing has changed, but they're pink under their freckles.

After lunch, we borrow bikes and ride into the hills; they blur green-bronze as we take our feet off the pedals and coast. Out here the sun hangs as wonderfully fat in the sky as it did in Florence, but it doesn't scorch. It soaks into the hills like oil into thick, well-risen bread, and we spread ourselves across them like happy little figs.

It's nearly time for aperitivo when we return. We take our

amaro behind the villa, to the grove where a gardener tends to young, bright green olives. He plucks two straight off the branch for us to taste and laughs mischievously when we choke on their bitterness. Theo jokes that it's our truest Italian aperitivo yet.

Dinner is served at a long table between the grove and the villa, covered by arching trellises of ivy and twinkling lights. We pass around heavy platters of wild boar ragù and pillowy gnocchi with greens and blistered tomatoes. The food here is rich and hearty, like it's meant to prepare the body to harvest crops instead of luxuriating with carafes of fine wine beneath a crepuscular sky.

Theo sits across from me, sun-kissed and windswept, wearing that lovely black linen thing from our second night in Paris. Fairy lights dapple their skin through the leaves. I want to touch them so badly. I imagine running my fingertip down the center of their chest to the point of their neckline's vee.

I let them catch me looking. I tip the last of my wine past my lips and show them the contours of my jaw, how my throat moves when I swallow. They bite their lip.

Soon, the villa's sweet, muddling magic sweeps us from one moment to the next, and we're retiring to a dark, warm sitting room. Signora Lucia brings out trays of crunchy, almond-flecked cantucci, and Fabrizio pours viscous vin santo into little crystal cups so we can dip the cookies before we eat them, as is the Tuscan way.

It seems it's also the Tuscan way to drape ourselves over antique couches and tell long stories in loud voices, because that's how we spend the rest of the night. I ask Blond Calum for his best emergency medicine stories, knowing I'll hate the answer as much as Theo will love it. The one he decides to share is about his first, long before he began to study.

He and Calum were thirteen, best friends who never paddled out to surf without each other, which was how he was able to act so quickly when Ginger went under in a cloud of red. A white pointer—a great white—had torn a hunk from his shoulder, and he would have bled out if Blond hadn't pulled him onto his board, paddled them both to shore, and pressed a towel to the wound until help arrived. Theo and I listen with our hands over our mouths.

"Cheers to that bloody shark," Blond says, raising his vin santo, "the reason I do what I do."

"Here, here," Ginger agrees, lifting his own glass. "Remarkable creature. Can't hold it against him, can ya?"

"I'll drink to that," Theo says. "Hey, how do you feel about *Jaws?*"

Eventually, the Calums drift off to their rooms with suspiciously similar timing to Montana and Dakota, and Theo draws me lazily to their side, letting out a long breath when I lean my head on their shoulder. I listen as they tell the Swedes a story about a bottle of wine the Somm's mother left in a window, and then as Lars asks how one bottle could possibly have been worth so much, Theo takes out their phone and dials the Somm on speakerphone.

"Hello, stranger," says the Somm's gruff voice on the third ring.

"Hey!" Theo says, leaning in. "Listen, I'm here in Chianti with a couple of Swedes, and I just told them about your mom's Romanée-Conti. They don't believe that it was worth forty-two grand. Can you back me up here?"

"It would have been, yes."

Lars shakes his head, smiling incredulously. "Unbelievable."

"Thank you!" Theo says. "That's—"

"But, Theo," the Somm interrupts, "you're forgetting the end of the story."

"I am?"

"We opened it, my brother and I, and we drank it," he goes on, "and it was the best goddamn wine I ever tasted."

A slight collapse happens around Theo's brow, as if this information has somehow injured them.

"I did forget that part."

"Hey, why'd you leave me hanging on that Scottsdale distributor thing?" the Somm asks. "Are you studying in Chianti? Have you been tasting? You remember, it was the Chianti subregions that got you on the written exam—"

"I know, I know," Theo says, eyes suddenly wide, "I have them now—"

"You better, if you want to pass this time."

Theo snatches their phone up and ends the call.

The others barely seem to have noticed, and Theo laughs it off, but they won't look at me. They drain their glass, mutter something about being tired, and they're gone.

— — —

I've only seen Theo cry three times: when they fell out of a tree and broke their arm at age nine, the first time they saw me after my mother died, and the day I left for New York. It's not that Theo doesn't experience huge emotions. They just muscle it down.

They'll squint and scrunch their nose, as if they're annoyed to waste energy on something so useless, then their face clears, and they keep going.

Right now, they're making that face.

I found them upstairs, tearing apart their backpack to get to their dopp kit. They're at the bathroom vanity now, peeling off their clothes.

"Theo, is there—are you okay?"

"Yeah," they grunt, stepping out of puddled linen and throwing on a T-shirt. "I'm just really tired all of a sudden."

"We can talk about it, if you want. You can tell me."

They try to open their kit, but the zipper is stuck.

"I don't," they snap.

With a furious yank, their kit explodes open and expels its contents all over the floor. They swear and fall to their knees, chasing bottles and tubes.

"Theo," I say, getting down beside them. They swat my hands away. "Theo!"

At last they go still. They sit back on their heels and look up at the terra-cotta ceiling, lip balm and toothpaste clutched in their fists, their face a vivid, mottled red.

"I'm—I fucked up."

"Okay. What happened?"

"It's not even something that happened. I think—I think it's something I am. I'm a fuckup."

"No, you're not," I say, not even beginning to know where this is coming from. I gently work their fingers loose, one by one.

"I am. I'm a fuckup, and I can't stop being one, no matter how much I grow and how hard I try—and I try so *fucking* hard—" Their voice breaks. They choke it back. "I can't change the fact that it's me. I'm me, and that means I'll keep fucking up forever."

"That's not true. You—"

"I've failed the sommelier exam three times."

That finally pulls my attention from their lip balm. I sit back, watching a muscle clench in Theo's jaw.

"I've been lying to you." Theo's voice is flat, sour. "I didn't plan to lie, just *imply,* but you were so impressed when you thought I had, and I'm taking it again when I get home, so I thought, you know, if he asked me a month from now it would be true. But, honestly, I'll probably find some new way to fuck it up, so I might as well come clean."

"Okay." I blink slowly, processing. "Is . . . is that all?"

Theo scowls, like this was the wrong thing to say.

"The bus bar is fucked too."

Oh, no. "Fucked how?"

"Upside down. Out of money. *Negative* money." They start snatching things up and hurling them into their kit. "I get all these big ideas, blow my entire budget on artisanal pickled kumquats and imported Persian saffron for one fucking cocktail, lose track of client emails, and it all gets fucked. I lost that big wedding gig because I got sidetracked with *you*." Their eyes flash—I can't tell if that's a confession or an accusation. "And now I—I don't see how it's not over. That gig was going to save me. I'm gonna have to sell the bus just to pay off my credit cards. So, I lied about that too. I'm nothing I told you I was. There you go."

They zip the kit up, climb to their feet, and drop it on the bedside table. Then they sit on the edge of the mattress and draw their knees up to their chin, looking absolutely furious with themself.

I sigh and pinch the bridge of my nose.

"Why . . . why would you lie to me about all of that?"

"Because I wanted you to think I had my shit together!" Theo says miserably. "I wanted you to think I'd grown. I wanted you to see me for the first time in four years and be amazed."

"That would have happened no matter what."

They roll their eyes spectacularly. "Whatever. I couldn't have you pity me, and I still can't, so just—please don't look at me like that."

"Like what?"

"Like you think I could do better," Theo says. "That's how Sloane looked at me too."

"Sloane? Did she—is that why she sent the wine?"

"I tried to talk to her about it, and she sort of laid into me about, you know. My nepo-baby complex."

I frown. "Your . . . ?"

"She tried to give me money. Called it an *investment,* like it's not charity. And when I said no, she went off about how I make my life harder on purpose just to prove a point."

"Ah. And when was this?"

"In Nice. After I left you with Apolline."

The pieces of the past few days begin to rearrange themselves.

"So, when we got to Monaco, you were . . . ?"

"In full self-destruct, yeah."

I pull myself off the floor and sit on the foot of the bed. Is that all this has been to them, with me? Self-destruction?

I don't know what difference it would make if it was. Does it matter if Theo is fucking me to destroy themself, if I'm destroying myself to fuck Theo?

I push my fingers through my hair and concentrate.

"How do you feel now?"

Theo answers after a long pause, their voice quiet but firm.

"I cannot build a life on being a Flowerday. I want to build a life on being Theo."

"Then don't use the family name," I say. "Or the connections, or the favors—you never needed any of that to be great." I choose my next words carefully. "But, Theo . . . maybe you should consider taking the money."

Theo fixes me with a hard look. "You'd take it, wouldn't you?"

"I would. And then I'd make it mean something."

"That's the problem," Theo insists. "I won't do anything great with it. I'd take Sloane's money and blow it, and that would always be between us. I can't risk that. She's my best friend, and I can't—I can't—"

The unfinished sentence hangs in the air between us: *I can't lose another best friend.*

"You don't know that's what would happen, Theo."

"Precedent says otherwise," Theo replies. "I want to do all these things on my own, and I—I just can't. It was stupid to think I could."

"Then use the money to hire someone to help you."

"What, and waste someone else's time too? I'm wasting enough on my own."

I put my head in my hands, nearing the purlieu of my patience.

"God, Theo, sometimes you just—"

They round on me, eyes wet.

"What, frustrate you? Well, we have that in fucking common. Don't you think I would fucking *love* to be different than this?"

"*You don't need to!*" The words burst out like bitter olive in a press, crushed beyond the limits of my skin. "Je te jure, Theo, I have never met another person with more to offer the world and less faith in themself. You are brilliant, and magnetic, and strong, and impressive and—and *vital,* and I cannot keep listening to you talk about someone I love like this, so please, for God's sake, *stop.*"

Theo is silent, eyes wide, lips parted in surprise. My heart fills my throat. I realize too late what I've done: I've said I love them. I go on before they realize it too.

"You have it backward," I say. "It's the rest that needs to be solved, not you. Will you hear me, please? You were good enough to get this far. You are good enough to fix it. You are good enough for anything you want, but you have to believe it."

Theo doesn't answer. In the dark room, we sit quietly on opposite ends of the bed, contending with our own hearts.

Slowly, Theo begins to unfold their body. They lie back on the bed with their face to the ceiling and extend an arm toward me, palm open. I ease myself backward, shifting my shoulders until our heads are bent toward each other. I lay my hand over theirs, and they twine our fingers together.

"I don't know where to start," they say.

I tell them, "Anywhere."

We lie on our backs with our arms and legs spread as if we're floating together on a wide sea. Theo takes slow breaths, in and out, until one comes out as a low, rueful laugh.

Gradually, we begin to shift closer. Theo's ankle hooks over mine. My fingers slip to the tender point of their pulse. When I turn my head, I find them already bent toward me, their eyes deep with desire, with some other enormous thing that doesn't look destructive at all. It looks like roots, like something that lives and grows.

"I want to change the rules," Theo says.

"The rules?"

"Our rules."

"*Oh.*"

"I think," Theo says, "we should be able to use our rooms."

I find my smile impossible to resist.

"I did say I would remind you—"

"Don't be a shit," Theo says with a pure affection that wraps tight around my heart. "Yes or no?"

Easy. "Yes."

Our clothes fall to the floor as we tumble across the bed, grasping and grinding and tonguing skin. Theo pushes my shoulders into the mattress and climbs on top of me. They bite my neck, leave a mark on my shoulder, rub the whole front of their body against mine as if they can't get close enough. I gasp and moan when they palm me through my underwear, and they bare their teeth at the sound.

"I missed you," they say, like they said last night in Florence.

"I missed you too," I breathe out.

They pull back to kneel between my legs.

"You know what else I missed?" they say.

They hook their hands behind my knees and shift me into a position that makes my breath hitch. It's an old favorite: my legs spread apart, their hips between them, the soft-hard swell of flesh over their pelvic bone pressed against the cleft of my ass. Like this, it would usually go one of two ways. Sometimes, when we'd had the time and foresight to prepare, Theo would push into me with blunt, slicked silicone until the buckles of their harness met the backs of my thighs. And sometimes, they would take me into their own body, pound their hips into me at such a smooth, relentless pace that it became impossible to tell which of us was fucking the other.

But neither of those things is on the menu tonight. It doesn't matter if I can feel how wet they are through our underwear, or that I'd happily accept whatever they chose to give. Fucking can encompass a thousand different things that aren't fucking, and our rules permit so many of them.

As if they can hear my thoughts, they say with tight, meted remove, "I want to propose another amendment."

"I'm open to that," I say, just as taut.

"I would like to get your cock out."

Something like a solar eclipse happens inside my brain. I stare directly into it and go momentarily blind.

"But," they go on, "I'm not going to touch it."

"You're—you're not?"

"No," they say, "you are. And I'll tell you how."

"I—I think that was already allowed, technically."

"Don't be such a fucking priss."

I smile, tipping my chin up.

"Don't like it so much, then."

Theo's grip hardens, but their expression does the opposite.

"Is that a yes?"

"Yes. Fucking—yes, but I'll need lube."

At the exact same moment, we reach for our toiletry kits on opposite nightstands. We stop, then burst into laughter.

"What's yours?" Theo asks. "Fucking organic unrefined coconut oil?"

I feel around my kit for its familiar shape, tossing it on the bed as Theo tosses theirs.

"Coconut oil can cause yeast infections," I say. "I'm a more considerate lover than that."

Theo eyes my travel-sized, fifteen-mil vial of lube. "That's not a lot."

"I packed refills."

"Hm." They nod thoughtfully, as if they're not currently bending me up like a Bavarian pretzel. "Sustainable."

I read the label on Theo's much bigger, sapphire-blue pump bottle, feeling lightheaded. "Aloe based? And you called *me* bougie."

"Shut up," they say, and I do.

True to their word, they don't touch me. I lift my hips at an instructive raise of their eyebrows, and they tug my underwear down until it cups the bottom of my ass, leaving me heavy and hard and exposed to the honeyed lamplight and the mild breeze carrying distant, wine-loose conversation through the open windows. They stare down at me, at the bright, wet glisten of anticipation already showing.

"Still so pretty when you're needy," they murmur, like I'm not meant to hear. I respond anyway, hitch a low whine in the back of my throat to make them claim it.

They look up then, directly into my eyes, and take their hand away.

"Hands on the pillow. Don't move them until I tell you."

Again, I do as I'm told. Theo shifts, widening their knees, then takes a small, blunt thing from their kit and slips it into their underwear. A pause—their teeth dig into their lip in a moment of disorientingly adorable concentration—and then comes the low rumble of their little vibe switching on.

A short *huh* punches out of them. They roll their hips forward, using my body to pin the pressure where they need it, and through the single layer of fabric separating us, the hum resonates into me, into the muscle they once trained with their fingers.

"Fu—uck," I exhale.

For a while, I'm happy to simply watch, pacified with how gorgeous they are grinding against my ass, making themself feel good. But it's huîtres gratinées for apéro, too rich and too filling to prime the palate and not enough for a meal. I pitch my voice up, rut uselessly against air, heart-wrenchingly untouched.

"*Please,*" I say. "Tell me to do something."

Theo kisses the bend of my knee and says, generously, "Get yourself wet."

My hands snatch up the nearest bottle—Theo's—and then I'm gasping at the shock of cold lube on warm, sensitive skin. Theo answers with an approving snap of their hips, so I make the sound again as I work myself over.

"What now, Theo?"

I can feel the plaintive look on my face, how readily I've shown them my throat and the whites of my eyes, and my heart swells at the thought that I'm being easy for them. I want to remind them how good they can be at something when they decide to be, how well they can take control, see a plan to completion.

"Go slow." They keep their voice low and steady even as their hips shift into a higher gear, core muscles flexing. "Tease yourself for me. Okay?"

"Yes. Okay, yes."

Theo gives calm, short commands, and my hand and body listen. They talk me through every change in pressure and speed, every twist of my wrist and slick glide of my palm. They push my knees toward my chin until my thighs burn, ease me through to blissful, slack surrender, *I know you can do it, beautiful, you can take more,* guide me right up to the precipice and then make me stop and watch them come instead. Then they start over.

I'd be screaming with frustration if I weren't so fucking happy to see it. So relieved, so proud. *This* is what Theo can do. The command, the deliberate force of will and want, the total inhabitance of their body, the fucking *range* to fuck me better than any person ever has or could, the *power* of that, the breathtaking endlessness of it. They're a catastrophe like an earthquake is a catastrophe, an act of the gods. They're the crumbling of an empire and the simple, immediate crash of glass on the floor for good luck. They're everything, and they're Theo. Singular Theo, everlasting Theo, Theo the superbloom.

Finally, somewhere in the valley of it, in the cleavage of hills and the ripe, red center of vines, Theo kisses my face and speaks in a voice I've heard in my dark, empty flat a thousand times when I'm bringing myself over the edge, "Come for me, Kit, let me see you." And that's so easy to give, because the only thing I want more than release is for Theo to be looking at me.

When I finish at last—at long fucking last, God—it's with

a broken half sob, my free hand knotted in Theo's hair, release spilling over my own skin. Theo's mouth falls open as they watch, and a second orgasm seems to take them by total surprise. A soft, awed sound wrenches out.

For a long time after, I just look into their eyes, and they stare wonderstruck into mine, and I feel the same magnificent fear from this morning, like I'm seeing a part of them I'm not supposed to. I nearly look away. But they wrap me in their arms, and they don't let go, even after they fall asleep.

I let myself wonder if maybe, just once, when I heard their voice in my ear in my bed in the 6th, they were on the other side of the world, hearing mine.

— — —

Morning floods across the wood and terra-cotta ceiling, turning everything to pure, pale wheat and apricot. The villa is quiet, and the smell of baking bread wafts up from the kitchens. Breakfast must not even be laid out yet.

I lift my head to look at Theo in this light while it lasts: the shape of their mouth, the dip of their collarbone, the gentle shadow cast by their nose that pools with the darkening freckles on their cheeks. It's been so long since I woke up peacefully beside Theo, and a whole life waiting to wake to *this* Theo.

When I'm satisfied, I slide out of the sheets.

In Paris, the quiet hours before I get dressed are my favorite hours of the day. I make the rounds to my houseplants, or write grocery lists, or mend socks with a darning needle and yarn, or fold the clean laundry hung to dry in the window. It's when I feel most full of possibility, like I could solve anything. So, this morning, I take a sketchbook down to the gardens and contemplate how I could help Theo.

It's not until I'm settling against a fountain that I realize one other person is wandering the estate: Signora Lucia, carefully clipping today's flower arrangements. I look on quietly as a breeze stirs her dress around her, surrounded by cosmos and zinnias, dahlias and roses. She sees me and smiles, waving with a gloved hand.

She really does remind me of my mother.

Maman loved Theo like a fourth child, and Theo loved her like a second mother. Outside of Ollie and Cora, there's nobody on earth who knows the exact shape and flavor and weight of losing her. That was one of the sharpest pains of losing Theo: losing this vestigial piece of my mother too, the deposit of her love in Theo's heart. It's been nice to talk about her without explaining anything.

Signora Lucia carries her flowers off toward the villa, and I sketch and think of Theo. It must be around seven now. Serving spoons clank against platters in the distance, quiet conversations twinkling to life on the terrazza. A few guests have come out for coffee and fruit, but most are sleeping off their late night. I expect Theo to do the same.

But minutes later, Theo comes tromping into the garden, dressed in boots and light jeans and a barely buttoned shirt.

"I knew you'd be here," they call, affecting the snobbish voice they used in the pool to tease me about my reading, "doing your morning taxonomy exercises."

I grin. "However else will I win the vicar's favor? I never learned pianoforte."

"Blow him," they suggest. "Hey, do you want to go for a bike ride before we leave? Apparently there's a trail that goes past an old castle. Twenty minutes each way. Could be cool."

"Aren't we loading up soon?"

"Not for another hour and a half. And I put our bags on the bus, so we don't have to go back up. We'll be fast."

I shift my weight, deliberating. My phone is in my pack, so I can't keep us on schedule. I'll have to rely on Theo. I can see the anxious hope in their eyes, a subtle, sunny glow.

"Alright," I say. "Which way?"

ROME

PAIRS WELL WITH:

Cardinale on the rocks, half-melted gelato

ROME

Luckily, Signora Lucia knows how to drive a stick shift.

We're on the motorway somewhere between Chianti and Rome, three across on the bench seat of the truck Lucia usually takes to pick up cases of wine from neighboring wineries.

Everything that could go wrong on our bike ride, did. Theo got lost, my bike blew a tire, a goat chased us off the road. For the first hour it was a charming pastoral misadventure, until our play fighting became actual fighting, and when Theo mentioned the bus leaving at nine, I stopped and stared and told them the schedule said eight. We were late for a bus that had already left, and nobody had looked for us because Theo had helpfully checked our names off when they loaded our bags.

By the time we could communicate what happened and get a concierge to call the tour company—Theo never got around to saving Fabrizio's number—the bus was an hour out. If they turned back, the entire group would miss the Vespa tour of Roman monuments scheduled for this afternoon. That was when Signora Lucia marched in, took up the receiver, and told Fabrizio she would handle it.

And now here we are, halfway to Rome in a half-rusted farm truck with the Italian ghost of my dead mother, who seems to only know two words of English, *hello* and *cow*.

Theo and I sit with our arms crossed, tense and separate. Under the engine and a cassette of Patty Pravo's greatest hits, I can almost hear Theo grinding their teeth. I fix my gaze on the miniature portraits of Mary and Jesus hanging from the rear-view mirror and try to recall how nice it felt to wake up this morning.

"Cow," Signora Lucia says boredly, pointing through the dusty windshield at some cattle grazing in a field. She has pointed out every cow pasture we've passed in what seems to be a perfunctory agricultural sightseeing tour. Theo and I both make appreciative *hmm* sounds.

We pass two more pastures before Theo finally unsticks their jaw and says, facing straight ahead, "Why don't you just say whatever you're thinking so we can get it over with."

Here we go.

"There's nothing to say," I tell them. "I should have checked the time before we left. I should have made sure you told someone where we were going."

"In other words, you should have known I would fuck up."

"I wouldn't have gotten us into this situation, no."

They nod hard and fast. "Right, and you never make mistakes."

"I knew the right time."

"Sure," they say. "Fuck me, I guess."

"Why are you mad at *me*?"

"Because I can hear the superiority in your fucking tone, Kit," Theo says, finally facing me. "Like you think I'm an idiot child."

I don't think that, but we've had this conversation a thousand times before, and it won't make a difference if I say so. Last night should be enough proof, but maybe that's the problem. Maybe they didn't really believe what I said then either. Maybe I just put a crust on top of everything, and this has broken it.

"There is one thing I'd like to say, actually," I attempt. "I don't think this is about the bus. I think you're feeling a bit raw from yesterday."

"Oh, cool, you're here to save me from myself *and* tell me how I feel," Theo says, cheeks flaring red. "Really taking me back to the good ol' days. It's a miracle I survived all this time without you, huh?"

"Don't put words in my mouth," I say, keeping my voice even. "That's not what I think."

"Pretty close to what you said back then."

"Cow," says Signora Lucia, pointing, and we both go *hmm*.

"Then?" I ask Theo. "Then, when?"

They don't say anything, and it hits me like I'm rolling down the motorway myself. Head over ass, scraped across the pavement, fifteen different French swears colliding in my head.

"You mean on the plane," I say. "You want to talk about that *now*?"

"No, I'm just saying," Theo says tightly. When they swat a piece of hair from their eyes, their hand shakes. "It's not like I'm making things up."

"I don't remember saying anything like that," I say, throat tight.

What I do remember is: my ears ringing as Theo shook me awake. The envelope in their hand—they'd gone looking through my bag for a snack and found it. The dull roar of the engines as we sailed over the ocean, the sour taste of sleep in my mouth. I remember Theo holding the pages out and asking what the hell they were, how I'd carefully folded them in thirds. My acceptance letter and the papers for our apartment.

We'd talked about Paris so many times. I'd been telling them stories about the pied-à-terre in Saint-Germain-des-Prés our whole lives. This was Theo's first time crossing the Atlantic, but when we were up late watching *No Reservations* or picking up Camembert from the cheese shop next to Ralph's, we swore that Theo would come with me one visit, and I'd show them everywhere Thierry and Maman took me when I was little, and we'd eat and kiss and drink kir with a splash of Lillet Blanc. And wouldn't it be funny, we said, if we never left? If we stayed forever, started a whole new life, opened up Fairflower on some flowering corner?

Theo knew I'd applied to culinary schools all over, including Paris. And so, when I'd gotten into École Desjardins a few months after we booked the tour, I'd had an idea: I would have Thierry sign the pied-à-terre over to me when he moved out. On our tour, Theo would see Paris for the first time, I'd introduce them to all the things they'd fall in love with, and then I'd surprise them. I had secretly rerouted our tickets home from Palermo with a two-day layover in Paris, and I was going to bring them to the pied-à-terre and give them our dream in an envelope. A blooming home in Paris, a new life, everything already prepared. They didn't have to worry about anything, didn't have to manage any of the difficult, tedious details. All they had to do was come.

I laughed and shrugged, *So much for the big romantic surprise,* and the color drained from Theo's face, and they said, *I thought you applied in Paris as a joke.* That was when it all fell to pieces.

The first questions were all *how* questions, ones I didn't expect because I thought we both knew the answers. How would I pay to study pastry in Paris? I'd borrow money from my dad. How would we move all our things across the ocean? The pied-à-terre was already furnished. How was Theo supposed to spend their time while I was at school? They could immerse themself in the French wine they'd gotten into lately, learn everything we needed to keep it flowing at Fairflower one day. How were they going to do that when they didn't even speak French? I'd teach them. How could it even work, legally? That one was easiest. I said, *I have dual citizenship, we'll just get married.*

And Theo said, *Do not fucking tell me this is how you're proposing.*

"What were you thinking?" Theo asks. "How could you design a whole life for me without even asking if I wanted it?"

I pinch the bridge of my nose, trying to trap all the frustration and grief there. They asked me the same question four years ago, and my answer ruined everything. But it hasn't changed.

"You weren't happy, Theo," I say. "And I was afraid that if you kept doing the same things, you never would be."

What gives you the fucking right, Theo said back then, *to decide that for me?*

I genuinely thought Theo would love the idea of no more rent to pay, no more double shifts or getting cursed out in the kitchen, no more rotating through the only five restaurants we actually liked, no ex-hookups to avoid, no credit scores to repair or worry about where they'd get insurance when they turned twenty-six. A limitless life in the most beautiful city in the world, where nobody had to know their family name. And us, together. We could do anything together.

They *weren't* happy. They hadn't been since they'd lost swim and dropped out. Timo worked them hard and nasty, made them earn every inch from busser to barback to bartender to bar manager with sweat and blisters and long nights that only made their shoulder worse. They were tired all the time. They picked up new passions and burnt them out in a week. And sometimes, there was a strange, brittle disconnect behind their eyes, like something was living inside them without being tended, something so essential it might permanently empty them if it died of neglect.

And the thing was, they never said I was wrong about that. But they were possessed of a fierce, stubborn conviction that it was their right to be miserable.

I told them, *I can't keep watching you give up on yourself.* I said, *I can help you.* I said, *I worry that sometimes you get in your own way.* And Theo said, *Do you hear how you keep talking about my life in the first person?*

"It wasn't a life I liked," Theo says now, "but it was mine."

Then, Theo had more questions: How long had I been planning this? At any point did I wonder if telling them to abandon their life, move to a different continent where they didn't know the language, and live in my family's pied-à-terre was actually

romantic or just controlling? Did I care that Theo hates surprises? And I thought, *Did I know Theo hates surprises?*

I reminded them of Fairflower, all the menus we'd thought
of, all our dreams, and Theo said that's all it ever was to them: a
dream. Something nice to think about, nothing more. I hadn't
known, and Theo wasn't surprised. They told me that I always
think I know better and never leave them room to correct their
own mistakes, that I live in fantasies and hear whatever I want
to hear. I hadn't known that either.

We went round and round for hours in those cramped airplane seats, through dinner service and tepid plastic trays of la-
sagna, letting loose everything we'd ever held back. We'd fought
once or twice as kids, but we'd never figured out how to fight
as adults in a relationship. We didn't know when to stop. I told
them how many times I'd bitten my tongue and let them make
the worst choices, and they told me they'd be embarrassed to let
their parents pay for their life the way I let mine. They said I only
cared about my own ideas of meaning and success, and I said at
least I wasn't afraid to try for them. I was so sure I could see their
exact, direct path to being happier, and they refused to take it.

Sometimes I wonder if that fight would have ended us if we'd
had it at home. If we could have aired everything, taken a night
to settle, and met in the kitchen the next morning, maybe we
would have stayed together. But we had it on a plane to London
with nothing to do but implode. The last two hours to Heathrow were silent, and I couldn't think of anything honest that
would convince Theo not to leave me. I wasn't surprised when it
seemed like they did.

"You didn't know what you wanted to do," I say now. "And
I thought that I could help you figure it out, and I was afraid of
what would happen if I didn't."

"You wanted to go to Paris," Theo counters. "You wanted
the life you wanted—the life you have now, actually, which seems
like proof I never even needed to be there. I was a plus-one."

I feel like putting my head in my hands.

"Theo," I say, sounding tired even to myself, "I don't know how else to say it. You *were* my life. You were always the whole point of it."

"Well, I shouldn't have been," Theo snaps. "Nobody should be that to anyone, Kit, that's how a person becomes a thing. That's how you forgot to ask if Paris was what *I* wanted."

And I take a breath and say, "I know."

The Patty Pravo cassette runs out, fading into thin white noise over the truck radio. Signora Lucia switches the dial off.

It's quiet inside the truck when Theo says, "What?"

"I know. You're right. So, please, do we—do we have to keep reciting the whole fight? It was painful enough before I knew I was wrong, so I *really* can't stomach it now."

"You . . . you think I'm right?"

It's strange to realize I haven't told them. It's such big piece of cargo, I forget not everyone can tell I'm carrying it.

"Theo," I say, "the Paris thing is the greatest regret of my life."

Theo looks at me, their eyes so intent on searching mine that I can't read anything else in them. Then they say, "Say more," which is such a Theo answer to a moment of quiet vulnerability that I have to try not to smile.

"You were right," I say. "I have a dream, and get so obsessively swept up in it that I can't see anything else. I didn't see you. I was treating your life as a problem to be solved, planning for the version of you in my head who wanted what I thought was best, and I was so sure I was right, I forgot I'd never even met that person. That's the fucked-up part. I never loved the Theo who would have gone along for the ride. I've only ever loved you."

I've done it again, forgotten to use the past tense when I say I love them. I wonder if Theo will notice this time.

"Yeah, that . . ." Theo says, their gaze far away. For a moment, I think I've been caught out, but then they say through a small, sad laugh, "That *is* fucked up."

I laugh too, can't help it. It comes out a sigh.

"If I haven't said it," I say, "I'm sorry. I shouldn't have done anything without you."

Theo doesn't say anything, but it's a soft silence. They nod and turn their eyes back to the windshield, which gradually reveals the distant outskirts of Rome. Squat roadside bars, stucco apartments, pointy cypress trees. I watch them roll by, a strange feeling within my chest like the moment a bubbling pan of sugar resolves into caramel. Like relief, like a turning.

After half an hour, Theo lays their hand on mine. Half an hour after that, when we've made it to the city, they finally speak.

"I should have checked the bus schedule again this morning," they say. "My bad."

The bus is so far from my mind, this surprises a full-throated laugh out of me.

"I could have checked too," I say.

Theo squeezes my hand.

"And to be fair," they say as the truck trundles between Flaminio's leafy pink and yellow houses, "there *were* days I wished I could just magically disappear all my problems and restart."

"I think everyone probably wants that sometimes."

"Now and then I still do," they say. "But if I start life over, I want it to be mine."

I nod. "I know."

Signora Lucia brings us to a bus stop on the edge of a piazza, across from the market where the tour group should be having lunch. We tell her "Grazie mille, grazie mille" over and over until she waves us off, and then we're running.

When we were young, Theo would get so angry when we raced each other. We're both fast, and Theo has always had power and defiance on their side, but I have longer strides and better reflexes. They were always one step behind.

Now, as we run across the piazza, I fall back. Theo advances at a thunderous clip, as if they could be unsheathing a sword instead of pulling their phone from their hip pack, hot Roman sun flashing off their hair like laurels on a gladiator. They're so gorgeous from this new angle.

They glance over their shoulder to find me one step behind them, and something blooms on their face. They turn away before I can name it.

— — —

Fabrizio scoops us up in breathless relief outside Antico Forno Roscioli as the group finishes lunch. The blessed Calums have saved us a few squares of crusty pizza topped with dollops of pesto and half of a sour cherry crostata, which we eat in big, messy bites washed down with the dregs of Stig's lukewarm Peroni. It was close, but we made it.

Six at a time, we're divided into groups, passed off to a grinning driver with a shiny helmet dangling from their fingers, and led away from the market to join our Vespa fleets. Theo and I are among the last to be assigned, but no driver appears. Instead, Fabrizio gives us a vigorous smile and says, "Amici, you come with me!"

Around the corner, we're awaited by a group of drivers and a line of vintage Vespas in a rainbow of pastels like a box of assorted Parisian macarons. A handsome middle-aged man wearing fingerless riding gloves shouts a joyous greeting to Fabrizio and kisses him hard on the side of his golden face. I'm beginning to suspect there's someone in love with Fabrizio in every city on this tour.

"This is Angelo!" Fabrizio tells us. "When I first come to Roma, he gave me my first job driving on this Vespa tour when I was only eighteen. I learn everything I know from him." He turns to Angelo. "And I was your favorite driver, no?"

"Sì," Angelo says. "All the girls want to take the tour when they see you. Very good for business."

"And now," Fabrizio says, "when my tours visit Roma, I bring them to you. And as a special treat, you let me drive like the old days, sì?"

Each rider pairs with a driver—two honeymooners with two sturdy older men almost identical to Lars, Stig with a tiny woman who wears a lot of nose rings and has to stand on her seat to jam the helmet onto his head, Dakota with Angelo. I count the scooters and come up one short. All that remains for Theo and me is a single canary-yellow Vespa with a matching sidecar.

"Fabrizio, no," Theo says as they realize what's about to happen.

"Fabrizio, sì!" Fabrizio replies, holding out a helmet for each of us. "One of you will ride in the sidecar, and one of you will sit behind me. Like this!"

He points to Dakota straddling the Vespa seat behind Angelo, her thighs pressed against his and her arms around his middle. One of us will be doing that with Fabrizio while the other squats in the sidecar like a picture-book dog with goggles on.

Theo plonks their helmet onto their head and turns to me. "Should we flip a coin?"

"We could take turns? Swap at the stops?" I suggest. I sweep my hair back and put my helmet on, and Theo instantly starts laughing. I frown. "What?"

"Look at you!" They pull out their phone to take a picture and show me the screen, my frowning confusion and the tufts of hair that stick out from the bottom of my helmet. "God, it's perfect."

"I look chic," I say. "I look like I ride motorcycles on the Amalfi Coast."

"You look like they shoot you out of a cannon at a circus for gay people."

"Even better."

"I know," Theo says, like they're surprised by how much they mean it.

I wink and tighten my chin strap, gesturing toward Fabrizio already seated behind the handlebars. "You go first. Keep him warm for me."

And, with a two-finger salute, Theo kicks a leg over.

The sidecar isn't as cramped as it looks, and once I get my legs situated it's almost comfortable. Theo, who continues to think this is the funniest thing that's ever happened, snaps a dozen more photos, and then Fabrizio cranks up the throttle and pushes off.

The other drivers fall into formation as we turn onto one of the wide main roads of Rome, Corso Vittorio according to a glimpse of a sign. Buildings rise up around us in stately blocks of ivory and cream, distinguished and lined with stone balustrades, propped up by Ionic columns with curling scrolls at their tops. The sky is a blistering blue, and the road bends west, toward the green rush of the Tiber. The engine purrs, and Fabrizio sings into the wind as he weaves through Roman traffic, and from my sidecar, I look at Theo.

They're a desert baby, brought back to life by sun and heat. Their grin grows wider and wider, the morning disappearing into Fabrizio's rearview. They lace their fingers together around Fabrizio's waist and put their face into the wind, gazing at Rome with honest wonder.

I think after everything, now that we've said what we needed to say, we might come out okay.

We cruise over an arched bridge to the round drum of Castel Sant'Angelo, atop which legend says the Archangel Michael sheathed his sword to signal the end of Rome's great plague. Honking cars race us to the travertine facade of the Palace of Justice and back over the Tiber and into winding nests of narrow cobbly streets, toward the Pantheon.

As we reach the temple, Fabrizio turns back to Theo and shouts over the engine.

"When we finish, come back here, down this street, and then the first left, and the first right after this into the alley, and you will find the hostel between the osterias at the end. Orla leaves your bags in your rooms at the top of the stairs."

"Uh-huh," Theo says. They're gazing in awe at the Panthe-on's ancient columns, not hearing any of this.

"Grazie!" I shout, happy to leave Theo's moment uninter-rupted. I'll remember for us.

We pull into an alley with an ancient faucet spouting crisp, clear water. I've read about these—nasoni, public faucets fed in part by the original Roman aqueducts—but I almost couldn't believe it until now. We catch water in our cupped hands, take turns pressing our fingers to the spouts to make them spray up-ward like a drinking fountain. Fabrizio tips his whole head side-ways and puts his mouth under the stream, and I catch Theo looking when I follow his example, taking cool water into my open mouth until it spills down my chin.

After, it's my turn to ride with Fabrizio. I wrap my arms around his firm waist, press my thighs against his, our shorts rid-ing up high enough for our sweat to mingle. He compliments the softness of my skin as he cranks the engine, and I thank him with my most flirtatious smile. Theo watches with open, curious hun-ger from the sidecar below. Two things that endure the passage of time: Roman antiquities, and the thrill Theo gets from seeing me with a man between my legs.

The tour goes on through a blur of stone and ivy, the ruins of the square where Julius Caesar was murdered, the grassy stretch of Circus Maximus once pounded by racing hooves and chariot wheels, temples to Hercules and Portunus so well-preserved a Roman farmer might amble through with a cow to sell at the Forum Boarium. We finish at the Arch of Constantine, barely changed from how it looked when victorious emperors paraded through seventeen hundred years ago, still proud and imposing on the backdrop of the looming Colosseum.

We tour the Colosseum on foot, our shoes on the same stones as thousands of ancient sandals. Fabrizio's voice is hoarse from use as he recites story after story, reenacts battle after battle. Then we go back out through the archways, past the ruins of the fountain where gladiators washed their wounds, to the top of the Palatine Hill and its wide overhead view of the Roman Forum.

On a long tour, days have a way of stretching impossibly beyond their edges. So many things spread out over such short hours, one after another, until it seems unimaginable that the day could have begun in a different place at all. Like there has only ever been here, and then here, this fountain and that drink and this sparkling pane of glass, each trapped in an instant happening in the memory forever, each instantly replaced with the thing after that. Perpetual fleeting everything, worn-out body and blissed-out brain. That's how this day goes on.

Fabrizio cuts us loose to explore the Roman Forum. Theo and I wander down the same main street where senators schemed and merchants traded goods and women practiced the oldest profession, everyone working or praying or gambling or spreading rumors, and past what still stands of the triumphal arches.

I imagine Theo and me in their world. I'd be the baker, baking loaves of sourdough under smoldering ash, olive leaves in my hair and flour on my tunic. Theo would be the roguish young charioteer who buys bread from me every morning and flusters the vestal virgins. We'd steal glances but never touch until we were alone, pressing each other into secret corners of temples, and when they bound their chest with leather to race, my name would be carved inside the straps.

"So crazy how two thousand years ago, they were feeling all the same things we feel," Theo muses. "They wanted to be loved, and eat good food, and make art, and fuck."

"The human condition," I agree.

We pause at the most impressive temple, one with ten thick columns still holding up the frieze over its portico. A sign says this was originally built as a temple to Faustina the Elder, the empress. Her husband, Antoninus, was so heartbroken when she died that he had her deified and her likeness cast into gold statues, pressed into coins, and enshrined in this temple. He wanted the whole empire to worship her the way he did, and the cult of Faustina spread.

"Kind of romantic to love your wife so much you start a cult," I say.

"I don't know," Theo says, an ironic lilt to their lips. "Did anyone ever ask Faustina if she *wanted* to be a god?"

I laugh, perfectly willing to take a nudge to the ribs if it means we can joke about this now.

"You're right," I say. "Very presumptuous of Antoninus."

On our way out of the forum, we realize neither of us ate enough lunch, and we still have four hours until group dinner. Hungry and overheated, we choose the first pizzeria we see, partially because the waiter is attractive and partially for the sheer volume of mist piping into the outdoor seating area. Everything from the chairs to the silverware is slightly damp, sparkling with tiny, cooling water droplets. When the hot waiter takes our menus away, there are two dry rectangles left in their place on the brown paper tablecloth.

"Is this too much mist?" Theo asks. "I feel like I'm at a Rainforest Cafe."

"No, it's nice," I say, watching a drop of water roll down the side of their neck. "Like being a cucumber in a grocery store."

I drink a limoncello spritz, Theo has a glass of chilled Orvieto, and we split a pizza. When we're done, we walk uphill to the Trevi Fountain, which is absolutely awash with tourists dripping gelato and sharing crispy fried supplì stuffed with cheese and tomato. We find a spot near the fountain's edge and sit together.

"And there waits our lover, Sexy Neptune," I say, admiring the fountain. "He always comes back to us."

"I think that might be less about us and more about him being a popular subject for fountain sculptures."

"No, we have a thing going on."

"Hmm. Hold on." Theo studies the fountain more closely. "I know this place. It's in the seminal rom-com—"

"*Roman Holiday,*" I say at the same time Theo finishes, "*The Lizzie McGuire Movie,*" and we laugh.

I look at them, freckles out, hair whipped wild by the helmet and frizzed from mist, beside me in Rome after all. My charioteer. They made their own life, and it brought them here, and I'm lucky enough to see it.

I think of Faustina in the Forum, Theo on the plane. I want to do better this time. I want to know what they want. And whatever they want, I want to give it to them.

So, this time, I ask.

"Theo," I say. "What do you want?"

It's an open question. It can mean whatever they want it to mean.

They consider their answer for a long time, watching water crash into the bowl of the fountain.

"I'm working on it," they say. "Ask me again tomorrow."

— — —

That night, we have dinner at the kind of family-owned side-street osteria a person would only find if they knew where to look. It's nothing special to see—flat and brown among all the ivy-draped alleys and heroic statues—but it *feels* special. The walls are covered in a riot of black-and-white portraits of great-grandparents, hand-painted pizza posters, grainy shots of sauce-smeared grandchildren, and signed headshots of Italian singers. Red-and-white-checked vinyl tablecloths drape each table, and mismatched plates overflow with pasta in a dozen shapes and colors.

After, Theo and I finally make it to our rooms. For our two nights in Rome, we're booked into an old apartment building turned hotel, our rooms at the top of five flights of marble stairs so steep we take the last one gasping on hands and knees. On a dusty, open-air landing lit by string lights, Theo unlocks their door and finds our bags dumped inside.

I reach for mine, but they take my key and say, "You should stay."

In Theo's room, we take turns rinsing dried sweat off with cold showers. Even then, it's too hot to consider clothing, and since yesterday at the villa—God, how can that be only yesterday?—there's no reason for modesty. We leave our damp towels in the bathroom and lie naked on our backs atop the duvet, careful not to share body heat by touching. Our heads soak wet halos into the pillowcases.

I'm not looking at Theo with any real intent. But there is the plain, extraordinary fact of their body beside me: the taper of their forearms from elbow to wrist, the ridges of their shins and the sturdy knot of bone at their ankles, the gingersnap hair that dusts each leg and thickens between them. Their chest is almost as smooth as mine when they lie like this, subtle swells a shade pinker at each peak. It's not only the beauty of their body but the casual presence of it, the way I'm allowed to lie beside it in a quiet room, that gets to me.

"Kit," Theo says.

"Theo," I say.

"You're hard."

I close my eyes. "I know."

Theo spreads their feet apart, indenting the bedspread in two soft points under their heels. One of their hands—those strong, lovely hands—skims down their stomach and between their legs. They lift it to the lamplight and show me the wetness glistening on their fingertips.

It's an admission and a question. I answer both by reaching down and pushing into my own palm.

And so we lie there on a bed in Rome, twelve hours after settling our scores, touching ourselves together.

There was one other time like this, when we were nineteen and high and eaten up with longing. A late night in my room, an endless conversation that had drifted to the people we were

fucking instead of each other. For years we pretended not to remember lying beneath the same blanket with our hands under
our own waistbands, the rustle of cotton and whisper of skin,
but I couldn't forget how it felt to learn the sound of Theo getting off.

It can't be possible for our history to repeat so exactly, for
us to be lying here loving each other and not saying it again, but
I wonder. I watch Theo's hand move, and I groan at my own
touch, and I wonder.

"Kit," Theo says, and for one thick moment I think they're
actually sighing my name in pleasure, until they repeat, "Kit."

"Yeah?"

"I wanna change the rules again."

"Yeah," I say readily, "yeah, okay."

"No kissing, no penetration," they say, "but anything else goes."

My hand stills.

"Anything?"

"Anything."

"Are you sure?"

They lean in and drag their mouth across the corner of mine.
It's not a kiss, but it's enough like one to make me shiver.

"Please," Theo says. I've never said no to anything Theo asks
for nicely.

In the space of a second, I jackknife off the mattress and twist
around, using the momentum to flip Theo on their back and pin
myself between their thighs. Theo lets out a scream that's mostly
a laugh, legs already lifting.

"Fuck, could you always do that?"

I shift forward, bracing my shoulders under the firm curve
of their ass.

"I have some new techniques."

Theo grins luxuriantly. "My little pastry school valedicto-
rian."

"Yours," I echo, heart aching.

I put my mouth to them until they're gasping, until their hips buck off the bed, until their hands are buried in my hair, gripping and tugging and crushing my face into them so hard my vision blacks out blissfully at the edges.

They finish loud, and as soon as they've caught their breath, they wrench me up by the root of my hair and throw me backward, crowding me until I'm sitting with my back to the headboard. Lube appears from somewhere—the nightstand, maybe, I don't honestly care—and they're pumping it into their open palm, and then—and then—

Theo wraps their hand around me.

The texture of their hand is different than I remember—more calloused, more scarred—but the shape of it, the pressure of each finger and the cant of their wrist, the way their palm accommodates me, it's all so devastatingly familiar I almost come at the first touch. Tears instantly prick at the corners of my eyes, and I can't find it in myself to be ashamed. Through the blur, I see Theo's face, their fierce determination as they spread lube over me with one hand and on the insides of their thighs with the other.

Then they're climbing over me and aligning their hips above mine, and for one delirious second I think they're going to abandon the rules and fuck me the old-fashioned way, and I'm more than ready to let them.

Instead, they twist their body to the side and sink down onto my lap. They close their strong legs around me, trapping my full length between their thighs, slick on slick, soft encompassing hard.

A stream of swears slips from my mouth so fast, even I don't know what language I'm speaking. Tongues, maybe. Ancient Latin. I'm so completely, suddenly surrounded that I can barely think, barely control the way my hands grasp Theo to keep them where they are, seated sideways with their shoulder to my chest and their thighs clenched tight. They shift their hips in a demonstrative tease, and I swear again as I understand what they're offering.

"You like that?" Theo says, staring into my face, seeing God knows what there.

"Love it," I breathe out. *Love you.*

They brace their hands on the bed behind them to lift a fraction of their weight off my lap, giving me room to move.

"Show me how much."

Everything—the room, the heat, the day, the ache in my heart—*everything* falls away when I push up into the slicked clinch of their thighs.

In the absence of thought, my body supplies, *glissando.* A half-remembered term from classical compositions. The smooth, continuous slide from one pitch to another, low to high, down and then up. An evocation of magic or emotion or grace, written into odes to the sea in summer. *That* is what's happening between our bodies.

It's so good I can't imagine ever needing more, until Theo shifts and I feel a new, wet heat against me, the familiar shape of their sex still messy from my mouth. They snap their hips, finding the friction they need, dangerously close to letting me slip inside. As they finish again, their gaze lands on my face like a comfort, like a command, and I'm done. I'm beyond recovery.

I'm so ruined that I don't realize until later, in a half-awake moment in the middle of the night, that we nearly broke the only two rules we have left.

— — —

The next morning, Theo's head is on my pillow and three new texts from Maxine are on my phone.

saw guillaume looking despondent at the cafe this morning. i think he misses you. at least parts of you.

And, you owe me updates on the theo situation. what happened after monaco?? if you've gotten your heart broken again i'll kill all three of us.

And, dinner on monday night?

I switch off my alarm before it wakes up Theo and reread Maxine's texts while I brush my teeth, puzzling out which Monday she could mean. Then I realize: She's talking about *next* Monday. As in, less than seven days away. As in, the tour is almost over.

For two and a half weeks, I've lived in this bubble outside of reality, where I spend every day eating and drinking and touching and looking at art, dazed from too many languages and not enough sleep. Where Theo is beside me, and we're friends again, and we share a pillow and wake up with the taste of each other on our tongues. I almost forgot that my life in Paris has been going on without me, and now it's so close that dinner with Maxine at our usual bistro is something I could be doing in a matter of days.

I spit and rinse, but the fizz of slight panic stays in my mouth. I count the time left. One more day and night in Rome, Naples tomorrow, and then the two-day finish in Palermo. Four days and four nights until I fly home to France, and Theo gets on a plane to California. There's nothing to stop them from blocking my number again if they want to. I feel certain that won't happen, not after all this . . . but what if it does?

Where have I been hoping this would lead in the end?

From the bed comes the rustle of sheets and a low, stretching grumble.

"Kit?" says Theo's voice, hoarse with sleep. "You here?"

"In the bathroom."

Another grumble and the creak of bedsprings, and Theo is shuffling into the tiny bathroom, pulling a T-shirt on backward. Their hair is wild, their eyes half closed, a streak of dried drool on their chin. I don't know how I could survive losing them again.

"Thought you left like yesterday."

"At the villa? Did it bother you that I got up early?"

They nod, fumbling for their toiletry kit. I place their hand on the zipper before they knock their deodorant into the sink.

"Wanted to wake up together," Theo says, which strikes me momentarily speechless. They rest their forehead against my shoulder, letting me prop up their weight.

I try to tell my heart to settle, that they're being tender because they're half asleep, but it clenches anyway.

Our packs are against the wall by the bed, mine repacked and zipped up neatly, Theo's tipped over and spilling half-folded clothes onto the carpet. I huff a laugh and begin arranging Theo's shirts into a more orderly pile, when my hand brushes something solid inside a ball of socks.

Part of a label pokes out, one I'd recognize anywhere. The little bottle of whiskey I gave Theo for our first anniversary, distilled the year we met. The one we were supposed to drink at the end of our tour four years ago.

They kept it. I thought they would have drunk it by now, or thrown it away, but all this time, they kept it. And when they were choosing which things to fit into their pack, they made room. They made the choice to bring it here, not even knowing they would see me.

"Where are we going this morning again?" Theo asks from the bathroom.

I cover the socks back up and move away from Theo's bag before they poke their head into the room.

My voice is admirably normal when I answer, "Galleria Borghese."

An hour and a half later, Orla drops us off at the Spanish Steps. Fabrizio takes us up into the huge green sprawl of the Villa Borghese Gardens, once a vineyard until Cardinal Scipione Borghese turned it into his personal party destination in the 1600s, as is an evil gay cardinal's right. His collection of art—some obtained by abusing the pope's funds, others by abusing the pope's influence—still fills the villa at the center of the gardens. Now, it's a public museum.

Fabrizio walks us through an introductory tour of the most

famous pieces, then lets us explore on our own. When I ask Theo where to start, they say, "Show me your favorite Bernini." So I lead them to *Apollo and Daphne*, and when I ask what they want to see next, they tell me to go on without them.

It's easy to imagine this place as Rome's hottest destination for fruity seventeenth-century art parties. Inside, it is the highest of high camp, from the trompe-l'œil fresco covering the ceiling of the salon to the thousands of gilded flourishes in the Room of Emperors.

I open my sketchbook and scavenge for details to bring home: the silly little face of the unicorn in the arms of Raphael's *Young Woman,* the eyes of the bejeweled woman in Titian's *Sacred and Profane Love,* the affectionate strokes Caravaggio used for the face of his lover Mario as the *Boy with a Basket of Fruit.* But every time I pass the room with *Apollo and Daphne,* Theo remains, fixed to the same spot.

I drift to the entrance hall, to the glossy marble sculpture of a topless woman reclining in a bed of flowing linens, apple in hand. I remember studying this one. *Venus Victrix,* the scandalous likeness of Pauline Bonaparte sculpted when her brother Napoleon married her off to a Borghese. She's an interesting woman—one of the great luminaries of being slutty and French, and for that I admire her—but I'm still thinking of Theo. Of last night.

In my head, I retrace our steps since we first touched in Cinque Terre. The edge in Theo's voice in Pisa when they agreed to keep hooking up, like they were throwing themself off some perilous ledge. The unknown emotion they fought in the grotto in Florence and their grip on my hair in the alley. The morning after in Chianti, that brash, invulnerable grin and their naked body in daylight, how they tried to protect themself with sex and jokes and then collapsed into me when they couldn't anymore. The way they pulled me into their room and their bed last night. The bottle in their bag.

The truth is, I haven't wanted to seriously consider what it all could mean. I've been so willing to believe that Theo would never want me back, because as long as I have nothing to hope for, I have nothing to lose. They can't leave me again if I don't expect them to stay.

But I'm beginning to think it could be possible. That there's a chance Theo could still love me.

Theo might love me. Theo might *love me.*

The tour is almost over, and if there's a chance Theo feels like I do, I can't let them go home not knowing.

If Theo loves me, then—then that's it for me. I want it all. I want to be with them for the rest of our lives, whatever that looks like, however they ask. I'd get it right this time, plan it out so they don't have to give anything up to fit our lives together. I'll never ask them to follow me anywhere again. I don't expect them to leave California, and I definitely wouldn't expect them to move to Paris. How could I, after everything? When it hasn't even made me happy?

When it—

I stare at Pauline and repeat the thought, testing its weight.

It hasn't made me happy.

I wish I could ask Pauline's opinion. Does Paris make me happy? Did coming to Rome make *her* happy?

Of course it didn't. She was happy in France, rouging her nipples and making love to men who weren't her well-bred husbands, getting caught with her skirts up behind screens. She posed nude for this, the statue commissioned to announce her as a wife to Roman society, simply for the delicious thrill, and her husband hid it away in a crate in the attic.

I don't think my life in Paris took my wonder from me, but I do sometimes feel like it's stored in a crate in the attic. I could take it down. I could ship it somewhere else—somewhere Theo would like to be. They could help me pry off the lid. They're so much better with tools.

Tonight, I tell myself, taking a deep breath. Tonight, after dinner, I'll take Theo out for a drink, and I'll tell them how I feel. I'll ask them if they feel the same. And if they do, I'll tell them I'll go wherever they want.

— — —

"Theo," I say, "I have a very important question for you."

It's night, and we're in Trastevere with our bellies full of pasta, at a tiny café table in a pocket-sized alley, perusing the wine list under a curtain of ivy. Mostly, Theo's perusing the wine list, and I'm reading the names of unfamiliar Italian appellations out loud just to hear Theo correct my pronunciation.

Theo lifts their stare from the menu, brows frozen in a studious furrow.

"Okay."

"If you were a wine grape," I say, "which grape would you be?"

They relax with a laugh. "Really? That's your question."

"You keep saying that every grape has its own characteristics and personality," I say, "so, which one is most like you?"

They think about it. "I feel like I have to be a California white."

"Well, you are a California white."

"Very original joke from the southern French white."

"Merci beaucoup."

"And le fuck you too," Theo says cheerfully. "I might be a Viognier."

"I have to tell you, that sounds French."

"It is, originally, but it's grown in California too. Full-bodied, rich texture. It might sound weird, but it makes a kind of oily wine? And I think that suits me. Something with weight, that likes to sit there and hang out for a long time."

"I can see that. What does it taste like?"

"Peach, mostly, but I also get tangerine and honeysuckle with it, and a lot of other florals. Which feels like me, I guess."

I ponder this. "You know, I think I assumed you would be a red, but that's perfect for you."

"Oh, Kit. *You* are a red."

"*I'm* a red? Why?"

"Come on. Deep, indulgent, immortalized in a million Renaissance paintings, made to be poured between ass cheeks at a bacchanal. You're a red."

"That does sound like me," I say, nodding thoughtfully. "But a light-bodied red."

"I'd say medium-bodied but light on its feet. Fruity."

"Naturally."

"French. Rhône-adjacent. If you're a grape, you've got to be Gamay."

"I've heard of that one. What's it like?"

"Well, versatile, first of all."

"Famously."

"Notes of pomegranate and raspberry. Soil. A lot of flowers too. Peony, iris." With a significant look, they add, "Violets, actually."

"You're very good at this. You do know that, don't you?"

"It's weird. I think I might almost be . . . afraid to be good at it?"

"What do you mean?"

"I've been thinking about something," they tell me. "Today, at the Borghese, I was like, what if I pick one thing in this gallery and spend the whole time with it? Instead of speeding through the entire museum for a hundred five-second hits of dopamine, what if I stand here and let this be the only thing I experience?"

"And how did that feel?"

"It felt . . . uncomfortable. Boring. And then I started to see things I hadn't noticed, like the details of the leaves, and the straps of the sandals. And I thought about how long it must have taken to sculpt, and to build up the skill to sculpt something like it, so I looked up Bernini."

"*You* looked up Bernini," I repeat, disbelieving. "After you made *me* have a Bernini jar."

"I know! But I looked him up, and he started sculpting when he was eight. Eight! He drew a little and did some architecture, but it was sculpting that he devoted his entire life to, until he was eighty-one years old. And then I thought about Gaudí with Sagrada Família. And I started thinking about having a thing that you throw your entire self behind, and about my sisters, and my parents, and how they've always had that, and they've never questioned it and always succeeded at it. And I was like, what's my thing?"

A waiter drops off our wine, a red Theo chose. They present the bottle to Theo and let them taste. Theo approves, so they pour.

"You were saying," I prompt when the waiter is gone. "Your thing."

"Right, so, first it was being the oldest child, and I mean, obviously I spectacularly failed at that."

I raise my eyebrows. "Did you?"

"Come on," Theo says with a roll of their eyes. "Sloane is everything the oldest should be. Brave, dependable—"

"Protector, leader, setter of examples?" I suggest. "I distinctly remember you being all of those things for at least one person. Me."

"Maybe so," Theo says, coloring faintly. "Or—yeah, I guess I was. But still. It was— I failed at being the firstborn Flowerday. I wasn't needed. I didn't have the family gifts. That's what I mean."

"Okay," I say, still unhappy with this characterization but curious to see where Theo is going. "I understand what you're saying."

"And so for a while my thing was house parties, and we all know how that went, and then it was swimming, and that was supposed to be the big one, so I went too hard and fucked my body up and lost that too. And after that, I think I got scared, and so I started putting a little bit of myself into a lot of things instead of all of myself into one thing. Like if I'm always just starting something, I can always be in that beginning stage when it's shiny and new and full of possibility, and if I never try to finish, I never get to the part where I fuck it up."

In all the years I wished for Theo to commit to being happy, I never thought to consider it this way, but it makes sense.

"So," I say, "where does this leave you?"

They sip, and they consider.

"Ask me a different question," they say. "Ask me what you asked me yesterday."

I lean back in my chair.

"Theo," I say. "What do you want?"

"I think what I want most of all," Theo says, "is . . . peace."

"Peace," I repeat slowly.

"I don't know if I've ever let myself have peace. I thought staying in one place my whole life would do it, but maybe I won't know peace until I choose one thing I want to do and put everything I have behind it and see it through. Even if I fuck it up beyond repair, even if I embarrass myself and my family and have to go live off the grid on Calum's shark-research boat. At least I'll finally know how it goes."

I want to take Theo's hand and tell them how long I've waited for them to decide this for themself. To believe in it. Instead, I satisfy myself with imagining leaving my life in Paris, chasing whatever dream Theo chooses. I picture myself balancing the budget for Theo's bus bar, or kissing Theo's hair while they make study cards for the master sommelier exam, or replacing the new pastry chef at Timo that Theo doesn't like. I could be happy there, as long as Theo wanted me with them.

I ask, "Do you want to know what I think?"

"Yes."

"I think you deserve peace. And you can do whatever it is you decide." I take a sip and add, "And you should have let me talk about Bernini more."

Theo laughs. "I guess so."

"And for what it's worth," I go on, "whatever you choose, you don't have to do it alone."

Theo absorbs this, then leans closer.

"I've been meaning to ask you something," they say. "I thought you went to pastry school so you could open your own place. You were going for the diploma in culinary management too, right? Why are you working in someone else's kitchen?"

The question catches me by surprise; I have to take a beat to think of an answer.

"I changed my mind," I say.

"Why?"

"I met other pâtissiers in Paris," I explain as simply as I can. "I saw what it was like, trying to start something from nothing in a city like that, and I realized you were right. Fairflower was a fantasy."

Theo's expression softens, something strangely sad playing around their eyes.

"A nice one, though, wasn't it?" they say. "Do you still think about it?"

"Of course."

"I do too," they say. "Sometimes, I wonder if—"

They break off, their gaze flicking past me.

"Oh, whoa."

"What?"

"That guy over there," they say. "For a second I thought that was your dad."

I look over my shoulder, scanning the tables outside the next bar until I see the man Theo must be talking about: sixty-something with a scruffy beard and a vague resemblance to Victor Garber, writing in a notebook with an expensive-looking fountain pen.

"Oh, huh. He does look like him, doesn't he?"

"It would be so typical Craig to just happen to be on summer sabbatical in Rome and not tell anyone."

"Oh, sure. He'll be the writer in residence at St. Peter's, and we'll find out when he shows up in a photo with the pope."

Theo laughs, and as they lift their glass back to their lips, a terrible thing occurs to me.

My dad's pattern. Deciding what he wants on some romantic whim, fixating on the fantasy, pursuing it without regard for how it will affect the people he loves or if they even want the same thing. That's what I did to Theo with Paris.

Am I about to do it again?

I said I'd do better this time, but here I am, about to present another dream of my own design, telling myself it's a better plan if I leave my life for theirs than the other way around. As if romance should mean giving up everything and disappearing into someone else. Theo has never asked for that, not then, not now.

"Kit?" Theo says. "Did you hear what I said?"

I blink myself back to the present.

"Sorry, what?"

"I said, should I pick out another bottle, or do you want to head back to the room?"

I see the promise in their eyes, and there's nothing I'd love more than to learn what they've dreamed up to top last night, but I can't. I've accidentally told them I love them twice now, nearly said yesterday it in bed. I'm one glass from saying it right here at this table. If I touch them tonight, I won't be able to stop myself.

There are only a few days left on this tour, but those are still days. If I offer them something they don't want, they'll be stuck with me thousands of miles from home with an American passport. What gives me the right? Because I still think I know best? Because I've grown bored of Paris, just like my father said I would, and I want a new dream to save me from boredom? Because of my ridiculous, incurable obsession with love?

I say the only thing I can think of to deflect.

"Do you remember what our score was?"

For a moment, Theo doesn't have any idea what I mean. Then it connects, and they set down the wine list.

"Five to three," they say. "Why?"

"Just—just wondering if we were still counting."

"Were you planning to catch up while we're out?"

"No," I say, "I'm too tired. I need to get some actual sleep tonight."

Theo nods, and mercifully, they don't bring up the room again.

I need to step back. I need to lock myself in my own room for the night and hope I've gotten ahold of myself by the time we get to Naples.

NAPLES

PAIRS WELL WITH:

Generous serving of limoncello, cannoli

There's a certain flavor to Fabrizio, a bacchanalian ripeness that I haven't yet identified. I'm sure if I'd asked Theo they could have named it right away, because the same notes are in the wine we're drinking.

"Body?" they ask me.

"Full," I say, feeling its weight on my tongue, the intensity of the flavors.

"Sweetness?"

"Barely. Sort of like a—a dark fruit at first. Maybe black currant? But it's more . . . savory?"

"That's good, savory how?"

"Um." I think about it.

"No wrong answers," Theo says, "whatever comes to mind first."

"Smoke? Or . . . dirt? Peppercorn?"

"That's good, really good. Keep going, past the first things you taste. What's back there?"

"It's . . . meaty, maybe? Leathery?"

Theo clasps their hands together, pleased. "It *is*. And do you feel how it's sort of coating the inside of your mouth, toward the front? Like, holding on to it?"

"Yeah," I say. "That means it has a lot of tannins, right?"

"Right," Theo says. "So, this wine is called Aglianico del Taburno. It's made with Aglianico grapes, which are grown a few miles inland from here, where it's warm enough for enough of the year that a late-ripening grape like that can thrive, and so they have deeper, darker fruit flavors because of the long grow- ing season, and grapes in hotter climates *also* have thicker skins, which means they let more tannins into the wine, because tan- nins are in the skin and seeds, so if you like tannic or savory wines or wines with dark fruit flavors you might like warm- climate wines, and— I feel like you're just staring at me now."

I shake my head, realizing I've forgotten my glass entirely. It's hard to remember anything else when I'm watching Theo light up like this. I can barely remember not to put my hand on their waist.

"No, that makes sense," I say. "Warm-climate wines. Meaty, leathery, ripe, full, but weirdly—"

"Smooth."

"Smooth. Kind of sounds like—"

As if on cue, Fabrizio swans by our corner of the table, half- open shirt billowing in the late-afternoon sun, melted-chocolate voice languid with laughter, a hot lick of breeze rippling the curls on his chest.

"—Fabrizio."

"Well," Theo says, "they are both from here."

We've finally arrived in Fabrizio's hometown of Naples, nes- tled along the coast at the shin of Italy's boot, and Fabrizio is in his element. He is making passionate love to his element. He's overflowing with compliments and kisses and historical morsels, continuously conjuring paper parcels of street food and reciting relevant stanzas of Neapolitan poems. He loves this city and its weathered streets with an irresistible intensity. The more we soak in his presence, the more I love Naples. And the more I love Naples, the more Fabrizio seems like her favorite child.

Naples has existed uninterrupted for nearly thirty centuries, and it exists so *much*. Shops and trattorias cram the ancient streets around Centro Storico, festooned with strings of flags and lights and drying laundry, ivy and satellite cables curtaining craggy stone facades. Every inch has something to look at, streaks of graffiti on yellow stucco or lintels with sculpted leaves or old bricks revealed by chipping plaster. Storefronts overflow with tables of puppets and figurines, hand-painted tambourines, paper flowers and cheap sunglasses. Yeast and oil permeate the air, carried by a million sounds all at once—scooters revving, arguments, laughter, old men coughing out cigar smoke, an accordion on the next street. It's a gritty, glorious feast of overstimulation.

Already, we've toured three separate astonishing churches and been whisked down Via dei Tribunali, where Fabrizio taught us the exacting legal requirements of Neapolitan pizza: that the dough must only be stretched by hand, the mandated temperature for fermentation, the clockwise spreading of crushed tomatoes, approved local sources for cheese. We've taken forks and knives to bloody red marinara and basil-flecked margherita with soupy middles, and we've stood at windows for pizza folded up with butcher paper, a portafoglio.

Which brings us here, to the terrazzo of a wine bar, all of us drunk on overindulgence. The muchness of Naples has caught up to us. Even Orla is boneless on her stool.

Today isn't only special for Fabrizio; it's also Orla's last day. Tomorrow we'll take the ferry to Palermo, and Orla will drive the bus back to its station in London. We're all devastated to see her go, and to thank her for hauling us around, we've coaxed her out to spend the day with us.

"What do you usually do while we're out?" Dakota asks her, tipping more wine into Orla's glass.

She shrugs. "Go hiking. Get a massage. Phone my wife. Read pornographic romance novels."

"I think I love you, Orla," Theo says. Orla raises her glass and winks.

In the thick of it all, I've barely been alone with Theo for more than a few seconds, but now that they're beside me, throwing around four-letter words and telling me how to use my mouth, I'm back on the ledge.

I could touch them. I want to touch them. Slip my hand across the back of their neck, press my knee against their thigh. They would *like* it, even. But everything I shouldn't say is right under the surface of my skin, and I'll sweat it out if we get too close.

I pull myself a few inches farther from Theo, tucking my hand under my thigh before I forget myself. The movement doesn't escape their notice.

"Hey," Theo says quietly. "You okay? You look like you're worried you forgot something."

Yes, my heart in California and my cock in a fifth-story apartment in Rome.

"Just—thinking we haven't had any Napoli pastry yet." I drain my glass and call out, "Fabrizio!"

Fabrizio tosses his handsome head toward me. "Sì, Professore?"

"Where can I try sfogliatelle?"

And so, Fabrizio wilds me away from Theo toward a pasticceria down the block, where I can busy myself with papery pastry layers and offload some sexual frustration onto him. It's always so easy, flirting with Fabrizio. He takes it so well and gives back even better, winks and raises his eyebrows and thumbs the edge of my jaw. I like him so much. It almost helps.

— — —

For dinner, Fabrizio takes us to a little osteria in the Spanish Quarter with walls covered in painted majolica tiles. An older woman bursts out of the kitchen to greet us in a white-collared red dress, her dark, wavy hair cropped close to her face and her eyes keen under strong, mobile brows. She is glorious, commanding the room with the brash, unflappable air of a woman who must have been mind-bendingly hot in her prime. Fabrizio lets her kiss him twice on each cheek and introduces her as his mother.

"It takes me many summers with the tour company to convince them," Fabrizio tells us, "but tonight, we dine in il ristorante di famiglia!"

The menu is a straightforward tour of Neapolitan staples: pappardelle in eight-hour ragù napoletano, pasta alla genovese, braciola, roasted squid, octopus cooked in white wine. For antipasti, Fabrizio's mother brings out plate after plate of eggplant involtini and fried nuggets of mozzarella. We devour more pasta than any human should ever eat and follow it with hunks of pork and beef stewed in the ragù. It is, unpretentiously and unassumingly, the best meal I've had in Italy.

Maybe it's the atmosphere of a traditional Neapolitan cucina. Maybe it's Fabrizio's father sweating under his heavy beard in the kitchen, stirring enormous vats of stew, communicating only by shouts through the kitchen window in the voice of a man who gets incredible deals from the local butcher. Maybe it's Fabrizio's mother, who dances in and out to deliver more parmigiana or squeeze Fabrizio's cheeks or interrogate someone on why they haven't cleared their plate. Or maybe it's how happy Theo seems to be here, nearly weeping with laughter at the photos of teenage Fabrizio and his brothers on the walls.

Just as Fabrizio's mother is beginning to nag him about the length of his hair, my phone sounds a long buzz in my pocket.

It's probably Cora, forgetting I'm in Italy and calling to chat about what she's been reading, or Maxine with a recipe question that's easier to explain over the phone. But neither of their names are on the incoming call.

I slip away from the table and out the front door.

"Paloma?" I answer.

"Bonsoir, mon petit américain," says Paloma's crisp voice over the line. "Ça va? Where are you?"

"I'm good," I say. "I'm in Naples."

"Ah, Napoli." Paloma sighs. "Beautiful city. Excellent fish. Are you eating well?"

"So well," I say, rubbing my chest where I can feel the threat of impending heartburn. "Maybe too well."

"As you should," Paloma says. "And your Theo?"

I press my shoulders to the restaurant's brick wall and lean my head back.

"My Theo is as brilliant as ever."

"Have you confessed your love yet?"

I cover the phone with my hand, like somehow Theo could overhear from all the way inside.

"Paloma, not that I'm not happy to hear from you, but is there a reason you called?"

"Yes, there is," Paloma says. "You remember the pâtisserie under me? The one with the macarons, and the old woman?"

"I do."

"Every Thursday I bring her dinner with fresh fish, so she likes me, and she tells me her secrets. Usually it is about François across the road—she thinks he is very handsome—but tonight it was about the pâtisserie. She wants to close next year."

"Oh, no," I say, still unsure why Paloma felt she needed to call with this news.

"And," she goes on, "she wants to sell it. She wants to find a young pâtissier who will do something nice with it and stay for a long time, the way she did. She asked if I knew anyone, and right away I thought of you."

"Oh," I say. "Oh, wow."

"And?" she prompts. "What do you think?"

It sounds like a dream. The kind of gorgeous, sugar-spun dream that is never as easy as it feels in my head. The kind of dream I was chasing when I lost Theo, the kind my kitchen in Paris wrung out of me.

"That's so kind of you, Paloma," I say, "but I have a job, remember?"

"Yes, the job you hate."

"I don't *hate* it."

"But you don't like it."

"That doesn't mean I can just quit."

"Why not?"

"Because I put all this time into it," I say. "It's what I worked for." It's what I lost Theo for.

Paloma laughs over the line, a short, sarcastic grunt.

"Crois-moi," she says, "ça ne veut rien dire, si cela ne te rend pas heureux." *That doesn't mean anything if it doesn't make you happy.*

I find myself without an answer to that.

The door of the restaurant opens, and people filter outside in knots of laughter and tipsy conversation, each flushed with the intoxicating joy of a good, simple meal prepared by someone who loves what they're cooking. I can hear Fabrizio's parents inside, making jokes with the cooks and foisting boxes of leftovers on the last guests. It seems like a good life. A messy and abundant life, possible because they share it with each other.

"Think about it," Paloma says.

Theo finds me as they exit, all curious eyebrows and Aglianico lips, and I rush out a goodbye to Paloma and hang up.

"Who was that?" Theo asks.

"Just Cora." I shove my phone into my pocket. "Where's everyone going now?"

"Different places," Theo says, "but wait until you hear where I got us invited."

"Where?" I ask. At first they just raise their eyebrows and lower their eyelids in that way of theirs that suggests something either very good or mildly illegal, which is usually also good. "*Where*, Theo?"

"Fabrizio wants to know," they say, "if we'd like to see his apartment."

I wait for the punch line, but it seems there isn't one.

"Are you teasing me?"

"Dead serious," they say. "He lives a ten-minute walk from here. Said he's looking forward to sleeping in his own bed tonight and asked if we wanted to share a bottle of wine."

"We?"

"*We.*"

I stare. For all our flirting and big talk about making sensual tantric love to Fabrizio, I never actually thought our tour guide would proposition us. But I think of his warm touch on the side of my face, how he chose us specially to ride with him in Rome, how he watched us work on the engine of the bus.

"Is . . . is this it?" I ask. "Do you think he wants to—?"

"There was a strong vibe, yes. At least one of us. Maybe both. It seems like he considers us a package deal."

"Oh my God, because we let him think we're together?"

"I don't think it's *not* because of that."

"Well." I put my knuckles to my mouth. "Do we—do we want to?"

"I mean," Theo says. "It's Fabrizio."

"It's Fabrizio."

"How can we not? Unless . . . you can think of a reason we shouldn't."

"No, it—it would be hot, if it's both of us."

"And if it's just one of us?"

The image flashes into my mind. Theo as seen from the foot of the bed, broad hands on their hips as they pant into a pillow. Or Theo reclined on a chair, learning that I've trained away my gag reflex. Heat coils in my gut.

"Then . . ." I say. "Winner takes all?"

It takes a beat for Theo to catch on, and then they're pink with indignance.

"What, after I smoked you in almost every city? No way. If it's just you, you can count him for double, because. You know."

"It's Fabrizio."

Theo nods, biting their lip. "It's Fabrizio. But if it's both of us, Monaco rules. It cancels out. Deal?"

"Deal."

— — —

"It's not that difficult," Theo says. "Just pick one."

"It is, actually." I scan the illuminated rows of different-colored boxes through the glass. "I don't know what half of these words mean."

"We don't have time for this!"

"Then *help me,* Theo," I say, feeling more than a little light-headed. "You're the one who actually knows some Italian."

"Yeah, weirdly, my job at a restaurant did not teach me the word for condoms."

We're in an alley a few blocks from Fabrizio's apartment, bathed in the glow of a Durex vending machine. Our hotel is on the other side of Centro Storico, and there's no time to run there for our own provisions. Instead, I'm squinting at boxes that say things like PERFORMA and PLEASUREMAX and, mysteriously, JEANS, trying to decipher which will bring the lowest element of surprise to group sex with the person I love and our sexy tour guide. We're already ten minutes later than we said we would be, and the German tourists behind us are getting impatient.

"I'm pretty confident the condoms are the ones that say PRO-FILATTICI," Theo says.

"Yes, like prophylactics, I guessed that, but the rest of the words? Which ones are the normal ones, without any flavors or tingling or anything? And which one is lube, Theo? *Which one is lube?*"

"The ones at the bottom!"

They point to the last row of the machine, which is filled with brightly colored plastic tubes of liquid with pictures of fruits on them. They're all marked LUBRIFICANTE.

"The ones that look like the sour squeeze candy we used to get from 7-Eleven when we were ten? I'm not using that."

Theo squats down to examine it.

"I don't think this vending machine sells artisanal fair-trade lube for delicate Parisian buttholes, Kit."

"How do you know it'll be for *me*?"

They look up at me with a perfectly flat, knowing expression and change the subject.

"Don't you think Fabrizio has condoms at his place?"

"We can't show up empty-handed, that's inconsiderate," I say. "And what if he doesn't? Who knows the last time he was home."

"Okay, okay." They take out their phone. "That box says 'Settebello Classico,' which means . . ." Typing, typing. "'Seven beauties classic'? What?"

"Just—get the natural lube." I sigh. "The one with the leaves on the tube."

"What if that means it's pesto flavored or something?"

"I guess that's a risk I'm willing to take," I say as Theo punches the buttons.

We determine that the Jeans condoms are so named because they're designed to fit discreetly in a pocket, so I buy a box and shove two in my shirt pocket, passing the remaining four off to the Germans for their patience. Then we continue along the route Fabrizio described to Theo, through the edge of the Spanish Quarter and uphill into a neighborhood whose buildings resemble the colorful stacked palazzos of Cinque Terre. Fabrizio lives close to Castel Sant'Elmo, on the third floor of a skinny, pink-red villa with yellow shutters and white iron balconies.

"So," Theo says, hand hovering over the buzzer. "We're doing this?"

Something wrinkles their face—not hesitation, but gentle concern, maybe. A possible out if I need it, and I'm afraid to lend weight to whatever is making them worry I might.

"We are," I say, reaching past them to hit the buzzer.

The whole way up the stairs, as I watch Theo's boots hit each step, I tell myself this isn't a bad idea, the way I did with Émile in Monaco. It'll be hot, and easy, and lovely, the way that sex should be, and I'll make sure everyone feels good. Like the times we had sex with a third person when we were together—just, without Theo's reassuring hand in mine, or the calm certainty that we'll come home to each other afterward, or the love.

Theo knocks, and Fabrizio—is not the person who answers.

"Hello!" says perhaps the most beautiful woman on the continent. "Welcome!"

We both stand dumbstruck on the doormat before this unexpected apparition of Venus with a dark, blunt-banged bob and plum-painted lips, a thin housedress falling midway down her thigh. She pulls the door wider, revealing Fabrizio in a fresh T-shirt and sweats, beaming.

"My friends! You are here! Benvenuti, come in!"

I have to nudge Theo in the shoulder to get them moving.

"Amore, questo è Kit, e quello è Theo," Fabrizio says to the woman before turning to us. "Friends, this is Valentina, my wife!"

"Your—" I clear my throat. "Your wife!"

Theo's eyes are as wide as mine. An entire conversation passes between us in the span of half a second.

I didn't know he was married! Did you know he was married?

Of course I didn't fucking know he was married, Kit, or I wouldn't have assumed he was inviting us over for sex!

Did he ever mention having a wife?

I don't think so? Is that weird? That's weird, right?

She's really hot.

She is insanely fucking hot.

"Ciao, piacere!" Theo says, leaning in to air-kiss Valentina and smoothly elbowing me in the ribs.

"So nice to meet you!" Valentina says in lightly accented English. "Fabrizio speaks of you so warmly!"

I accept an air-kiss of my own, casting about for something to say. The apartment is small and cozy, filled with soft pastels and well-loved wicker furniture and dangling wind chimes. Candles burn on the low coffee table, and through the open balcony doors, I can see Mount Vesuvius in twilight on the horizon.

"This place is incredible," I tell Valentina. "Thank you for having us."

Valentina smiles, brushing hair from my eyes. I consider the possibility that this is some kind of partner-sharing situation—I could probably get on board after enough wine—until Fabrizio calls out, "Orla! Our friends are here!"

Theo's eyes are the size and shape of an arancini.

"Orla?"

"Yes, did I not say? We always have Orla for drinks on her last day of the tour. This is why I invite you!"

"You—didn't say, no, but—hi, Orla!"

Orla comes around the corner holding a bottle of wine. Her shoes are off, and her socks are patterned with little koalas. I should have recognized her hiking boots by the door.

"Evening, darlings! Valentina, love, where did you say the opener was?"

Valentina floats off to show her, and Fabrizio says, "Come, sit, we have room in the kitchen for everyone."

Theo and I exchange another look.

This is cool?

This is cool.

"We're coming!" I say, stepping out of my shoes.

"Not how we thought we'd be," Theo mumbles, "but yeah."

And so we find ourselves around Fabrizio and Valentina's table in an adorable kitchen with sea views and yellow countertops and shelves of antique teapots filled with seashells. Orla opens the wine, Fabrizio pours, and Valentina sets out dishes of marinated olives and crusty bread. Above the toaster oven hangs a framed photo of the two of them laughing in tiny swimsuits, up to their perfect thighs in crystal clear water off a white sand beach. Mon Dieu. He really has been married this whole time.

"So, Valentina," Theo says, already recovering their charm by sheer brute force, "what has Fabrizio told you about us?"

"Oh, I have heard that you are an expert on wine," Valentina says, "so I hope you like this one. I took it from the cellar at his parents' restaurant, though I do not always know if his mother has good taste."

Fabrizio gasps theatrically and fires off a string of Italian; Valentina ignores him.

"It's perfect," Theo says, amused.

"And I hear that you are a pâtissier in Paris, very impressive," she goes on, smiling at me. "And that you are star-crossed lovers who fell back in love on Fabrizio's tour!"

My face, previously warm from the balmy night and Valentina's compliments, goes cold.

"Oh, we're not—" Theo begins.

"We're just friends," I say before I have to endure the rest of Theo's sentence. "We split up years ago, that's true, and the tour did bring us back together."

I turn to find Theo's eyes sharp and searching.

"Right," they say. "But . . . as friends."

"Ah, I see," Fabrizio says, sounding disappointed. "Colpa mia."

I set my attention upon the olives in front of me, studiously avoiding Orla's sympathetic gaze.

"Well, even so," Orla says, "you're friends again, and that's lovely. Some of my best friends in the world are my ex-girlfriends. I've got one in Copenhagen who lets the wife and I borrow her flat when we're in the mood for herring."

"Oh, I hear Copenhagen is so cozy," Valentina says. "Can we come next time?"

"Fabs, you haven't taken this girl on the Scandi tour yet?"

"I tell the company to never send me on the Scandinavia tour," Fabrizio says. "Too cold. Not enough sun."

"Oh wise up, that's when you let your lady keep you warm. Valentina, love, I'll take you."

Theo laughs, and I laugh, and it's okay.

We talk for an hour while the sun sets. Orla and Fabrizio tell stories of their wildest tour happenings, and Theo and I talk about the strangest people we've encountered at our jobs. Valentina tells us that she was working in Rome as an English tutor when she met a Vespa guide who wanted to learn English to travel the world, how they kissed for the first time on Rome's oldest bridge because he wanted to join her to history. Orla tells us how she met her wife as schoolmates in Derry and waited fifteen years to confess how she felt. It's simple and warm, the kind of magical human thing that happens in transit when like brushes against like.

"My mother, she would tell me to hold the bottle like this"— Fabrizio holds the wine by its bottom, palm to base with his arm fully extended—"and when I am big enough to hold it this way and touch it to my lips, I am old enough to drink it."

"And what age was that?" Theo asks.

"Eleven!" And we fall apart laughing again.

Everything is going well until I lean over to refill Theo's wine, and a condom falls out of my shirt pocket and into the olives.

"*Oh God,*" Theo whispers.

I try to intercept before anyone notices, but the foil wrapper is now coated in olive oil and shoots out from between my fingers. It lands with a small, wet plop beside Fabrizio's glass.

The table goes silent.

"So sorry about that," I say. "That's—that's really a design flaw, isn't it? If anything should be easy to grab when it's covered in oil—"

Fabrizio claps his hands together with delight.

"So, you *are* together again!"

"What?" Theo says.

"Yes, of course, when two lovers are reunited, the sex is better than ever. All you want to do is make love, day and night." He takes Valentina's hand, glowing with the romance of a poet, and plants a kiss on the inside of her wrist. "When I return home from a tour, Valentina and I—"

"Fabs, darling," Orla says. "Spare them."

"We're not—" Theo says.

"That's not what it's for," I say.

Fabrizio pauses halfway up Valentina's arm.

"It is for something else, then?"

And it's been such a long day with so much to process that I can't think of a single excuse.

A twinkle appears in Fabrizio's eye.

"*Ohhh.* You think I invite you here for—ah, I forget the word in English." He turns to his wife. "The sex with three people?"

Valentina helpfully supplies, "Threesome, amore."

"Threesomamore."

"No, amore. *Threesome.*"

"Ah, yes. Threesome."

Theo and I lock eyes.

Do we tell him?

Of course we don't fucking tell him.

"We—" I start.

"We weren't—"

"I wouldn't say we—"

"I mean, I may have gotten the impression—"

"We just—we—" I'm losing the plot. "Maybe we—"

Theo glances at me, eyes huge. "I guess we *might* have . . ."

"We . . ." Fuck it. "Did. Yes, we did think you wanted to have sex with us."

After a beat, Theo adds, "Respectfully."

Orla sits back and takes a hearty swig of wine.

"And we're so sorry for presuming," I say. "And to you, Valentina."

"Oh, no need for that," Valentina says. "This happens sometimes when he tries to make friends." She takes Fabrizio's face in her hands and wobbles it side to side. "Look at this man, who could resist you?"

"I keep telling him he's got to flirt less with the guests," Orla says to us, "but I don't think he knows how to stop."

"I cannot help that I am so full of love," Fabrizio says earnestly, "and also so very good-looking. It is my cross to bear."

"You wouldn't believe how many people finish this tour thinking they could have slept with Fabrizio if they'd had the opportunity," Orla goes on. "I reckon we could sell T-shirts. *Nearly Fucked Fabs: The European Tour.*"

"I am providing memorable customer experiences!"

Orla snorts and says, "Love, it's alright to like the attention. You'd wear a ring if you didn't."

"Yeah, to be fair, I had no idea you were married," Theo chimes in. "Sorry, again, Valentina."

"That is my idea, actually," Valentina says, releasing her husband. "Once, not long after we were married, he forgot his ring at home and came home from the tour with twice as much in tips, so now I tell him to leave it with me. People tip more when they think he is available."

"Especially the Americans," Orla adds.

"Oh my God." I bury my face in my hands. "*I'm* Americans."

"Professore, no!" Fabrizio says. "With you, it is not just for tips."

When I lift my head, Fabrizio is looking at Theo and me with pure, bare sincerity.

"Every tour I enjoy the people, but on some tours, I meet people I think could be my friends," Fabrizio says. "And I want to bring you to my home and introduce you to my wife because I hope that after this trip is over, we can stay in touch, if you like. I hope we do not become strangers when we leave Palermo."

There's something so admirable about his directness. *I like you. Stay in my life.* It's perfectly simple, when he says it like that.

I turn to Theo and find them smiling.

"We'd love that," Theo says.

"Che bella!" Fabrizio says, raising his glass. "Then, let us drink to that! To friendship!"

Valentina adds, "And to love!"

— — —

"I have a question for you," Fabrizio says to me after we've finished the wine.

We're alone in the kitchen. Theo's out on the balcony with Orla and Valentina, their laughter occasionally drifting like sea breeze through the half-open door. All the olive brine made us crave something sweet, so I volunteered to make dessert from whatever's on hand, and now Fabrizio is playing sous while I improvise a gâteau au yaourt—French yogurt cake, the first thing I ever learned how to bake.

I'm wrist-deep in a big mixing bowl, white and sky-blue porcelain passed down from Fabrizio's parents' honeymoon in Siena. A delightfully weird sea monster is glazed into its bottom. Fabrizio says it's supposed to be a dolphin, the symbol of one of Siena's seventeen contrade, but it has scales, and eyebrows. God bless medieval zoology.

As I massage lemon zest into sugar with my fingertips, I realize I haven't once stopped to think of the next step. I'm going by heart, making best guesses and dreaming of finishing it with Valentina's homemade apricot marmalade instead of the traditional lemon glaze. This might be the most fun I've had baking since my first week on the job.

"What's your question?" I ask Fabrizio.

"You are in love with Theo, no?"

I nearly tip the bowl.

"*Fabrizio.*"

"Oh, they cannot hear," Fabrizio reassures me with a wave of his whisk. I've put him in charge of the dry ingredients. "Too much noise from the street."

I sigh.

"Is it that obvious?"

"If I am honest, yes. But I hear from Orla."

"*Orla.*" This is what I get for assuming all women in safari hats can be trusted.

"You must know we talk about everything. The tour is the same every time, but the people are different. The guests are our entertainment."

Satisfied with the sugar, I reach for the little glass pot of yogurt Valentina took from the refrigerator and add it in.

"Well, I hope we've given you a good show," I say, genuinely meaning it.

"I think right now it is a tragedy. Tell me, why are you not together? You do not tell Theo how you feel?" He reads my face, then puts down his whisk in despair. "*Why,* Professore?"

"Because I don't know if I deserve to."

I crack the eggs and add vanilla and, as I whisk it together, tell Fabrizio the most simplified version of our story. Our lives together, the Paris mistake, the breakup, my father, how I never let Theo go, what I almost did last night in Rome before I caught myself. When I'm done, I have Fabrizio sprinkle the flour and baking powder and salt into my bowl while I go on mixing.

"I understand," Fabrizio says. "You love Theo. You do not want for Theo a selfish lover who takes away choices."

"Yes."

"And so, you take away the choice to be with you."

"I—" My hand falters on the whisk. "No, that's not—"

"This is what it sounds like to me."

"I—I just want to do the right thing for Theo."

"Sì, and only you know what this is?" He's at the pantry, searching for the last ingredient, a neutral-flavored oil. His tone is casual, as if he delivers axis-shifting insights to all his house-guests. "Ah, it is as I fear. Only olive oil. Okay?"

"Uh—sure," I say, barely hearing him.

He sets the oil beside his mother's mixing bowl and takes in my expression, then reaches out with easy affection to stroke my cheek.

"When I met Valentina," he says, "there was another man who loved her. He was the son of a rich man, with a good job close to home, and her mother liked him very much and me not at all, so I believed she will be happier with him. So, when he tells her he loves her, she says to me, 'Fabrizio, what should I say?' And I tell her, 'I want you to be happy.' And when he asks her to marry him, she says to me, 'Fabrizio, what should I say?' And again I tell her, 'I want you to be happy.' And the night before her wedding, she comes to my door, and she says to me, 'Fabrizio, what should I do?' And I tell her again, 'I want you to be happy.' And she says to me, 'Fabrizio, idiota, all I ever want is to be happy with you.'"

The oven dings, preheated.

"What I mean is, if I say how I feel sooner, Valentina's father does not have to tell the priest why his daughter is not coming to her wedding," Fabrizio says with a grin. "It was not for me to protect her from my heart. It was only for me to let her see it and decide if she will keep it."

He glugs oil into the bowl and takes the whisk from my hand, replacing it with a well-seasoned wooden spoon. I should start folding if I want the batter to come together. But I'm frozen on the spot, overpowered by the plain truth. Maybe it's not a matter of whether I deserve to tell them. Maybe it's that they deserve to know.

From the balcony, laughter grows. The door slides open.

"I will say one more thing," Fabrizio adds in a low voice.

"How Valentina looked at me the night before her wedding—this is how Theo looks at you."

— — —

Near midnight, full of wine and olives and cake, Theo and I call a cab back to the hostel. We make it two blocks before we dissolve into long-delayed, incredulous laughter.

"I can't believe that just happened," Theo says, wiping their eyes.

"I think we might be friends for life? With Fabrizio? Somehow?"

"What the fuck." They smooth a hand down their face. "God, this whole competition was so . . . stupid. We're being stupid, aren't we?"

"It definitely hasn't been my finest work," I say. "Sexually, yes, but not intellectually."

"It's stupid," Theo concludes. "And it's immature. We're *adults*."

"That's what I keep hearing."

Theo shakes their head. "But when I first saw you in London, it was like I was an insecure twenty-two-year-old again."

Ever since they crashed in that first day, I've wondered what they felt when they saw me. I didn't want it to be that, but it's nice to be reminded that they never hated me. They still thought enough of me to care what I thought of them.

"When I saw you, I thought I was dreaming," I confess. "I couldn't possibly get that lucky."

Theo frowns like they don't understand.

"Lucky?"

"I didn't think I'd ever get a chance to make things right," I say. Afraid of giving myself too much credit, I add, "And I don't know if I have, but—"

"I think so," Theo cuts me off with a small smile. "I mean, it's a process, or whatever. But I'm not mad at you anymore. It wasn't one person's fault."

"That's good," I say, warmth pooling in my chest. I wish I could dip their fingers inside me and let them feel it. I settle for confessing something else, pouring a little out. "The competition . . . when you suggested it, I said yes because it was an excuse to keep talking to you. That was all I really wanted. Although I did enjoy the sex."

"I . . . I didn't understand it when we started, but I think I wanted to prove I was over you," Theo says. "To you, and to myself. And maybe I wanted to make you jealous."

"Why?"

"Because of this thing I have where I need to win the breakup, which I've realized is meaningless," Theo admits. "It doesn't leave room for me to care about you as a person. I don't want to not care. I want you to be happy."

I watch the traffic lights change in the reflection of Theo's eyes and think of Fabrizio's story. *All I ever want is to be happy with you.*

"I'm happy right now," I say.

Theo nods. "I'm happy you're happy."

I feel it in the pit of my stomach: Fabrizio is right. I have to say it. Theo should know they have a choice.

I love them. I should tell them. I'll tell them in Palermo.

"So, should we call it off?" I ask. "The competition?"

"Yeah." Theo nods. "Cut it loose."

"Okay." I make a sweeping, pinching gesture in front of my face like I'm pulling some invisible mask away from it, and cast it off into the air. "Done."

Theo's brows draw in realization.

"Was that the thing from *Face/Off*?"

I smile. I knew they'd like it. "That was the thing from *Face/Off*."

"God," they groan, grinning, throwing their head against the headrest. "One of the greats."

"As we've learned, I *can* eat a peach for hours."

"Speaking of, let the record to show that I was in the lead and would have won."

"It's *done,* Theo."

"I'm just! Saying!"

PALERMO (DAY ONE)

PAIRS WELL WITH:

Bitter amaro, sfinci di San Giuseppe

The first time I almost tell Theo I love them in Palermo, we're at Mercato di Ballarò.

"*Quanto,*" they say, enunciating. "Not quando, that's *when.* Quanto is *how much.*"

"Quanto," I repeat.

Theo nods. "That's the only word you need."

"Quanto?" we ask the leathery old woman grilling stigghiola under a thick cloud of smoke, and she sells us skewers of lamb guts for two euros. Quanto to panelle (crispy chickpea fritters) and quanto to pani ca' meusa (lamb spleen sandwiches). On and on through the noisy, endless street market, to rickety carts and steaming gingham-covered vats, between pungent bins of fresh-caught fish and produce stands so overfull that artichoke leaves cascade to the ground. We taste everything we can. Somewhere ahead, Pinocchio bobs above the crowd like our merry little North Star.

"I feel so much pressure to pick the best arancini," I say, eyeing yet another cart selling them. "It's like, we only get one chance to have our first arancini in Sicily."

"I think all fried rice balls are precious gifts from God," Theo says. "Ooh, but those are *really* big, holy shit— Ciao! Quanto?"

Once, when we first moved in together, I accidentally killed my thyme plant. I'd carefully caramelized onions and figs and made pâte feuilletée from scratch for this one perfect galette, and when I went to snip some sprigs for the finishing touch, I knocked the plant out of the window. While I was mourning my exploded thyme on the sidewalk, Theo was substituting a spoonful of Aleppo pepper flakes in total disregard of my vision. It was improvised on instinct, and it was better.

I love ingredients because they have memories. Stories, histories, personalities. A peach has a memory of every finger that's touched it. A vanilla bean cures for months. Sometimes when I take a first bite, I try to name every individual ingredient, to find the gardener who pruned the tree that yielded the olives for the oil coating this specific pan in this specific kitchen watched over by one specific cook, who came to work thinking of his mother's skillet back home.

Theo cares about all of this, but they're an instincts-first eater. They understand ingredients like old friends who don't need anything when they come over. They know when to apply their knowledge and remind me when to think less and simply open my mouth. They question me, surprise me, challenge me. Taste is what I do; Theo makes me better at it.

Theo buys an arancini the size of a grapefruit and splits it down the middle, gasping as it reveals a center of spiced yellow rice and dark ragù. When it hits their tongue, they close their eyes and wiggle their shoulders with pleasure.

I almost say it then. It's so clear in my mind. *I'm in love with you.*

The man dunking whole octopuses into a huge vat of boiling water bellows at the top of his voice, "Polpo, polpo!" And the moment passes.

— — —

The second time, it almost slips out on a laugh.

We're on the stairs of Teatro Massimo, the opera house near the city center, digesting between market crawls. Theo counts the steps, finds a spot, then lays their long body down.

"What are you doing?"

"*The Godfather Part III,*" they say, as if this should be obvious.

They speak up into the sky, their head nearly resting on the stone. "This is where Mary dies at the end."

"How could I forget." I climb up and gaze down at them. Their sunglasses have slid onto their forehead, and their freckles are on glorious display. "You know, I didn't think Sofia Coppola was *that* bad."

"That's because you have a soft heart and you liked *The Virgin Suicides*."

I offer them my hand, and they give me that familiar look, eyes narrowed, mouth taut at the corners like, *If I say one word I'll kill us both laughing*. That look made our homeroom teachers stop assigning seats in alphabetical order to keep us separated.

They take my hand and, instead of letting me pull them up, they pull me down beside them.

Sometimes, when people first meet me now, they think I'm a serious person. They see an art degree drinking espresso in a Parisian kitchen and imagine some Nietzsche-reading gourmand. They don't know how loud my laugh can be, or how shamelessly I'll commit to a bit, or the dirty jokes Theo and I taught ourselves in Elvish to use at the Renaissance festival when we were thirteen. It's a shame, because I like that about myself. My favorite parts of me are the ones that Theo brings out, the ones that grew to match theirs.

It almost comes out as we're laughing together on the steps. The stones reflect the sun like we reflect each other, and I think, *I love you.*

Theo says, "Is that guy choking on a sausage?"

I say, "What?"

There is, it turns out, a tourist on the sidewalk choking on a hunk of street meat. We sit up as Blond Calum leaps into action, deploying an expert Heimlich maneuver to completion. The gathered crowd cheers, and the tourist gives Calum a grateful hug. He's a hero. It's no longer our moment; it's Calum's.

"Damn," Theo says, as Calum is enveloped by six arms—
Dakota's, Montana's, Ginger's. "He's definitely getting laid tonight."

— —— —

The third time, the words stick in my molars like candied orange
peel.

Secreted away in the monastery behind the Chiesa di Santa
Caterina is a tiny dolcería selling sweets made from the nuns' recipes. I learned in Venice that most of Italy's famous sweets orig-
inated in monastery kitchens, crafted by monks and nuns with
no indulgences but sugar and flour. These nuns make Fabrizio's
favorite cannoli in Palermo.

In the piazza between the church and the monastero everyone
still buzzes with Blond Calum's heroism. Theo's helping Montana fix a broken dress strap with safety pins and keeps glancing
from Montana to the Calums to Dakota and back, observing
everything.

Our eyes meet.

I'm gathering valuable intel, go get cannoli and I'll tell you what I find.

Inside the dolcería, every confection suggests the simplicity
of a kitchen with only a handful of ingredients and the obsession
of a thoroughly cloistered nun. Almond paste molded into clam-
shells and stuffed with cream and apricot jam, or sculpted and
painted to make glossy, lifelike figs and pears and peaches. A few
extravagant cakes are topped with piped curls of white icing and
piles of sugared fruit—a sign declares these TRIONFO DI GOLA—
TRIUMPH OF GLUTTONY. God, if I could title my memoir.

I order cannoli for two, Theo's with extra pistachio bits and
candied orange. Outside, under the fountain of San Domenico,
Theo can't believe the size of them.

"Jesus, it's like a burrito." They take their cannolo without
having to ask which one is theirs, then notice the plate in my
other hand. "What's that?"

"I got you something else," I say, showing them a small, domed cake coated in white icing and topped with a candied cherry.

Theo tilts their head. "Is it supposed to look like—" They glance up at the saint in the fountain, then whisper, "—a titty?"

"Yes, they're called St. Agatha's Breasts," I say. "I saw them and knew you had to see it too."

"I extremely do," Theo says, taking it from me happily. "Oh, that reminds me . . ."

They report the status of the Calums-Dakota-Montana sex polygon, which is that every side has now been consummated except for Calum-on-Calum, but the sudden exhibition of Blond's livesaving skills may be reigniting a nostalgic flame in Ginger. Montana and Dakota are doing their best to encourage this, because Montana is a completist. I listen with my mouth full of thick, sugary mascarpone and find myself rooting harder than ever for the Calums. Seems like a waste to never have sex with the person who pulled you from the mouth of a shark.

Over Theo's shoulder, Ginger Calum swipes a bit of mascarpone from Blond's chin with his thumb. I wonder if he's spent his life the same way I have, finding small ways to look after the person who saved us when we were young. I hope he gets as much joy from it as I do.

"Incredible cannoli, by the way," Theo says, chewing a bit of orange. "You're so good at ordering for me."

My eyes meet Theo's. They must see the softness on my face, how sweet it tastes to be told I've taken good care of them. Pink blooms on their cheeks. This has always been the part they've been least willing to see, how caring for them is something I *want* to do and something they can allow themself to have.

They don't turn away now. They lift their chin and hold my gaze. The moment falls over us like a net in the sea.

I'm going to say it as soon as I find the right words. *I'm in love with you. I love every part of loving you, even the parts you don't think you deserve. You are the love of my life.*

I begin to say, "I—"

Theo's phone rings. It's Sloane, and they've just started speaking to each other again, so Theo needs to take it.

"Of course," I say. "Of course."

— — —

The fourth time I almost tell Theo I love them, we're under a vault of stars.

The Martorana is nearly a thousand years old, and it looks like a place out of time. It's a physical record of the island's history, with its Spanish Baroque facade and Romanesque bell tower grafted over the original Byzantine dome and radiating Islamic niches. Inside the basilica, golden Greek mosaics glitter from the floor to the vaulted ceilings.

I remember the night Theo drove us out into the desert and held me under the blackberry swirl of the Milky Way. They kissed me as deep as the sky, every point of skin contact as sharp and hot as a star. They showed me the galaxy, then made me feel it. That's one of Theo's natural gifts, the way beauty moves through them like stained glass. It illuminates them, and they transform it in kind.

They stand in this luminous church and look at the ceiling of the nave, which arcs upward into a heaven of deep blue tiles and blazing gold stars. Another galaxy for Theo.

What I want to say is, *Do you know that you refract light?* But *I love you* could be close if I said it right, hushed in reverence beneath a mosaic sky.

I step toward them.

A bell rings; the church is closing for the day.

— — —

The fifth time, we've just eaten one of the most interesting meals of our lives.

The first restaurant in Palermo with a Michelin star sits

within the stone archways of what was once Antonello Gagini's Renaissance sculpting studio. In a way, it's still an artist's workshop. Blood orange–glazed veal sweetbread with fennel confit, sea anemone with salted ricotta and sauce Choron—what was all that, if not art?

Throughout dinner, Theo made quick-and-dirty use of the wine list to win over the sommelier, jotting down notes and ideas on a napkin while carrying on conversation with the Swedes. They were in peak form, all chaos and intent, a rough touch and a smooth result. It reminded me that Timo hadn't yet had their Michelin star when I left California. Theo helped them get it.

I remember what they said in Rome, how they still dream of Fairflower. I may not believe in it for me, but . . . for us? Some sweet future where Theo does their best things and I do mine, and we discover that in our years apart, we learned what we needed to actually do it?

Maybe it couldn't have worked then, but maybe it could work now. I don't know where, or when. But maybe when Theo believes in one thing and throws their whole weight behind it, anything can happen.

We're in an alley beside the restaurant, and Theo is chatting easily with the bartender on his smoke break, and I'm looking on from down the sidewalk. Theo is just—Theo is *cool*. I'm so proud to know them, to have the privilege of being important to a person like them. I want to be by their side forever. I want to build something with them. Something new, something we could only make now. I want to invent it with them and trust them with it.

They return with a paper bag, which they offer to me.

"Seemed like this one was your favorite."

Inside is a tiny to-go portion of the saffron panna cotta we had for dolci. I know what it meant when I did this for Theo in Paris, hoping to show them I was sorry for ever hurting them, that I still cared and wanted to make things right.

I look up to find handsome, enduring Theo thumbing the

same knuckles they bruised for me when we were children. I know them. I know this person better than I know anything, better than Bernini or Middle-earth or the importance of good butter. And they know me, and they're still looking.

This must be the moment at last. Here in long-awaited Palermo, at the end of the day, our stomachs full. This is where it's all led.

I take their hand, gently lace my fingers through theirs.

"Theo."

They can't hear it. Someone else yells their name at the same time, twice as loud, beckoning us out for drinks. Theo gives me a look, and I know they want to go. They're too curious about what might happen, too afraid to miss it.

I untwine our hands.

"Let's go."

— — —

We move through bar after bar, terrazzo after sticky bar top after dance floor, through the thick fog of Sicilian night. We take shots of bitter amaro and order Negronis with prosecco. I keep waiting for another opening, for a quiet moment with Theo, but there's so much happening. Everything keeps exploding around us, spilled drinks and stolen kisses and cherries flaring at the ends of cigarettes.

We lose our friends in a dark, cramped bar with live music, a woman playing an upright bass and a man on the saxophone, the crowd thick and surging and full of smells. Theo is holding a drink with fish bones in it, complaining that my alcohol tolerance doesn't make any sense, that I should be drunker. We can barely hear each other, so we bob wordlessly, eddied by the bodies around us, floating on an incandescent tide.

The band starts up a new song, and I recognize the first chords. Even with the words in Italian, I'd know it anywhere.

"Is that—" Theo shouts. "Are they actually playing—"

"'Can't Stop Loving You,'" I confirm.

Phil Collins, in a dive bar in Palermo. We're alone in the crowd, staring wide-eyed at each other, swaying impossibly to a song we've sung together a hundred times, never knowing it would be the story of our lives. Nothing could convince me that isn't some kind of sign.

Theo leans into my ear and says, "Will you—?"

I can't make out the end of their sentence.

"What?"

They try again. "Will you please—?"

"I can't hear you!"

The music shifts, dipping into the end of the first verse, quieter now, *I could say that's the way it goes, and I could pretend and you won't know—*

This time, I hear Theo when they look into my eyes and say, "Kiss me."

They look like their heart might break, as if they're begging mercy for a lost cause when they reach out to cup my face.

"One kiss, and I'll never ask you again," they say. "I'll get over it one day, I swear, and we can be friends, but I—I just need a better kiss to remember it by."

The crowd pushes us together, and I feel like I'm somewhere else, like I'm everywhere, like every heart in the room must be synced to the hammer of mine.

"Remember what, Theo?"

And they answer, "How it feels to be in love with you."

The band kicks off the chorus. Theo's drink hits the floor as I pull them to me.

"I can't believe you got to say it first," I say over the music.

Their lips part. "You're—you—?"

"I never stopped," I tell them, finally. "Theo, *I never stopped.*"

When they smile, it's gold in the sky, unfolding green hills, a country of endless possibilities, the relief of the last turn before home. I take them by the waist and kiss them with everything in me, everything we made of each other, my mouth to their mouth like we sculpted them with our own hands for this, and Theo holds my face between their palms and kisses me back, deep and sure.

I understand, finally, in the heat of their mouth. They love me. I love them. It was always as simple as that.

— — —

We had two rules left. No kissing, no penetration.

We start with kissing.

We kiss on the crowded street outside the bar, one of dozens of couples pushing each other against rough stone walls under strings of hot lights, Theo's tongue in my mouth and my hands in their hair. We kiss on our way back to the hostel, my lip caught between Theo's teeth. We kiss on the stairs up to our rooms and again in the tight, humid hallway, gasping with slack mouths, hands everywhere. We kiss as if we're inventing it, as if everything else we've done together since we got to Italy was chaste and *this* is sex.

I back Theo into the door of my room and lick into their mouth, swallowing their moan like vin santo, heavy and sweet and lingering.

"Since we're being honest," I say, out of breath, wrenching myself away long enough to get out the room key, "I want you to *fuck me.*"

"I was about to say the same to you," Theo pants.

Then we're crashing inside, grappling across the wall, tearing at each other's clothes. I spare half a breath to thank Italy for inspiring us to button our shirts less, because those are gone in seconds, whipped over our heads so we can press chest to chest, skin to skin, lips sliding wet and raw into another fit of furious kissing. By some miracle I manage to undo Theo's shorts without looking, and Theo tugs my drawstrings loose, and then we're nearly naked.

For a moment our eyes lock, and we stand motionless in the amber nighttime glow of Palermo through the window, arrested under the intensity of each other's attention.

And then Theo smiles, and it's the most beautiful thing I've seen on the entire tour.

"It's so weird when your face gets that serious," they say.

"Yours too."

"Like, who are we?"

I laugh, and I say, because I can, "I love you."

"I love you," Theo says. They love me.

They reach for their shorts on the floor and dig something shiny and gold from the pocket—I think it's one of those fucking Jeans condoms from last night, but instead, they hand me a single euro.

"Flip for it?"

When we were together, this was how we decided who would be fucking whom when we both wanted the same thing. Heads for Theo, tails for me.

I toss the coin across the room.

"I want everything."

Theo's eyes darken.

"Everything?"

"Everything."

They pull me close by the hinge of my jaw and brand my mouth with a kiss, and then they shove me onto the bed.

I can see their mind working behind dilated pupils, strategizing, making plans for me. I was already hard, but being looked at like that by them makes me *ache*.

"Hands and knees."

A warm shiver courses through me, and I do as I'm told. Theo climbs onto the bed behind me, strips me bare, and sets directly to work with their mouth.

I have long believed that being eaten out by Theo Flowerday is enough to make a person understand why erotic writers of history called an orgasm a crisis. The dedication, the skill, the endurance, the total uninhibited enthusiasm, the swimmer's breath control—they lavish me with it, rim and tease and press with their tongue until I'm whimpering and sinking down onto my elbows, widening my legs and rolling my hips.

"That's good," they say, breath shockingly cool on wet skin. Another whimper slips out. "You're being so good. You want more?"

"Please," I say, voice already wrecked. We've barely even started.

I direct Theo to the lube in my bag and watch over my shoulder as they slick up their fingers with the swift confidence of an expert. It occurs to me distantly that Theo has done a lot of fucking since the last time they fucked me, and knowing them, they'll have picked up a million new ways to be good at it. They were already the best fuck I ever had, and now they may be even better.

I may go out like Raphael tonight in this hostel bed. Theo may actually kill me.

They ease me open with smooth, deliberate purpose. I haven't let anyone inside me like this since I left home, but Theo is patient, as promised. They kiss the small of my back and work their way inside until the stretch becomes more pleasure than pain, and then something past pleasure, a breathtaking fullness, as if some missing piece of me has been returned at last. And then their fingertips graze that bundle of nerves inside of me.

"*Fuck*," I gasp, my back arching at the shock of sensation. Theo smiles against my skin.

"Right where I left it."

"More. Please."

They push in again, brushing the same spot, and a broken sound wrenches out of me. My shoulders finally give. I scramble to pull a pillow under me, tucking my chin into my shoulder, desperate to watch as Theo balances on their knees and lines their hips up behind me. Their fingers are buried so deep that their palm presses against my ass, and when our eyes lock, they reach around with their slicked left hand and—Jesus, *fuck*—wrap their fist around me.

"I'm gonna fuck you like this," Theo tells me, voice rough but determined, "and just when you're about to come, I want you to tell me. Then we switch, and you fuck me until we both finish. Okay?"

"Yes," I manage to say. "Fuck, yes, that sounds perfect. I want that."

"Until then," Theo says, "I want you to be a good boy and take it."

"Yes," I say, more aroused than I've possibly ever been in my life. "Yes."

They brace their pelvis against the back of their own hand and fuck me like they said they would, using the steady, relentless roll of their hips to guide their fingers in and out, fingertips skating over that sensitive spot inside me. Their other hand matches the rhythm, so that every time they push inside, their hips push me into the tight circle of their fist. I was right— they've never fucked me like this, never pinned me between two points of pleasure and held me there with their full strength. They're stronger, surer, and I feel so fucking *good* beneath them.

"God," Theo groans. "You're such a little slut sometimes."

My heart clenches, a weak, grateful sound breaking loose.

"You like that?" they ask. "You like when I call you that?"

"Yeah, yes, fucking—love it. Feels good. Feels like—praise."

"It is," they say in the lowest, gentlest part of their voice. "You're so good. So sweet. Such a perfect slut for me."

I let my mouth hang open so they can fuck all the sounds they want from me, one of my hands braced against the headboard to take it better. It's so good like this, so good when it's Theo, so good to be home in capable hands. Complex thought evaporates into sparkling firmament overhead, and far below, I bite the pillow and want only very simple things, to be held and fucked and told I'm pretty, to be good for the person I love.

"Theo," I stammer, barely holding myself together. "Theo, I'm—I'm close."

"Yeah?"

The last thing my body wants is for Theo to stop stroking me, but I find the fortitude to reach between my legs and guide their hand away, down the wetness I've been steadily leaking onto the sheets.

"Yeah."

All at once, Theo's hands and body leave me.

The parts of me that had gone pliant and molten instantly cool like volcanic rock. Hard with need, with intent, with a consuming desire to release everything that's been locked inside me for so much longer than we've been in this bed. I gather myself, wanting to use my strength. I want to be the one giving. I want to hear Theo beg for me the way I did for them, to—

Something light smacks into the side of my face.

I blink down at the bed. It's a condom. The foil wrapper says, JEANS.

"I—I thought we didn't save any of those."

I turn to see Theo naked atop the sheets, propped up on their elbows with one knee bent, freckled cheeks red with exertion and a halo of sweat on their brow. They're smirking, pleased with their performance and now their comedic timing.

"Fabrizio slipped me one before we left," they say. "Come on, I wanna see you."

In a second my feet are planted on the floor and I'm dragging them to the foot of the bed by their ankles as they laugh out a yelp of surprise.

"Is this the manhandling you were talking about?"

"Yes," I say, standing between their legs, tugging them closer so their hips are nearly at the edge. "Come here."

"Zut alors, I feel like a sack of flour— Oh *fuck*."

I cut them off with a touch, the flat of my thumb drawing a blunt, smearing circle just the way they like, the way I did to that peach in Monaco. I bite back a swear when I feel how astonishingly wet they are, even though it's the first they've been touched tonight. All this melting softness, all because of how much they enjoyed fucking me. I'm kneeling before I know it, half hunger, half supplication.

"What are you doing?" they demand, watching me on their elbows. "You're supposed to fuck me."

"Let me taste," I say. "Please." And God knows Theo will never deny me a meal.

I fill my mouth with that innate, vital bittersweetness of them, pull them between my lips and savor. My tongue dips briefly, indulgently—Theo moans—and I decide that's enough to satisfy the craving.

"Thank you," I say, adoring the crease of annoyance between their brows as I stand. I grip their hips, not quite pressing where they want me. "Did you want me to keep going?"

"Fucking cocktease," they whine. My heart sings. "Do *something*, please."

"I will, if you can be a good—" I pause. "What should I call you?"

Theo blinks, like I've asked them to solve my riddles three in the middle of sex.

"Uh—definitely not girl."

"No, obviously. Boy?"

"Sometimes," Theo says. They lower their gaze to the point where our bodies nearly meet, biting their lip at the sight of us. In a quiet, raw voice, they say, "I could be your bottom, if you want."

My body answers for me, visibly twitching.

"Yeah?" I breathe out. "You want me to top you?"

Theo looks up with wide eyes, something wild and new in
them. They nod fast and hard.

I press the condom packet to their lower lip.

"Then be a good bottom for me."

With no further instruction, they rip the packet open with
their teeth.

When I'm ready, I guide their hands to the backs of their
own thighs, pushing their knees up toward their chest, and they
catch on quickly to this too. A vulnerable blush spills like wine
down their throat, but they don't look away. They hold my gaze
and open themself to me.

"That's perfect," I say, taking them by the waist, voice shaking. "God, I fucking adore you."

The ease of the first push shocks a gasp from us both, as if
their body has kept a place for me. One roll of my hips and I
sink to the hilt, and we're there together, fluid and engulfing and
known.

"Fuck me," Theo begs. So I do.

It's furious and desperate and deep, the sounds of our bodies
filling our little half-dark room. Theo takes it beautifully. They
hold their head up to watch as long as they can, stomach muscles shaking with the effort, lip bitten between their teeth, hair
bouncing across their brow. When they collapse onto the bed,
they fall back in glorious surrender. I'm barely in control of
my body, but I'm so absolutely inside of it, aware of every nerve,
every rippling touch, the most of everything.

I always loved how similar our bodies were, that we were almost the exact same height and size, as if we were so entwined
that we grew to mirror each other. I loved how easy it was to
touch myself and pretend I was touching them, how we had the
same insatiable appetites. And in this bed, in our bodies, I'm
overwhelmed with the understanding that we never stopped reflecting each other. We've become a perfect match, two lovers
with equal capacity and equal desire to fuck and be fucked.

I surge onto the bed, catching one of Theo's legs to hold them open as I crush our mouths together.

"I love you," I say, trembling all over, our faces close enough to share breath.

They wrap their arms around my neck and press their forehead to mine.

"I love you," they answer. "*I love you so fucking much.*"

That's all it takes to send me over. I hold back just long enough to watch their mouth drop open at the first crest, and then I'm swept out to sea with them, plunged deep and locked in Theo's embrace, hot tears in my eyes. I've never come so hard. I've never been more thankful for anything. I've never loved Theo more than I do in this moment.

Love took root in me before I learned its name, and I've sat in its shade for so long now without eating its fruit. This feels as if I've finally taken a piece into my hands and split it open. It's so sweet inside.

Sour too, slightly underripe—but so, so sweet.

PALERMO
(DAY TWO)

PAIRS WELL WITH:

Granita and brioche,
fourteen-year whiskey

PALERMO

When we arrived in Sicily, Fabrizio told us the myth of its creation. How three nymphs danced across the earth, gathering the best of everything, the most fertile soil and the most fragrant flora, the ripest fruit and the smoothest stones. They met at the bluest part of the Mediterranean, where the heavens overhead were brightest, and they danced there, casting their treasures into the sea, and so the island was formed.

As I walk with Theo to Palermo Centrale in the light of a warm Sicilian morning, sharing granita di caffè with one spoon, I think it must be true.

It's the final day of the tour, and we're finishing with a day trip to Favignana, one of the tiny islands off Sicily's northwest coast. We meet the group outside the train station, clutching tickets to the port in Trapani, where we'll catch a boat to the islet. Montana waves when she sees us, sunglasses flashing glamorously in the sun.

"Hey, we lost you guys last night!" she says. "Where'd you go?"

Theo and I glance at each other, failing to hide our laughter. Montana's gaze skims down to our hands, fingers laced together.

"Oh my God, no way!" she gasps. "Oh, wow, I'm so happy for you!"

Theo arches a surprised brow. "You are?"

"Duh, everyone knows you're, like, butt-crazy in love with each other."

"They—they do?"

"Yeah, Calum and Calum are always talking about how they hope you figure it out," she says, as if this is common knowledge. "Ko, come see!"

Dakota drifts over, looks at our hands, and says flatly, "Slay."

By the time our train arrives at Trapani, it seems everyone else on the tour has heard that we're back together. We stand outside a gelateria across from the pier, eating bubbles of fresh brioche stuffed with gelato and bemusedly watching people pretend they're not watching us. The Swedes are gossiping in rapid Swedish. The honeymooners who gave Theo directions in Chianti are whispering. Even Stig seems invested in our saga.

"Are we . . . tour famous?" Theo asks me.

I shake my head, amazed. "I think we're their Calums."

"Let's give 'em a show, then."

I lean in and give Theo a solid, deep kiss. They taste of coffee and pistachio and sunscreen, like the love of my life.

Aboard the ferry, Theo and I find a spot at the stern of the boat and watch Trapani shrink in the distance as the blue waters grow vaster. We lean side to side, taking each other's weight, the wind whipping our hair into one swirl of brown and rose gold. The sun kisses the tops of our shoulders.

I close my eyes and drink in the sea air, as if it could carry this moment into my body forever.

"You brought yours, right?" Theo says.

I unzip my bag and show them what I promised to bring to Favignana with us: the envelope containing my unsent letter from four years ago, the one I planned to bury at sea on the last day of my solo trip.

In return, Theo opens their hip pack to let me see their own promised cargo: the little anniversary bottle of whiskey.

"Amici!" Fabrizio's voice is warm behind us. We turn to find him bursting through a thin crowd of passengers, arms held wide. "Is it true what I am hearing? You are together at last?"

Theo slips me a small, private smile, which is answer enough for Fabrizio. He scoops each of us up, pressing congratulatory kisses to our cheeks. He promises to order extra prosecco at tonight's dinner and prances away, alight with the joy of romance renewed.

Theo touches their cheek, still smiling.

"I just don't have the heart to tell him," they say.

"No," I say. "I don't think he has to know."

— — —

Last night, after we cleaned ourselves up and climbed back into bed together, we couldn't fall asleep. We were too high on each other, too restless with delayed touches and full of things we'd been meaning to say. Theo wanted to see my sketchbooks, so I took them out and flipped through while they sat behind me, peppering kisses across my naked back.

At the top of my shoulder, they paused. "Oh."

I didn't realize they'd reached my tattoo until they smoothed their finger across it.

"*Surpasses all jewels*," they said in a quiet voice. "I just remembered why I know that."

When I turned to them, I saw tears in their eyes.

And suddenly we were in a different bed. We weren't two adults reunited; we were two wide-eyed children in a bedroom with stars on the ceiling, during the worst summer of my life.

It happened in a way I think my mother would have loved. It was almost a fairy tale. A silent curse from an enchanted garden, an eternal slumber. For so long I held on to that idea to make her death seem less pointlessly cruel, but in the end, it was a single, stupid accident. She slipped and hit her head in the greenhouse, went to sleep certain she hadn't seriously injured herself, and never woke up. There was no sickness, no terrible event. One day she was there, and the next she wasn't, and life as I knew it went with her.

I was thirteen. Ollie was sixteen, and Cora was ten. None

of us knew what to do, not even Dad—especially not Dad. But Theo, somehow, did.

They were close enough to our family to know what each of us needed, and removed enough to do the things none of us could. All summer, they skateboarded two miles each way from their house to mine. They asked us our favorite meals, wrote lists of ingredients, and assigned Ollie to grocery shopping. They knew I loved baking and Cora loved cakes, but that Maman's recipes were unusable for now, so they borrowed cookbooks from the library and shoplifted issues of *Good Housekeeping* from the drugstore. And, when I couldn't fall asleep for days at a time, they climbed into bed with me and read out loud from my favorite book, *The Silmarillion*.

"Maman read it to me when I was six," I told them.

"In French, right?" Theo asked in that simple, direct way of theirs. "Well, I'm reading it in English, so it's different."

By then, I had known for years that I loved Theo. But in my bed in the desert that unthinkable summer, I knew that no matter what happened between us when we were older, they would always be the person who did this for me. That would always matter more than anything.

I never could find words to tell them what it meant to me, but when Theo's thirteenth birthday came that autumn, I tried to put it in a card. On the back, I wrote a few lines from my favorite chapter of *The Silmarillion*: the story of the mortal man Beren and the elf princess Lúthien. Beren, after many long, hard years in the wilderness, saw Lúthien dancing on the glades of Doriath in the light of moonrise and fell in love.

For Theo, I wrote a line from Beren's speech to Luthien's father, the king: *And here I have found what I sought not indeed, but finding I would possess for ever. For it is above all gold and silver, and surpasses all jewels.*

I never told Theo, but I thought about getting a tattoo of

those last three words for years. I finally did it a year after our breakup. I still wanted it. It still meant something to me. I'd had the gift of being loved to the center of my soul twice in my life, and even if both of those people were gone, the love had been there. It was still there, in the shape it had made me into.

When Theo touched the ink in the sea near Saint-Jean-de-Luz, I was sure they'd put it together. I couldn't decide if I was disappointed or relieved that they didn't. But last night, when they recognized it, when I was reminded of what it meant to me, I looked into their eyes and knew. I just knew.

"I love you more than anything," I said. "But I can't do this."

It was the last thing I wanted to say and the only thing I could. I lost Theo once by chasing a dream without considering its cost. I can't take that risk again, not even if the dream is them.

The problem is, I can't promise I won't repeat the same mistakes. I can't know if this will end, or when, or how, and I don't know if we could come back from it again if it did. If there's a chance that one day I'll never see them again, and I could change that fate now by never taking the chance, then I'll stop here. I'll make the bargain.

They were silent for a long time, their cheek against my shoulder blade.

Finally, they said, "Neither can I."

We live on different continents, they said. We have different lives.

One of the core truths of Theo is, ninety-nine times out of a hundred, they'll sacrifice what they want to protect what they have. Our friendship is a sure thing, and they would choose that sure thing over anything.

"But I still love you," they said.

"Yeah," I agreed. "I still love you."

We kissed, and we cried, and we told each other we were doing the right thing. That these are the kind of painful choices adults learn to make to keep something for life. One day it wouldn't hurt so much, and we'd be grateful we had done it.

Then Theo said, "What now?"

They looked so heartbreakingly gorgeous then, with their mussed hair and bruises on their collarbones and wet, pink-rimmed eyes. I had to let them go. But I thought a thing like this deserved a true goodbye.

"What if we're together for the last day," I said, "just to see what it's like?"

— — —

"You got us a *boat*?"

"I mean," Theo says, looking down at the thing from the pier, hands on their hips like a captain surveying his vessel, "technically, it's a dinghy."

I marvel at the little boat floating on the crystal clear water that surrounds Favignana. Its round, inflatable walls gleam pristine white like Italian meringue in the sun. It has two horizontal rows of benches and an adorably small motor on the back, and thanks to Theo, it's temporarily ours.

"You *got us a boat*."

Theo hops down onto the dinghy's deck with steady sea legs. The sandwiches in my hands are beginning to leak juices through their wax paper and down my wrists, but I barely notice.

"You said, 'Go get us sandwiches, I'll find something to drink,' and you came back with a *boat*."

"Oh! I have drinks too!" They dig a shopping bag out from under a bench and show me a sweating bottle of white wine. "It's not that cold anymore, but it's a good one."

"Theo, *how*?"

"I made friends with a guy at the enoteca, don't worry about it," they say dismissively, as if charming a stranger into lending out a boat on a remote Mediterranean island is something anyone could do. "Come on, we only have it for two hours. Pass me the sandwiches and get in."

When I was sixteen in New York, I envied every person in the Valley who got to witness Theo's career as a house-party king. I wanted to see them like that, strutting cocksure around the room like a young James Dean, magically conjuring up the object of anyone's desire. I wasn't sure I'd ever see the return of that Theo, until now.

"James fucking Dean," I say faintly to myself, and I do as Theo says.

Every place we've stopped on this tour has been so singular, but Favignana truly is unlike anywhere else. The island is tumbled together from sun-bleached beige rock, so uniform in color that even the blocky houses lining its streets are the same shade of eggshell. The beaches are quiet here, natural pockets of white sand between jagged stone shores and the occasional tuft of scruffy yellow-green grass. And the water—the water is so brilliantly clear that boats seem to magically float on thin air.

Since the island is too small to get lost on, we have time to explore on our own. Theo and I have already wandered most of the dusty roads hand in hand, past homes with every window frame and door painted an identical shade of deep sea blue, past cactus-lined terrazzos where old women hang sheets on their lines and old men crack mussels. Eventually, we found our way back to the shoreline, where we split up to gather lunch.

I'll admit, I was a bit smug about the food. I found a yellow truck near a cove selling fresh-caught fish and ordered two overstuffed sandwiches of tuna kebab and tomato, dripping with onion agrodolce and spritzed with lemon between oily, herb-rubbed bread. They smell incredible, but they are undeniably not a boat. Theo takes this round.

Aboard, I ask them, "Do you know how to drive this thing?"

Theo shrugs, wrapping a confident hand around the throttle. "I'm sure I can figure it out. I'm the Crocodile Hunter."

"The what?" I ask, but it's drowned out by the crank of the engine.

As with almost anything Theo has ever put their mind to, it takes them only a few minutes of hands-on trial and error to get the hang of it. Soon, we're skipping like a stone across the turquoise bay, following the curve of the island.

I'm trying very hard not to think about how this time tomorrow, I'll be on my way to Paris, and we'll be apart, and I don't know when I'll see Theo again. Instead, I memorize every detail of this moment. The sunlight on the waves, the hum of the motor and the rush of wind, the silvery fish darting beneath us. Theo, with their dust storm of freckles, hair in the wind, smile radiant.

Theo steers into a secluded cove within steep, curving walls of rock and throws the anchor. There, we float, eating and taking turns drinking from the bottle.

"Fuck," Theo moans as they chew. "Why is this, like, the best sandwich I've ever had?"

"I have a theory about this," I say. "I call it the contextual sandwich."

"Contextual sandwich?"

"Yes," I say. "Sometimes, a perfect sandwich is not just about the sandwich itself, but about the *setting*. The *experience* of eating the sandwich. Context can elevate a great sandwich to a spiritual experience."

"I'm following," Theo says, nodding thoughtfully. "I think it's that and also the onion agrodolce."

"The onion agrodolce is everything," I agree. "I want to make a baby with it."

"Ooh." Theo sits up, inspired. "Onion agrodolce, on the fly."

"Well, I already said, I would take the onion agrodolce and make a baby."

"Something you can eat, Kit."

"Why not the baby? Like Saturn devouring his son."

"Kit devouring his onion baby," Theo imagines. "I can see the painting now."

"Art historians hate him."

"And they're right to."

"But actually . . ." I chew and swallow another bite, considering the question. "I think I'd keep it simple. Bake it into a nice focaccia. Let it do its sexy little thing."

"Hm. Focaccia has lots of olive oil, right?"

"Correct."

"Okay, I'll take the olive oil and emulsify that with an egg white," Theo says. "Add lemon juice, basil simple syrup, Gin Mare, bit of soda. Mediterranean gin fizz."

I imagine a bistro table somewhere close to the sea, set with both. A pillow of focaccia with sweet-and-sour onion on a chipped saucer, a juice glass with fizz and a single, fresh basil leaf shipped in from a farm in Cinque Terre. I find that I don't want to come up with the next dish; I want to sit here with this complementary pair.

"Do you ever think," I ask Theo, "about how amazing it is that a drink or a plate of food can be so good separately, but if you pair them together the right way, it becomes an experience?"

"Well, yes," Theo says with a swig of wine. "That is a sommelier's job."

"Huh. It is, isn't it? You're an experience maker."

"Yeah, I am," Theo says, preening slightly. I love to see it. "I think that's what I like most about everything I do, the bus or the somm stuff or anything. I like creating an experience. I like tasting and smelling and feeling things, and listening to what's meaningful to someone, and then trying to distill all of that into a glass."

"What did you think of the wine pairings at that first dinner in Paris?"

"Oh, fuck. Those were inspired. The Châteauneuf-du-Pape they paired with the gigot d'agneau?" They groan at the memory.

"Honestly, that might have been my favorite meal of the whole trip."

"Really? We've had so many incredible ones since."

"I know. Maybe I just have a soft spot for French food."

"Oh, you do?" I say, smiling. "Any particular reason?"

I'm flirting, setting them up for an easy, dirty joke about how the French go down easier, but Theo says plainly, "Probably because I'm in love with you."

We said it so many times last night, but my heart still clenches.

"What about you?" Theo asks. "What was your favorite meal of the tour?"

I think about it. "Maybe dinner at Fabrizio's family's restaurant in Naples. That ragù, *God.*"

"Ooh, that was a good one," Theo agrees. "My favorite drink, though—that might have been the Pomerol we had at the chateau in Bordeaux."

I smile fondly. "Oh, Florian."

"Oh, *Florian,*" Theo echoes.

"Be honest—did he take it better than me?"

"Not better," Theo says fairly. "But like a champ."

"Maybe I'll go back to Bordeaux one day."

"Send me a video if you do."

"I'll ask him," I say, more intrigued by the thought of Theo wanting videos from me than the idea of topping God's perfect farmhand. "My favorite drink was the vin santo we had in Chianti, with the cantucci."

"You would pick the only drink that came with a cookie," Theo teases. "Favorite sight?"

"The Duomo in Florence," I say. "Definitely. You?"

"Roman Forum is up there. But I have to give it to the Sagrada Familia." They finish their sandwich and wrap the remains back up in the paper. "Can I tell you a secret?"

"All of them, always."

"I think," Theo says, "being in Sagrada Familia with you, listening to you tell me about it—that was when I started to realize I still loved you."

The tide laps quietly against the sides of the boat, swaying us from side to side.

"It was?"

Theo nods. "Yeah."

"An architecture lecture made you realize you loved me?"

"It was the Gaudí story, man," Theo says, laughing. "It got me."

"It's romantic, isn't it?"

"That man really loved that church." They've pushed their sunglasses up into their hair, and their gaze holds mine as they pass the bottle back. "It was also just . . . I knew I loved you when I listened to how you talk about something you love. I don't know if you know how beautiful it is, the way you give your whole heart to what moves you. You're always looking for reasons to love things, and when you do, it's never halfway. I've always loved that about you."

"Theo," I say softly. I set the bottle on the floor of the boat and take their hand. "I need to tell you something."

"Tell me."

I take a deep breath and say, "My nose is about to start bleeding."

"Your—?"

"My nose, yes."

"How— Oh, fuck, there it goes."

They pull their hand back, grimacing as wet warmth begins trickling into the dip above my upper lip. I'd be embarrassed if we had any reasons left to be. As it is, I have to tell myself not to laugh so it doesn't overflow into my mouth.

"Dude, are you okay?" Theo asks, handing me a paper napkin. "Does it always happen this often?"

"Before I saw you in London, it had been over a year," I say. "But since then—twice a week? Maybe three times?"

"Why?"

I smile, a bead of warmth rolling over my lip. It's just so ridiculous. Theo's brows shoot up.

"Because of *me*? They're—*love* nosebleeds?"

I nod. "Always were."

"That's *disgusting*," Theo says, lunging forward, sliding a hand into my hair.

They swipe their tongue across my lips and push it into my mouth, and we drink in the mingled flavors of us: the acidic burn of green grapes and vinegar, a heady combination of bitter orange and lavender, coppery blood turned sweet and ripe as a pomegranate in Proserpina's palm.

I pull them into my lap, and they push our swimsuits aside and take me right here, floating in our hidden blue cove under the Mediterranean sun. I spread my fingers to touch all of them I can reach, so that when they're gone, I won't have to imagine anything. I'll only have to close my eyes and relive this, their grinding hips, the smell of summer on their skin, their body living forever in my body's memory.

Rilke wrote, *He makes a home in your familiar heart, takes root there and begins himself again.*

After, we strip down to our bottoms, our chests unceremoniously bare, and jump in. I tread water while Theo swims laps around me, ripples of light sliding over them. I count their efficient strokes. They know exactly where they're going.

— — —

At a seaside restaurant near the busiest part of Favignana—that is, one of the streets not wandered by cattle—everyone seems reluctant to finish their last dinner of the tour. Even after all these days on a bus and nights in strange beds, all the blisters from long city walks and Florentine sunburns and daily translation failures, it always seems like home could wait one more day. I don't know if I'll ever be ready to take my final sip of wine wearing shoes that stood before a Botticelli only days ago. I can't imagine walking into my apartment and kicking them off into the pile with the rest.

Around tables laden with fresh-caught seafood, the strangers we met three weeks ago talk and laugh and feast in now-familiar ways. The honeymooners touch hands on the tablecloth. The Swedes finish all their vegetables first. Dakota and Montana photograph every dish from a dozen dynamic angles before they throw their phones down and dig in. The Calums laugh too loudly—although, tonight, they sit closer than usual. A conspicuous bruise on Blond's neck looks about the size of a man's mouth. When Theo catches Montana's eye, she gives them a thumbs-up, and Theo and I raise our glasses. Montana smiles victoriously, running her fingers through Dakota's blond hair.

Between primi and secondi, Fabrizio stands and makes a toast.

"For nine years now, I do this tour," Fabrizio says, holding his glass of prosecco aloft. "Since I was twenty-five years old. If I am honest, sometimes I cannot wait for this dinner. Sometimes the people are not so good, and the weather much worse, and I wish to be home soon as I can. And sometimes, this dinner breaks my heart, because the people are so kind, and the sky is so blue, and the wind is so warm, and the love in my heart for food and wine and history shines back to me from all of you, and I do not want to say goodbye. Tonight, amici, my heart is broken."

People sigh. My own heart aches. Beneath the table, Theo reaches for my hand.

"Grazie mille ragazzi," Fabrizio says with shimmering eyes, "thank you for coming along with me. I hope you will remember me well. Salute!"

"Salute!" the room calls back, and we drink to our dear, delicious, devastating Fabrizio.

— — —

Before the end of dinner, we sneak away to the smallest, emptiest beach we can find nearby. We stand before the setting sun and take out the whiskey, like we always said we would. Theo has another day and a half on their own before they fly home, but I leave first thing in the morning, so this is our last chance. Funnily enough, though, Theo has a layover in Paris.

As we drink, Theo asks, "Which city was your favorite?"

I consider my answer for a long time.

Finally, I admit, "I haven't been able to stop thinking about Saint-Jean-de-Luz."

"I was going to say that one too," Theo says. "All the others I felt like I was visiting, but Saint-Jean-de-Luz felt like a home, you know? Or—I guess Paris is home to you, so maybe not."

"No, I know what you mean," I say. "There was something about it, a sort of . . ."

"Peace," they finish for me.

I nod, letting the tide wash up to my ankles. Theo passes me the whiskey, and I savor its burn.

"I think these might have been the most important three weeks of my life," Theo says. "There were so many things I didn't even know I was capable of until I was doing them. And I never would've known if I hadn't come. And now, when I look at my life back home, I feel like I can see actually see it clearly from here."

"I know what you mean about clarity," I say. "You know I've been trying to read *A Room with a View* for two years now?"

Theo shakes their head. "Really? You?"

"I know. It's been like that with so many things. Baking for myself, or making up recipes, or painting, or drawing. I just haven't had it in me. I packed that book and all those sketchbooks because I was hoping that something here would bring it out. And now I feel like . . . like I'm starting to come back to life. Like I'm a plant and someone finally remembered to water me."

After a long moment of thought, Theo says, "You used to get this look on your face when you were baking—this *smile,* like you were exactly where you were supposed to be."

I consider this, the differences between now and then, when I was baking my own recipes in my own kitchen. I think I could feel that way again, under the right conditions.

"I might need a new job," I confess. Theo laughs quietly, and so do I. "What about you? What'll you do when you get home?"

"I think," Theo says, tipping their chin up with a declarative air, "I will try to figure out what the one thing I want to do is, and then really commit to that thing."

"That sounds like a good plan."

"And I think maybe, *maybe,* I will talk to Sloane about the money. And maybe I could even move out of the Valley, to somewhere new," they say. "I don't know. There's so much world out here."

"There is," I agree.

"Most of all," they say, "I want us to stay friends."

God, I didn't realize how badly I needed to hear them say that until they did. I touch their cheek with my fingertips, swimming in the clear-water blues and greens of their eyes.

"I want that too," I say. "I don't want you to ever not be in my life."

"Good," they say fiercely. "And I'll come visit you."

I raise my eyebrows, teasing. "Will you?"

"I will." They put their arms around my waist. "And you'll come visit me, and there could be . . . benefits."

"Benefits," I repeat. "I'll always want your benefits."

Theo laughs.

When we finish the whiskey, I take my unsent letter and roll it up as tightly as I can, then push it through the bottle's opening and screw on the cap.

Theo hooks their chin over my shoulder, pressing their cheek against the side of my neck. I imagine us in five, fifteen, thirty years. Best friends an ocean apart, reappearing once every couple of years to burn the bedroom down, then slipping back to our own lives. Always orbiting each other, never fully out of reach.

I could love that ongoing, extant Theo again. There's so much romance in that, so much beauty in learning how much my heart can endure. Sometimes I think the only way to keep something forever is to lose it and let it haunt you.

I reel my arm back, ready to throw our letter in a bottle to sea, but at the last moment, Theo stops me.

"I want to keep it," they say. "Maybe I'll want to read it, one day when I love you less."

PARIS (AGAIN)

PAIRS WELL WITH:

Tarte tatin aux pêches,
espresso from the second-best
café in Bastille

PARIS

It feels like there must be such a tremendous distance between Palermo and home, between where Theo is and where Theo isn't, but the flight only takes two and a half hours. I close my eyes to Ravel in my headphones, and when I open them, I'm once again arriving in Paris alone. This time, I'm here because we chose it. That has to count for something.

At home, everything is how I left it. The embroidered pillows on the sofa, the shelves of my and Thierry's books. Maxine has washed and changed the bedsheets, even spritzed them with the lavender oil I keep beside the bed. The plants in the windows are happy and verdant, their leaves plump and shiny in the early afternoon light. The detailed list of plant care instructions I left on the chalkboard by the kitchen has been erased and replaced with a stick-figure drawing of Maxine and me riding a giant strawberry.

The first thing I do, once I've unpacked and showered and applied all the nice skincare products I couldn't pack, is go to the market. I pick up the basics to ready my kitchen for everyday use again—eggs, butter, milk, ripe tomatoes on the vine, a fresh loaf of peasant bread, paper cartons of berries, lemons, heavy cream—and then carefully select the ingredients for a tarte tatin. Summer will end soon, and in a few months autumn will bring quinces; today, I choose peaches.

I haven't made a tarte tatin since pâtisserie school, and it turns out I've forgotten how tricky they can be. A quarter of

the peaches stick to the pan. Not my best work, but if I'm being honest, Guillaume isn't the best fuck. Both will do in a
pinch.

It's a twelve-minute bike ride from my apartment to Guillaume's, and I spend it reflecting on what exactly I've been doing
with him. I like him, but I like a lot of people. He's sweet, and
he manages the best café in Bastille, and last month he physically
mailed me a poem, which means he's probably at least a little in
love with me. I never asked him to be, and I've never suggested
it would be a good idea. But I *do* bring him a tart every so often,
which Maxine says is "evil, misleading boyfriend behavior." I haven't been trying to mislead him. It's just that the way he smiles
every time is so lovely.

He gives me that smile when he answers the door to me and
my tart, which makes me feel even guiltier that I'm here to break
things off.

I know, the same as I've known since I was nine years old
in the desert, that I'll always love Theo. But I can't keep doing
what I've been doing with that love. It doesn't feel fair to go on
burying it in other people, showing them all the flowers Theo
has frescoed over my heart without telling them I've already put
someone else's statue in the fountain at its center. Guillaume is
the first on the list. Tomorrow I'll call Delphine, and Luis, and
Eva, and Antoine, and—maybe I should write this down later.

Guillaume takes it reasonably well, but he lets me know in
no uncertain terms that I will *not* be getting my plate back. Fair.

When I get home, I do the next thing on my housekeeping
list: I call my dad. He answers as if we last spoke a few days ago,
which doesn't surprise me. He's not in Rome, but he is currently
writing in residence at the Ace Hotel in Manhattan, even though
his apartment is only six blocks over. He's been translating a German vampire novel for fun in his spare time. I tell him about the
tour, about the food and the paintings and the sea, but not about
Theo. The closest we get to addressing our last conversation is a

vague mention he makes of wanting to visit Paris and "leave work at home this time."

"I'm not sure how much longer I'll be living here," I tell him. "I've been thinking about making some changes."

On the other end of the line, he's quiet for long enough that I think he must not have been paying attention. My suspicions seem confirmed when he says, "Did I mention my editor is leaving? I had dinner with him last week."

"Oh?" I begin trimming the basil plant in my kitchen window, ready to ease myself out of the conversation.

"I was telling him how happy Violette would be to know you'd wound up back in France."

My scissors still.

"You were?"

"He's moving abroad for his wife's job, and they have two sons. Sixteen and eleven. He asked me how the three of you adjusted when we moved from France. I said, well, Ollie was old enough to be excited about it, and Cora was too young to remember much. But our Kit—he was the one Violette worried most about. Our sensitive one. He's the most like his mother, and her heart belonged in France."

My throat tightens. He doesn't like to talk about my mother, especially not with my siblings and me. I think it hurts too much to draw attention to all the pieces of her in us, like how I spoke only French the first few months after losing Theo so I wouldn't have to hear the English phrases and inflections I'd adopted from them. This is the first time in years he's said something like this to me. It's the closest he's ever come to saying he regrets taking her away from France for the last six years of her life.

I glance at the watercolor paintings that hang on the kitchen wall exactly as they have since Thierry hung them years and years ago. The centermost one is a garden scene, all green except for the brown shape of a little fox curled up in the roots of an orange tree.

"Do you think I should stay, then?" I ask.

"I think," he says, "that I'm thankful you have my spirit, but her heart."

That night, I scroll job listings in bed, half-heartedly searching for something that might make me happier than my current one does. There are plenty of openings for part-time bread makers and sous chefs and cake decorators, but the more I try to imagine myself doing any of them, the harder it gets to ignore what I don't feel: the startling rush of possibility I felt when Paloma told me about the pâtisserie in Saint-Jean-de-Luz.

I type out a text to Paloma: can i call you tomorrow?

When I've sent it, I swipe back into my messages, to my conversation with Theo. I haven't heard from them all day, and I tell myself it's nothing to be concerned about. They've probably been busy enjoying their time alone in Palermo, sunning themself on the beach and eating arancini. I'll hear from them tomorrow. We promised.

I fall asleep thinking of them. The curve of their shoulder, the slant of their smile. Their hands covered in pizza grease, an apricot-flavored kiss. I miss them so badly already. But I've learned to love that ache.

— — —

The next day, I go back to work, and it feels better than it has in a long time—not because I've decided to stay, but because I've decided to leave. I find that I can put up with any amount of tweezering when I can imagine my own tasting menus while I do it. It's good to feel like I'm working toward something, even if I don't yet know exactly what that will be.

I still haven't heard from Theo. I sent one text this morning, asking if they've eaten any more granita and brioche since I left, but they haven't responded. I catch myself leaving my phone face up on my station all morning, even though it's expressly forbidden. Maybe Theo's preparing for their transatlantic flight tonight. Maybe that's all it is. Any minute, they could send me a

photo of a priceless sculpture's cock and balls, and everything will be fine.

Maxine meets me for apéro at our usual café. She's happy to see me, once she's finished scolding me because Guillaume has started charging her for coffees again. I tell her that I'm trying to break things off with every hookup in my rotation, and she says it'd be faster to send out a newsletter.

I tell her everything that happened on the trip—even the horny parts, which are more interesting to her than the parts where I experience new heights of human emotion while staring at old churches. She understands how we arrived at the decision we made, but she doesn't agree with it. I find it harder and harder the longer I talk to explain why it makes sense.

It made perfect sense two days ago, when I was so afraid of my own predisposed selfishness, so sure I'd carry on the family curse. But I keep remembering my dad's words. *Your mother's heart.* I wish I could talk to her about it, have her tell me I've done the right thing. I wish she could tell me if she ever doubted what she gave up for love.

"What about you?" I ask Maxine, eager to change the subject. "Did you go on any dates while I was gone?"

Maxine scoffs, reaching for her glass. "Darling, I don't even know the last time I met someone I'd consider putting my mouth on."

"Maxine," I plead. "There has to be someone."

She considers, leaning back in her chair, an elegantly rolled spliff dangling from her manicured fingers.

"Did you say you got Fabrizio's personal number?"

"I did," I say, unable to suppress a smile. Another North American victim of Fabrizio's charm offensive. "But listen to *this.*"

— — —

Maxine offers to stay over, knowing how much I hate sleeping alone, but I tell her I'll be fine. I should get used to it. I walk home through dusk, stopping at the market on the way. I have an idea I want to test.

The sun is gone by the time I get home. Theo should be on their layover now. Somewhere just outside the city, they're ordering a bitter coffee at Brioche Dorée and browsing French liqueurs in the duty-free store, looking out of airport windows into the same night as me. Tomorrow we'll be back on separate hemispheres, but for a few short hours tonight, we're in the same city.

I lay all my ingredients out on the kitchen counter and get to work making the madeleines I dreamed up while looking at *The Birth of Venus*.

It's all going well, until I turn on my stand mixer. It's been so long since I used it, a screw must have come loose somewhere without my notice. It rockets across the narrow kitchen, bouncing off the refrigerator and toward the framed paintings on the adjacent wall. In a fraction of a second, the garden scene I noticed last night takes a direct hit and tips sideways, the hanging wire on the back tugs the decades-old nail out of the wall, and it crashes to the kitchen floor.

Miraculously, the glass hasn't broken. A corner of the frame has split, but the painting itself is unharmed.

When I turn the frame over to check the back for damage, I see something I never knew was there: an inscription, written in French and dated two years before my parents met.

I have to sit down when I recognize my mother's handwriting.

Thierry,

Happy birthday, my dear brother!

Please do not let your girlfriend hang this one in her house. I would like to see it again! HA—just kidding. I hope one day I can be more like you. If I can give my whole heart to love without fearing the cost, I will regret nothing.

Love, your sister Vi

My breath catches.

I read the last sentence again, and again.

I put my hand over my heart. I feel it pounding, feel it breaking. Feel the love forever regenerating.

I've been willing to accept being wrong about so much. About the choices I made when I thought I knew best, about the dreams I believed would materialize if I simply decided they should. About Paris, about what Theo wanted. About love meaning a person must give up everything, and love meaning a person must give up nothing. About what we deserved from each other. I've gotten down on my knees and begged myself to understand that I'll never do it all right like I do in my fantasies, that a love that's ended is the only kind I can have, because I can't possibly lose it.

But before all of those things, I was a boy in a ridiculous fairy-tale hamlet. I was a child with his mother's eyes and heart, a heart she wanted to give over to love. And I have the one chance of my life to do the same, and I'm in my kitchen making madeleines because I'm afraid of the cost. God, she would *never* let me hear the end of it.

What am I doing? What have I done?

The clock on the oven says a quarter to ten. Theo should be boarding in an hour and a half.

If I run—if I catch the fastest cab in Paris—if I buy the first available international ticket on the way to the airport—if I can get to the gate in time—

If I can catch Theo before they get on the plane, I can tell them I was wrong. That I was afraid, but I don't want to be anymore. That being with them is worth anything. Everything. Whatever it costs, however it ends. The only thing I'd regret more than losing them is never getting to love them the way I could love them now.

The chance I'll make it is so small, but I have to try. I have to.

I turn off the oven, pocket my keys, snatch my wallet and my passport from the bowl above the fireplace, charge toward the door and throw it open and—

On the other side of my apartment door, wide-eyed and breathless, their pack still on their shoulders and their right hand raised as if to knock, is—

"*Theo.*"

They stare.

"Hi." They scan my frantic expression, the passport in my hand. "Were you going somewhere?"

"The airport," I say faintly. Theo is here. Theo is here, at the pied-à-terre, on my doormat. "How did you—"

They hold up a yellowed, crinkled envelope. It's been unfurled from the tight roll I put it in, and one side is ripped open.

"Return address."

"You—" I try to form words, to get my head to stop spinning. "You opened it."

"I was on the plane from Palermo," Theo says, "and I realized, I'm never going to love you less."

I'm gripping my passport so hard I think I might tattoo its crest into my hand.

"There I was, on another plane without you. And there you were, in Paris without me. Everything we've been through, everything we said to each other, everything we've done to try to be better, and we're right back where we started. And somehow, we talked ourselves into believing that means we've grown up. But, Kit, I *have* grown—I've grown into someone who's better for you. And you've become someone who's better for me. And I know you want to put our friendship first, and I'm so afraid of fucking that up. I'm so, so afraid of fucking everything up all the time. I don't know how we would make it work, I don't even know where we would live, or what my life is supposed to look like, or what happens if I take the wrong chance, but—but that's not the worst mistake I could make. *This* isn't the worst mistake I could make. The worst mistake I could ever make is pretending I'd be happy as just your friend for the rest of my life. And I'm sorry if that's not what you want to hear, but I couldn't go home without saying it."

They let out a huge breath, as if they've been holding it since I opened the door. Bright tears blaze in their eyes. Their hair is dirty from traveling, their face red from running, and if I could commission an oil painting of them in this state of absolute, screaming perfection, I would.

"Also," Theo says. "It would be so great if I could crash on your couch tonight, because the next flight out is tomorrow."

"Theo," I say. My voice shakes. Every nerve in my body sings together a three-movement opera. "Fuck the couch. Come get in my bed."

And, with all the momentum of twenty years and a hundred thousand miles, Theo smashes into me.

The force of their kiss knocks me backward into my apartment, toppling the shoe rack and at least two of Thierry's hand-thrown vases, which shatter on the floor by our feet. I barely notice. I'll make it up to him. Right now, I'm being thrown up against the wall, and I'm fisting my hands in Theo's hair, and I'm kissing them like we're twenty-two again, courageous and astonished and pushing our luck. I'm kissing them like we're twenty-four, full of dreams and fears, and like we're twenty-six, lost in each other's memory. I kiss them like now, twenty-eight, wiser and steadier and evolved and still so fucking gone for each other.

"To be clear," Theo gasps, breaking away from my mouth, "when you said you were going to the airport—"

"I was coming to get you," I say. "You keep beating me to it."

"Nice. I love winning," Theo replies, smiling hysterically. They're still wearing their backpack. I think I might be stepping on my passport. "And that means you—you feel the same—"

"I love you," I say. "I want you back."

"And you're not going to change your mind in the morning?"

"Theo." I look directly into their brilliant, searching eyes. "If a priest lived in this building, I would take you to his door right now and tell him to marry us."

"Oh," Theo says. "I was thinking it'd be fun if Fabrizio officiated."

"You were—" My heart stammers. They're not even joking. "There are so many things I want to ask you, but Theo, I swear to God, if you don't get in my bed right now I *will* die."

So we go, Theo's pack thrown down on the carpet, shoes kicked off into different corners, clothes removed so quickly that buttons go flying and skittering across the floor. Theo kisses me hard enough to bruise, and I'm so thankful, I'm so fucking unbelievably, shatteringly thankful for this.

— — —

The next morning, I wake Theo up with cinnamon rolls.

"You finally found the perfect recipe," they say after their first bite. They're resplendent, sitting in my kitchen chair wearing nothing but a pair of my underwear, hair matted in the back from sex.

"This is the same recipe I used the first morning we were together," I tell them.

"Oh. Well. Maybe that's why I like it so much."

I place a cup of black coffee beside their plate, following their gaze to the kitchen wall next to the chalkboard.

"I can't believe you bought one of those," they say, smiling at the calendar I brought back from a roadside souvenir stand in Rome, the one featuring a hot priest for every month. "Wait, what am I saying—of course you did. You're Kit."

"Forgive me, Father, for I have sinned," I say, kissing their temple. Then I look more closely at the calendar and realize the date. "Wait, Theo, weren't you supposed to take the somm exam today?"

They reach for the sugar bowl and dump a spoonful into their cup.

"I think I know what I want my one thing to be," they say. "And I don't know that I need to pass a test to do it."

I sit in the chair beside theirs, holding my coffee cup between my palms, letting its warmth spread into me.

"Tell me."

"Imagine a bar," Theo begins, "but it's also a bakery. New menu every week, only five or six special items dependent on what's in season, plus a permanent selection of local staples. French-focused, but with Spanish and Italian elements. Everything sourced directly through personal relationships with farms, vineyards, fishmongers, chocolatiers, bakers. And the concept is, every dish is designed to pair with a drink. A customized cocktail, a specifically chosen glass of wine. Every pairing is designed to tell a story, so when you order, you're ordering a full experience."

I nod. I adore this idea. "And what's this place called?"

"I was thinking," Theo says, "Field Day."

It dawns on me slowly. Fairfield. Flowerday. Fairflower was our first dream. This could be our new one.

"If you want," Theo adds. "It's just an idea. I don't even know where we could open it."

I look at Theo, bathed in morning glow, and I picture them in the sea with me, swimming back to each other, meeting again and again. I see sand as white and fine as sugar.

"I might have a suggestion."

EPILOGUE

Notes on aroma, Saint-Jean-de-Luz on a winter morning:

Cold, crisp seawater. Fresh linens, washed just yesterday, already mingled with lavender and neroli. Yeast, bread crust, brown butter, lemon rind, thyme dried by the sun in a kitchen window. Wet paint and sawdust from the turn-ups of my jeans, the apricot jam Kit brought back from Les Halles for me when I was too busy under a sink with a wrench to go grocery shopping. Possibility.

"Say it again," Paloma says to me as we walk back from the post office, our arms full of packages. "Faster now."

"Veux-tu m'épouser?"

"Now like you mean it."

"Veux-tu m'épouser!"

"There you go! Your pronunciation is getting better!"

I grin. Paloma smells faintly of sardines and sweetened coffee. "I'm a fast learner."

Last summer, when I landed back in California with one of Kit's sweaters and a whole new idea of what my life could be, I started learning French. I had plenty of help—long emails from Paloma, Cora over the phone, podcasts and apps and Maxine with the air of a sexy drill sergeant. And, of course, Kit. Always Kit and our never-ending conversation, our video calls to test recipes or sketch out plans. Sometimes I'd make him quiz me. Sometimes he simply sat on the other end of the phone and read a novel aloud in French while I soldiered through chores.

(Sometimes we'd get naked. For an intermediate French speaker, I have acquired a truly impressive vocabulary for dirty talk.)

"Sounding lovely, Léa!" Paloma calls toward the open window upstairs as we reach our destination. Her little cousin recently switched from flute to clarinet, much to the neighbors' dismay. "Much less like a dying cat!"

"Shut up, Paloma," Léa says, sticking her head out. "Hi, Theo!"

"Hi, Léa!" I call back. "See you for dinner tonight!"

"Is Kit coming?"

"Of course."

"Mama!" Léa shouts, disappearing. "We need another chicken!"

The boxes in my arms are stacked so high, I hear Kit's laugh before I see him.

"Didn't I just pick up our packages last week?" he says, taking a few. His face comes into view, and for a moment I'm amazed all over again that this is our life. That I get to wake up every morning to the rush of the ocean and this person, this beautiful, irreplaceable person with paint streaked across his nose and a smile made only for me. He leans in and kisses my cheek.

"You did," I say. We're there so often these days, the old man behind the desk knows us both by name. "Gilles says hello."

With Kit's help, Paloma and I get our packages inside and pile them on the floor by the pastry case.

"Those are for Mikel," Kit says, pointing Paloma toward a box of macarons. When we bought the bakery from the old woman who owned it, we bought her recipes too. We both thought some things should stay for good. "And tell him I haven't forgotten that he still has my copy of *Candide*."

"You know you're never getting that book back, right?"

Kit returns to his arsenal of paint buckets, still smiling. "I know, but it's fun to bother him."

"Do you know how many of your friends are coming on Sunday?" I ask Paloma.

"Everyone, love," she says with a grin. "Fucking everyone. They're your friends too."

Paloma leaves us to clock in at the fish counter, striding away with such merry yeoman's swagger that she nearly bowls over a woman just outside the door. They both apologize before splitting, and then the woman turns, and I see that pretty, familiar, heart-shaped face.

"Oh my God," I gasp, leaping over boxes. "*Sloane!*"

My sister yelps as I full-body crash into her, throwing my arms around her and lifting her off the ground.

"Ow, Theo, those are my ribs!"

I set her down, feasting my eyes on her for the first time since I moved abroad almost a year ago. She never shaved her head like she was threatening to, but her hair is much shorter than it was, just above her shoulders and almost back to our natural color. I rub my hand through it to mess it up, enjoying her scowl. "What are you *doing* here?"

"Friends and family menu tasting?" Sloane says. "You literally invited me."

"Yeah, but you're so busy, I didn't think you'd actually come, and you never said—"

"I bailed on my schedule for the week," she says with a casual shrug. "Hi, Kit."

Kit, who is looking at Sloane and me with the soft amusement of someone who once watched us fistfight over the last cupcake at Este's third birthday party, says, "Hi, Sloane." And then he's scooping her up too.

While Kit gets back to work on the mural he's painting across the shop's back wall, I give Sloane the investor's tour of what will soon be Field Day: the new ovens we installed together, the dry storage bins thoughtfully organized by Kit, the mosaic tiles we laid by hand into the wall behind the bar. Our vibe is Old World meets New World, cozy and bright and similar enough to the way it was left to keep the neighbors comfortable. We've added café tables and a corner bar, an espresso machine in the corner, plants in every window. Welded into the base of the pastry case is the front bumper of my old bus bar, taken before I sold it to a friend of Montana and Dakota, its battered old VW logo reflecting lights Kit strung overhead.

I finish by showing her what we've been prepping for our first menu tasting this weekend. Ribbons of mint, jars of dark red and orange spices, cinnamon sticks, blitzed pistachio. I just finalized the cocktail menu yesterday, but I haven't finished naming them all yet—in my notebook, they still have placeholder names after the nights that inspired them. The Caterina, the Émile, the Estelle.

Sloane leans against the walk-in door, smiling, saying nothing.

"What?" I finally ask.

"Nothing," she says. "You just look so happy here."

"I am. It was scary, at first. But I really am happy."

Truthfully, it was more than scary. It was terrifying. I had the jitters every day of my six months tying up loose ends in the States, applying for my visa, making sure Timo would be okay without me, saying goodbye to the kitchen guys I'd worked alongside since I was nineteen. There was so much logistical wrangling, so much paperwork, budgets and business plans and all the things that are hardest for me. But one thing I've learned is that I never really know what I'm capable of until I'm doing it, and the only way to find out is to march on. And when it's hardest, Kit is there.

I love this life. I love this life with an enormity that would have frightened the hell out of me five years ago, because I wouldn't have trusted myself to keep it. Instead, I swim in the Atlantic before breakfast, and I hold on tighter every day.

Later, while Kit and Sloane are busy gossiping like middle schoolers, I start unboxing all our deliveries. There are the expected orders—barware, sifters, nuts shipped in from up the Pyrenees—and then there are the things that started pouring in once we put out word about Field Day opening next week. A case of wine with a handwritten note from Gérard and Florian, and another from the Somm with a card from Timo's bar staff. A parcel of pure drinking chocolate from Santiago, pouches of Australian wattleseed and dried Dorrigo pepper from the Calums, flaky Mediterranean sea salt from Apolline. A good-luck package containing two flax linen aprons, a gilded jigger, and a postcard from Este.

The rest of our out-of-towners start to arrive tomorrow. Maxine is taking the train down from Paris; our parents land in the afternoon. Cora and Ollie coordinated their flights with the Swedes. Valentina has even persuaded Fabrizio to leave Rio in January to come up to France, and Kit nearly fell out of bed laughing when she texted us a photo of him begrudgingly swaddled in a wool sweater. Every night after dinner the past week, Kit and I have stood at our window overlooking the bay and gone over the menu again, determined to make it the most it can be. Not perfect, but the *most*. That's us. That's Theo-and-Kit.

Across our little shop, Kit glows in pink morning light through our big front windows, striped by the shadows of the letters spelling FIELD across the glass. I love the paint stains on his hands, the old cardigan rolled up to his elbows. I love how good he is to me. I love how good I am to myself when he's around.

I think of the question I've been practicing: Veux-tu m'épouser?

He was the first great thing I ever let myself want. This time, I'm keeping him.

ACKNOWLEDGMENTS

That was a lot of book, wasn't it?

When one opens a new page to write, it's important to have a goal in mind. My main goal with this one was to love writing it, and to write a book that loved being a book. I think I got there. I know I've never been loved back by a book quite like this one.

This book had me leaping off a sailboat in the Mediterranean and standing in my kitchen rubbing lemon zest into white sugar. It kissed me good morning and told me to read some Rilke before I clocked in. It asked me to be smarter and more curious, to learn a dozen new things every day. It was my pleasure to write it, and I owe such a tremendous debt of gratitude to so many people for that.

Thank you to my tireless agent, Sara Megibow, and my faithful editor, Vicki Lame. Thank you to the entire team at St. Martin's Griffin for all the work that went into editing it and putting it into such a beautiful package and sending it out into the world, including Anne Marie Tallberg, Vanessa Aguirre, Meghan Harrington, Alexis Neuville, Brant Janeway, Melanie Sanders, Chrisinda Lynch, Lauren Hougen, Laura Apperson, Sam Dauer, Jeremy Haiting, Devan Norman, Kerri Resnick, and Olga Grlic. Thank you to our cover illustrator, Mira Lou. Thank you to our incredible audiobook actors, Emma Galvin and Max Meyers; our director, Kimberley Wetherell; and the Macmillan audio team, including Elishia Merricks, Emily Dyer, Isabella Narvaez, Ashley Johnson, and Tim Franklin.

Now, I'd better start listing the resources that went into this research quickly, or it'll be another fifty pages. I'd only been to Europe a few times when I came up with the idea for this book, and I would have been literally and figuratively lost without the dozens of guides—physical, literary, and virtual—who showed me the way. Thank you to the travel YouTubers, whose content was indispensable when I was searching things like "streets of Naples ASMR 4K" at one in the morning, including Oui in France, Tourister, Abroad and Hungry, Chad and Claire, Days We Spend, Euro Trotter, and whoever has been uploading old episodes of *Rick Steve's Europe.* Thank you to the writers and editors of the many books I used for reference, including *Cork Dork* by Bianca Bosker, *Italian Hours* by Henry James, *Wine Simple* by Aldo Sohm and Christine Muhlke, *The Sommelier's Atlas of Taste* by Rajat Parr and Jordan Mackay, *Bouchon Bakery* by Thomas Keller and Sebastien Rouxel, and *Wine Folly: Magnum Edition* by Madeline Puckette and Justin Hammack. Thank you to the travel bloggers whose writing and photos helped me step inside every scene, including Along Dusty Roads, Bordeaux Travel Guide, and Florence Inferno. Thank you to the *TravelMag, AFAR, Lonely Planet, ArchDaily, Atlas Obscura, Condé Nast Traveler, Travel + Leisure,* and Michelin Guide contributors whose work helped in both writing and planning my own travels. Thank you to the hosts and producers of the podcasts I listened to for context, including *Half-Arsed History, ArtCurious, Stuff You Missed in History Class,* and *Wine for Normal People.* Thank you to random commenters on the subreddits of each of these destinations for their recommendations. Thank you to the documentary *Somm.* Thank you to the poet Louise Labé for helping me understand the sexual and romantic derangement of someone from Lyon. Thank you to the Uffizi Gallery for uploading a three-dimensional virtual tour of the Buontalenti Grotto without ever imagining what I would use it for. I would apologize, but I do feel I was honoring the spirit of the place.

Thank you especially to Anthony Bourdain for *World Travel, No Reservations,* and just about everything.

As for the brilliant experts and locals who taught me about history, food, and drink, a written thanks here hardly feels like enough. Thank you to my Florentine history guide, Gian; to my Barcelona chocolate guide, Carla; to my tapas guide, Boris of Food Lover Tours (who told me the wine bottle story that Fabrizio tells in the Naples section); to Pierre, who drove me around Paris in an antique Citroën; to Angelo for the Vespa tour of Rome; to Ciao Florence Tours for a sweaty and magnificent day trip through Tuscany; and to Michelle for the Parisian pastry tour. Thank you to Sara of Villa Le Barone for answering my questions about which specific flowers and trees would be in bloom during late August/early September in Chianti. Thank you to my friends Carol Ann, Brenden, and Joey for joining me in France and Spain and speaking more French than me. Huge, huge thanks to Sarah Looper of il Buco for looking over my pages and saving my life with your big somm brain.

Thank you, as always, to my best friend and writing partner, Sasha Peyton Smith, for always encouraging the most indulgent choice; to my family for your unwavering love and support; and to the love of my life, Kris, who was unflaggingly patient as I made so many messes in the kitchen and accumulated so many bottles of wine over the course of writing this book. Thank you to all of my friends who devoured early drafts and told me exactly how horny was horny enough.

And of course, thank you, Reader. I hope you finish this book with a desire to have a second helping of something delicious, try something you can't pronounce on a menu, and make the most indulgent choice. Settle for nothing less than the most.

Love you. Sluts forever.

ABOUT THE AUTHOR

Sylvie Rosokoff

Casey McQuiston is a #1 *New York Times* bestselling author of romantic comedies, including *One Last Stop, I Kissed Shara Wheeler*, and *Red, White & Royal Blue*, whose writing has appeared in *The New York Times, Condé Nast Traveler*, and *Bon Appétit*. Born and raised in southern Louisiana, Casey now lives in New York City with a poodle mix named Pepper.

DON'T MISS THE SPECIAL COLLECTOR'S EDITION

of the beloved *New York Times* bestselling novel, now featuring new case stamps, illustrated endpapers, an exclusive bonus chapter, and more!

"[A] fireworks in the sky, glitter in your hair, joyous royal romance that you'll want to fall head over heels in love with again and again. A+."

—*ENTERTAINMENT WEEKLY*

ST. MARTIN'S GRIFFIN

Don't miss the special collector's edition

of the celebrated *New York Times* bestselling novel,
now featuring case stamps, illustrated endpapers,
pink stained edges, an exclusive bonus chapter, and more!

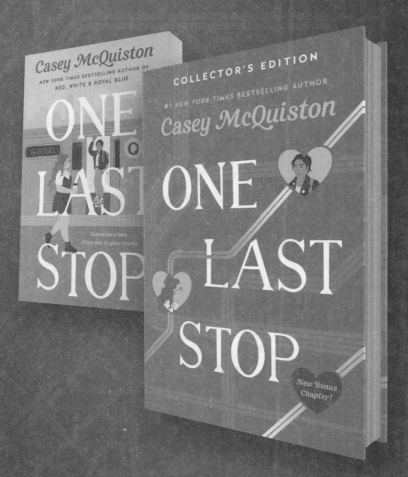

"McQuiston is leading the charge for inclusive happy-ever-afters,
radiant with joy and toe-curling passion."
—NPR

ST. MARTIN'S GRIFFIN